Bree Donovan received both her BA and MA from Rutgers University, Camden. She is currently working on completing her PhD. Bree's main areas of study are: psychology, philosophy, world politics and animal rights. She hopes to continue writing unusual stories that combine the fundamental elements of humanity with the supernatural world. Most importantly, she is a dog mom.

Blackthorns

of the

Forgotten

by

Bree T. Donovan

Blackthorns of the Forgotten

Cover and art design by Daniele Serra.

IFWG Publishing International
Gold Coast

www.ifwgpublishing.com

For my mother, Mercedes, the first person to read to me, and Gerry Huntman, who believed in my ability to write a story.

A note about the written form of Irish dialect: I did my best to write the speakers as they would sound, but also not overdo it. I hope you, dear reader, will be able to hear the characters in their own voices.

I had the honor of visiting the locations mentioned in this book. My apologies if my descriptions of these places are not one hundred percent accurate.

Part 1

"Come not, when I am dead,
To drop thy foolish tears upon my grave,
To trample round my fallen head,
And vex the unhappy dust thou wouldst not save.
There let the wind sweep and the plover cry;
But thou, go by.

Child, if it were thine error or thy crime
I care no longer, being all unblest:
Wed whom thou wilt, but I am sick of Time,
And I desire to rest.
Pass on, weak heart, and leave me where I lie:
Go by, go by."

Alfred Lord Tennyson

Prologue

Tullamore, Ireland
1972

A Time to Dance, A Time to Mourn

Gillean Faraday always heard the music. Even in the blissful semi-conscious state he was presently in—naked and content as a child in the womb. The wind colliding with the trees reminded him of the waves beating against the unyielding rocks lining the shore. A bird's distant call floated on the air like the lone charm of a tinker's whistle. A shiver ran up his spine at the sound, a prelude to the chimes riding on the wind. The sound was imperceptible to everyone but him. Something inherent stirred in Gillean, something which he had spent most of his life fighting against. He was constantly beckoned to the sweet notes mingling in the shafts of early morning light, and most disturbingly, held hostage by the low, haunting melodies hiding among the shadows, the sounds that live in the dark places.

Local folks spoke of ghosts and spirits where he lived as easily as they discussed the dreary weather. It was mostly tradition. Not many would dare lay claim to actually witnessing the kind of paranormal happenings about which Gillean possessed a begrudging certainty.

The rain battered against the window of the thirteenth-century stone castle. He remembered when he was a child and the chilly, rain-swept November day when his parents had first taken possession of the crumbling old building. It had been in a substantial state of disrepair then and had only gotten worse since. They dreamed of turning it into a family-run hotel.

At first it was all charm and mystery, but soon the reality of the situation hit them with the full power of the eastern wind. Many bitter nights the family was forced to go to bed fully clothed—coats and all—because of the lack of electricity. Delight turned into dismay for the ten-year-old boy. That was when Gillean vowed to escape his imposing home and newly acquired homeland as soon as he was able.

He missed the continual warmth of his birthplace, Brazil. His family had never returned once they settled in Ireland, not even for a holiday. As he grew from a boy to a young man, Gillean couldn't differentiate between his real memories of the tropical island, and what were merely dreams of a far-off place. The castle was dubbed *Teach na Spioradi (Home of the Spirits)* in honor of the myriad fairies that purportedly ran rampant in the country. The structure, now heated by modern technology, filled to the brim in the spring and summer months with guests from around the globe. These short-term visitors provided the captive audience the budding musician treasured. But it still seemed like a hostile takeover to a young man who dreamed of leaving the troubled island and its dark shades of green. Being held prisoner in an ancient tomb was torture to Gillean.

He rolled over with a grunt, rubbing his numb hands together. "Christ, I hate Ireland!"

The woman who shared his bed wiggled her way onto his stomach. She too was naked.

"You come back to Paris with me."

Her French accent was as alluring as her warm, voluptuous body. Gillean reluctantly thwarted her efforts to engage him in a kiss.

"I can't." He stroked her blonde hair with the great desire to return to their love-making. "Right now I am expected to be studying. And you best return to your own room, or we'll both be hearing it from my mother to be sure!"

She tried once more to place her lips on his.

"Now, now, I am an adult and a paying guest," she purred. "I bet your *maman* has many things to do keeping her other guests content. Trust me, *Cher*, she is not worried about where her son is at…" — she leaned over to glance at the antique clock on the table next to the bed — "one in the afternoon."

He gently pushed the woman back onto the bed, sat up, and reached for his trousers.

"Ah, you don't know Mrs. Faraday. She does indeed know where both her sons are at any hour of the day or night. I assure you, she is very concerned with her youngest son's time management skills right about now!"

He slipped on a heavy wool jumper, the kind a sailor would wear for extra warmth during a jaunt at sea. Gillean felt much like a sailor, wishing for the wild, windblown ocean, and heading for undiscovered destinations.

"I'm sorry, but I must go and make an appearance. Besides" — he grabbed for his guitar standing beside the bed like a dutiful wife — "I have to practice before this evening."

"I say you get all the practice you need right here with me." She patted the mattress, moving her slender calf seductively in and out of the covers. "But, you may be close to an expert already, and at such a young age. How old are you?"

He tried his best not to be persuaded by her provocative gestures, but the older, more experienced woman was difficult to deny for an arduous man of nineteen.

"Old enough to please a beautiful woman like you, no?" he smiled, his dark eyes hooded by even darker eyebrows.

"You are young enough to be my...little brother," she laughed. "But old enough to be my lover if you choose." She kept her languid eyes on him as he moved about the room getting ready to leave.

"A tempting offer, but as you are scheduled to return to your country in a few days, I'd say our love affair is ill-fated."

He bent down to give her one last kiss but thought better of it. No matter how much time he gave her, she wanted more. Gillean Faraday would never be constrained by the demands of another.

"We'll always have Tullamore," he joked.

She grabbed for him but he was already heading for the door, guitar in hand, his head cocked towards her in a gesture of farewell.

"And maybe I will wait for you, little singer, and we meet again." Her eyes seemed to change from deep blue to pitch black.

"Please return to your room, madam. We wouldn't want any of the guests to talk. After all, I do have to *perform* for all of them tonight."

He blew her a kiss and was out of the room, making his way down to the Great Hall, pausing at the sound of a recognizable song surging like a musical wave from down below. Gillean shook his head in an effort to clear his mind. He laughed at his own suppositions. So now it seemed the resident ghosts had also taken up music, or perhaps he should have just stayed in bed, alone.

He was able to go undetected, or so he thought, past the spacious first floor kitchen where his mother was making one of his favorite foods: butterscotch fudge. His older brother sat at the table warming his hands over a cup of tea. In about an hour's time the heat of a roaring fire would pervade the space, and several employees would be preparing the guests' afternoon meal.

Gillean's mother, Ena, was a compact lady, but she condensed terrific energy, wit and strength into five feet of Englishwoman. People would constantly remark that her younger son took after her in stature and personality. But, had they met her father, Gillean's beloved grandfather, they would have said otherwise. Perhaps that was why Ena and Gillean were always at odds with each other. Ena saw her son as being untamed and undisciplined. He had too much of the dreamer in him. He was so like her own father, Colonel James Klnsey, who, having been in both World Wars, had filled Gillean's head with tales of his own great adventures. She knew her son had a wonderful way with people—especially the women. He possessed a genuine warmth and sincerity that came across in his daft sense of humor, but most of all in his tender, poetic music. When she'd first heard him play, she'd wondered where on earth he'd come upon such a gift.

Gillean scoffed at his mother's disbelief. He suggested it was bestowed upon him by one of the spirits that shared the *Teach na Spioradi* with them. When Gillean had bravely endeavored to play for the hotel guests a year earlier, Ena worried her son might rashly decide to give up his university studies for a near-impossible career in music. Young people these days were so intent on pursuing the unattainable. But visitors repeatedly espoused the brilliance of her son's music. There was no denying that he was headed for something other than a university degree in French Literature.

"I don't know, Mother," said Joseph, helping himself to another biscuit. "I think your plan may backfire and innocent people could get hurt."

Ena turned the thick, sugary confection with a wooden spoon, and looked up to address her eldest son. He was the one with the level head. He never gave her a moment's worry. Even when her boys were children, Joseph took to looking after his brother without any prodding from his parents. It was simply Joseph's nature to be responsible and dependable.

"For goodness' sake, Joseph, it's not as if I've rigged a bomb to go off. I'm simply taking on a new employee. I think she might do our Gillean some good, that's all."

Joseph diligently brushed crumbs from his gray vest. He was twenty-five going on forty, as his little brother was so fond of saying.

"Uh, huh, well, I don't want to be around for the fallout. I won't be able to resist the urge to say 'I told ya so' this time."

"Just hush up now, and get me a cup of tea, will you."

Ena sat at the table taking a moment's respite before she began to roll out the fudge. She was hoping she could hear what was about to transpire in the bar down the hall. So far the music continued uninterrupted, but she knew her Gillean. He wouldn't be able to resist such a calling.

———————————

Gillean entered the bar with his guitar behind his back. As he came through the door, a Bob Dylan tune—the same one he had heard drifting through the hallways—was still in full folk swing, broadcasting from a transistor radio set upon the hearth. All the spotlessly polished chairs and tables were pushed back to the far corners of the room, leaving an aged but shiny plank floor. A young woman glided across the wood, jumping and pirouetting with all the poise of a seasoned ballerina.

Gillean placed a hand over his mouth to stifle his delighted surprise. She took no notice of his entrance, her eyes half closed. But he took notice of her. She looked to be his age, a slight lass in her black leotard and knee-length pink skirt. Auburn hair fanned out around her like ginger flames sparking with her movement. Her feet, clad in tatty pink slippers, barely made contact with the ground.

As quietly as he could, Gillean perched on a barstool, taking up his guitar, and joined in the next verse. It was second nature to follow a Dylan song. The man's work was part of Gillean's nightly repertoire. Watching her dancing the few brief moments while he played was hypnotic. It was a high he did not want to relinquish.

Just as he was immersing himself in the experience she stopped, turning her head in his direction and switching off the radio.

"I beg your pardon. I didn't know anyone else was here."

She was a local girl. He could deduce that much from her accent. Gillean noticed her slate eyes resting on him. He stood in front of her, smiling like a boy who had successfully captured a firefly.

"No need to apologize. It was smashing! I would have liked to continue. Women are always so quick to put an end to a man's pleasure."

The corners of her mouth turned up into a wry grin. He liked the sarcasm he saw there, even more the taint of it in her voice when she responded, "And men are always so quick to introduce themselves into places they are uninvited."

He shook his head in awe of her candor, his laughter spontaneous.

"Well, bein' as how I live here, I would have to say that *you*, my lovely, are the uninvited one."

Her pale face flushed crimson as her eyes anxiously searched the room.

"Oh." She dabbed with her sleeve at the sweat beading her forehead.

"I do apologize. Mrs. Faraday said it would be alright for me to practice here. You must be one of her sons. Please, forgive me."

Gillean was touched by the girl's sincerity. He reached for her hand, bending down to kiss it.

"Not at all, I quite enjoyed the experience. I'm Gillean. It is a pleasure to meet such a talented dancer. I don't think I've ever seen anyone dance ballet to Dylan. You do him a great honor."

He reached behind the bar, tossing her a hand towel, which she caught with an appreciative nod.

"Gillean, is it?" She wiped her cheeks.

"The one and only. It's obvious by the tone of your voice that my mother already told you all about me. This is the part where you run from the room screaming."

Her gaze was cast directly on him as if she could see right through him. He found the intensity of her stare unnerving. He'd been drawn to more beautiful women, but it was that unassailable quality of astuteness she exuded that made her so enticing.

"I have no fear of the infamous Gillean Faraday. I've confronted much more frightening figures than you, and I must say you are quite the musician."

She smiled now. He liked the way it lit her face.

She continued, "You have a most unusual accent—not quite Irish, not quite English. Perhaps you really are an intruder."

Gillean found this attractive too, her ability to notice something about him few others did. So many foreign guests hardly took note of the numerous cultural influences in his speech, and the local Irish didn't care.

"Well now, there have been many times I have felt like a stranger in a strange land," he admitted. "My mother is English and my father Irish. We traveled a great deal when I was a boy, but mostly I remember living in Brazil before ending up in jolly Eire."

"Brazil? Very exotic," She rested her feet in a dancer's stance. "Now, would you be singing in Portuguese or Gaelic?"

His dark eyes momentarily rested on her strong legs, then moved leisurely upwards to her mouth.

"Whatever you wish, my lovely. But it will cost you. Everything exquisite in this world has a price."

She rolled her eyes at his apparent show of conceit.

"You're already too dear," she declared.

"My price," he continued, undaunted by her disdain, "is the revelation of the identity of this spellbinding dancer."

"I'd say a man of the world such as yourself has seen far better than the likes of me, your basic country lass," she answered in a matter-of-fact tone. "Besides, I have work to do. So if you'll excuse me..."

"Ah come on!" He was tickled by her complete lack of interest. "You could at least let me try and guess who you are." He touched her arm, meaning to make her stay.

A slight smile returned to her rosy face. "Go on then, have a go, but make it quick. I have your mam to answer to."

"You leave Mam to me." He winked. "Now, let me see... Ah! I know! You are a world-famous ballerina, perhaps with an international dance company, and are hiding out here at the *Teach na Spioradi* for refuge from the throngs of adoring fans. Lord knows you would be safe here," he added cynically.

"Not even close. I'm far from world famous, dancer or otherwise. I'm seeking not refuge, but gainful employ."

"*Employ?*"

"My name is Adara. Your kind mother hired me to do some baking and work in the gardens."

"Mother hired you, ya say?"

Gillean was incredulous that his mother would take such an action without consulting him. Ena made it a point to make sure he felt some sense of obligation to the family operation by including him in the bigger decisions such as staff.

"I do hope my working here doesn't offend you."

He caught himself, not wanting to appear unsettled by a woman—even though *this* woman did so, and then some.

"No, of course not, I just... I mean to say—"

"What's the matter? You don't associate with the hired help?" she asked, holding the towel close to her chest in a defensive gesture.

"Yes...*No!* That's not what I meant! I..." He took a moment to compose himself, practicing the same breathing techniques he utilized for singing. "It's a pity. I'm an aspiring musician, and I thought maybe you and I could do it together...I mean this...." He offered his guitar as a visual aide. "What we did now, again, sometime?" He was beginning to sweat.

"Are ya serious?" She placed her hands on her hips, looking like a formidable interrogator.

Gillean made one last effort to smooth over the situation. He liked this girl. It was not just her enticing body that attracted him, but her strength. She was a challenge. He had stumbled at the starting gate while she was running yards ahead.

But he was always able to gain ground with his charisma. The door to the bar pushed open and the graceful dancer who stood defiantly against it was shoved unceremoniously against Gillean. He instinctively put his arms around her to keep her from falling.

"There you are, *Monsieur*! Dismissed me already, I see," remarked the amorous Parisian, assuming the musician and dancer to be in an embrace. "I was so hoping you would join me for some afternoon tea."

"*For Christ sake, ya almost knocked the girl over!*" Gillean shouted at the woman. He no longer found her the least bit appealing.

"I…I didn't see her." The French woman acquiesced to the dancer, "Pardonnez-moi, mademoiselle."

"No worries." Adara quickly regained her balance, moving away from Gillean. "I'm quite fine. No one expects you to see through doors." She glanced sharply at a gobsmacked Gillean. "Please, enjoy your afternoon tryst, uh, I mean *tea*."

His heart pulsed. Gillean did not want her to go, but he also did not want to be so captivated. He had no time for such trifling feelings. He allowed the confounding Adara to take her leave.

"Perhaps you will consider my offer? I'm extremely good at what I do!"

"Perhaps you'll let me know when music is your *first* priority."

She glided deftly through the open doors with dignity and an air of superiority. Her accusatory words held all the power of a slap in the face. He shouted after her.

"*Music is my only priority, missy! You come tonight to hear me, I dare you!*"

"I'll have work to do, *Monsieur!*" She turned down the hall, her left hand caressing the wall.

———————◆———————

"**M**ay I say it now, Mother?" Joseph said, standing next to the kitchen door from where he and Ena had been privy to the entire exchange in the bar.

"No, Joseph, you may not. This is only round one!"

His mother took the fudge from the oven and called to her youngest son.

Ballina, Ireland

1980

The boy's heart expanded at the crackle of the needle settling into the grooves of vinyl. He lovingly took up his fiddle. He'd taught himself how to play by listening to the recorded music. His bow coaxed the sweet, clear notes from the tired strings of his second-hand instrument. He closed his eyes, lashes still damp with tears, and tucked his chin into his beloved companion. His bruised body swayed like the fragile branches of a young willow.

The voice on the record lifted the child's spirit with the gentlest of hands and set him down amidst the swells of melody which they created together. Time and place held no meaning. They were one in heart, mind, and music.

The boy continued to play as the heavy steps of his father's steel-toed boots ascended the stairs with purpose. This time the boy would play until the song was finished. He would play until the end, until their music would be the last, beautiful sound he heard.

They gathered around the gravesite: a teacher, a priest, and three older women who lived up the street from the deceased—otherwise unrelated people connected only by death. Each mourner was happy for the rain. The cold, heavy drops meant they could hide underneath their umbrellas, no need to look one another in the eye. Only the dead child's schoolteacher had the courage to step forward, lay a yellow rose on the coffin, and turn to the huddled few.

"I know we all wish things could have been different. No child should ever lose his life, especially—" Her throat clutched as the absence of the boy's parents, or any sort of concerned family member, was as awful a sight as the miniature casket. "Let this be a lesson for us." She stared at each of them, regardless of whether they returned her gaze or not.

The priest placed his arm around the tearful woman. The two shared the same excruciating mixture of emotions: guilt, grief, bewilderment—and a numbing sense of the pathetic, human tragedy that now lay unseen and beyond help in a little wooden box.

"One of the children told me how much our lad enjoyed music. I was told this was his favorite musician."

The older man had buried quite a few children in his lengthy religious career, but most were victims of disease or accidents. He held his black umbrella over a tape player and pushed the *on* button with a shaky hand. The music of Gillean Faraday floated in the air, hung on every drop of rain, marked the fiddle which lay atop the child's resting-place. The voice sang of the wonders of the stars and ocean journeys.

But underneath the lyrical imagery, each person standing silently by would swear they heard only one relentless word.

"*Why?*"

Chapter One

Ireland 1996
Tunnel of Light

It had been a long day. The train's movement was as soothing as a mother's lullaby. Fatigue and sadness clouded Gillean's brown eyes. He hated the idea of leaving his family, but the music playing inside his head would not be silenced. He was finally free to compose songs for his own recently acquired record label after more than two decades of being a commodity for others. The constant demand for "hit albums" from smug businessmen who appreciated artistic expression about as much as Gillean liked being cooped up in boardrooms, was gone. That particular, long-standing discomfort had been mercifully extracted like a decaying tooth. Instead, an inner calling drew him back to the days of his musical roots as a soulful storyteller when music was about creative expression, not the money to be gained by disinterested third parties. The fruition of this inspired endeavor weighed heavily upon him for the past few months, but there never seemed to be enough hours in the day to accomplish all he wanted.

After completing a successful and exhausting world tour, he took great pleasure in idle days spent in his beautiful home nestled in a hamlet on the east coast of Ireland. His four children offered endless, unconditional love which did much to nurture his ego. Gillean willingly accepting love and adoration; it was as natural to him as songwriting—as breathing. Extending himself to others, baring the more knotty parts of himself, especially his fears and failings, was something akin to an unnatural act. The famed artist trusted only one man completely: Gillean Faraday.

Gillean made the difficult decision to leave the comforts of hearth and family to take an unaccompanied journey. Relations between him and his wife had been, at best, strained for years, and no matter how much either one pretended that all was well, they continued to silently drift apart. Gillean believed the time in seclusion would provide him with a clearness of vision.

The singer-songwriter didn't lack for material. He knew *what* he wanted to say. A hungry pack of emotions gnawed at him. He had simply closed the door on the unmanageable feelings. They were unwelcome guests. He was afraid of what embracing them might mean. Most of all, he was fearful that his message would fall upon deaf ears. His treasured fans were always supportive, but the media could be brutal in its criticism. He was beginning to feel like a rag doll pulled from all directions. Although his loyal listeners clamored for more, they differed on what it was they demanded from him—the man who each considered their own personal singer. Pressure was building in his core like the heat in a train's engine and like the vapor that eventually has to be released; Gillean knew he must discharge the negative energy. He was deeply puzzled as to why so many wanted so much from him constantly. He simply wanted to write and perform songs, not to be burdened by concern with whom or how many people approved of his work.

He unknowingly spent an hour staring into the darkness as town after town sped by in a blur. The large window he was seated next to offered the perfect view of himself.

Night crept stealthily across the sky like a highwayman. The window, a mirror of the night, reflected Gillean's face. It appeared so much older than he recalled and stared back accusations. He slowly dragged a hand across his cheek, shaking his head at the drained man regarding him. The pronounced lines around his eyes and mouth were like the markings of an intricate roadmap on his sallow skin, reminders of the countless miles of travel, nameless faces in crowds, the pain of the early tests of endurance, and defeat. *Where does time go when it gets away from you?* he considered. *Where had Gillean Faraday gone?*

After the train cleared a tunnel, darts of rain pelted his window-mirror, creating a canvas of fog on which Gillean's finger traced the letters of his name; he was reliving a childhood memory. The dormitory of his boyhood boarding school had afforded ice-cold showers during the dark, early mornings of the winter months. The pre-dawn ritual commenced yet another day of dread, loneliness and violence.

Gillean's imaginative personality and propensity towards the artistic rather than sport were two inherent attributes that set him apart from the other students. Gillean was a walking target for bullies. Luckily, his older, footballer brother, Joseph, held no reservations about placing himself between Gillean and anyone who meant to do him harm. Joseph's protection was a double-edged sword. Gillean, though thankful to be safe from being target practice for arseholes, wondered if the temporary discomfort of a few square punches was preferable to the long-lasting humiliation of having a protector.

Much as he wanted, Joseph couldn't provide full-time protection. There were occasions when his accusers confronted Gillean for being a puny wanker, queer fish and other crude descriptors; he firmly planted his shiny, black regulation shoes, taking the blows, instead of running away.

Evenings when the rain and fog misted the tiny window next to his bed, Gillean would write his name. It was a secret consolation that even when the morning sun arrived, his name would exist on the glass, as if written in invisible ink. He might be unimportant and even reviled, but those letters scrawled in the dark assured him of future distinction and respect.

The ensuing years had been generous to Gillean. One illustrious lover had taken to calling him his "selkie". That was back in the days when Gillean embodied the volatile mixture of the wild spirit of youth, and the quintessential brooding of the great artists of Eire. His body was the instrument through which he explored all possibilities of passion. He wanted his music to reflect his experiences and to speak to the experiences of others. His art was meant to elicit the feeling of kinship. Men and woman could feel someone understood. This desire to connect in every way with his fellow humans allowed him quite an array of lovers, some of whom were not the kind to take home to Sunday dinner, as it were. But they all held something in common. They all exacted a fee from Gillean for their services, some more costly than others. Regardless of the outcomes of these opulent relationships, each was a part of Gillean and his music.

His long chestnut hair and dark, repining eyes complemented his unpredictable moods, which vacillated between outrageous daring and bouts of self-doubt and depression.

Some evenings after a set in a small local venue, he would be soaring to the heavens.

Drinks all around for the bard of Ireland!

The following week he would be sat alone in a pub, digging through the pockets of his worn, corduroy trousers for the two quid needed to buy himself a couple of pints, hoping they would quell the hunger in his empty belly. Relishing the easy, liquid comfort, the stinging words from his mother invaded his moments of peace. She advised her son that his little dalliance with music was well and good while he was at university, but now that he had completed his studies it was time he set about finding a real, stable place of employment.

He'd sat on that bar stool praying for a sign. The bartender, noticing Gillean's guitar, offered him a free meal along with a few pounds to play a set. Gillean took this as reinforcement from the heavens not to pack it in and go home. He was meant for a different kind of life. He'd believed he would one day look back on these lean times and smile, proud that he hadn't given up on himself and his dreams.

Now that day was here. His graying head rested involuntarily against the cold glass. His leaden eyes closed without his consent. The fleeting question, "was it worth the sacrifice?" played over and over in his head to the monotonous clacking of the train's wheels.

"Excuse me, lad. I think this is me seat."

Gillean sluggishly turned to the sound of a mysteriously familiar voice. Beholding the man standing next to the empty seat adjoining his, Gillean was both surprised and frightened.

"*Sully?*" He rubbed his disbelieving eyes.

"*What?* This can't be! *Gillean?*" The man looked down at his ticket as if it would confirm his presence.

Gillean was waking up with a sudden burst of adrenaline. "What are you doing here?"

"What am *I* doin' here? What are *you* doin' here?" Sully raised his eyes to heaven. "What's *he* doin' here? Not again with the singer!"

The sarcasm was noted. "Lovely to see you, too." Gillean reached out to place his guest's well-worn satchel into the overhead compartment. "And what the hell kind of luggage would a…*creature*…like you have?" he asked, making room for Sully to sit. Gillean knew better than to believe there was any chance of escape. Besides, he wanted some answers from the enigmatic man.

"Don't go askin' me about *my* baggage when obviously ya have plenty of yer own." The feisty man plopped himself down with a great sigh.

"I beg your pardon?"

This peculiar visitor had first appeared while Gillean was out walking through the misty woods one lonely afternoon. He'd presumed one of his mates, or his manager, must have been having a go at him. But he quickly came to the realization through the course of several unsolicited visits that Sully was not of this world.

The riotous being had descended from a Blackthorn tree (also known to the Irish as *Wishing Thorn*) with all the grace of a drunken leprechaun, knocking Gillean to the frozen earth.

"Beg yer pardon!"

The intruder attempted to brush dirt from Gillean's black leather jacket as both men struggled to their feet. Gillean was not a tall man. He stood only five feet, seven inches. His visitor was the same height.

Gillean's impulse had been one of retreat until he was firmly on his feet and staring at a man who could have passed for his twin, save for the brilliant green eyes and the apparent twenty-year age gap between them. Same dark, shoulder length hair as the twenty-something Gillean had sported, same cheeky expression.

"Who…are…you?" Gillean stammered. He quelled the great desire to reach out and place his hand on the man's face, an echo from Gillean's past.

The mischievous, childlike man smiled. "Ah now, perhaps ya should be askin' me *what* I am."

"Fine, then. What are you?"

"'Tis not the time for ya to know."

The young man gave his back to Gillean and started to walk away. He took a few steps, then swung round to the baffled Gillean. "Would ya be havin' any chocolate with ya?"

Still in shock, Gillean thrust his hands into the pockets of his trousers, mumbling, "Let's see, chocolate…chocolate…" His fingers retrieved several pieces of foil-wrapped candy. His admirers were forever presenting him with such trinkets of affection.

"Here." He shoved his open hand toward the stranger.

"Belgian." The little man happily accepted the offering. "How classy."

"Who sent you here?" Gillean protested. "What's this about? He zipped up his jacket against the renegade wind blowing in from the east. "Whatever it is, I don't find it entertaining."

"I don't see what the big deal is about yerself either. All those people falling o'er ya just 'cause ya can sing a little ditty."

The man gave Gillean the once over with his powerful eyes, all the while licking chocolate from his lips. Gillean thought him reminiscent of his own petulant son.

"Bloody hell! You're not…" Gillean could not give voice to the un-thinkable possibility.

"Not?" Gillean's visitor repeated with total innocence.

"Do you mean to claim a relation to me?" Gillean would have made the sign of the cross had he been any kind of believer.

The man's unrestrained laughter could have woken the dead.

"Listen to ya now—such ignorance!" He paused a few moments, savoring the remaining chocolate. "I'll tell ya this one thing. I am not a part of you in the way ya think."

"Mind telling me exactly what part then?" Gillean couldn't help being beguiled by the peculiar youth; in his eyes burned the reflection of ancient fires.

"'Tis not time yet."

"Not time?"

"I'm here, so it must be approaching." The green-eyed man handed Gillean the crushed colorful candy wrappers. "You'll have to keep yer eyes open and wait." He drifted away from Gillean as if the wind were moving him along like a fallen leaf from the great wishing tree. "All in good time."

"Just a moment. Where are you going?" Gillean called. The vaporous air enfolded the man. He was disappearing as swiftly as he had arrived "What is your name?" Gillean yelled in desperation.

"Sully," a disembodied voice called back.

"Sully?"

Gillean quickly processed his memory banks. No match found. *Sully.* The echo of a lone fiddle riding on the wind kept Gillean planted beneath the tree, enchanted for the rest of the afternoon.

Gillean's conscious mind could not let the memory go. The best he could surmise was, apparently, Sully was meant to be some sort of guide—but for what? And why did Sully look so much like a young Gillean? His entire body quivered whenever he ventured to consider what or who Sully was. Creating magical and ethereal characters for his songs was one thing. Irish folksingers had done so for centuries. It was their legacy. Confronting a being seemingly from the hallways of his imagination was too much to be believed.

A few stiff drinks of Jameson and the confirmation from his family and friends that they were not having a go at Gillean had done little to dispel Sully back into the parallel universe he came from. After the first encounter in the woods, Gillean reckoned he would write a song about the bizarre occurrence, hoping to be done with it. But the situation proved none too simple. Sully was not one to be rid of so easily. Gillean caught bits and pieces of the unknowable man, but like grabbing at frayed fabric, he was left with just shreds of evidence of their encounters. And always, the sublime notes of a fiddle whirled around him like the wind.

Gillean recalled his last exchange with Sully to be a particularly vivid and disturbing experience. It was the eve of the summer solstice. Exhausted from an outdoor concert, Gillean stumbled bleary-eyed into the bathroom. He lacked the hand-eye coordination to grab for a toothbrush. Lurching out of his trousers one leg at a time, he peeled off the rest of his sweat-soaked clothes, rinsed his teeth with a hefty slug from a half-full bottle of wine set on a bureau and headed for bed. A soft projection of moonlight sliced though the open curtains. The surprising brightness unsettled Gillean.

He moved to close the curtains. *"What the hell?"* he muttered, peering into the meadow surrounding his home. His body tingled on the verge of fight or flight. The silhouette of a man stood, or more like floated, over a small patch of grass. The visitor was completely engulfed in the black shroud of night. In a show of defiance, Gillean opened the window and climbed out. Only one could have the audacity to manifest at this hour, and in such a manner.

"I have my mobile in hand," he lied. "I will phone the Garde if you don't identify yourself."

Before Gillean could feign a call for help, the man moved behind the disoriented singer. Cold hands settled upon his shoulders; terror registered for a brief moment, but was soon released by the tranquility of the visitor's soft, even breaths. He didn't speak, but as if by telepathy conveyed the request for Gillean to close his eyes. Gillean hoped that in doing so, the eiderdown of his mattress soon would be cradling his weary body carrying him into another, more pleasant dream.

"Close…your…eyes." The words seeped into Gillean's ear.

With shut eyes, it was as if Gillean had been ushered into that pleasant dream he ached for. Water mirrored the gloaming sky. The tart smell of dirt from trails leading into a forest of hawthorn, juniper and pine trees filled Gillean's nose. It was the tempting, secretive forest of fairy tales. Even if Gillean could speak, he had no desire or need. The beauty and peace of the place he witnessed behind his eyes stunned him into an appreciative silence. After a few moments of taking in the spectacular view and inhaling the purest air, Gillean's companion spoke.

"Here is my home. No one can hurt me. I am protected by all that you see."

Was he a hallucination? Wiping cold sweat from his face, Gillean pivoted to face the perplexing figure. He couldn't be certain the entity possessed a body. But he damn sure had eyes! Eyes that shone with an unearthly glow. An unsettling intuition nagged that, like himself, this…man…had searched his entire life for this place. Was Gillean entrusted with this man's happiness? He swallowed the urge to cry as he remembered the name.

"Sully?"

The hands that patted Gillean's were warm with humanity.

"You must be open to every possibility in heaven and on earth."

The words assaulted Gillean as if he had been jerked about the neck with a steel chain. He staggered backwards. The mention of heaven unhinged Gillean more than the entire experience. He'd rejected the traditional ideas of heaven and hell, loathing the Church's extended tendrils of power over Ireland.

"What kind of ghoulish priest prowls the neighborhoods of artists?" It was a rhetorical question. "Get out! If I see you here again—"

Gillean's body shook with shock and rage. Slowly unclenching his jaw and fists he incredulously found himself on the inside of the closed bedroom window. When he wheeled around, only his empty bed awaited him. He dove under the covers. But he could not un-see the earlier vision.

"Fuck Ireland!" he kicked at the firmly tucked corners at the end of his bed.

———————————

Gillean's brief reverie ended. The reality of the present train ride re-asserted itself.

He shuddered as Sully fired back, "Looks like we're both goin' to find out why I got stuck with ya."

"Who? Stuck with me? You…I…ARGH!" Gillean exclaimed in total exasperation.

Sully began to laugh, his wide grin like the Cheshire cat's.

"Sod you, Sully. I came here for some peace." Gillean grunted, and turned his back to the man, twisting his body into a fetal position.

"Look here." Sully elbowed Gillean's side.

"Ouch!"

"We are clearly in this together, so there's no need to get in a snit." Sully winked at the weary Gillean. "Come on, let's have a song, shall we?"

"A song? No. I'm exhausted. I'm going to sleep. I pray you will do the same."

"You? Pray?" Sully feigned disbelief. "Fine. Suit yerself."

"I will, thank you."

With that, Sully burst forth—full throttle: "Oh my old man's a *dustman, he wears a dustman's hat!"*

"Oh, Sully, please. Shut it."

"Come on then, come on." Sully gave another, sharper shove of his elbow.

"Ouch!"

"Sing!"

Gillean sighed with disgust. "Okay, okay, ya damned imp. *He wears cor blimy trousers and he lives in a Council flat!"* he offered with high theatrics.

"Now that's got it!" Sully exclaimed with delight.

Together, the two men filled up the silence of the otherwise empty compartment as the train propelled itself forward through the darkness and into the undiscovered.

Chapter Two

The Promise

Gillean woke to find himself once again alone. He glanced out the window. Night held firm its grip.

For a moment he had forgotten Sully's appearance and their rowdy duet. But when he stood to stretch, Gillean noticed the weathered knapsack on the overhead.

"Damn you, Sully," Gillean muttered.

Glancing around like a guilty child before filching a cookie from the jar, Gillean surrendered to the sudden urge to see what was contained in the carry-on of his guest. He felt only the slightest pang of remorse as he reached up, pulled the sack to him, and undid the tie. In order to justify his intrusive action, Gillean decided to place his hand inside and retrieve only the first thing it touched. His fingers brushed against a wood surface. Wrapping his hand around the object, he gave a slight tug. He uncovered an old fiddle with an envelope stuck between its strings.

"What have we here? Was that your music?" Gillean examined the instrument briefly. He'd never seen a wood of this sheen before. The fiddle glowed a soft purple. Perhaps it was simply the reflection of the artificial light. Gillean carefully placed it back inside the knapsack. "We'll see about that later." He turned his attention to the envelope where he noticed *Gillean* was penned in black ink! He opened the note with trembling hands. The swirling, feminine strokes were as beautiful as the woman who'd brushed the paper with her felt pen: Ciar! Gillean's body shook as he read the first few lines.

My Little Gilly,

It's been a month since you left Prague. Your phone calls have been slight consolation. You told me you need time—time to think, to be alone, away from me and all that we have shared—time to clear your head. But my sweet, misguided singer, you will not find what you search for so desperately, away from me and our great passion…

"Oh God."

Gillean fell back into his seat, his legs like jelly, and his empty stomach stirring with bile. His throat stung. He shut his eyes tight. But she was there. Behind his closed eyes she came to him more clearly than any daydream.

Gillean had been on tour in Prague. The day held the promise of bright, crisp, early autumn. He was doing his usual tooling around the city, the sun spilling into the city streets like saffron. He ducked into the local art museum to escape the blinding daylight when he stumbled upon the most stunning woman he had ever seen, a young artist preparing for a showing of her work later that night. Her paintings depicted the ultimate struggles of life—more specifically, spiritual life—and of the constant battle between good and evil.

Her images were startling and thought-provoking to say the least. She did with color and canvas what he had tried to do with music. Being a man prone to such lofty considerations, Gillean felt an urgent need to have a long discussion with the woman, whose name meant *darkness* in Gaelic. The pale hair which fell to her waist and the bewitching indigo eyes seemed a far cry from the shadows.

Their first conversation caused him to believe he had known her before. He promptly arranged for many other prolonged meetings. Although she offered herself to him, time and again, she was politely refused. Gillean had been down that road before. He was not about to make the same mistake and begin the great chain of pain all over again. But what existed between them was becoming more powerful, not so easily denied. His desire for her was like a single, pointed thorn digging deep inside him, into a place where even his music had never taken him. She told him a true artist would never let himself be bound to any man's vision but his own. The days and nights spent in her company made him feel alive, or more correctly, aware of how threadlike the veil is between this world and that of the spirits. She was a bolt of lightning and he, her conduit.

But there was something underneath the current, a foreboding sense of loss and misery. Gillean explained away these uneasy feelings as mere shame for giving himself to a woman other than his wife. The more time he spent with Ciar, the greater the imperative to unearth the briar. He needed to leave, because of how much he wanted to stay. Gillean didn't have the courage to tell Ciar goodbye. He hoped his explanation of needing time to himself and his subsequent absence would speak to what he could not. Leaning his head against the seat, the question came to him: *How the hell did the letter come to be in Sully's bag?*

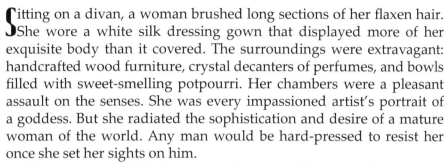

Sitting on a divan, a woman brushed long sections of her flaxen hair. She wore a white silk dressing gown that displayed more of her exquisite body than it covered. The surroundings were extravagant: handcrafted wood furniture, crystal decanters of perfumes, and bowls filled with sweet-smelling potpourri. Her chambers were a pleasant assault on the senses. She was every impassioned artist's portrait of a goddess. But she radiated the sophistication and desire of a mature woman of the world. Any man would be hard-pressed to resist her once she set her sights on him.

She summoned Sully from the train just as Gillean was falling off to sleep. She smiled at him as if greeting a beloved friend.

"My, how our wayward little boy has grown into a fine young man. You must tell me all about it, Sully." Her pitch-black eyes took him in like a coiled snake an ill-fated mouse.

"Ciar," Sully nodded. "I think ya know very well what became of me."

"Oh?" She tucked her long legs beneath her, but not before she exposed her thigh. "I couldn't begin to know what goes on in your insignificant world of do-gooder spirits. I'm far too preoccupied with my own affairs."

"*Affair* being the key word," Sully baited her, as he moved about the room. "Playing the part of an artist this time round I see. What an insult to those who truly have the gift."

His eyes came to rest on a golden vase in the shape of a guitar filled with red roses. He didn't have to look at the tiny card lying next to the bouquet. He knew who had made the romantic offering.

"Explain to me, why yer interested in a mere earthly musician who also happens to be me charge?"

Disregarding his query, she studied him, apparently pleased with what she saw. "Yes, you have come a long way from the broken child you once were."

He cringed at her reference to his childhood. Much to his dismay, she was one of the few who knew about his brief and anguished life as a human.

"Look at you," she continued. "All spit and fire. I'd say it's a struggle for you to remain *angelic,* isn't it, *me boy*?"

She moved from her seat, her tall frame circling him.

"Not with the likes of you around, it isn't." He backed away from her. "And ya know full well I'm not an angel."

"Now, now, don't be cross with me. That's not my fault." She moved with him, not allowing the physical connection between them to be broken. "You have your assignment, as do I. Did you think I wouldn't notice your interference? That goes against the rules of your own collective. Intercepting my letter meant for Gillean was a mistake." Her feathery hair touched his cheek. "You're a little late if you're thinking of saving the singer, or are you just jealous because I have his full attention? Either way, he's a done deal, lad."

Sully held his ground, determined not to let her see how much she frightened him. With her surreptitious charms, she had the power to make a man do horrendous things…such as being the instrument of his own child's death. Shoving his shaking hands into his pockets, Sully acted unperturbed by her pronouncement.

"I'd say I'm right on time. If Gillean was such a done deal, ya wouldn't have felt the need to bring me here or write him such a pitiable letter." His eyes did not betray him, only flashing a warning as his stare intensified. "What's the matter? Losin' yer touch, old girl?" he taunted.

She hissed at him, "You stupid, broken boy!" In an instant she turned from a flirtatious woman into the seething, dark force she truly was. "You couldn't even save yourself from being crushed by your own father, and yet here you are, once again in my way."

She smiled maliciously, her eyes revealing an intense cruelty and her half-open mouth baring predatory white teeth. "You'll manage to muck things up. You don't have a chance in hell to save the likes of Gillean Faraday. He's more than your charge, isn't he? Which *is* every bit *my* business. You have only yourself to blame for whatever happens to him. I'll make sure he's sorry for ever laying eyes on you."

She placed her hands on his chest pushing him backwards. It was as if she had placed hot irons against his skin. His eyes tearing from the pain, he remained conscious long enough to hear her last noxious words. "You went too far by crossing me, Sully. You violated your duties. You entered my world. And now I have the right, the obligation, really, to punish you."

———————————◇———————————

Gillean jolted awake. A piercing scream, like the wail of a siren, or an animal suffering a mortal wound, had sliced into his rest. The resonance was so deafening he let go of Ciar's letter to cover his ears. As his mind registered the shrieking whistle of the train, his eyes focused again on the surroundings. A single, stunning beam of sunlight shone down on an unidentifiable heap lying in the center of the floor.

"Christ on a cracker!"

Gillean jumped up and moved cautiously to the center of the car. There, lying face down on the threadbare carpet, was his companion. Gillean knelt to gently turn the man onto his back. Sully's eyes were closed.

Perfect black fingerprints riddled the once-crisp blue linen shirt. Gillean tentatively undid some of the buttons. Sully's chest was covered with angry-looking indentations that aligned with the marks on his shirt. Gasping to compose himself, he leaned into Sully's face, frozen in a grimace of pain.

"Hey, hey, young man, come on now, time to wake up."

Sully blinked open his eyes. Gillean noticed instantly that something was terribly wrong. The light that once shown through the green portholes was gone. Sully's eyes were now a cold, dark green— resembling the moss gathering at the bottom of the bogs. He was slowly regaining his senses.

"Gillean?" his voice crackled. "What happened?"

"Hush," Gillean admonished. "First things first, can you sit up?"

"I think so."

Gillean placed his arms around Sully, pulling him into a sitting position.

"We need to find you a doctor," Gillean said.

Sully sputtered, "A doctor will be of no help to me." He sounded tired and weak, looking down at the raw incisions in his chest.

"What happened? Did someone attack you? What the hell are these?" Gillean demanded answers to ease his awful sense of helplessness.

Sully stared blankly. "I don't know. I don't know what to do now."

The door to the compartment unexpectedly opened. A child no older than nine or ten years of age came towards them. Her hair was pulled back into two red braids which swung across her back as she walked. The delicate white dress she wore fell almost to her feet, which were covered with ballerina-like slippers. As she moved closer, the rustling of her dress coalesced into the sound of whispering children. She carried a guitar much too large to be her own. When she came upon the two men, she sat next to Sully, placing a delicate hand on his head in a gesture of love and concern. "You weren't supposed to do that, Sully."

Gillean looked at the two in confusion. "He wasn't supposed to do what? Who are you?"

Sully grabbed on to Gillean, who recoiled at the burning sensation caused by Sully's touch.

"Mother of—" Gillean turned to the girl. "Do you know what happened to him?"

The girl looked to Sully.

Sully made the introduction. "Gillean, this is Keelin."

The girl nodded to Gillean, then rested her sorrowful eyes on Sully. She spoke earnestly. "You knew they would send me. Forgive me. I told them I didn't want to. I tried to tell them."

"No tears, me girl. Ya did nothin' wrong." Sully comforted the distraught child. "I'm ready to go with you. I understand."

"*Wait!* What the hell—"

Gillean corrected himself. He could hardly believe he'd swear in front of a child. Then again, he could hardly believe any of what was happening.

"Pardon me, Keelin. Sully, what do you mean you are ready to go? You're not leaving me—I won't allow it. Not until you tell me what's happening."

Sully tried to stand, but was stopped short. He moaned and willingly allowed himself to rest against Gillean's chest.

"'Tis nothin' ya should be troublin' yerself about. You will be right as rain, I promise. I just need to take me leave of ya now."

"I won't accept that," Gillean said stubbornly.

He was used to getting his way. But being a famous performer was of no worth to the suffering young man who lay in his arms.

"Why don't you tell him?" Keelin coaxed.

"No. It doesn't matter. Just take me back."

Gillean spoke up. "Tell me, Keelin. It does matter. Tell *me*."

The girl looked from Gillean to Sully as if weighing the pros and cons of Gillean's request. Her darting eyes indicated the difficulty of her position. She spoke quickly like taking a dose of bitter medicine. "He disobeyed an important edict."

"*Don't, Keelin.*" Sully struggled against Gillean, but the singer held him firmly.

"What edict?" Gillean inquired.

"He tried to save you. He tried to do work which was meant for you. He knows that is forbidden."

"Come again?"

She smiled briefly. It was there, in the way the corners of her lips turned down ever so slightly, that Gillean saw the girl's sorrow. Her mouth, like the pieces of fractured light in Sully's eyes, betrayed their attempt at simplicity. These two before him were anything but lighthearted spirits. Was this child telling Gillean that he shared responsibility for their woeful state?

The girl kept her eyes on Sully. "Our choices come with consequences."

"Whose choices and consequences are we talking about?" Gillean felt sick, not wanting to know, as he was sure it was something terrible for Sully.

"Sully is mortal now; a human, as you."

"Are you telling me—" Gillean's mind glossed over several possibilities, none of which made sense. "Then what in God's name was he before?"

She shook her head, the crimson braids falling into her lap. "'Tis not for you to know."

Surprised at how quickly anger had overtaken him, Gillean quipped without thought to the girl's age or circumstance. "What sick cult has gotten its claws into the pair of you? That's the same rubbish answer I keep getting from your friend here. Show me the great Oz who decides when the hell it's time for me to know what's going on for *my* benefit?"

Keelin was not upset by his fervor, keeping her tone even as if Gillean was the child. "The answers you seek don't always come wrapped in familiar packages. You have been silently pleading for help for a great while, haven't you? You entreated the universe, and Sully was the one who was sent to you."

"Is this true?" Gillean asked Sully. "Did you do something on my behalf that brought terrible punishment?"

"Gillean," Sully tried to put him off.

"Tell me. Is this true?" Gillean persisted. "The letter from Ciar, does it have anything to do with what happened to you?"

"Yes," Sully sighed. "But it's over now. You are free of me. You should be pleased." He tried to muster a laugh but failed miserably. "I won't be yer shadow any longer."

"Keelin, is this the only choice he has?" Gillean persisted. "To go with you?"

"Yes it is," Sully broke in. "Carry on, *please*."

"There must be another way for him," Gillean pleaded. "What is it?"

Sully looked away as Keelin spoke. "You tell me, Gillean. What is your choice?"

"*My choice?*" Gillean's patience for the child's paradoxical responses was wearing thin.

She waited.

Gillean's stomach churned. "Alright." He took a breath. "He stays with me, and he remains safe from whatever edict-producing powers that did this to him."

The girl heartened, placing a hand on each man. "If that is what you want."

"Don't do this," Sully beseeched her. "Take me with ya. 'Tis what I want."

"But it is not what Gillean wants. Haven't you learned your lesson yet, Sully?" She turned to go, handing the guitar to Gillean. "Don't forget this. It has always taken you where you need to be."

Gillean took one arm from Sully to accept the guitar. He smiled at the girl, grateful for her assistance.

"The Powers be with you both." She kissed Gillean, then Sully, on the cheek. "And remember," she cautioned, "they will be watching you, Sully."

Chapter Three

Vicissitudes

Shortly after Keelin's departure, the train pulled into a station. It was around midday. Gillean insisted they leave the train to tend to Sully's wounds. A good number of people were disembarking. Gillean wondered why he had not noticed any other passengers until now. Could one of these people have witnessed the bizarre happenings during the trip? There was no indication from anyone that anything unusual had transpired during the passage. Fathers were reunited with their children and wives, lovers embraced—and the pair of the singer and his injured companion did not stand out among the crowd of weary travelers.

The station was tidy and welcoming, the afternoon warm and sun-splashed. Gillean, assisting Sully with an arm around him for support, remained alert for a sign that would tell them where they'd been deposited. A white wooden post with painted black letters spelled out a strange word for a point of arrival.

Sully put up a brave fight against the obvious pain. Gillean wrapped him in a leather jacket, partly to keep the shivering man warm, but also to hide the terrible burn marks on his shirt and skin. He wanted desperately to find them shelter, so Sully could get a proper rest. It was imperative he have strength enough to be questioned at length about who he really was, and had been.

"Do you know where we are? What does the word on the sign mean?"

Sully drew in a breath and said, "*Athruithe sa Saol*. It means 'vicissitudes of life.'"

"Vicissitudes?"

"Changes, changes in life."

Gillean took umbrage to the simplistic explanation: he was Trinity-educated. "I know what vicissitudes means. I never heard of such a town. Are we still in Ireland?" He scanned the area for something familiar.

"I wouldn't know." Sully leaned against his companion. "You are the erudite, all-knowing one."

Gillean gave Sully's shoulder a squeeze. "Come on now. We'll manage, no worries, right?" He said it as much to reassure himself as the disheartened Sully.

"Gillean, I have to sit awhile. Why don't ya go on without me, I'll catch up."

Gillean shifted both his suitcase and Sully's cloth knapsack over his free arm.

"Hardly, you heard what Keelin said. We are in this together. We'll find a place to stay straight away. Can you manage for a little longer?"

The guitar hanging over Sully's shoulder swung against his side as he winced, "Uh-huh."

Sully was making his best effort not to be a burden. Gillean felt he'd been pushed into the deep end of a pool. "Good. We'll settle at the nearest bed and breakfast we can find, which shouldn't be too difficult. If this is Ireland, we should find an inn with a welcoming innkeeper in no time."

Gillean held to the hope that they were still in Ireland, and not some cosmic delusion he seemed to be experiencing by the hour. The one thing that remained constant was Sully, and he was hurt. Gillean put aside the issues and concerns that had taken him from his own home and family, sweeping them under the carpet of his subconscious, fully focused on helping the ailing man.

They'd walked along the pleasant, tree-lined dirt road for a quarter mile when they came upon the rear entrance of a large, stone farm house. Cows and horses grazed quietly in the fenced-in acreage, paying no mind to the human newcomers.

"Round here, that's gotta be us!" Gillean cried with enthusiasm, leading Sully to the front of the house. "Can you manage the stairs?" He tried to get Sully to smile. "Or I could carry you up and tell the proprietor we desire the honeymoon chamber."

It worked. For the first time in what seemed an age, a cautious grin slid across the young man's lips. It was not the contagious smile Gillean had become accustomed to, but it was welcome all the same.

"I'd like to see ya pull that one off, Faraday," he answered with a slight spark in his eyes.

Gillean led Sully up the first of a series of steps. The wooden exterior was a soft yellow, reminiscent of the wild daffodils blooming in the Irish fields. The wrap-around porch offered various-sized wicker chairs and a view of the verdant countryside surrounding it. There were no other houses in sight. The seclusion offered by the inn was perfect. A large sign bore the family's crest as well as the name, "Ballyhugh".

Upon entering, they were immediately bombarded by the sweet smell of baking. Cinnamon, butter and vanilla swirled with the dust in the shafts of late afternoon sunlight, bathing every piece of homey furniture in a golden glow. The two men walked further, stepping onto a well-worn, rag rug. As they basked in the comfy feeling, a kindly older woman appeared from a back room. Her predominately silver hair was flecked with streaks of the black color of her youth. She offered them her hands and a warm, genuine smile.

"Hallo, lads! Welcome to the Ballyhugh. My name is Rene McHugh.

Gillean reached for her hand. "Good afternoon, Mrs. McHugh, I'm Gillean, and this is my mate Sully."

The woman gave Gillean's hand a strong squeeze, but as she reached for Sully's, she took a step back, apprehension clouding her hazel eyes. "Oh my," she breathed. Sully stared at the floor. He was abruptly and uncharacteristically quiet.

Gillean broke the uncomfortable silence. "Sully is feeling a bit under the weather you see, Mrs. McHugh. I'd appreciate it if we could have a room directly, if you have one available."

The woman kept her eyes on Sully as Gillean spoke.

"Mrs. McHugh?" Gillean pressed.

"What? Oh, yes! Yes, of course! I'm sorry. Sure we do have rooms for the both of ya."

She turned her attention back to Gillean, who was worried she might recognize him. The last thing he wanted was for anyone to know his identity, or to call attention to himself. Gillean winked, trying to speed along the process. "Thank you, Mrs. McHugh. I'd appreciate it if we could sign in now. Sully desperately needs to rest."

Whatever her concerns, she quickly responded to Gillean's request. "Certainly. If ya would just follow me." She motioned to an oak counter to their right.

Sully whispered a line from one of Gillean's songs as they walked: *"Follow me, and I will show ya to yer heart."*

"Shut up!" Gillean's voice was well above a whisper.

"Pardon me?" Mrs. McHugh came around the counter. The stunned look on her ruddy face made it obvious she had heard.

"Ah," Gillean stumbled over his words, "I said, RIGHT UP! We will be going RIGHT UP to our room!" He cleared his throat. Mrs. McHugh opened a ledger, studying Gillean with curiosity. She was the perfect Irish hostess, keeping her thoughts to herself, and went about the proper business of helping her guests to settle in.

"I won't keep ya but a few moments. Ya need not tell me how long ya plan on stayin'. We'll take care of such business tomorrow. If I can just get ya to sign in."

She offered Gillean a pen and turned the book towards him. He hesitated with the pen in mid-air. He considered how many times had he signed his name—on a photograph, an autograph book, a cocktail napkin—and, in his earlier, wilder days, various parts of a woman's anatomy. He had signed it with great flourish and confidence then, knowing the cache his signature carried. At this moment, he wanted as much distance from fame as possible. He leaned over and pressed pen to paper.

He turned the book back to the woman. "Very well, Mr..."—she leaned in to make out the surname—"Mr. Kinsey. 'Tis two rooms you'll be needin'?"

Gillean breathed a sigh of relief. The earlier look of recognition on the woman's face had vanished when she read his name. He said a silent "thank you" to his mother's clan, and answered her query.

"One will do, please."

Mrs. McHugh cast a quizzical glance at Sully as he inquired, "*One room?*"

Gillean confirmed, "Yes, one room. With a king size bed if you please."

Mrs. McHugh stared at the men a moment longer, raising an eyebrow. "I daresay this is a most unusual request. If yer quite certain."

"Quite."

As she turned her back to obtain the proper key, Sully turned to Gillean. "What are ya doin'? One room? That won't rouse suspicion too much, will it?"

"Just shut it. If you think I am going to let you out of my sight for one minute you're wrong. You are MINE!"

Mrs. McHugh appeared holding out a key to Gillean, a dubious look on her face. "You gents on holiday, is it?"

Sully leaned onto the counter. "Not exactly. Ya wouldn't be havin' yer honeymoon chamber available would ya, Mrs. McHugh?"

Gillean forced a laugh that was something between mortification and fury.

"Oh ho! Sully!" He hugged the man close. "He is such a lovable imp, isn't he, Mrs. McHugh? Imagine... The honeymoon chamber. He's the limit!"

Mrs. McHugh kept her distance, but endeavored to remain the calm professional. "Yes indeed. The limit." She came around the counter and proceeded to the back of the house. "If you two..."—she hesitated as both Sully and Gillean regarded her—"*men* would come this way. Your room is up this staircase."

"Thank you, thank you Mrs. McHugh!" Gillean said, pulling Sully along. When they reached Room 203, she stooped at the door.

Her face flushed as she gave them some final direction. "Well, everythin' you'll be needin'—towels, robes, extra blankets—you'll find in there. I'll return in a bit with some tea and scones for ya. Breakfast is at 8AM. Are ya all fixed then?"

"Yes, very good. You're magnificent, Rene, truly." Gillean gave her one of his trademark Faraday smiles, known to make many a woman's knees, including Mrs. McHugh's, weak.

Her hand fluttered to her cheek as she giggled. "Ah, 'tis nothin', Mr. Kinsey, nothin' t'all. You and yer friend just give us a holler if ya need anythin'."

With that she shuffled down the stairs.

"*You're magnificent, Rene.*" Sully mimicked. "Is that how ya treat women?"

Gillean put the key in the lock and opened the door.

"Let me tell you something, my friend," Gillean enthusiastically replied as he walked into the Victorian-style sitting room and over to the bed. "If there is one thing I do know, it's how to give a woman pleasure, and to receive in kind. You ought to try it some time."

Sully wearily placed the guitar onto the floor. "Gillean, I died when I was seven years old. Pleasure-seeking was not top on me list of obligations when I was returned." He rubbed his chest, looking uncertain. "What yer describing sounds like a jumped up schoolboy."

Gillean was about to fire back a round of questions at Sully's revelation when he noticed how pale his companion had become. "Yeah, yeah, you're a perfect being." He took Sully by the arm and led him to the four-poster bed. Gillean's tone softened. "Time for you to rest."

Sully kicked off his boots and climbed into the bed, settling with evident discomfort under the soft, down quilt. He gave the impression of being fragile and innocent.

Uneasy about Sully's wounds, Gillean inquired, "Are you sure you don't need a doctor?"

Sully yawned, "No, I'll manage."

Gillean sat down on the edge of the bed. He had to ask Sully one thing before he fell off to sleep. "You said you died when you were seven. Does that mean you're an...an angel?"

Sully struggled to keep his eyes open. "I'm no heavenly being. I never was."

"Who was Keelin referring to when she said *they* will be watching you?"

Sully weakly held one hand in the air. "Yer not to worry." He turned his head, suppressing another yawn.

"I'm sorry. I just want to understand what happened to you, but you get some sleep." Gillean started to rise from the bed.

"No," Sully reached out to him. "You should understand. I want to tell ya."

Gillean sat back down.

"Contrary to what most people believe, angels are not born into this world as human. Angels are spiritual beings who come from another dimension entirely. They may help, and sometimes even reveal themselves to humans by taking on their form. So ya see, I am not an angel, as I was once born human, like you."

Gillean was listening in rapt attention. "Go on," he encouraged.

"People like me, who die an unfinished life; we are called *ath-teagmha*. It means 'rerencounter'. We are sent back to earth to rerencounter life as entities who offer guidance and assistance to those humans who share dreams similar to the ones we had in our lifetimes."

Enthralled, but confused by the lofty concept, Gillean's eyes requested more.

"We connect with the energy of kindred souls."

"So, you're not an angel, but some sort of guardian?"

"Yes, because we are souls that share the same purpose or desire."

"And what would that be?" Gillean could hardly wait for the answer to a question he had pondered for most of his life.

"'Tis not the—"

"Sully, don't even dare!" Gillean would have shaken his companion had he not been in such a sorry state.

Sully closed his eyes. He appeared to be drawn inward by his own musings. "Ya give me too much credit. I don't have all the answers. This is why we must travel our own paths."

"So you have no idea why yours and mine happened to collide?"

"When me father beat me, the one thing that would console me was lookin' out into the vast, night sky—"

"Hold on!" Gillean abruptly stopped Sully's exposition. "Your father *beat* you?"

Sully ignored the question. "I watched the night sky wonderin' about the stars and all the planets far away, *dreamin' of the universe*, as you once sang. I believed if life was so unhappy on earth, surely there were other planets where people cherished and cared for one another and were able to resist the temptation of evil."

Gillean's eyes filled as he imagined the anguish Sully must have endured during his brief lifetime. "And you played the fiddle."

Sully's face registered surprise. "I did."

"But why *me*?" Gillean lowered his graying head. "I have certainly been less than an honorable man."

"Ya have the heart of a troubadour, and the soul of a voyager. You, too, look to the stars when life here gets too unbearable. You envision other planets where beings live much different, more peaceable lives."

Gillean smiled. "Does this connection between us have something do to with why you look so much like me?"

"Unfortunately, yes. Nothin' could be done to help that. I am a reminder of your aspirations when you were young. More's the pity for me, eh?" Sully laughed.

"What about Keelin? Did she die as a child, too?"

Sully turned his head away.

Gillean placed his hand on Sully's arm. "These things must be difficult for you to talk about."

Sully spoke with his face to the wall. "That is why the Elders chose her to take me back. I have already broken a serious rule. Keelin was a human child whose father used as a replacement for his wife's affections."

"Christ Jesus!" Gillean gasped, thinking of his own daughter, Antonia, only five years old herself. He recalled holding her when she was born. He'd felt for the first time in his life that he was actually capable of killing—*would* kill anyone who ever tried to harm this precious being.

"I believed there must have been a reason why I found Keelin, and so I took her with me. I presented her to the Elders, and pleaded they provide her refuge. They agreed on the condition that I never again interfere in the life of another human."

"Oh, Sully, but for me? Why did you feel you had to rescue me?"

Sully swallowed hard. "About Ciar—"

"You don't have to say another word." Gillean raised his hand as if making a pledge. "I'm done with her."

"I don't think it will be so simple. Ya don't know her."

"And you do?"

Sully nodded. A violent cough overtook him.

"Put this business out of your head. Ciar is my problem." Gillean rose from the bed.

"She is *our* problem," Sully corrected between raspy breaths.

"Good night, Sully. Sleep well." Gillean brushed his hand over the man's hair.

"Good night, Mr. Kinsey."

———————————————◆———————————————

Sully valiantly fought the urge to sleep, waiting until he could hear Gillean's even breaths of deep slumber. He rested in a reclining chair, giving off the occasional rattling snore to assure Sully his movements would go undetected. He had risen from the bed, checking the grandfather clock. Because of the cracks along its wooden belly, Sully was dubious it would be working, but its elderly heart ticked away. The face registered 3AM. Turning the door handle and making ready to leave, he took one more look at the sleeping Gillean.

Sully's heart constricted as he thought of what Gillean had taken on in choosing to take care of him, but he would not put this man at further risk. Sully was the one who had done the unforgivable deed; it was he who should be punished. The irony was not lost on Sully. He wanted to warn Gillean about Ciar, but she had correctly predicted Sully's total incompetence He quickly scribbled a note, leaving it on the coffee table.

"Goodbye, little singer, good luck to ya," Sully whispered, as he closed the door.

Chapter Four

Hide and Seek

The moon hung low and large. He had been walking for nearly a half hour when he was confronted with her voice.

"Sully! You're pong at hide-and-seek. Please return to Gillean before I have to take you back with me."

Keelin was walking by his side, tugging at his sleeve. Sully took her hand in his and kept walking.

"No, Keelin. I told ya, I do not want to stay with him. I will not. He'll work out what he has to on his own, and I—"

"You'll pay a high price." She gripped his hand. "You don't know what you are doing. Return to Gillean before they know what you have done."

He stopped walking and looked into her clear eyes, which transmitted pure honesty and caring. She was everything good in the world.

"Ya mean they already know and have sent ya to collect me. I'm deeply sorry I hurt ya."

"You didn't hurt me, silly." She gave him her toothy grin. "And the Elders aren't aware of your leaving, *yet*. I came here to warn you. Please do as I say, go back to him."

She shook his arm in desperation.

He leaned down to kiss her forehead. "I won't. If ya truly want to help me, you'll return to the Elders and forget all about me. Ya didn't lay eyes on me tonight. If anyone asks, ya have no idea where I am."

"You have no more time. "Ya won't reach whatever place ya think yer going. Or Gillean could come looking for you himself," she persisted.

"He won't. I took care of it, me girl, go back. Don't come to me again. Get on."

He gently nudged her aside, quickening his pace.

"Sully! Sully!" she called after him in vain.

"**S**ully!" It was daybreak and Gillean was wildly pacing the room, holding another letter and wondering desperately what had become of his new companion.

After a frantic search of the bed and breakfast and nearby grounds, Gillean concluded Sully meant what he had written in his hastily scrawled late-night missal. He was gone. Sorry for the trouble he'd caused and wished Gillean strength of heart. Sully wrote of his firm belief that Gillean would be better off without him, and concluded with a final plea for Gillean to keep his distance from Ciar. She was not to be trusted.

Gillean agreed with Sully's summation of the artist, which was why he reached for his mobile and dialed her number. He'd have to be careful. He was a man in a cage with a tigress, but he meant to get some answers. He would help Sully, even if the way in which to do so was not apparent to him at the moment.

As he waited for Ciar to pick up, he glimpsed the guitar Keelin had left with him. It was a full week since he'd laid his hands on an instrument. *Odd*, he thought. This hadn't occurred since he was seventeen. Gillean chuckled at the idea that beings from another dimension would cause him to reassess his priorities.

"Care to share what's so funny, Gilly?"

She'd caught him off guard.

"So, you are at home." Gillean stood with phone in hand.

"Of course I am. I have been making many delightful preparations in the hopes of coaxing you back to me."

Even in the midst of what had transpired, Gillean could not quell the anticipation she aroused. When he'd first met his wife, Adara, he had been infatuated with her, no doubt. But he was a wild heart and his attention was easily diverted. She had been his greatest challenge. Unlike his other lovers, Adara didn't ask anything of him, but rather offered her support. She didn't wait around pining for him when he would unexpectedly take off for weeks on end, but did not refuse him when he returned, either. She was continually there to take back his gypsy soul, offering a shoulder to cry on, and the tender reassurance that he would be a success.

Despite his best efforts at not settling down, a seed had begun to take root. Over time it grew into a deep, abiding friendship and love. He'd never told another living soul, not even Adara, that from the first he'd been in total disbelief that such a genuine and caring woman would ever fall for him. The boys in the popular band he opened for, however, had no reservations about this fact. They teased him mercilessly.

"Come on, Faraday. She's much too smart and independent for the likes of you. Why don't ya stick to the eye candy type—the no-brainers? That's more your speed. After all, you're just an opening act. You'll never be the main event," they would poke at him in hysterics.

This brought a painful echo of his childhood, when he'd been shuttled off to boarding school, alone and ridiculed by the rest of the lads for being the smallest and because of his eclectic background. Many nights he had lain in his dormitory bed, listening to the lonesome, howling wind. On many nights he lay in his dormitory bed, hunkered down underneath the flimsy covers listening to the lonesome howling of the wind, while the first of the trenchant briars began twisting their way up the wall that was being erected inside his heart. Gillean had vowed to make those who derided him sit up and take notice someday. He wouldn't always be the butt of everyone's jokes. The impenetrable wall would keep him safe.

Three years after first meeting Gillean, Adara informed him she was moving to America. She had been accepted to a prestigious dance company. Gillean had had no idea she was even considering a life separate from his. A terrible panic seized him. His career was just showing signs of promise. How could he set sail without his anchor? He took her to the top of the highest tower of the *Teach na Spioradi* on Christmas Eve, the sky a bowl of stars above them. Falling to his knees, he begged her to marry him.

Joseph readily loaned his brother the money to purchase a tiny ruby engagement ring. That was the only time Gillean ever asked a family member for financial aid. Good old Jos had come through for Gillean once again. His elder brother was only too happy to concede victory to Ena. Gillean was finally going to settle down and marry "the right girl."

Fixing her halting eyes on him, Adara inquired, "What? I don't even get a song for this momentous occasion? Ya know, Dylan would have one at the ready."

Gillean bounded up from the icy ground. He was truly mad about this woman. "Every song I sing is for you." He kissed her hands. "Stay with me and allow me such an honor."

"Just don't forget about this moment, and our promise, when you go soaring out there." She pointed to the December sky as he hugged her to him.

Like a bothersome bug, Gillean brushed away the feeling that he was taking away something essential to her, rather than giving her what she ought to have.

"You don't worry, missy. No amount of success would mean anything to me without you," he assured her with a kiss.

Gillean succeeded beyond his wildest imagination. But with the spoils of fame came the temptation of other, beautiful lovers. He felt it his right not to deny himself anything he earned. The vow he'd made on such a long-ago Christmas Eve floated away like so many flakes of snow. He reasoned with his twisted conscience that he deserved everything offered to him. He'd worked for it—suffered, sweated and bled for it. If his wife and those on the outside of his life could not understand and accept his perspective, they damn sure were able to accept the money and gifts he gave them. He was lost. He no longer knew what love was, let alone how to be a lover. The treasured ideals he'd once sung about—fidelity, simplicity and family—were illusions to him. Not even those basic things he dreamed of for himself were immune to the corruption of power and fame.

But he'd swallowed the lies and sour emotions like pieces of spoiled apple. He wanted his family to be safe and happy. He was willing to pay any price for them, but now such a price was too high—the sacrifice of his nefarious pleasures. That was what he had seen in Ciar: an escape. She offered him the chance to live without rules or demands, just reward. The wounded Sully caused Gillean to ponder if Ciar and her beguiling trappings were the grandest of illusions.

"Tell me you will come and see me," Ciar responded to his thoughtful silence.

"That depends." He felt as if he'd just moved forward a pawn.

"Upon what?"

"What have you done with Sully?"

"I beg your pardon?"

"Look, Ciar, I don't have time for games. If you are going to claim you don't know him, so be it. But I have to ring off. I have things to see about." He was amazed at his own calm in the face of her possible wrath.

"I suppose you suspect sweet Sully has gotten his teeth into me too, or maybe even your wife?"

He didn't like where the conversation was going. "Tell me how you know him. You can leave out the unfounded accusations." Rattled, he was in need of a stiff scotch.

Ciar explained, "I knew Sully when he was a child. Poor lad, he was a disturbed little boy."

"It would go to show he'd be a little off, considering his father beat the tar out of him!" Gillean interjected.

"Oh, is *that* the story he gave you?"

"*Story?*"

"My little Gilly, you're too good a man. You take what people tell you at face value, after all these years. It's one of the reasons you are so special to me, but it's also one of the reasons people take advantage of you."

"You mean to tell me Sully was not abused by his father?"

"Abused? No. Sully got into a lot of trouble—and not just the usual rambunctious boy kind of trouble—when he was still quite young. His father, not knowing what to do with him, sent him away—I don't know where. I thought that would be the last time I'd see him, until one night, years later; we met at a party in London. One thing led to another... It was a meaningless affair."

"Wait a minute!" Gillean shook his aching head. "How could you have known Sully when he was a child? He was born here in Ireland. He lived and di—" He had enough sense to not finish his statement.

"That's right; I didn't get the chance to tell you, did I? I'm not Prague born. I didn't call it my home until I was fifteen. I spent some time in Ireland with a cousin when I was a girl. In fact, I'm named for our shared grandmother. Her family lived up the road from Sully's." She sighed. "That was a lifetime ago. Easy to forget, I suppose."

"Hmm..."

"Come now, that is ancient history. I swear to you, I have not seen him since. But I don't blame you for being upset. Sully is cunning."

"Yes, you suggested he has knowledge of my wife, is it?"

"I didn't want this to come between us, but, yes, I'm certain of it. But, please"—the seductive tone was familiar enough to Gillean—"let's not talk of trifles. It's time you concentrated more on what you and I could have if you would simply let go."

"I'll have to get back to you, *darling*." Gillean was in no mood for her niggling.

"When will you realize it is I you are meant to be with? We are soulmates. The universe doesn't make mistakes."

"Perhaps not, but people do. I have to go now."

"Gilly?"

"Goodbye, Ciar."

Gillean turned off his mobile so that no one could reach him. Grabbing his one travel bag he moved about the room preparing to leave. His hand on the door, he looked back one more time at the guitar propped against the wall. He saw the face of the little girl, Keelin, the look of love in her eyes for Sully, her anguish in not being able to help him. Gillean had promised her he would keep Sully safe, but he had no idea where the man was. Or did he? Gillean swept the guitar under his arm. Home. He was going home.

Ciar rested the phone back onto the receiver, giddy over the fact that Sully himself had set the perfect trap, while having the audacity to believe that he could snare her. Sully and his ridiculous dedication to the *truth*; she had no such naive notions. She could lie whenever it suited her. And as far as Sully was concerned, Ciar celebrated in her unparalleled talent for spinning the most elaborate of tales. She was a bit disappointed the much-anticipated confrontation with her adversary was quickly approaching an easy win.

Chapter Five

Wild Flower

Sully walked for most of the morning, his pace checked by the sting of his burns, and his senses on high alert lest he make contact with any other person. Keeping to the pastoral back roads, he noticed cows and sheep were the sole witnesses to his passing. By noon, hunger, the throbbing of blistered skin and exhaustion, caused him to collapse under a willow tree standing on the edge of a farm. He slept for hours. He woke shivering. It was night once again. He was thankful for the darkness but wished for the warmth of Gillean's jacket as he rose unsteadily from the ground.

"Man ought to get somethin' for his troubles, I'd say." He hadn't the slightest clue where to go, or what he was supposed to do. "Maybe I can find me some tinkers to take up with."

He brushed off his dirty, wrinkled clothes, gathered up his knapsack and set out on the road once again. His immediate need was food. He hoped to find a tree or bush offering ripe fruit ready for the taking. He remembered from his childhood that a person needed money for just about anything, but he had none.

"Ah, lad, ya've fallen a long way from grace," he said, bemoaning his fate.

"Come on, Sully, over here! Over here!" It wasn't so much a voice as a collection of voices, children shouting, each trying to outdo the other. "Over here!" Their laughter and mirth were infectious.

Scanning the area, he saw no one, not even the usual farm animals. All good souls were in their homes at this hour—at dinner tables or sitting by their hearths. How could anyone know the plight of one forsaken being? His eyes fixed upon a grand house looming ahead. It sat back from the road and, like the Ballyhugh, was surrounded by voluptuous trees and a thriving meadow. Funny, he hadn't noticed it before he'd fallen asleep.

Wildflowers moved gently with the evening breeze. They appeared to be gossamer dancers, silently swaying in the moonlight. The urging of the voices, the brisk night air, and the wave of those flowers overtook Sully. He possessed the irresistible urge to take off his boots and walk through the grass. He glanced again at the building. A few of the rooms were bright with lamplight.

He removed his boots and the socks he'd hated having to wear as a boy and slipped like a fey into the opulent meadow. He broke into a run, throwing his arms out as he went. The pain in his chest could not compete with the rush he felt from releasing the pent-up joy of a seven-year-old who had been forbidden to run free. The grass underneath his feet was soft and wet; the breeze lifted his hair as he ran. Wind chimes sounded from a back porch, filling the air with sweet, alluring music mixing with the children's laughter.

He stopped to catch his breath, gazing out over the enormous stretch of land on which sat the house. Sully couldn't comprehend that any human could be so lucky as to have all of this in their possession. He spied the crescent moon residing in his post of velvet sky and shouted, "Ha! But no man could own you!" He waved at the golden sliver as if signaling to an old friend, then took off at full throttle in the direction of the house.

"Wahoo!" he yelled.

The secretive moon concealed itself behind a collection of drifting clouds, forcing shadows on the world below. Still, he saw her standing at the open gate, but too late. He had built up too much momentum to stop. She held her ground, a look of disbelief on her face. Their bodies crashed to the ground, his landing on top of hers.

"Have you gone completely mad?" she screamed.

Sully quickly disjoined himself from her and inquired, "Are ya alright? I'm desperately sorry."

She was quiet for a moment, then spoke in a more collected tone: "I think so. Are *you* alright?"

Auburn hair fell across her face. Gray eyes, their character reflecting much suffering through the years, nailed him to the spot. She was wearing silk pajamas with a matching robe. Her slippers had been sent flying willy-nilly as a result of the collision.

"No, just me pride is a bit dented. But I am glad you are in one piece." He smiled shyly.

Her mouth opened slightly at the sound of his voice, her continued stare causing him to become self-conscious. He was woefully inept at being human.

"Pardon me, again. It might do nicely if I help set ya right!" He offered her his hand.

She sat up smoothing her hair. She was not a young woman, nor was she old. She had a regal but delicate bearing and a self-protectiveness about her that told Sully she kept herself closed to others she did not know.

He helped her to her feet and was about to tussle his way through an introduction when she spoke again.

"What are you doing home? And what in God's name are you doing jaunting in the meadow at this hour?"

"Huh?"

She stood looking at him, as if trying to decide whether she wanted to continue the conversation or leave him where he was. "I see you have thought about what I said to you before you left."

He kept quiet, shifting his weight from his left foot to his right.

"Well, you won't get my forgiveness so easily as running through the grass like a nymph. Don't just stand there; help me look for my slippers." She bent over, searching for the lost footwear.

"But, I—I'm—"

She stood up straight, regarding him with bewildered amusement. "You are helpless, that's what you are! Now come on and help me with the slippers you knocked to high heaven."

"My name is—" Sully choked.

"Mr. Kinsey, I know. Clever one, Gillean. You think you could travel the country unnoticed with your mother's name? I received a phone call this morning from a B&B to verify your charge account. No doubt your travels will be in the local news soon enough. Sorry you couldn't get your proper rest, dear."

"*Gillean?* What? I—I'm trying to tell ya…"

She wasn't paying attention to him. She was busy rooting through the grass for her slippers. "Don't try and be cute with me. It won't get you anywhere. You will still be sleeping in your study." She lifted one slipper from the ground, waving it victoriously in front of him.

Sully's mind was racing. All he knew was that he did not want to take his leave of this woman just yet. She was special, and in desperate need of something. That much was clear from those winter eyes.

"*Adara!*" He pointed at her as if he had solved a cold case.

"Very good. Nice of you to remember *my* name, at least, Mr. Kinsey."

He pulled the other slipper from his pocket and handed it to her.

"How did that get there?"

He shrugged like a renegade thief. "Magic?" he offered.

She threw back her head and laughed, revealing the charming young girl she'd once been. He must have been a sight with no shoes, wrinkled trousers and a burned shirt. He endeavored to remain composed.

"I don't need to sleep inside. If ya have a barn, I'll be just fine."

"What are you talking about? Sleeping in the barn? Honestly. I may not have completely forgiven you your tantrum, but have I ever sent you to sleep in the barn? Besides, you look like hell. I hardly recognized you. You need a long, hot shower, my beloved husband." She proceeded to the house calling after him. "Then again, maybe you should sleep in the barn. That's where all little piggies belong!"

"Touché, Adara!" Sully was tickled by the woman's sense of humor. "Yer really funny."

"Your flattery is comical. Now get a move on before the media set up camp out here as well!"

She was almost at the front door but stopped to wait for him.

Good God. She thinks I'm Gillean!

Sully pleaded for any power to take mercy on him and his plight. He must escape this potentially devastating situation, but in a way not to cause more harm to Gillean or his wife. Gillean's own words provided him the guidance he needed: *one thing I do know is how to pleasure a woman.*

Gillean had been so smug in his statement, but it was obvious his wife was not pleased with him. Her eyes could not hide years of disappointment. She struck him as an intelligent, sensitive woman. How could Gillean have been taken in by the likes of Ciar? Granted, her artistry was deception, but Gillean already had all he could possibly want.

That is it! Sully's predicament was not a punishment. Keelin had somehow seen to it that he arrive here. Certainly she could have persuaded the Elders to agree to such a thing.

Now he had the benefit of fully experiencing Gillean's life and with the experience would come solutions. Now he could truly help Gillean unimpeded by any laws or rules, but also without any powers. It would be a great challenge, but Sully deemed himself ready. His life as a child had been snuffed out, overcome by the dark forces which occupied men's hearts. He would make sure that his second chance would not be wasted. Not only could he help Gillean find his way back but perhaps, just perhaps, he could help the striking woman to see the obvious beauty she overlooked in herself.

Once inside, Adara walked ahead with Sully keeping a respectable distance. The beauty of the Faraday inner dwelling astounded him. The home was huge, filled with the luxuries which made it beyond the means of an ordinary person. Each of the rooms he passed was appointed with hand-painted vases containing fresh flowers, grand furniture, and precious pieces of artwork. The many pictures displayed of Gillean, Adara, and their children at various stages of their lives encouraged Sully. He sensed Gillean's love for each of his four children.

Adara turned around. "The children will be disappointed they missed you. Ena asked if she could have them for a fortnight. I didn't have the heart to tell her about your little trip."

"Ena?"

Adara resumed walking. "Yes, Ena, your mother for heaven's sake. Honestly, Gillean Faraday, if you're trying to convince me you are innocent of treachery, you are doing a terrible job of it."

The hallway was dim, with only the light of a small table lamp. Sully hesitated, wishing for the right words to tell her about himself, praying she wouldn't put him out.

She stopped with her back to him and drew her robe tighter around her slight waste.

"I'll give you the night to think of a proper reason as to why someone named Ciar would call here claiming it was urgent she should speak with you. I thought we were done with such nonsense years ago."

Appalled at Ciar's audacity, Sully stood behind Adara assembling his words.

"I would like to talk—" He broke off as the pain from his wounds took his breath. He bent over clutching his chest.

"What is it? Are you hurt?" She reached for him.

Sully shook his head, wanting desperately to be any place than where he was at that moment. He cursed his vulnerability and the stupidity of his plan.

"I'm…fine…"

"The hell you are!" She lightly moved his hands away, seeing the burn marks in his shirt.

"Don't, please." Sully tried to back away.

Paying him no mind, she unfastened the buttons. His skin was covered with blistered pieces of flesh.

"Gillean, oh Gillean…"

She took his hand and led him to a black-and-white-tiled bathroom. It was bigger than any living room he had ever seen. Sitting him on the edge of the porcelain tub, she turned on the light and knelt in front of him to get a better look. Her eyes were on his chest. She didn't bother to look at his face, Sully assumed, because she believed it was the same face she had seen for the last twenty-some years. *People are so utterly blind*, he thought.

"You need a doctor," she said in all seriousness.

"Adara."

"I've never seen burns like this. What in heaven's name were you do—" She raised her head to finally look at him. "You're not Gillean." The sudden change in her expression showed no alarm, only the obvious question.

"No, kind lady, I'm not."

"Well if you won't let me fetch a doctor, at least let me put something on those burns. And you'll need something for the pain, of course."

She was up and rooting through a well-stocked cupboard of first aid supplies. She knelt down again with a yellow tube, squirting the contents onto her finger.

"I'm sorry, but this is going to smart a little."

<hr />

A flash of memory; the sterile smell of hospital, the biting pain of broken bones, and unexplained bruises, a concerned doctor questioning a large man standing by a child's bedside gripping his hand, meaning to keep him quiet. "I turned me head for a second, and he took a tumble down the stairs. I didn't have a chance to get to him, ya see?" A tall blonde woman with coal eyes impatiently pacing the corridor outside the door, her hatred more painful than the beating the child had received, and one hundred times more terrifying.

<hr />

"Are you quite ready?" Adara was smiling at him with her finger in mid-air.

Sully blinked his eyes and was once again in the bathroom with Gillean's wife. He could hardly believe she wanted to minister to his wounds.

"But ya don't even know who I am."

"I don't need to know right now. I am certain you don't mean to do me harm, and you need medical attention. Now prepare yourself."

She smoothed the paste onto his chest. It felt like a hive of hornets.

"OUCH!"

Adara quickly removed her hand.

"I'm sorry!" they apologized simultaneously.

"Now ya know why I don't want a doctor," Sully declared wryly.

"On my word, I've borne four children into this world, and no matter how old a man may be, he's still a wee lad when it comes to pain."

She held her hand out again as if to prove she would be gentle.

"Some men more than others."

"You aren't going to cry on me now, are you?"

She sat back, her face flushed, her hair pulled into a ponytail. The thin lines around the corners of her eyes and mouth hinted at the story of her tumultuous life as Mrs. Faraday.

"Yer something'," Sully said, running a hand through his matted hair. "Providin' first aid to a man who not only trespassed on yer private property, but mowed ya down in yer own driveway and almost lost yer precious pair of slippers."

"Hey, I love those slippers. They were a gift from my—" She caught herself.

"Yer husband, from Gillean?" Sully finished her thought.

"Enough talk, patient! You won't distract me with your attempts to draw me into conversation. I am putting this cream on you, and if you behave in a civilized fashion, I may allow you to tell me who you are, and why you are here before I throw you back into the meadow."

Sully shook his head. The whole situation was unfathomable.

"Don't look so baffled. You are a relative of Gillean's, I gather by your looks. I assume you are here to do his dirty work."

She placed her hands on him again. He squirmed, trying not to feel the sting. Her warm fingers blending with the cold liquid made it bearable.

"Dirty work?" he repeated between gritted teeth.

"You're here to tell me he has taken up with this Ciar woman. Of course he wouldn't want to tell me himself. No, no." She made sure she covered each sore with the ointment. "He's too sensitive, cares too much for my feelings to have to look me in the eye. Or maybe he simply pays someone to clean up his messes. It's more his style."

Sully placed his hands over hers, entreating her with his eyes to listen. "I promise ya, Ciar is not and will not be a threat to yer marriage. Yer husband may have his faults—after all, he's human, right? But he loves ya. And he didn't pay me anythin'. Would I look this wildly stunning if he had?" He mustered a faint smile to assure her.

She stood, putting the cap back on the tube and grabbed for a bottle of tablets. She handed him two with a glass of water.

"Pardon me skepticism, but if that were true, why would I be left alone, tending to a strange man in my bathroom?"

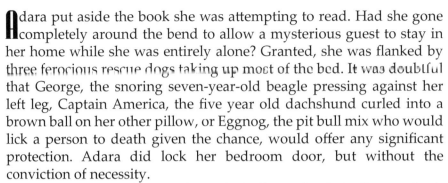

Adara put aside the book she was attempting to read. Had she gone completely around the bend to allow a mysterious guest to stay in her home while she was entirely alone? Granted, she was flanked by three ferocious rescue dogs taking up most of the bed. It was doubtful that George, the snoring seven-year-old beagle pressing against her left leg, Captain America, the five year old dachshund curled into a brown ball on her other pillow, or Eggnog, the pit bull mix who would lick a person to death given the chance, would offer any significant protection. Adara did lock her bedroom door, but without the conviction of necessity.

The young man sleeping down the hall was clearly in distress. But it wasn't simply compassion that drew Adara to him: he reminded her of her husband. The lad possessed the endearing combination of a gentle soul mixed with a touch of the devil-may-care attitude. But there was something about him which was completely alien to the young Gillean who now stood before her in memory, the slight young man in blue jeans that fell to the tops of sneakers which had been worn well past their prime. His dark hair needed a good brushing. His brooding eyes captured her with their mystique. There was the promise of profound passion in his glance, and a most definite hint of the high price to be paid for falling in head first.

An afternoon from a lifetime ago came to mind. She was dancing in the auditorium Gillean was set to play the same evening. It was a rare treat to have this time to herself—better than sneaking a stolen hour in a cozy café with coffee and a good read. Being on the road with Gillean and their six-month-old son, Arlen, occupied most of her time. Adara was extremely proud of her husband's rising success but giving up her dancing had been more difficult than she'd expected.

Gillean arrived several hours before the sound check. Arms and legs akimbo, he looked none too happy as he addressed her, just as she was moving into an arabesque penchée.

"What are you doing here?"

She looked to the band's piano player, who had been kind enough to accompany her. "Thanks so much, Kev. You'll need the rest of afternoon to prepare for the show."

"Ya sure, Adara? This was fun. I got some time yet."

A heated Gillean charged to the foot of the stage. "Yes, she's sure! We have a concert tonight. And I'd thank you to be in top form for it."

Kevin raised his hands in the air as if Gillean had pointed a pistol.

"Take it easy, Faraday."

Adara quickly intervened. "Gillean, it's not his fault. I asked him to play for a half hour." She turned to the keyboardist. "Go on, Kevin. It's tea time. And, thank you."

He hesitated, but appeared to know full well the singer's stormy nature. "Okay then. See ya tonight."

Kevin took his leave, but not without casting a look of disgust at his fellow musician.

"Aren't you supposed to be helping me?" Gillean sounded like a ten-year-old boy with a school project.

"I've got all the t-shirts, posters and programs ready. No worries," she assured.

"Well, by all means, take the afternoon to flit around the stage while I make ready for the biggest concert of my career! Do you see all the seats in here?" He motioned to the empty theatre.

"Gillean—"

"No, truly. I'll be fine."

"I needed a break from the baby and…"

"And *what*?"

"Nothing. You're right." She stroked his arm. "I should have been with you. I'm sorry."

"I'm sorry too." He knelt and kissed her hand, "Your humble servant, Mrs. Faraday." His gaze hinted at repentance. "I'm acting the complete bastard. I'm just so damn nervous, ya know? However"—he hung his head—"I have absolutely no right to be terrible to you."

"There's no reason to be nervous. You'll be wonderful, as ever."

He grabbed at the thin material of her leotard, and getting to his feet, he held her close. "I need you with me."

"I know," she said, pacifying him.

He whispered in her ear, "If you repeat to anyone the bit about my being nervous, I'll lock you out of the bus tonight." He nuzzled her damp hair.

"Don't worry, my love. All your secrets are safe with me."

———⊰✖⊱———

Adara's sleepy eyes drifted to the window to take in the night sky dappled with pieces of starlight. She had lost her husband out among those stars. He shone with them now, competing for the attention. She remained on earth, but she had long since given up searching for a way to reach him. And now this peculiar man had appeared. Letting sleep take her, she drifted off thinking he must be very rare indeed.

Chapter Six

Be a Dancer

Sully woke to a splendid assault of the senses. His empty stomach reacted with rumbles of hunger. The mattress beneath him cradled his body in comfort. The smells of delicious food were overpowering. Was he in a purgatory, a waiting room of sorts for more of the same delights when he entered heaven?

"Excuse me for letting myself in, but when you didn't answer my knock earlier, I was concerned."

Sully palmed his tired eyes. Who was this woman in the doorway?

"It's gone on afternoon now. You needed the sleep, I see." After Adara set a sterling tray laden with various breakfast items on the table next to him, she pulled a posh armchair to the side of the bed to sit down.

He sat up and leaned against the oak headboard.

"What… Yes, I'm sorry." Stretching his arms over his head he asked, "Did I sleep so late?"

"Was there somewhere you needed to be?" She smiled, handing him a scone.

Sully put his hunger before his manners. Taking a generous bite, he then spoke with a half-full mouth, "Thank you."

She was wearing blue jeans and a white jumper that fell to her knees. Her ginger hair was piled on top of her head, fastened with a colorful barrette. She appeared younger in the morning light and dressed casually. Looking at her now, Sully could see Adara was quite the beauty: not the obvious, socially endorsed kind, or the sort that relies on overt physical allure like Ciar, but with a grace and dignity bestowed by the wisdom of time. Wisdom Sully desperately wished for.

He accepted the cup of tea she proffered.

"You don't remember my seeing you off to bed last night, do you?"

She poured herself a cup.

"No."

"But, you do remember me?"

"Yes, of course, Mrs. Faraday.

"Adara, please," She took a sip of the licorice-scented tea. "You were so tired. I hadn't the heart to send you out to the barn."

"Hmm…" Sully was now sampling the scrambled eggs. "

Adara leaned her back against the chair, appreciating Sully's hardy appetite. "I don't recall anyone relishing food that I prepared as much as you."

He offered a bashful glance. "Pardon me." Sully dabbed the corners of his mouth with a linen napkin. "But, 'tis very good."

When Sully had satiated his hunger and took a last sip of orange juice, Adara removed the tray. She sat on the edge of the bed. "Let's have a look at those burns."

The throbbing pain was blessedly absent. "I can hardly feel them."

She reached over to unbutton his top.

He flushed at the direct gesture.

She paused. "Don't worry, I'm not going to attack you. I just want to check on your injuries."

"It's not that." He noted his new pajamas. "Ya changed me clothes!"

Adara laughed, a rich, full chuckle, inviting like a warm fire.

"You really do think I'm a desperate woman! I gave you a pair of Gillean' pajamas before I sent you to bed. You took care of the rest." She started up from the bed. "But if I honestly make you feel uncomfortable, perhaps it's best if…"

Sully fingered the soft material. The unique musk of Gillean permeated the purple silk fibers. Odd, yet exciting, feelings churned inside like the muddied waters of a once-pure stream as he breathed in the scent. She was almost out the door when her words registered with him.

"No! Wait, please." He motioned for her to sit. "It's me who is the desperate one. You've been so kind. I meant no offense."

"No offense taken." She remained standing. "I would like to see that you are fit to stand trial."

"Trial, did ya say?"

"Meaning you tell me who you are, and why you've come here."

Sully didn't know how he could explain himself in a way that wouldn't leave her questioning his sanity. A few hours ago he was sure he could help both her and Gillean, now he wasn't convinced he could help himself. He lay back nervously.

"Alright," he agreed.

As she unbuttoned his shirt, her eyes met his.

"Well, go on, Doctor. Am I gonna live?" Sully asked.

She attempted to open his shirt. The fabric appeared to be fused to his skin. But when she let go, the shirt fell away like petals from a flower. She sat back to marvel. His chest was unmarred, as if there had never been an injury.

"Astonishing!" Adara gasped. "It's completely healed."

Sully looked down, amazed with what he saw as well. The source of his pain had literally disappeared overnight.

"Well, how do ya like that? Must have been yer good care and these grand pajamas."

She covered her mouth as if to swallow unexpected emotions. Keeping her back to Sully she drifted towards the window.

Buttoning up his shirt he went to her feeling terribly confused.

She was quietly crying, hiding her face in her hands. This woman carried great pain, wrapped up as tightly as a steel drum. Perhaps she feared what voicing her pain and disappointment would mean.

"Adara, what is it?" The sound of her weeping struck at his core. *"And ask ye why these sad tears stream? Why these wan eyes are dim with weeping? I had a dream – a lovely dream, of her that in the grave is sleeping. I saw her 'mid the realms of light. In everlasting radiance gleaming; co-equal with the seraphs bright, mid thousand angels beaming."*

Her cries softened. She tilted her head towards him, tears falling freely from her eyes. "That's beautiful."

"Isn't it though, the words of Alfred Lord Tennyson. I read him when I was a boy." Sully paused for a beat. "I didn't understand much of it then, but I could see the beauty of how the words came together, like a gathering of angels. I could envision such lovely pictures in me mind when I would read his poems."

"You read poems for your studies?" she asked.

"For companionship."

"Tennyson is a bit lofty for a child. Were you terribly lonely?"

"Ah!" he said, brushing aside her concern. "'Twas a lifetime ago."

She cocked her head to one side. "Who are you?"

He inhaled deeply, wishing a reasonable explanation would flow from his lips. "Me name is Sully, and—"

"Sully." She interjected with a question. "Are you here on Gillean's behalf?"

Inside the gray of her eyes there shimmered a hidden violet, the place which housed a piece of Gillean. Sully wanted to step into that light.

"I speak only for meself, and the truth of the matter is that Gillean loves you."

"No. He doesn't." The veracity of her emotion reflected in the certainty of her voice. She redirected his attentions, dismissing the topic of her husband's honor. "The bath and shower are in the connecting room. I've also left you some clean clothes."

"I will tidy meself up. But first, ya must tell me why."

"Why?"

He dabbed at the remaining tears on her cheek, "*Why these sad tears stream.*"

She moved to the closet, gathering towels. "I can't tell you without using some *colorful* language. I rather like the peace we've established."

"Oh, well, if ya have the colors"—he took the linen from her—"ya see the pictures in yer mind. Now let the words come."

"I did see the pictures," she brightened. "Your presence here, it caused me to think about my life with Gillean. How it was years ago." She allowed him to lead her back to the bed. They sat side by side. "I saw Gillean and me a lifetime ago, when we were young, like you."

Sully nodded.

"Gillean swept me up with his passion. Soon, what he wanted became what *I* wanted. They were one and the same."

He patted her hand. "Ya must have wanted somethin' of yer own, before Gillean. What was it?"

She shook her head.

"*What was it?*" he prodded.

Her back stiffened.

"What I meant…" Sully studied her. "I know what it is to be robbed of yer dreams, to be carried away by the desires of someone else, someone close to ya. It's a terrible thing when dreams die."

"What can you know of dead dreams?" She pulled her hand away. "Your whole life is yet to be lived. Why are you here? You must have better things to do with your time than stroll down memory lane with a failed dancer."

He folded his hands in his lap. "I promise ya, I'm where I'm meant to be. So," he said, nudging her with his elbow, "yer a dancer."

"*Was* a dancer, past tense."

"Can ya tell me true that when ya hear music, yer feet are completely motionless?"

She crossed her legs. "Dancing the hazelnut with my children is an altogether different animal."

"Was dancin' yer great passion?"

"I don't want to—"

"Yes or no? Was dancin' yer great passion?"

"*Yes.*" She nearly shouted.

He leaned in, meaning to share a secret. "Ya see, love is where things can begin again. It gives ya the nimble hands to pick up the pieces of broken dreams." He eyed the carpeted floor, then her. "Go on, be a dancer."

"You're mad!"

"Possibly." His eyes sparkled. "Dance for me."

"*What?*" She looked as if he had suggested she jump out the window.

"Dance for me, Adara."

"It's not practical. Dancing isn't like riding a bike." She squared her shoulders in a gesture of pride. "There's no need to feel sorry for me. I chose to forgo my dreams. Gillean couldn't have made it on talent and desire alone. The machine doesn't work that way. I made sure Gillean didn't have to wait years for his chance. I was ignorant to the full cost back then."

"Blah, blah, blah… I'm hearin' excuses when I should be seein' some beautiful dance moves."

He hopped from the bed, pulling her with him; using his body, he shoved the substantial piece of furniture against the wall along with the armchair and night table. Seeing the wood surface underneath a Persian carpet, Sully bent down, put his hands to the middle and began rolling up the rug. "This is perfect! Just like a Ceili!"

Adara's eyes were on the considerable amount of dust which had collected underneath the bed. "I don't dance jigs."

Sully dug into his knapsack and retrieved his prized possession. "And now, ya shall have music!"

He drew the bow across the strings, pausing to tighten or release the tension to obtain the proper sound. His chin lay on the rest of the lower bout. The chords he elicited from the instrument were rich, bittersweet. She had heard the classical composition before, but not like Sully's earnest rendition.

"I can't dance to this." Her eyes didn't leave his face.

"Take off your shoes, Adara."

"Sully, really."

Pointing his bow at her like a conductor he commanded, "Take 'em off!"

"Fine! Now you will see. You have no idea."

She slipped out of her trainers and took a few paces towards the window. Sully watched with great attention as she placed one hand on the sill, her feet instinctively moving into position one. When he resumed playing, her feet slid gracefully across the floor performing several traveling turns, moving into a full arabesque.

Here was her alchemy, Sully noted, it radiated from Adara as she elegantly moved around the floor. He could scarcely believe this woman had not danced in years. He knew nothing about technique, but that didn't matter. The way Adara took flight after years of binding her feet to the ground was sublime.

Adara landed all too soon. She went to him, sweaty and flushed. He lowered his fiddle and bow to one side. She reached out to touch his face, brushing her lips ever so lightly against his cheek.

"Thank you," she whispered. "You know, you could walk out the door right now, Sully, and we would still be connected. It's entirely incomprehensible, but it's there. Isn't it?"

Sully may have been relieved of his duty as far as the Elders were concerned, but he did not understand the tumultuous and thrilling emotions for Gillean and the connection to Adara. He didn't understand any of it. He moved to the bed to rest his fiddle, and grabbed for a down-filled pillow.

"Now that we have established you *can* dance, let's see if ya know how to play!" The pillow thwacked her in the forearm.

"You little devil!" she cried, landing a pillow of her own squarely across his face.

"Madam, this is war!"

With that, the two dealt each other strategic blows, all the while scrambling round the room breathless and laughing. They kept at it even though the delicate pillows began to break apart from the force of their play. Feathers took to the air, falling like January snow.

Ciar was waiting, calling from the open window of her Porsche 944 as he walked from the train platform. The trip had been an exhausting one. Amazingly, Gillean and Sully had traveled to the outermost edges of the island. Gillean was relieved to be back in Bray. Relief turned to irritation at the sound of her voice. She had one thing in common with Sully, neither could be ignored. Gillean plodded over to the car, wanting nothing more than to dismiss her.

"Why did you come here, Ciar?" He held his suitcase firmly in hand.

She lit up a cigarette, tossing the burning match out the window, dangerously close to where he stood. "You may not believe this, Gilly, but I'm the one person you can trust."

"You're right, I don't believe you. And I don't trust you. So if you will please excuse me—"

She exhaled a puff of smoke in his direction. "Going home to the wife and children?"

He took a moment to decide if she should know his plans. "Yes, as a matter of fact, I am going home. I suggest you do the same."

Leaning onto the opened window, her oceanic eyes latched onto him. She was so damned beautiful. Gillean cursed himself. For a moment he was carried back to the time he was first introduced to her and her work. There was no denying their exhilarating effect.

"Promise me this. After you return home to your wife and family, if you discover that I was right, and Sully is not who he appears to be, will you at least consider what I have to offer you?"

His tone softened. "I can't say I was not completely smitten by you—what man wouldn't be? But I have a life that I am obliged to. I'm sorry if I led you to believe I could promise you anything. That's not who I want to be."

"Little Gilly, you're not as complex as you'd like to be. You are an artist, like me, insatiable. You want the same things I want; and they are *not* found in tedious family life."

"I have to go now." His neck craned to identify his car in the small lot. "I hope you will respect my wishes."

She smiled at him with confidence. "I hope you will remember what I said. I'll be waiting for you. Don't be afraid to call."

"I need to get back to my family."

"And to find Sully?"

"Yes." His eyes narrowed. "I intend to find Sully and help him if I can."

The car window hummed upward to close while she tossed out the burning cigarette. She offered him one last thought. "I'd be more concerned with what Sully is helping himself to!"

She waved, driving away with a gratified smile.

Chapter Seven

Monsters and Men

Gillean stumbled up the stairs two at a time. Ciar's prediction mixing with the recognizable laughter echoing from a bedroom catapulted him onward. He dreaded what lay on the other side of the door, and flinging it open, he radiated anger.

"What the bloody hell is going on?" he demanded.

Adara and Sully stood motionless, as if a force of nature had blown its way into the room. The only movement was of the feathers that continued their descent upon the three occupants. Gillean eyed Sully's pajamas, *Gillean's* pajamas! Adara's hair was uncharacteristically wild and unkempt. Neither was wearing shoes. They looked as if they had just been caught attempting to steal the crown jewels.

"Gillean," Adara spoke, showing no remorse for her husband's lurid discovery.

He was not as tolerant as to allow her an explanation. He dove towards Sully, violently dragging him away from Adara.

"*You lying tosser! Get over here!*"

His vigor was much more than a man of his small stature. His eyes were black portals of fire and jealousy. Sully did nothing to resist as Gillean continued to berate him.

"To think I actually fell for your lies! I trusted you, and *you!*" Gillean turned towards Adara.

"*Stop it!*" she yelled, moving towards him.

"What? Do you want me to leave go of your lover then, Dara?" Gillean shoved Sully up against her, his breath on her face. "Look at how pathetic he is! He won't even fight for you."

Gillean heaved Sully in the opposite direction, sending him crashing to the floor. He landed roughly in the corner of the room. Sully tried to stand as Gillean came at him again.

"*No!*" Adara tugged at Gillean's arm.

He shrugged her off as he loomed over the stunned Sully. "Leave us, Adara. This is between me and Sully."

"Is it?" Sully stopped the enraged man in his tracks.

"Is *what*?" Gillean boomed.

"Is this between you and me, or maybe you and Ciar?

"Where do you get off accusing me?"

"Or maybe Adara?" Sully tossed out the explosive question. "Who is it ya *need* today, Gillean?"

Gillean's body shuddered with a rage he could barely contain. Here stood Sully, a man he had trusted, a man he not only felt sympathy for, but also a kinship with. Why had this man betrayed him? Why was Gillean the least bit distressed over someone he hardly knew? The nebulous questions only fueled his fervor.

"Don't take a superior attitude with me, you worthless piece of—" Gillean lunged for Sully, twisting the pajama top into a balled fist.

"Why don't ya speak to Adara?" Sully lifted his chin, his face defiant. "Why don't ya speak to her of yer feelings? Or are ya too much of a coward?"

The pounding of Sully's heart against Gillean's clenched hand caused a strange sensation within him. His own heart constricted. He had to look away from the pictures in Sully's luminous eyes. He was thankful Adara could not see his face.

"*You get out of here, Gillean Faraday!*" Adara's scream was that of a banshee.

Gillean recoiled at the sound.

"Dara, no."

"You heard me. *Get out!*" She opened the door and gestured to him. "How dare you make this between you and Sully? You don't even care enough to be upset with me." She pointed a finger at him. "It's impossible for you to conceive I could love someone other than you. Have I got it right? You simply assumed Sully must have seduced me." She chuckled. "That would be the only way I'd succumb to another man, because I'm so bloody over the moon for you!" She placed her hands on her hips, her eyes emitting hoary sparks. "Here's a news bulletin for you, Mr. *the-entire-world-revolves-around-me* Faraday. Perhaps, just perhaps, I've had my fill of you and *your countless* lies."

Gillean blinked back raw, hot tears. "What? Please..." He needed her calm, to stay and restore the balance of their normal, predictable life. He needed her to remove the unnerving sensation he felt standing close to Sully. This was not who he was. His sudden change in attitude failed to stem the flow of Adara's fury.

"What if I may not desire you any longer?"

Confounded and repentant, Gillean looked to Sully, who stood with his head bowed. Reality settled over Gillean like a sodden blanket, muting the intensity of his emotions.

He held Sully with his impassioned stare as he asked his wife, "Where are the children?"

Adara cooled in the wake of Gillean's composure. She gathered the hair from her heated face.

"They're fine. They're with your mam."

"I need a drink, and then some sleep. We can talk about this in the morning." Gillean forced his eyes to meet Sully's. "I promised to look after you, Sully. I don't know what the hell to think now. But don't leave this house until we speak further."

Sully held Gillean's glance, then slowly, as if with regret, turned to address Adara. "If that's what ya both want."

"Yes, of course." Adara swept her bare foot over a pile of feathers. "I can prepare another room for you."

"No, I'll be fine here." Sully replied.

Gillean nodded, "Right. I'll see you both in the morning. Adara, I'll be sleeping in the study." Not wanting to be trapped in those infinite green eyes, Gillean departed to the first floor, his strength and self-assurance already exhausted from the volatile exchange.

Adara did not follow her husband. Sully stood with one foot pressed against the wall, arms folded across his chest. He held the look of a man headed to the gallows, so great was the regret in his troubled eyes—the same eyes through which she had rediscovered herself.

"Don't do it, Sully. I know what you're thinking. Leave him be for now."

"I must speak with him." Sully fell to his knees. "Oh God." The sob caught in his throat. "I didn't mean for any of this to happen. I'm an idiot. Why was I sent here?"

"Hush, now." She pulled him into a comforting embrace. "Don't blame yourself." Leveling her lips with his ear she continued, "You gave me the courage to uncover what I have kept buried for such a long time." She held him as he continued to cry mournful tears. "You did nothing wrong. We did nothing wrong."

"How can you say that?" He raised his damp face to hers. "I was meant to help, and now Gillean is devastated, and you—"

"I am stronger than ever, dear man," she soothed. "Gillean will finally have to answer for the mess he has made. It's been a long time coming. You were the catalyst for a much-needed change."

"But, ya must still love him."

"I will always love him, but I no longer believe my place is with him."

"You don't mean that."

"I'm sorry, but you have given me a great gift. I won't be too quick to let go of it either. I think it best that you do as Gillean suggested. Get some sleep. We'll each be better to talk in the morning. Will you be alright, now?"

Dabbing at his face with a sleeve, Sully spoke in a more controlled tone. "Yes, maybe you could go and have a word with Gillean?"

She kissed the top of his head. "I'm going to take a nice hot bath and then to sleep. Listen to me." She held his face in her hands. "I meant what I said. You were the fresh breath of air that was needed here. I recognize there are powers greater than us, connecting to the powers within each one of us." She giggled like a jubilant child stumbling upon a hidden treasure. "You, my sweet man, you made me believe in the limitless sway of the universe. We are a part of something so exceedingly magnificent. You gave that to me. You gave me the sky."

It wasn't enough for Sully. "Sleep well, Adara."

"Good night. Try not to worry about Gillean." She stopped at the doorway. "He's a tough character. I know him much better than you do. He'll come out of this on top, no doubt."

———◦———

As she walked the hallway to her room, Adara's heart soared. She had been married to one of the world's most admired and beloved musicians for over twenty years, but the most divine music she'd heard was borne of the impetuous young man who insisted she should dance. Sully was the embodiment of the philosophy her husband ceased to espouse. The broken pieces she reached for were not connected to Gillean, but to the one who appeared to want nothing other than her happiness and to assure her that she was loved. Sully reminded her of the tragically romantic Irish poets. Adara's sleeping desires had been aroused after years of lying dormant. She wanted to give herself and her love to him—to extend the acceptance he seemed so terribly in need of, and to fall into the green of his eyes like a cool, refreshing stream on a hot summer's day. She wanted to lose herself in him.

Chapter Eight

Sacrifice

Sully fought a fruitless battle against sleep. He intended to make sure Adara was settled so he could speak with Gillean alone.

His heart ached with an alien desire. It was Gillean's face he saw when the feeling washed over him like a temperate wave. He acknowledged his complete failure as any sort of worthwhile being. All he could hope for was to unite Gillean and Adara, perhaps even stronger for the hardship they'd endured. Adara may have her doubts about her husband, but two decades of marriage and four children spoke volumes to their bond. Sully's presence had upset the balance, confused the issue. Once he was gone, she would come to realize she could make a better life with Gillean. Adara had reclaimed her power. Sully had seen as much in her dancing.

Sully had unintentionally drifted off when a fantastic force took hold of him; a tornadic wind of tremendous intensity blew the door off its frame, the hinges and screws hitting the floor like hard rain. The undulating air lifted him high into the heavens. The stars emitted blindingly sharp, silver light. When the assaulting burn of air and light was too much to endure, Sully plummeted downward into a pit within the bowels of unyielding darkness. His body shivered uncontrollably from biting cold. He could not lift his head, or move in any direction, paralyzed, save for the shaking of terror.

After what seemed agonizing hours, an isolated beam of light shone through the open door. Its candle-like glow created warmth enough to diminish his trembling and reveal Keelin making her way towards him.

"K...K...lin?"

She knelt beside him solemnly.

"I tried to warn you. I tried to help you," she said, her tone desperate with an assertiveness he'd not heard before. "I even tried to hide you, but you still would not listen!" she cried.

"What happened? What's happened to us?"

"The child you were in life and the re-encounter you were, are no more. Because you chose to disobey the directive, you have lost your history and your home with us." She spat out the words as if they were poison. The little girl, the messenger assigned to deliver his ill fate. Sully understood he had brought it on himself. He wished Keelin could be spared the task.

"Where am I to go?" His voice was ragged and cracked.

"You have the choice as to your final destination. You will die there, with no hope of redemption. Your spirit will fade into oblivion, having no place in the universe."

He tried to remain composed for Keelin's sake. "I'm sorry if I got ya in trouble. I would never purposefully hurt you. I hope ya know that."

"I do, Sully." She lowered her head. "I have to send ya off now. I promised them the debt would be paid."

He wrestled his way onto his feet. "Then that is what ya shall do."

The girl slipped her hand in his as they walked, swathed in darkness. Pitch blackness prevented him from seeing where they were headed. Explosive expansions of thunder rolled down the length of a single, jagged stroke of lightning. Keelin navigated the murky terrain without difficulty. It wasn't long before they reached what appeared to be the edge of a river where a ferryboat waited, a hooded man stationed at the rudder. Mist enveloped the water.

Keelin pointed to the faceless man. "You must go with him."

The smell of sulfur permeated the air. Sully tried to swallow over the lump in his burning throat.

"I will do."

Sully was resigned to his fate. He was desperate to hug Keelin, but it was not permitted.

"Thank ya for tryin' to help me." He smiled down on her. "Promise me one thing?"

"If I can," she spoke through tears, "you know I will."

"Please look after Gillean and Adara. Make sure they put things right between themselves."

She shook her head furiously. "I can't. I won't do it!"

"Why?" He stared at her in surprise as she nudged him ever closer to the ferry.

"Because I want to help *you*!"

She flung her body towards him, hurtling them both into the water. Smoke rose thick and heavy from the river, the sounds of dreadful moaning undulated beneath the restless waves. The ferryman reached out in an effort to snatch up his prize, but Keelin, bobbing next to Sully, pushed his head downward so that he was under the boat. Water quickly filled his nose and mouth. He blindly paddled forward, resurfacing on the other side of the vessel, but he was drifting away.

Keelin swam directly towards the boat. The Ferryman's gnarled hand took hold of the girl, easily hauling her up from the briny waves. The ghastly old man claimed his one promised soul.

She shouted to Sully with her last breath. "Go on now! You have one more chance to save the life you have chosen."

"Keelin! NO!"

Sully gulped down water and air in a fruitless attempt to swim back to her.

The Ferryman was swift, commanding his craft and the child closer to the other side of the shore, churning the restive waters in their wake. Falling onto the warped wooden planks of the boat's keel, the little girl blessed Sully, the one being who had risked himself to rescue her from a wretched life on earth-because of love. Sully knew full well how to give it—now he would need to learn how to receive it, as she had, in order to be free.

Chapter Nine

The Letter

Downstairs in the study, Gillean poured himself another drink while he absentmindedly sifted through the piles of assorted mail on his desk. The first two whiskeys had just about taken the edge off. He intended on getting good and knackered so he would not have to digest all that was on his proverbial plate. It was piled high with heaps of shame and self-pity, complemented by steaming sides of betrayal and anger. A feast surely not fit for a man of his means, but here he was washing down the pungent meal with the liquid sedative of choice of both kings and peasants.

He busied himself with the chaos of a month's worth of fan letters, bills, and the usual junk mail in an effort to create some order, even if it was a meaningless endeavor. It kept his mind from replaying the scene which transpired earlier and the feelings it had aroused. It was like walking into the middle of a bad film, only this was the cinema of his life. Try as he might, he could not stop the projector from flashing the images onto the screen.

As he picked up an invitation to yet another fund-raising gala, the question pricked at him like the ever-present thorn of Ciar. How could it be that she was the person to be trusted over Sully? Gillean had been so sure of the man's genuine nature. Gillean was no babe-in-the-woods as far as people were concerned. He had come across players, users, and abusers of all sorts during his extended career. A significant part of his business was merely staying alive.

At one time, he fell from grace in a most public and humiliating way. Overnight, *Ireland's Perfect Man* had become its most flawed. He had not asked for any of it: the expectations, praise, or criticism. He'd just wanted to play his music for anyone willing to listen. Somehow the musician became the music. The collective belief was held that he was what he sang about—every note, lyric and song. One by one, his own creations had chipped away at his real surface, defacing the once smooth edifice and weakening the supporting beams of the structure. And when he could no longer hold the crumbling walls together, his fans—the very same ones who had showered him with roses—assailed him with stones. He was not blameless. He had done wrong, living life according to his own rules and giving himself to whomever he pleased. He betrayed Adara, his one steadfast supporter, and his children. But most of all, he betrayed himself.

Nothing hurled at him from the outside could have hurt him as much as the hole he had hewn in his heart. Even when all seemed lost, he got up, brushed off, and offered himself once again to the people. Slowly but steadily they took him back, no more the favorite but instead, the prodigal son. Invariably there was always one disgruntled patron ready to remind him he was no longer a perfect man, but a forgiven one—fortunate enough to be given a second chance. He bowed in their presence, suffered their judgments, and once again held out the hope that he could play his music for anyone who would listen. Only now he wanted something in return: recompense for his ordeal.

He was beginning to feel the effects of three drinks. Was Sully the ultimate deceiver? But Gillean saw the authenticity in the man's bright eyes and childlike magic. *Hold on*, Gillean realized, making the connection: *child!* Yes, what about the little redheaded girl he'd questioned? She could not be capable of duplicity. That much he had to believe, or by God, Gillean could trust in nothing at all! He dutifully carried the guitar she had given him. When he looked to the corner of the room where he'd left it, his heart leapt into his throat. A fiddle now rested in the place where the guitar had been, its wood glistening a deep purple hue in the firelight.

Dizziness overcame him. He clutched at the edge of the glass top desk. His hand rested on a particular envelope. Although it was plain in appearance, it held an air of import, as it was sealed with wax. He turned the letter over. Squinting for lack of glasses, he was able to make out his name in heavy print on the front. There was no stamp, return address or postmark. Sober enough to be intrigued, Gillean rummaged through a drawer to retrieve a letter opener and his spectacles. He ran the blade under the red seal and unfolded the parchment paper. Taking another sip of spirits, he began to read.

Dear Gillean:

My greatest wish is that this letter reaches you. It is with much thought, and a heavy heart, that I write. I hope you remember me, and the recollection is with fondness. My name is Keelin. I met you in the company of the spirit we called Sully. I, like Sully, am going against everything we re-encounters are directed to do. But, also like Sully, my disobedience is fueled by the love for a friend. You see, Sully loved you so much; he risked all he was in an effort to save you from the things that haunted you and caused you unhappiness. As a result, Sully has lost his place among our kind. The decision was made to banish him forever, and no memory of his existence as the boy he was, or the spirit he became, should survive. But I believe with all my heart that this tired Earth needs more, not less, souls of his kind.

Gillean brought the letter closer to his face, tears obscuring his vision as he continued to read.

Sully paid a high price for rescuing me. His action brought me precious peace. I have become, as they are, a being with the ability to guide humans, but only from a distance. Upon my acceptance, Sully was forbidden to ever interfere in such a direct way again. But Sully, being Sully, could not resist when he saw how troubled you were. He truly loves you, and whatever he may have done, please know he did so out of this great love. He is no angel, no perfect being. But he is a being with a heart full of good intentions. Sadly, he has a habit of making the wrong choices, and unintentionally hurting the ones he loves most.

I shall never see my friend again. I am grateful for the chance to sacrifice myself in an effort to save him. I don't know what will become of me. We are a pair, Sully and I, tampering with the natural order of things. Who can say what will be? But as far as Sully is concerned, you do have a say. You could help to save him. Please forgive my selfish gesture in asking you to reach out to him, but he has done so much for me. He is my best friend. I feel I owe him as much.

If someone can truly love and trust in him, he would have the chance to return. Your connection has already healed his wounds. Sully doesn't know this, but I do, and now you do too. He does not have an unlimited amount of time. I was able to persuade the Elders to give him this chance, but it is only until the dark moon. As I write this to you, I see such time will be in four days. If he does not receive this precious gift, he will die. He will cease to be on any spiritual plane.

All I ask is that you search your heart and remember things are not always as they appear. Please bear this in mind when you return home. I am forever in your debt. I trust you will do what you believe in your heart to be right.

I wish you a long and happy life filled with love. I wish the same for my beloved Sully. I am entrusting to you the proper documentation needed for whatever happens to him. Please see that all is as it should be in the end, or the beginning.

Ever Yours,
Keelin

Gillean could hardly keep his head up, his mind being so muddled with whiskey and emotion. Placing the letter on the desk, he shut his eyes for a few moments to recompose then deal with the magnitude of the situation. For Gillean alcohol was often the precursor to disquieting dreams. It could also serve as the hole in the dam of sleep. Gillean was swept away by the flood of dreams.

"Oh, sweet Jesus."

Gillean pressed an open palm against his pounding head, wishing for a bottle of aspirin or caffeine delivered intravenously. No need to mess with the middleman of the digestive system. Beams of sunlight seemingly infused with atomic power blasted his exposed skin. He draped an arm over his stinging eyes to block out the over-exuberant light. His stomach protested from too much wine and not enough food. He would have to face the inevitable. Gillean would have to sit up and assess the damage inflicted by a night of wild abandon in Rio de Janeiro. He wondered who he might find lying next to him—the certain "mystery guest." His memory was temporarily on hiatus.

He rose up on unsteady elbows, slowly turning his head left then right. All that accompanied him on the bedraggled picnic blanket were a few empty bottles of cheap alcohol, scatterings of sand and his guitar. His companions had left him behind, abandoning him to the elements without shelter. So much for artistic camaraderie.

He reached for a bottle that showed some promise. "Hair of the dog," he pronounced while raising the warm spirits to take a healthy swig. "UGH!" He brushed the sleeve of his undone shirt against chapped lips.

Gillean was about to let his fatigued body fall backwards onto the blanket in defeat, but instead pushed himself forward. He was situated in a snug, grassy valley at the foot of a hill. One of his newly made acquaintances—Niles, was it, the self-proclaimed poet with stringy, blond hair and an overblown sense of himself?—had declared that the collective should gather at this meaningful location, deeming it ideal for "true artists." Niles had planted his skinny bum on the ground with as much purpose as a settler planting a flag on native soil.

"Tourists." Gillean swirled the coarse word around his mouth with some additional wine. "They think they actually know a place because they carry around a goddamn guidebook." Every element of Brazil, its narrow, rutted roads, the songs of hundreds of hummingbirds, the taste of the humid morning air, was imprinted onto Gillean as surely as a firstborn is to its mother.

"Serves you right," he addressed his absent parents. "You've kept me as an inmate in your blasted castle." Gillean quickly dismissed the guilt over the pound notes he had nicked from his mother's coffee tin.

He supposed that back in Ireland, his parents were frantic over their runaway offspring. But Gillean had been utterly compelled to return to the place where he could actually *feel* the music pulsing like blood throughout his body.

The sun tucked itself behind low lying clouds, rapidly assembling like a gray army. He brushed strands of dark hair from his mocha-colored eyes, allowing them to fully open and take in the horizon. Sitting up on the blanket and tucking his knees underneath himself, he stared at the mist rising up from the hill. The gauzy air covered everything with its delicate veil. Gillean wondered if he was indeed back in Ireland. These moments of feeling lost inside a primordial pocket of earth were one of the few things he treasured about his home in Tullamore.

Through the dissipating mist an image took form as if it was slowly being born from the earth's womb.

An imposing stone figure stood in the distance at the top of the hill. Gillean lifted his head to get a full view of the world-renowned soapstone and concrete arms with the span of an ethereal eagle spread out as if offering an embrace.

"O Cristo Redentor."

Gillean had spoken in his first tongue. Despite not being a religious man, he was still awed by the sight. Flashes of past carnal pleasures came to him like a list of sins to a penitent kneeling in a confessional.

He had been the man of the hour. After finishing an impromptu set with the local musicians, Gillean was sought after by several sun-kissed women, their tans fresh, their bodies still smelling of lotion, and their soft hands seeking to touch those that could command a guitar to sing. He was ushered out of the restaurant by the doting group, picking up additional members and refreshments as they made their way into the Tijuca forest, seeking the perfect location to get to know one another better. None of the women were natives, but rebellious Europeans looking for a party and an escape.

Now, a massive Jesus seemed to be entreating him. For what purpose, Gillean was uncertain.

"'Tis quite a sight, isn't it?"

The question was delivered to Gillean's back. He hugged his knees closer to his chest and closed his eyes, believing as a child playing hide and seek that if he did not make a move, he'd be invisible. He would refuse to be held accountable for anything he may have done under the influence. This wouldn't be the first time he'd been confronted by the jealous partner of a lover the morning after.

"One of the original designs was to have Christ holdin' a globe in his hands," the voice continued, as if encouraged by Gillean. "I don't care for that idea very much. Makes him seem too greedy. To me, his hands would be held open to people, not filled up with no room to spare."

Gillean kept his eyes and mouth shut.

"Mind if I join ya?"

Gillean shook his head.

"Was that a nod of affirmation, then?"

The damn brogue. Not only had Gillean's peace been disturbed, but by an Irishman no less. He wanted to see the face of the person who addressed him, the person who seemed to have materialized from nothing more than the bits of leftover morning. But Gillean wasn't going to give in so easily. Let the intruder take up the challenge if it was so important for him to remain.

"*Está bem-vindo aqui*," Gillean spoke.

"Thank ya for the welcome."

The stranger knelt and brushed off a corner of the blanket. Gillean turned his head to get his first look at the man. He was young, probably no older than Gillean, and handsome in an unconventional sense. His body was unusually slim, but had the defined muscle tone of an athlete. He wore black trousers and a pale blue linen shirt with the sleeves rolled neatly over the elbows. His dress implied that he did not wish to be associated with those his age: young people like Gillean who simply woke up, fell out of bed, and pulled on blue jeans and whatever shirt wasn't too wrinkled or dirty from off the bedroom floor.

Gillean couldn't see the man's face, just the top of his head, which was a crown of black curls. He was busy gathering the empty wine bottles, placing them on a far corner of the blanket. Who requested maid service? Gillean's stormy temper flared.

"Now look here!"

The man merely glanced up, undisturbed by the harsh tone, and offered Gillean a tall, silver thermos.

"Nothin' like a hot cuppa to get the blood flowin'." His lips curled into a smile. "Coffee. Yer welcome to it."

Gillean was caught in eyes of shifting color, like a prism, as sunlight shone on the man's pale face. Something inside Gillean pitched like the fit of an impudent child.

"You weren't here before this morning?" Gillean broke the momentary silence and accepted the thermos.

"Should I have been?" The man's arm brushed against Gillean's as he settled himself. "I gather it was quite the party."

Ignoring the jolt of adrenaline which shot through him like the caffeine he was about to ingest, Gillean turned his attention to opening the thermos.

"Ya play the guitar, I see." The green eyes rested on the battered six-string. "I play the fiddle meself."

"You don't say." Gillean gulped down the coffee, which burned his throat.

"Used to, anyway."

"Why *used to*?"

"Time and place for everythin'."

"I cannot imagine a time when I wouldn't play the guitar."

"I know."

Gillean's eyes narrowed, handing back the plastic cup.

"Do I know you?"

The man's expressive eyes studied Gillean. There was no hint of judgement in the gaze, but a most unusual openness, and an air of expectation about his reply.

"Am I familiar to ya?"

Gillean chuckled.

"Everyone is familiar to me. There isn't a story I haven't heard."

"Yer after stories, is it?"

"I'm not after anything."

"I don't believe that. I think ya want somethin' so badly, not even the arms of *O Cristo Redentor* could encompass it all."

Gillean leaned back on his elbows, his shirt open to welcome the hot sun onto his brown skin. The cool morning breeze carried the scent of spices, coffee, and the sea. Together they dissipated the annoyance he would have felt at such a bold observation.

"Am I so different from you?" Gillean regarded Corcovado Hill. "Isn't there something you want with all your heart and soul?"

"Indeed there is."

"What?"

"The connection."

"Pardon?"

"I want to find the other piece of meself."

Despite his youth and vigor, there was a fragility about the stranger. Gillean was not one to be bound to needy people, but this man didn't seem of the grasping sort. He had a self-assured and confident manner about him. Gillean suspected the lad with the luminous eyes would be hard pressed to tell a lie. He knew that such a trait made a man vulnerable, easily trampled upon. To wear one's heart on the sleeve was the best way to ensure pain.

Gillean was learning quickly how to play the game and keep clear of the snares of love and romance. He could don the cloak of the romantic artist when it suited him, but he could toss it off just as easily when he claimed victory. He wanted to believe in the truth of *real love*, but one had to be extremely careful when navigating such turbulent waters. He had yet to stick a toe in. He was quite comfortable singing about it from the safety of the shoreline. From a distance, it seemed like a mirage.

"It's like when yer a child and lose a tooth." The man took up his explanation. "Yer tongue is constantly probing the empty space to fill in the gap."

"Why do you feel so empty?"

"Why do you?"

"I never said…"

"I don't feel empty." The man reached for one of the bottles of wine. "Half-full. There's a difference, ya know."

"I'm sorry for you."

"Are ya now?"

"You're a hopeless romantic."

"And you?" The green eyes rested on Gillean's guitar as if to illustrate that a musician was the ultimate romantic.

"You don't know me. You want what doesn't exist. You're like the first design for that statue. You want to hold on to only one thing. But me, ah! I'm standing there like ole *Christo*. My arms are open wide to the world. Bring it to me! I want to see, feel, hear, taste everything!"

"And then?"

"Then what?" Gillean laughed, tickled by the amazing adventures a hungover morning in Rio could conjure.

The childlike eyes were upon him. "What's left?"

The tantalizing imagery faded. Gillean's throat closed. He was enveloped by an unfamiliar ocean of innocence.

"Will there be only you, then?" The man asked.

"Who else? In the end, it's always been just me."

"No." The man breathed deeply.

"No?"

"There is yer other half."

Gillean shivered despite the heat of the midday sun. He wanted to get up and take his leave of this perplexing visitor, but something invisible anchored him to the ground.

The man unbuttoned his shirt and exposed his back to Gillean.

"Ya see these?"

A chaotic pattern of vicious scars crisscrossed the protruding knobs of spine, no doubt made by a belt which had struck and opened the flesh on many occasions years ago.

Gillean gasped, holding a shaking hand to his mouth.

"Ya have them too, me friend. Only yours aren't so easily seen. Ya hide yer eyes and heart from them."

"Are you mad? No one has ever beat me in such a brutal way." Gillean caught himself, not wanting to appear coldhearted to the man's misfortune. He softened his voice. "What I mean to say is, what you had to endure must have been terrible, but I have not…"

The man buttoned up his shirt and faced Gillean. "But, ya want to feel it all."

Gillean's head throbbed. He yearned for the softness of his bed delivering him into the glorious netherworld of sleep. He most certainly did not want the array of disturbing emotions being stirred within him.

"He surely felt it all." The man nodded to the statue on the hill. "But he just wanted to love. By his stripes we are healed."

"The Book of Isaiah." Gillean massaged his temples, avoiding the stranger's gaze.

"Ya don't need to memorize scripture, blindly accepting it as fact. Question *everythin'*, and then reach yer own conclusions—find yer heart."

Gillean rubbed harder. "What the hell kind of drugs are you on?"

"By love we are healed." The man stood and brushed grains of sand from his trousers. He squinted into the distance. "'Tis good that ya keep yer arms open." He turned to Gillean. "Just be sure yer ready to grab on when that piece falls into yer hands. The wheel will keep goin' round even if ya miss."

Gillean forced his aching body to stand.

"I hope ya find yer way back, Gillean." The visitor extended his hand.

Gillean didn't bother to ask how the stranger knew his name. He was pierced by the incisive eyes that dug under his skin. He grasped the man's hand, not knowing why, but placing his other hand over the top. He wanted to hold on, tether himself to this other, if only for a few moments. Was it his exhausted state, or the exotic locale that made Gillean aware of an energy so pervasive he could neither let go, nor hold on?

"The center." Gillean pronounced.

"Say again?"

"Rio is believed to be at the center of a magnetic field; a place of cosmic forces."

"Is it now?" The man lightly pulled his hand free. "Safe journeys." He unfolded a cap from the pocket of his trousers and settled it on his head. Without comment, he started towards the city, then spun round to wave. A smile lighted his face in satisfaction and anticipation.

Gillean imagined this beaten and gentle soul being swallowed up by the pushing and shoving of a gritty city. His eyes stung at the sight of the traveler walking towards the looming statue with its extended, but empty, arms.

"Wait, Please!" Gillean called out. The blanket wrapped around Gillean's ankles. He fought against the binding material. "Have I missed it?" he whispered, falling back onto the sand.

Chapter Ten

Do you see?

Sully descended the stairs to the first floor. The memory of his time with Keelin and her sacrifice was transforming into a hazy recollection of a bizarre dream. He came to the open door of the study. Gillean lay sprawled across the desk. Sully hesitated, thinking it might be best to go while the coast was clear, but he owed Gillean more than abandonment. They were obliged by a promise made to one another. The least Sully could do was assure Gillean he need not view his unwanted guest as a rival; their friendship may be irreparable but, the Powers willing, not Gillean's trust. Sully took a tentative step into the room, quietly inquiring if Gillean was awake. Receiving no response, Sully approached, careful not to cause the hard wood floors to creak and wake the sleeping man.

Gillean was lost to the world of slumber. Sully lovingly placed a hand on Gillean's disheveled hair. He studied the creases—*laugh lines,* people referred to them—ingrained in the musician's face. Sully knew that during Gillean's prolific years he had smiled more times than frowned, accepted insults and injury with the same grace as he did accolades and confirmation.

Sully didn't blame Gillean for being angry. Adara maintained their union throughout the difficult years, because she had loved the young, aspiring musician who saw the light and tapped into its energy. Sully reached for the energy through her. The same principles that govern light preside over darkness. Neither is good nor evil, blind or sighted on their own; only those who master one over the other can utilize those powers for their own gain. It was that desire which disconnected Gillean from Adara, not his misdeeds. Gillean had long since left her behind, waving from a window of their life. This was the opening through which Ciar had slipped in, seeping like slick, black oil. Tunnel vision blocks light. Gillean never saw her coming until she was right in front of him, disguised as a gift.

Ciar was drawn to Gillean's radiance in order to extinguish it. She seduced Gillean by providing him an avenue to return to the tempestuous ways of his youth. It was possible Sully maintained enough power to lead Gillean in the charge of renouncing Ciar and her inscrutable intentions.

Adara told Sully he was an instrument of change. Wasn't it so that with change—good or bad—there comes pain? Gillean might end up hating him, but Sully would gladly accept that if it meant the troubled singer could at long last find peace.

Lost in his musings, Sully started when Gillean shifted positions, still embraced in an intoxicated sleep. Taking a step back, Sully read his own name mentioned in a letter underneath Gillean's arm. Leaning over the desk and holding his breath in trepidation, Sully slowly pulled the paper away. He shrunk back in alarm as Gillean let out a cough, but the sleeping man turned his head and slept on. Sully moved quietly to sit on the couch by the hearth where the fire still burned.

His hands shook as he pressed the letter to his wet face.

"Oh Keelin, darlin' girl, ya shouldn't have done this."

He stood, crumpled the letter in his hands and threw it into the fire. Watching the flames engulf and destroy Keelin's words of love, he wasn't sure what good it would do. He surmised Gillean had already read it.

Gillean! Sully turned, exhaling a sigh of relief. Gillean was still sleeping. Sully's mind raced. What to do?

What was Keelin referring to when she wrote of leaving Gillean with the proper documentation? He hurried back to the desk. Next to Gillean's arm lay some official looking papers. These must be the ones Keelin referred to. Sully grabbed at them in haste, bumping against the desk. Gillean stirred, lifting a sleepy and disoriented face.

Sully held in his hands a certificate recording that Sullivan O'Shay had been born at midnight, the twelfth of December, twenty-seven years ago in the town of Ballina, County Mayo. The more ominous document recorded his death. He didn't have a chance to note the fateful date.

"Sully, what are you doing?" Gillean's faculties slowly returned. He tottered to his feet, hitting his knee hard against the desk. *"Feck it! Give them to me!"* He was reaching for the papers.

Sully raced to the fire with Gillean stumbling behind him.

"No! *Leave it!*" Gillean yelled as Sully tried to toss the papers into the flames. He was determined that Gillean should not feel any obligation.

Gillean threw himself on top of Sully. They crashed to the floor. Gillean held Sully's wrist with surprising strength for a drunken man, preventing Sully from putting the papers in the fire. "I won't let you do it. You still have a chance!"

Sully freed his hand from Gillean' grip. "Not this way. 'Tis not the time!" Giving Gillean a shove Sully staggered up from the floor, hurriedly casting both certificates into the blaze.

Gillean was behind him, panting like a marathon runner, his hand on Sully's back. "It's not going to be that easy. Both of us are staying right here and face our fates like men. *Do you hear me?*"

"Don't be an eejit, Gillean. Do ya hear *me?*"

Sully grabbed the half-full bottle of whiskey from the desk, throwing it against the hearth. Hunks of glass splintered into pieces, the alcohol slowly sliding down the brick and combusting into orange-blue flames, piercing as Gillean's eyes on Sully.

Gillean bent forward, taking in more air. Sully's arms ached to hold the man and tell him how much he loved him, ask for his forgiveness and a chance for a life with him, the one person who felt like home. But he didn't speak any of those words which would have been smooth and sweet as caramel on his tongue. Instead he raised his shoulders and spat out the *necessary* words.

"Ya have a wife who has given ya her love, sacrificed for ya time and again. Wake the hell up, Gillean, and put things right with her!" Gillean looked as if Sully had slapped him across the face. But Sully continued his verbal assault. "If yer so keen on *bein' a man*, that's what ya need to do." Sully stared at the fire, resolute. "My time with you is done." His voice softened. "I know what me fate is, and I accept it. Yours is about to change for the better. *Please,* trust me."

"Trust *you?*" Gillean blinked back the tears. "Sully..." His eyes were the color of honeyed wine as they held Sully's face in a most tender attitude. Lifetimes of himself and Gillean inhabited the sparks of gold.

"God damn you, Sully," Gillean whispered. He breathed in awe of the exquisite feeling of oneness.

"Do ya see it, Gillean?" Sully asked in amazement.

Gillean's hand gently cupped Sully's face. "I haven't missed it." He drew Sully into a deep kiss.

"No..." Sully pulled away, refusing himself bliss beyond any he had imagined. "I...I can't."

Gillean stood immobile, looking as if a wrecking ball had smashed into the room. "Was I wrong?" his voice cracked. A look of realization crossed his clouded eyes. "You love Adara."

Sully's right hand folded into a tight fist. "Yes, I love her." He caught the look of surprise on Gillean' face as a fist made contact with the man's jaw. It only took one hit to put Gillean out. Sully knelt down to place an open palm on the bruise rising on Gillean's cheek.

"But I love you as no one else, Gillean Faraday. Yer place is here. And mine is out there, somewhere else."

Before leaving the study, Sully made sure Keelin's letter and both certificates were nothing but ash, then he affectionately picked up the black leather jacket from the chair behind the desk and exited into the night. He fondly regarded the spot where he had literally run into Gillean's wife only the day before. It was inconceivable that this was the last time he would see Gillean or Adara. What had begun as a journey of such optimism was ending in dashed expectations.

Chapter Eleven

Absence of Light

Sully glanced once more to the majestic Faraday house. Perhaps, given time and Sully's absence, Gillean and Adara would strive for their true selves. He turned from the house with trepidation for what would become of him. He squeezed his hands open and shut repeatedly, steeling himself for the anomaly of his existence. He was a being with no past, nothing to justify or record his presence on earth or in the heavens. Yet he was a living, breathing man with limitless potential and unfulfilled desires. He was also a marked man, singled out for an unknown destination because he had reached out in love. Arriving at the bottom of the grand driveway, he walked out into the road. The inky sky smothered the world like black snow, muting all sound.

Sully could barely spot the silhouette of a person meandering up the road, so thick was the darkness that sucked the air and light from the waning crescent moon sky. With the blithe spirit of youth, a lad swinging a small satchel in one hand moved through the night closer to where Sully stood.

The boy, a teenager as he appeared, whistled as he walked; seeing Sully, the teen stopped for a moment and called out. "Da?"

Surprised by the greeting, Sully turned around to see who the boy was calling to. No one else was about.

"*Da, you're home!*"

Oblivious to the car rapidly gaining behind him, the teen ran towards Sully. The vehicle swerved recklessly from one side of the road to other.

"*I missed ya, Da!*" he persisted.

Sully rushed towards the boy shouting, "*Look out, lad! Behind ya!*"

The boy jerked his head at the sound of Sully's warning. He tried to escape from the car's erratic path.

Sully's movements were swift. The car came within a hair's breadth of the boy, just as Sully dove forward pushing the young man to the side of the road. He was out of harm's way when the car made violent impact with Sully's body.

Ciar watched in delight as her adversary landed on the hood of her car, his blood spattering the windshield like tiny pellets of red rain from an enraged heaven. She continued for a few hundred yards, her prized casualty clinging to the hood, then braked hard so he fell in a twisted heap in front of the car's dimpled front end.

She quickly exited the car. Her time was short. Gillean's son would surely be summoning help. She could not over-indulge in her victory. The rapture of the moment could ruin her. Ciar knelt down beside him, reveling in his suffering.

"Hello, dear Sully." She seized hold of his cold hand.

Through half-open eyes her face came to him. Tremendous pain shot through his body. His mind moved through time. Was this the result of another beating from his father? A glimmer of his past, a real image of the child he used to be, gradually came to him like a picture developing in a pan. She was the one who'd tempted his father and transformed him from a frustrated, working-class man into a perverse beast. His father had gorged himself on all she offered. So full and satisfied was he, when Ciar dictated he should rid himself of his one obligation—his child—her demands must have seemed a mere pittance for the gratifications she offered.

"So now you know how it ends," she whispered into his ear. "You are ever the fool, Sully. Would I harm Gillean's firstborn? That would leave a bad taste in his mouth to be sure."

"Ya can tell me nothin' true." He choked on the fluid in his mouth.

"You will die here. You will die because no one loves you, no one trusts you enough to save your pathetic life; certainly not Gillean."

The boy sprinted up the road, shouting for assistance. She leaned even closer to Sully, his blood catching in her golden hair. "You were always a worthless, abject, little being. Go on to the nothingness you deserve."

Sully summoned every ounce of his waning energy to speak to her. "The...lad is...okay..."

His resistance infuriated her.

Agony splintered throughout his body. "And...*I* loved, *I* loved..."

Ciar tucked her chin against her chest, saying nothing to the over-wrought boy who was now inches from her and Sully. She retreated to her car and drove away, leaving in her wake an expulsion of fumes and screeching tires.

Gillean and Adara, hearing the dreadful sounds slicing through the quiet night, met at the front door of their home and raced into the street. Locating his son by the sound of his tormented cries, Gillean's found his feet couldn't move fast enough.

"*Arlen!*" he shouted.

Gillean and Adara came to the area of asphalt where their son knelt next to a broken man.

"Son, are you alright?" Gillean questioned, as he and his wife embraced the boy.

Arlen pulled away, trying to speak although in obvious shock. "I'm okay, but Da, I...I thought he was you!"

Gillean looked at the man lying in the road. Blood clotted under his nose and in the corners of his mouth, blue-green bruises swelled on his face. Before any glimmer of recognition, Gillean hurriedly turned his head away in revulsion.

"He saved me. That man saved my life!" Arlen cried.

"What do you mean?" Adara smoothed her child's hair.

"There...there was this sports car, a woman, she must have been drunk, I don't know." The words came quicker than his breath. "She was driving all over the road. I...I thought I saw Dad out walking."

Adara interrupted. "Don't try to explain it now, sweetheart,"

Gillean's son shook his head vehemently. He was insistent they know what had transpired. "The man tried to warn me, shouted at me to get out of the way, but... He knocked me to the grass." Arlen wiped at his nose, swallowing the tears. "The woman got out to check on him, I think, but then she drove away. Why would she leave him to die?"

"Steady now." Gillean placed a reassuring hand on his son's arm while fishing for his mobile in the pocket of his trousers. "We'll need to get an ambulance." He dialed the three numbers, eyes focused on the boy.

Adara began to wail in horror. "*Oh God, Gillean, it's Sully!*" She placed her head on Sully's chest.

"Best you take Arlen inside now." Gillean tried to pry her away. "I'll stay here to wait for the ambulance." He couldn't bring himself to look at the willful man who had caused him to question everything: his fears, his marriage, and his life. The man who'd managed to capture Gillean's heart only to abandon him, endear himself to Adara, and save his son.

Adara raised her head to him. Her eyes were the color of lavender fields set aflame. "He didn't betray you. How could you think that?"

Gillean choose to ignore the remark and keep to the task at hand.

"Please, take Arlen to the house. I'll stay with…I'll stay here."

Keeping her hand on Sully's chest, Adara turned a deaf ear to Gillean's request and her son's insistent questions regarding the state of this man his parents obviously knew. She stayed silent until the sound of distant sirens penetrated the bubble of their shared disbelief. A voice came from her lips, but she was not connected to it. "Come with me, luv. Leave Daddy here to deal with this." She did not look down or say goodbye. She took hold of her son as if he was the only real thing to hang on to.

The dead man's eyes seemed to follow Adara and Arlen, arms encircled round each other, as they walked to their home.

Gillean spoke to Sully. "I don't know how you managed it, but she deeply cares for you, old chap." The ambulance was only moments from arriving. "She'll probably find some way to hold me accountable for this." The sirens almost drowned his words. *"Bollocks, Sully! Why didn't you stay?"* He reached over to close Sully's eyes, the once brilliant green windows of an intricate soul. "I would have given you a chance, or if you wanted her…"

He rubbed the sore corner of his jaw where Sully had struck him in order to make his getaway. The impetuous action had spared his son. Flashing red-blue lights momentarily blinded Gillean. It was in the whirlwind of light and sound that Sully was swept away. As the rescue team approached, there was no body on the ground, no bloodstained pavement, nothing to indicate that anything of a brutal nature had taken place. The paramedics found only Gillean kneeling in the grass, his arms gathered around himself, rocking back and forth.

Finding no trace of an accident, the paramedics examined Arlen at Gillean's request. The boy was physically unharmed. Leaving the Faraday house, the medical technicians sniggered to one another. They knew from years of experience that nights of a full or dark moon brought the batshit crazies out of the woodwork. This wasn't the first time a celebrity had lost hold of his senses. They were anxious to share the story with their comrades about the eccentric musician alleging a bloody hit and run accident had taken place outside his spacious grounds. They joked that Gillean Faraday must be hard up for publicity.

Epilogue

For days after the accident, Gillean continued to root through the soot and ash for any scrap of Keelin's letter, or the certificates. He could find nothing. It was as Keelin wrote: Sully's existence had been voided. When Gillean tried to speak to Adara and Arlen about the matter, he received only blank stares. They had no memory of Sully.

But something surely afflicted Adara. She retreated into a world of silence. She was evening snow—cold, beautiful, drifting, scattered to the wind and night. She fashioned an airtight cocoon made of the hardiest threads, filaments of unresolved anger, uncertainty and a palpable solitude, allowing no one in.

The mind's eye is not always privy to what lies deep-seated in the heart. This was where the cord between Adara and Sully remained intact. It coiled inside a stolid, hidden place. They'd stumbled upon each other in life, but the impact was lasting. Sully bequeathed Adara a single gift. But, she placed it deep within the recesses of her mind.

Time had not allowed for Adara to save him, but what lay arrested in her was enough to keep him in the periphery of her heart. She closed and barred a door that Gillean had so freely entered and exited for over twenty years. When she did speak to him, she repeatedly expressed her single wish, like a sacred mantra, to be left alone with her children.

Gillean was exhausted from fighting something he could not see, an adversary with no name, form, or face. But somehow he could not escape the idea that each time he looked in the mirror, he beheld the answer. He was the only one to maintain a faint memory of Sully. At first he believed he had cracked under the pressure of the recent happenings in his life, and his more vivid recollections of time spent with the spirit-man were a figment of a disturbed mind. But Sully's words wrapped tightly around Gillean's heart, squeezing with each beat. Sully was an inextricable part of Gillean. Sully's earthly absence was a constant reminder of Gillean's failure to recognize what could have been. He had allowed his fears and ego to overshadow the light. He felt abandoned and rejected. He could find no refuge from what he had been so quick to extinguish. Sully was not the only one to receive a grave sentence for his refusal to heed the warnings.

Gillean requested his manager arrange an extended European tour as soon as possible. He hoped his music, the hectic pace of life on the road, and the noise of the crowds, would subdue the echoes inside. When he returned, he would speak to Adara about how to share their children in what would be their new and separate lives.

Driving to the airport, he noticed an overgrown field. Flowers shot up like rebellious children, their colors rich and luxuriant. The heather, laurels, thistle, and daffodils possessed his faculties like heady wine. He wanted to savor the vision. His driver navigated the car around a particularly complicated bend, bringing into view a haunting sentinel at the far end of the field; it stood alone and resolute, a Blackthorn tree.

Part 2

'Twas that friends, the belov'd of my bosom, were near,
Who made every dear scene of enchantment more dear,
And who felt how the best charms of nature improve,
When we see them reflected from looks that we love.

Sweet vale of Avoca! how calm could I rest
In thy bosom of shade, with the friends I love best,
Where the storms that we feel in this cold world should cease,
And our hearts, like thy waters, be mingled in peace.

—Thomas Moore, "The Meeting of the Waters"

Chapter One

The Teach na Spioradi

Ireland, 1997

Edges

Rain lashed the trembling window, driven on by a ferocious easterly gale, the first of the spring storms. It would be the first of many this season, in a cycle of restoration that had repeated itself for untold years and would continue long after the last whisper of human breath circled the earth—the restoration cycle of the forty shades of green.

Adara's fingers curled around what had been a steaming cup of tea when her husband brought it to her. Although the contents had long gone cold, she took no notice. The sheets of liquid that streamed down the window appeared like phantoms grasping helplessly for a point of contact, but lacking solidity, slid away, leaving a trail of regretful tears for what they could never be.

She spoke little, only when necessary, floating further and deeper into her silent world. Upon returning from a six-month tour, Gillean had brought his taciturn wife to the *Teach na Spioradi*, believing the familiar setting and the affable memories of the place would ease the necessary and difficult steps to be taken. It made no difference to Adara. She allowed herself to be swept up in the embrace of her doting mother-in-law, suffered the well-meaning visitations of family and friends, seeing and hearing them through one end of a lengthy, unlit tunnel. Not even her children could reach the place where she curled up inside herself.

Her most treasured time was alone, near a faint source of light. There she could savor the taste of words as they found expression within a safe corner of her mind.

"Break, break, break, On thy cold gray stones, O Sea! And I would that my tongue could utter the thoughts that arise in me."

The words of Tennyson lingered on her tongue with all the sweetness of summer strawberries.

A fervent hand pulled at her, the persistent presence of someone

93

outside the room disturbing her peace, the one and only thing she would defend. She set the cup on the windowsill, unfolded her legs from beneath her, and stepped into the hallway.

She saw no one, but the presence was unmistakable. A tender ache took hold of her—the heartache of being in the midst of something exquisite yet devoid of recognizable identity. Whatever was surrounding her was simply beyond her grasp. She turned her head to the sound of water splashing against glass—the shower in the bathroom at the end of the hall. Gillean, yes, it would be him, but the entity she yearned for was not her husband.

She walked a few steps, her stockinged feet padding along the floorboards. Warmth encircled her like the embrace of a beloved. She drew her arms around herself as a radiant light washed over her, streaming in from the stained-glass window, its etching depicting a gathering of angels. She was caught in a dazzling, prismatic web. Colors bathed her body, as if she were being cleansed in a rainbow. This was true tranquility.

And yet the longing still clutched at her. She did not know why, or for whom, but all she could feel was overpowering sadness and grief, the certainty that the colors would soon fade, and she would be left alone in a monochrome castle. Adara fell to her knees.

Don't go! *Please!"* she choked out, her voice rough from disuse.

A gentle breeze lifted the sheer curtains of a second window. Sunlight tumbled in like a gleeful child. Through the shafts of light images took fluid form. She saw herself dancing around a bedroom. The freedom of her feet as they skimmed the floor then allowed her body to take to the air with the flawless precision of her youth. A man who had read her dreams by looking into her eyes. They were playing like innocent children, fighting with pillows, the soft touch of feathers against her cheek and the sound of the man's laughter riding on the night air. Her breathing quickened as the memories cascaded over one another in her mind.

She watched as a single shape disclosed itself in the sunlight. The intensity stung her eyes but she could not—would not—look away. Just when she believed the brightness would blind her, it was gone; and in its place, in front of the window, a figure appeared. Softly focusing behind a veil of tears, she could make out no identity—only penetrating green eyes.

This was the poetry, the longing. Here was her missing voice. As soon as the realization came to her, the image was gone.

Gillean had just donned a thick, cotton robe, when he heard Adara's sobs through the closed bathroom door. Tossing a hairbrush into the sink he bolted down the hallway to find his wife leaning precariously out of an open window. Rain streamed in, mixing with the tepid, late-March air.

He grabbed at her, placing one hand around her slender waist, the other over her head as he hauled her inside. She was completely soaked, as if she had joined him in his shower.

She struggled against her husband's hold. *"No. Bring it back! Bring it back!"*

Gillean staggered at the first words his wife had uttered to him in an age. Her eyes were the deepest shade of violet. They looked past him, as if searching for something—someone—that had been right there a moment ago. Her hair, a fiery red, stuck to her cheeks and shoulders. She shivered uncontrollably.

"Adara! Adara!"

He pulled her to him, hoping the contact would break whatever spell she was under. She smelled like damp earth and clover.

He was exhausted, drained from the tour and the constant state of helplessness watching his family splinter apart before his eyes. Some unseen hand had taken a mallet and smashed their house of glass. The memories and past experiences counted for nothing. They were merely slices of a life which no longer existed, or perhaps never had.

The question resurfaced time and again—whether he was alone in a hotel room reaching for sleep, with the adoring voices of hundreds of fans still ringing in his ears, or more often, cradled in the arms of Ciar. He wondered why he could never fully rest, why he never felt whole, *real.*

"Leave go of me." Adara shoved at him.

"What the bloody hell's the matter with you? Hanging out of windows, are you *trying* to off yourself?" The words came without the benefit of forethought, just as they had when he'd lived in this place years ago, and she had aroused the passion in him with her dancing.

Adara began to shake again. Water dripped from her fragile frame. She appeared sorrowfully lost.

"I'm sorry, Dara-Day." He spoke the name of love from their youth. "What's the matter? *Please*, talk to me."

She stared at him, saying nothing more. He attempted to take her arm and lead her to the bathroom to dry off, but she resisted.

"What have you done, little Gilly?" Her eyes were empty of expression.

"*What?*" He backed away from her.

Ena chugged up the stairs breathing laboriously, her stiff knees cracking with the movements of an older woman.

"Glory be to God, Gillean! What have you done to her?"

Ena brushed by her son, casting him a look of aspersion. She took the woolen shawl from her shoulders, wrapping it snugly around Adara.

"Is this how you look after your wife? I thought I taught you better than that."

"Mother, I...I didn't know. I came out of the shower and found her like this." Gillean was once again ten years old, caught sneaking off, shirking his chores to play in the castle battlements. "Honestly, I don't know what's wrong."

"You'd better get to finding out. She needs help, Gillean. Or haven't you noticed?" Ena smoothed her daughter-in-law's sopping hair.

"What am I supposed to do, Mother?" Gillean threw up his hands in disgust and pity for the shell of the woman who was his wife. "She wants nothing to do with me."

"What have you done, little Gilly?" Adara repeated in a childlike voice.

Gillean and his mother exchanged disturbed glances before she took Adara for a hot bath.

"Bring it back, Gillean! Bring it back!" Adara shouted over her shoulder, her severe eyes confining him to the spot where he stood now shaking.

The spirit hovered above watching the distressing drama unfold but was unable to intervene. Here was an angel of the scarcest kind, an earthly being granted a second chance, the wings to fly because of his disobedience, and because he had given his life for an innocent—a child.

It was a child who had saved him, but it was love for the imperfect man, a love both pure and complicated, that induced him back to earth. No matter what incarnation either of them cycled through, their bond was eternal.

The man's wife loved the angel because he had shown her how to love herself, yet she did not make the connection. She cast her love outward, still not recognizing what was within. Her nameless yearning had brought him to the precipice of materializing, but he could not advance any further. He was trapped in a netherworld of waiting.

The angel was aware of all these things, most especially the torment of standing back. He could do nothing, help no one, until he was called for by name—called by the man, his wife, or the child. What the angel did not know—or rather, would not acknowledge—was that the love growing inside him was as rare and unusual as his existence. It was this efflorescence of love that suffused the air around his charges. He was like a live wire waiting to be tapped. But as with most sparks there resulted a flame. And sometimes not even the best intentioned of beings can confine a wildfire.

Chapter Two

Reckonings

Gillean walked the wooded path with heightened awareness. While his mother saw to calming Adara, his wife's words would not release him. *"Bring it back,"* she had entreated him. Finding her as he had, Gillean could have easily made the argument that his wife was not in her right mind. But the fact that those three words were the first she had spoken in weeks made the case for her lucidity. Much to his dismay, Adara's request was the only thing she had done recently that made sense.

The more haunting, ominous question, *"What have you done, little Gilly?"* required an answer to preserve his own sanity. He could no longer avoid the memories so neatly tucked away. Mid-tour he'd met up with Ciar in Prague. He finally gave himself to her, not out of love or even desire, but from the insufferable turmoil Sully's death had brought about. Adara's silence merely stated the obvious. She loved Sully, and Gillean concluded Sully must have loved her. Adara remained firmly ensconced in her emotional wasteland while he thrashed about like a drowning man refusing to go under.

Gillean had presented his grief, confusion, and pain to the intense artist, hoping she could mold it into something beautiful. But he had held back. He did not speak to Ciar of the spirit-man. He would not let the name cross his lips. An armored centurion guarded the place where those memories were kept. Gillean believed if he uttered the name, he would be opening Pandora's Box. Oddly, Ciar did not speak of Sully either. Her earlier warnings were not repeated. She wanted Gillean, and he obliged without conscience.

He was consumed by the image he did not want to reclaim, the name his lips could not speak, the pot of churning feelings he did not wish to stir.

Sully.

Gillean stood underneath the Blackthorn tree, releasing the name like a dove to the sky. Dusk smoothed over everything with its gray brush. Twilight subdued the lushness of the land. The air carried tiny filaments of severed willows. He lifted the collar of his overcoat. The evening wind tripped in, rustling the leaves of the robust tree.

Gillean felt entirely alone, and a bit stupid for supposing he could command the presence of a dead man. He had once believed in the magic he wrote and sang about. His zealous fans still had no doubt. But the magic he now practiced was the sleight of hand it took to assure his supporters that he was still their sincere, beloved bard of Ireland. He shrugged, realizing this too may be beyond him once he and Adara were divorced. How could the man who sang of love everlasting face his scrutinizing public without his wife of over two decades?

He walked deeper into the woods, his feet sinking into the wet ground. The familiar scent of burning peat mingled with his growing anger. Each intake of breath brought another regret to mind. Why had he made this backwards country, one where religion, superstition and war ruled supreme, his home? Wasn't he the one who was going to be different? Why had he opened himself to another man only to be left raw and exposed like a carved-out corpse?

It became more difficult to walk, his shoes making a sucking sound as he extricated them from the mud. Shoving his hands into his pockets, his fingers touched something. Chocolate! Cupping the small, heart-shaped pieces in his palm he deduced Ciar must have left them for him. But it wasn't Ciar he was contemplating when the wind strengthened, forcing him to button up against the sudden chill.

"Sully?" He breathed the name. "Are you here?"

"Turn round, Gillean."

Gillean remained as motionless as a soldier in a minefield.

"Turn round and look what the wind brought in."

Gillean did as directed. Behind him stood the man he remembered, except he no longer held the resemblance to Gillean he had in years gone by. Sully possessed the same radiant green eyes, but the cheeky grin was replaced by a more thoughtful, mature expression.

"I insisted on keeping my name. 'Tis me virtue." His smile reflected just a hint of the playful boy, but his voice had changed, revealing a new poise, along with his taller stature.

Gillean was at a loss for words and eyed Sully from head to toe. His dress was smart, with a bit of the old world about him—with his Irish linen shirt, complemented by a blue vest, white trousers, low black boots, and a tweed cap sitting atop curling black hair brushed behind his ears.

Gillean remembered the desolate, powerless feeling of holding Sully in his arms after the accident. One moment he was looking down at the bruised and bloodied body of the man who had commandeered his life. The next, Sully was gone, with no evidence of ever having existed.

"How…?"

Sully reached out tentatively. "Walk with me?"

Gillean nodded silently, thankful to place his hand into Sully's. He turned his head, not wanting his companion to see the tears of relief. The two started off towards a field of feral thistle.

Sully began his exposition. "I did tell ya that angels are not humans because they are not born into this life."

Gillean nodded again, taking note of the feel of Sully's skin. He feared his companion might evaporate before he could ascertain what had happened on that dreadful night.

"When I died on the road, I became as the re-encounters had commanded: without my past as a human child, but also having no future with them. So in essence, I was never born."

Gillean stopped. "So you're an angel now?"

Sully squeezed Gillean's hand. "Aren't I? Some forgiving spirit decided to fetch this tired old nobody from that road and slap some wings on him."

Gillean glanced behind Sully.

"'Tis figurative, Gillean."

"Why can I see you? How is it you can come to me?"

"So you can know me. I'm not a being in the sense of having a physical form, but if called upon, I must make myself recognizable."

"Called upon by whom?"

"You."

Gillean stepped back, releasing Sully's hand, and reflecting on the three words that had beckoned him to return to the Blackthorn. "What about Adara?"

Sully fell momentarily silent as a soft breeze glided through the patches of thistle. "If she should call upon me, I am obliged to answer."

"Have to, or *want to*?" Gillean prodded with suspicion.

"I don't desire as you do."

"Bullshit!" Gillean spat. "You and I… Something happened that night. Why would you lead me to believe that you cared about me?"

"I *do* care about you. I'm standing here, aren't I?"

"You said you loved Adara, and then you walked away, or did you wager I wouldn't remember that bit after you clocked me?"

Sully's eyes caught him in the same accusatory stare as his wife's.

"And you said ya trusted me. Were you lying then?"

"I did trust you! But I don't trust who or *what* you are anymore, or what you want."

"I want to help you."

"*Oh please!* How? By driving me mad?"

This was going all wrong. Gillean was thrilled to see Sully apparently alive in some as yet to be understood form. But now the sleeping emotions of the past several months woke with the ferociousness of a hunted dog. He backed Sully up as he came at him with a purposeful step, pointing his finger with the authority of a school master.

"I want to know about the relationship you have with my wife. Why is she wasting away? It's for you, isn't it? She won't tell me, but *you* bloody well will."

Sully spoke in a flat tone, his body unmoving. "You wanted to see me because of your jealousy? You want to blame Adara? Not a chance. Ya see, I have the same memories as yerself. And I recall that I told you what ya needed to do if you cared for—" Sully bowed his head.

"For who? For *you*? Were you unsure as to how I felt about you? If *I* recall, I told you—*showed you* in no uncertain terms. I suppose you thought that was easy for me?"

"It's not always about you," Sully put forth with a solemn stare. "What have you done to make things better? And I mean for your family, not just for *Gillean Faraday?*"

"Listen to me, you God-forsaken creature—" Gillean spoke through clenched teeth.

Sully threw back his head and laughed.

The unnatural glow of his eyes gave Gillean pause.

"Takes one to know one!" He folded his arms across his chest. "*If* ya should genuinely want my help, I'll be waiting."

"*What makes you think I want anything from you now?*" Gillean yelled. "And just what the fuck happened that night?" His finger pressed harder against Sully's chest.

He ignored the intense pleasure of being near the man once again, and instead fired off his hurt-filled questions. "Why didn't you tell me about yourself and Adara? And who was the woman in the car?" He paused for a breath, saving the best for last. "And how did Ciar know I would find you with my wife?"

Sully took off his cap, running the brim through his fingers as if Gillean had simply asked him the time of day. "You're a right jackass."

"I thought angels were supposed to be all sweetness and light," Gillean scoffed.

"You think ya know a lot of things, Gillean, that's your problem."

"Then enlighten me. Let's start with how you are acquainted with Ciar."

Sully placed the cap back on his head, straightened it, and smoothed his shirt. "Like I said, I'll be waiting."

Chapter Three

Hide and Seek

Gillean entered the castle through an underground door he'd disc-overed when he was a lad. He'd made good use of it as an adolescent, coming and going unnoticed at all hours of the night. It was one of the few benefits of living in such an unusual home.

He was glad of the furtive entrance, wanting to avoid the barrage of questions his mother would most certainly launch into, and not ready to be assaulted by the accusatory eyes of his wife. He needed time to think and digest what had just happened. He needed a drink.

Gillean knew every inch of the old fortress. Navigating the dark passageways like a bat in a cave, he heard the echo of long-ago laughter—his and Joseph's as they played hide and seek in the dank spaces running underneath the main halls. Back then Gillien's greatest challenge was avoiding the tickling hands of his older brother. Now he was searching for an escape from the sticky web of his own mistakes and missteps. He was stumbling through life, wreaking havoc on anyone who had the misfortune to be in his vicinity.

At least that's what Sully had so smugly indicated. The mere idea of the man-angel, reincarnated demon—whatever the hell he was—made Gillean's blood boil. Who was this infernal creature that he should judge Gillean? He was sure there was something going on between *the angel* and Adara. Maybe the whole outlandish story was an elaborate plot hatched by the two in order to convince Gillean he was mad.

"Angel, my ass," Gillean mumbled, as he swooped into the hotel bar, waving his hand to the grad student wiping down tables.

The family business was still in operation, although much scaled down. After the deaths of his grandfather and father, Gillean had tried his utmost to convince his mother to sell the old place. But Ena, being as stubborn as her son, insisted upon staying in the home her husband had so loved. These days, however, neither she nor the rest of the remaining family had much to do with the day-to-day operations of the hotel. It was now open four months of the year and serviced a more well-to-do clientele.

The preoccupied singer on the run pilfered a bottle of whiskey.

"Night now, Mr. Faraday!" the bartender called.

Gillean located an unoccupied guestroom downstairs. Tossing his coat onto the bed, he opted to forgo lamplight and instead opened the drapes, letting in the natural light of the night sky. He grabbed a glass from the bedside table and poured himself a double. Taking a few quick gulps, he fixed his gaze on a distinguishable cluster of stars: Orion, the Hunter.

As a boy, he and his grandfather would climb to the highest point of the castle and Gillean would proudly identify as many constellations as he could. His granddad's arm draped over Gillean's shoulder provided a sense of confidence and security. At only ten years of age, he was weary from traveling the globe—making friends only to be uprooted and transferred to other, foreign soil. Eventually Gillean learned to keep to himself no matter where he was. His grandfather became his best friend. It hurt less not having to say goodbye to anyone when the inevitable request would come for his father, a world-renowned archeologist, to embark on another dig.

Gillean's da had believed he was providing his family the greatest benefit by exposing them to as much of the world as possible. Dr. Milo Faraday assured his protesting son that precious few children were privy to such rare opportunities, and didn't it make Gillean quite the spoiled little boy not to appreciate the rare opportunity given to him.

At seven years of age Gillean had enjoyed a period of happiness and stability when the Faradays returned to his place of birth. They spent the next three years settled in one place, the beautiful and romantic Brazil. He had just begun to breathe freely, believing the family was finally going to put down roots, when his father was offered a prestigious teaching post in Ireland. Once again, Gillean was instructed on the advantages of living in his ancestral homeland. And when the opportunity presented itself to purchase the *Teach na Spioradi*, his parents announced this would be their "real home".

But Gillean spent most of his time at Boarding school. His parents' hands were full enough—getting the castle ready for guests and discharging his father's duties as a professor—without having the added responsibility of bringing up two children. Not once did Gillean express to his parents his feeling that they regarded the raising of himself and Joseph as the one full-time responsibility they did not wish to take on. Why else had the children been sent away only a few months after settling into their "real home?"

Stargazing with his grandfather was one of, if not the only thing Gillean could rely upon. Many a song was inspired by those treasured evenings.

He poured another drink, closing his eyes; he could envision his grandfather's white hair, neatly trimmed mustache and dancing blue eyes. The bergamot scent of the man's aftershave and his gentle voice were always in the back of Gillean's mind.

"Don't ever feel you are alone, my boy. You have the stars, the same ones that have been shining down on young men for thousands of years. No matter where you go, you will always have the same sky. And you will always have the old chap here, too."

The ringing of his mobile jolted him back to reality. He flipped it open, nearly shouting.

"Hallo!"

"I hope that's excited anticipation I hear in your voice, Gilly."

He sat down on the bed, uncharacteristically lighting up a cigarette; he'd only recently resumed the unhealthy habit of his rebellious youth.

"Greetings, my beautiful painter." He blew a dense cloud of smoke high into the air, praying there wasn't a smoke detector in the room.

"Everything alright?"

He took another generous sip of alcohol. His throat burned from the combination of whiskey and smoke.

"Fan-fucking-tastic," he gasped.

"Yes, certainly sounds like it," she laughed. "What's the matter? Life in the Emerald Isle not so magical?"

"A little too magical, maybe." He took another puff, licking his lips.

"Have you spoken with her yet?"

"I tried to, but—"

"Oh, please don't."

"Don't what?" He crushed out the cigarette in what he hoped was an ashtray.

She was quiet.

"Ciar?"

"Don't call me, don't come to me, don't contact me again until you are free to be with me—fully."

"Darling, it's not so easy. She's not well, and I have four children to consider."

"Of course, take all the time you need. Maybe I will be waiting, and maybe I won't, *little singer.*"

Her words hurtled him back to another time, another face; or was it? He held the phone out as if he had no idea what it was used for.

"Do you love me, Gilly? You've yet to tell me. Do you?"

He shut his eyes, considering the stinging irony of her question. The man who had spent most of his life singing about love—of nature, family, exploration, and for one true heart—now doubted that he'd ever known the genuine character and course of love. Surely he loved his family, most especially his children and grandfather. He must love Adara. She was, after all, the person he'd built a life with. But when he considered love in all its complexities, it was a man he'd felt on the verge of hating who had taken full hold of Gillean's heart.

He was aware that his answer would irrevocably alter the direction of his life. Maybe this was his destiny. He was no longer sure of anything, except that everything changes and he could count on nothing.

"Yes, Ciar. I love you," he heard himself proclaim.

"Say it again, little Gilly," she whispered.

Chapter Four

Apollo 8

Gillean returned to identifying the constellations, but their nature had changed. The stars appeared as a constantly moving collective of fireflies. Fatigued, he stretched out on the bed. He'd finally decided upon a course, but its direction felt far from secure. He would need more than the aid of the North Star to guide his floundering ship.

Closing his eyes, he was thankful there were no images or voices to taunt him, only darkness. A single word stuck in a groove of his consciousness, kept coming at him—much like the Beatles' Revolution 9. Only the word was not a number, but a pronouncement from his inner self. *Liar. Liar. Liar.*

Despite his inebriated state he became aware of another presence. It dolefully pulled at him, meaning to keep him from rest.

Gillean rose impatiently from the bed, momentarily latching on to the nightstand for support. He called out in a raspy, heated voice, "What the hell do you want, Sully?"

Gillean paced the room.

"Damn it to hell! I know you're here, ya sneaky bastard. Let's have at it then so you can leave me alone, for good!"

Stumbling into the adjoining room, he found Sully sitting cross-legged on the floor, facing an open window. His back was to Gillean, apparently taking up his tacit vigil of the sky.

Irate, Gillean knocked a lamp from a desk and demanded, "Answer me!"

Sully raised his head. "Do you remember Apollo 8?"

"What?"

"The space mission, Apollo 8. Do you remember it?"

Gillean hovered above clenching his fists. "And you're asking this, why?"

"Three men boarded a craft and became the first earthlings to fly to the dark side of the moon."

"So?"

"And ya fancy yourself a star gazer. Ya don't even know the significance of such a happening."

Gillean yanked the curtains closed, eliminating Sully's view. "I'll ask you one more time, what do you want?"

"What do *you* want?" Sully raised his voice. "Is it this?" He waved his hand across the dimly lit room, "To hole up with alcohol and cigarettes placing secret phone calls? My, how sophisticated you have become, my friend." His eyes heaved allegations. "You're a genuine artist."

"Did you just call me a liar?" Gillean scoffed.

The word sounded even more menacing in the spoken form.

"Aren't ya now?"

"Get up!" Gillean roughly took hold of Sully's arm. "You said you would come to me if I called you. Well, I don't believe I asked for you, so what business could you possibly have here now? Is it with Adara, perhaps?" He jabbed at the man's shoulder with an open hand. "Maybe you could restore her sanity while you're trespassing." His laugh was hollow. "Ha! Get it? You're an angel and you're trespassing." Rocking on his heels, Gillean regarded Sully with watery eyes. "Go on, ask me to forgive you your trespasses."

Sully lifted his shoulders, "Ya think this is funny, that *you're* funny?" He stepped forward, forcing the inebriated man to rock to maintain balance. "Ya think this is all a big joke, do ya?"

Gillean's voice wavered. "I don't think any of this is funny."

"Then make it right," Sully spoke softly. "Ya have it within your power to do so."

Gillean threw his hands in the air, retreating to the other room. "And so does she!" he retorted.

"*She*?"

"Adara, ya stupid plonker! I assume you mean to make things right with her, don't you?"

Sully followed, placing a warm hand on Gillean's back. "'Tis a bigger mission than that."

Gillean turned a stormy face to the statement. "I've had about all I can stomach of you and your holier-than-thou attitude. You've got what you wanted from me, just like everyone else. So I suggest you walk, fly, slither, whatever it is you do, and leave me alone."

"And if it's Ciar you're wanting, you'll be climbing into bed with the devil to be sure," Sully admonished.

Gillean stared blankly at the pictures his mind flashed at him, his safe life with Adara and their children, the forbidden life he had begun to imagine with Sully, and of his current life with Ciar—the latter being one of deceit and self-indulgence miles away from what he used to hold sacred. He blamed Sully's presence for the ugly reminder of the conflict raging within.

"You forget, Sully. Your silver wings are tied to my steel guitar strings." Gillean smiled self-righteously. "You are obliged to follow my wishes. And I am telling you, insisting that you get the hell out of my life." He set for the door. "I wonder how you should know the devil so well."

Chapter Five

Worlds Collide

Gillean thrust the door open without the courtesy of knocking and promptly marched over to his wife, who was in the midst of hurriedly packing suitcases.

She looked incredulous as he barreled his way into the room. It was a little before six in the morning. The sun had yet to begin its steady climb into the misty sky. Gillean was in the habit of sleeping well past noon whenever he had the chance.

His bloodshot eyes glanced at her half-full travel bags.

He deduced that Adara had reached a decision of her own. Without a word to him, she continued gathering her things.

"Going somewhere, Dara?" He slammed shut one of the cases, confronting his unnerved spouse.

Gillean's harshness was as predictable as the tides. He was of a stormy nature, keeping his true feelings in check when he was in the public eye. He had matured that much in the years she had been with him. But this gave him all the more reason to let loose when he was not under such relentless scrutiny.

"Jesus wept. I don't know what has possessed you, Gillean!" His mother shouted from the doorway. "You ought to be ashamed of yourself." Marching determinedly to Adara's open suitcase, Ena reached for the clothing neatly stacked on the bed. "*I* am, to be sure. And if your father was alive—"

"Oh spare me, mother. He's not. And if he were here, he'd not have a clue as to what was going on in anyone's life but his own, as usual."

Gillean was in rare form. Being exhausted allowed him to speak his mind completely uncensored.

Striking like lightning, Ena slapped Gillean hard across the face. She had never raised a hand to either one of her sons, not even when they were children. The sound was as ugly as the gesture itself.

Ena's handprint colored her son's pale cheek. "Like father, like son then, I'd say."

Gillean's eyes watered from his mother's unprecedented action. "Mother, if you don't mind, I'd like to speak with my wife—alone."

Adara spoke up. "Put your knives away."

"I'm sorry, my dear. I didn't mean to upset you. I don't know what came over me," Ena stammered in apology to her daughter-in-law, and not her offended son.

"Like mother, like son." Adara turned her back to them and resumed her packing.

"I'll leave you to your privacy," Ena said quietly. "Gillean, please come and speak with me when you're ready."

The beleaguered woman bowed out of the room.

"May I ask what you are doing? Where do you think you're going?" Gillean put to his wife.

She retreated to the bathroom, where he could hear water running.

"Oh, Mother of..."

Gillean was about to follow her in. His dependable wife had become as unpredictable as the March storms that blew in fast and fierce from the sea.

Adara returned with a cold cloth, pressing it with care against his reddened cheek.

He put his hand over hers, his fingers brushing against her wedding ring. "You don't have to do that."

She had insisted on keeping the tiny gold band, even years later, when he offered to buy her a much more elaborate symbol of his love and success. She preferred his original offering. Noticing the bluish circles shadowing her eyes, he wanted to be twenty again, and she seventeen. Gillean believed he would have done many things differently, given the chance.

"I'm going home, with our children." She slid her hand from under his and turned her attention to the suitcases.

"Why do you say that as if I am not welcome to come with you?"

"Why do you act as if you intend to come with us?"

He thrust the cloth in the air. "I never said—"

"You didn't have to."

She drifted back to him. "Leave that on your skin. It will calm your nerves."

Her impulse to care for him produced an agonizing sense of culpability. He'd done nothing to assist her these past few months.

She reached out and pulled a few hairs from his shirt and studied them like they were rare artifacts, much like his father poring over dirt-covered bones and clay objects unearthed at a dig.

"Look here, lad!" his father would say enthusiastically. It was one of the rare moments when the old man was actually animated. "Come here, Gillean, and see what life is all about."

Gillean protested; why was it so important to gush over things that had been buried in the ground for centuries. *Life?* The people were dead and gone, and yet his da attached such value to these grubby items, finding them enormously more fascinating than his own living sons.

He shook free from the memory. Adara was running her fingers the length of the long, black strands. She was lost again, wandering in the hidden retreat of hers.

"Hello!"

She turned her face to his, looking as if he had broken some prayerful meditation. She carefully tucked the hairs into the pocket of her jeans, which were now a size too big. Her eyes were a striking, rich violet. "Please excuse me. I have things I need to attend to. I imagine you do as well."

Gillean was panicked by her resolve. She was more than ready to sever their bond. He was desperate, knowing he was to blame but not wanting to own it. He didn't have the strength. He was forty-three and tired. He found that age brought more questions than answers.

He thought of Sully, a being who unwaveringly knew right from wrong. This ignited Gillean. *Sully!* The dark hairs that damn near enchanted Adara. They must be Sully's. Gillean relished the one true power he possessed, the one thing he could depend upon—Sully's steadfast faithfulness to him. Gillean could wield it as a sword in whatever way he wanted.

The clouds were lifting for him as they did amidst the sun-speckled Maumturk Mountains of Connemara. Everything was so blessedly clear. Adara groped her way in the darkness of ignorance. Gillean would hold on to his little nugget of certainty, polishing it until the time was right. But not now. He had to let Adara lead the way. She would be the one to trip up the haughty little spirit. He shoved his attachment to Sully into a corner of his mind reserved for things best not thought about. But there was no such corner of his heart to hide the feelings Sully engendered. Gillean's consolation was that he could guarantee Sully would be sorry for judging him so harshly.

Chapter Six

Winter Magic

February in Ireland is a time of tranquil comfort. There are few tourists who brave the wet, windy, winter months to visit a country when daylight is at a premium. The colorful lights, joyous music, and general atmosphere of wondrous excitement shepherded in by Christmas and Solstice festivities fade away with the old year. February is in the infancy of the new.

Adara imagined more enjoyable places she would rather be than an abandoned gardener's shed on a snowy February evening. Invisible fingers of dying light spread from underneath the wooden door. The air crept along the rotted floorboards, rising up in a lonesome whisper, rustling yellowed newspapers and decayed leaves. Adara had chosen this shed on the outer edge of the Faraday property, believing she would not be disturbed. She was a bit apprehensive at the task she set about, so foreign to her was the concept of summoning a spirit.

It was exactly a fortnight since she and Gillean had left the *Teach na Spioradi* and gone their separate ways, deciding to wait until the spring months before telling their children of the breakup. Her husband assured her he could be reached any time on his mobile. But he gave her no word of where he would be, or with whom.

Adara was less disturbed by this fact than she was by the pieces of hair she kept close to her person at all times. The thin strands represented the wire twisted around her heart. With every breath, a piercing sensation stung her chest. Pisces' season was leaving Ireland, kicking up the snow and frost in its wake.

Not knowing how she could continue on in such a state, feeling as if she were fighting for each inhalation of breath, she had sought the advice of an elderly traveler the previous day. Adara stumbled over her words, seeing with absolute lucidity her vision in the castle, but having no verbal grasp for the right description. Since that day, she'd experienced inexplicable happenings, seeming only to affect her.

She would return from shopping trips laden with bags, fumbling for her house keys, and she would see him; not a full person, but an obscured image on the periphery of her vision, like a sideways glance.

She could swear the telephone was ringing, but when she asked her children why they didn't respond, they looked at her askance. Only she heard the chimes. And when she found a pair of pajamas that Gillean left behind, she knew her impassioned reaction was not that of an impending divorce.

Holding the soft material close to her cheek—it was not her husband's familiar cologne she smelled—she was transported inside the deepest part of herself, taking in the unique scent of burning turf fires, the majestic ocean, and the wintry air of Bray Cliff—something ancient and timeless.

Adara, desperate for answers and communication with the one entity she believed could bring her peace, sat alone in the chilly shack following the elderly gypsy's instructions.

"I...I don't even know what kind of spirit this is, or even if it is a spirit," she had told the kindly woman.

"Ya don't need to know, dearest. Ya believe it to be a good spirit and wish to summon it. There is nothin' more ya need do other than follow these steps I've written down."

And so Adara had. She chose an isolated spot—one where she was certain she would not be interrupted—and waited for the first traces of darkness. *The gloaming, as* the Celts referred to this ephemeral time, is when day falls from the sky slowly, like paint sliding down a canvas, the colors mixing into a beautiful, indescribable shade of twilight.

She lovingly spread out the filaments of hair on a rickety table, and lit a tall, indigo candle. The tinker woman told her that indigo is the channel for opening portals. The color also lends the ability to see the world from a parallel point of view. Adara shifted on the uncomfortable stool, whispering a personal apology before reciting the words the traveler had given her.

"Please forgive my disturbing your rest, whoever you may be, but I believe I need you."

Concentrating on the high orange flame and listening one last time for any sounds of intrusion, she found only the noises of the countryside making way for the evening that remained. Taking a deep breath she recited the invocation given to her.

"I call upon the spirit so close, to the one whose heart knows mine the most. Bring your essence to me. I evoke thee. I ask thee, please draw near."

She shut her eyes tight, shivering not so much with cold, but with expectation. A few moments passed. When nothing happened she searched the shadows for some entity.

No one.

Feeling a little more than silly, she stood to blow out the candle. Before the breath left her, she looked to the door and he was there—like a ghost, an angel. The man she had come to trust more than anyone.

The glow of his ethereal eyes seemed brighter than that of the candle. He was no longer a flickering image, but a man standing before her.

Her heart expanded, hacking through the wire of pain that had imprisoned it all these months. She felt enveloped by the tremendous waters of the sea. Her toes dug firmly into the warm sand just as a spectacular wave crashed against her. Its fury almost took her down, but the memories of him inundating her consciousness gave her the strength to stay upright, feeling the cool spray of brine against her face that was titled towards the sky and his beaming eyes.

Her gaze lingered on him. He wore white trousers and a simple white cotton shirt. A smart cap covered his untamed hair, the hair she'd found on Gillean's shirt.

The same unmistakable aura that had drawn her to him before was present in his generous smile. Without saying a word, he put her at ease purely by taking her in with his compassionate green eyes.

"Sully." The name released itself from her center, like a gem loosened from the earth.

"'Tis himself." He did not move, but his smile remained.

"I hope I have not disturbed your peace." She looked away, ashamed. She thought she must be dreaming and longed to touch him, feel his body to prove that he was indeed there.

"I'm always here. But I cannot come to any of you, unless ya ask for me." He regarded her with his intense eyes. "And I cannot touch you unless ya reach for me first."

She rushed to where he stayed against the door, placing her arms around him. He was real. She could hear his breathing, his lungs taking in air. Pressing her face to his chest, she could count the beats of his heart.

It all came back to her—not just how he looked, but how he made her feel. How she cared for him, and how his brutal death had submerged her in relentless agony. He was the echo that remained in her heart. Now she was free.

"What has ya so troubled?" He sounded overly cautious.

Overwhelmed by the magnitude of the moment and the protracted emotional war she and her husband had been engaged in for the past few months, she cried. "You're upset with me." She backed away from him awkwardly.

"Why would ya believe such a thing?" Sully said.

"You aren't as I remember you. You're so reserved, so distant. Why have you changed?"

"I'd like to think I am merely new and improved, eh?"

"Oh what's the use," muttered Adara. "Everyone has changed. My whole life is changed, why not you as well?" She paced the floor with renewed energy. "I have no idea who you are." She took refuge on the other side of the room.

"Yes ya do," he said in a low voice. "Look at me, Adara."

Her eyes obeyed, searching his for answers.

"That is why ya called to me. You know ya can trust me. Ask me. Ask me what ya want to know."

"It's not Gillean, it's you, isn't it?" she blurted out.

"Me?"

"I know what my husband is up to. People tell me I'm distraught over his leaving. But, as ever, we will eventually work things out, they say."

She slowly moved towards him. The room was barely lit by the waning candlelight. "I knew that wasn't the reason for my pain. It was you. The things I remembered tonight... *My God!*" she cried, placing her hand over her mouth. "You died saving our son!"

Sully remained impassive.

"If I ask you to stay here with me, can you? Will you?" Adara gripped Sully's arms in desperation. "I know you want to tell me the truth. I think you want to stay."

Sully eyes moved over her like fingertips, transmitting great sorrow. She shook him. "*Tell me.*"

He cast his eyes to the floor.

Adara touched her hand to his cheek, "Stop thinking about Gillean. He is the captain of his own ship. I need to make some sailing plans of my own. Will you stay and help me? *Please?*"

Sully shook his head mournfully. "I cannot."

"Gillean remembers you, doesn't he?" she asked. "He's spoken to you."

"Yes."

She smiled ruefully. "You think he will want your help?"

"I don't know, but if he should..."

She reached around him and opened the door. The night was cool. Her head finally felt clear. "You will do what you must." She took his hand, proffering a walk in the same meadow where they had first met a lifetime ago.

Chapter Seven

Inspiration

Adara did not dare ask Sully about his present state of being, as if delving into the obscure subject would somehow cause him to vanish once again. She spoke of Gillean's leaving, and of her intentions to gather up the threads of her undone life.

Sully listened thoughtfully, walking by her side, and keeping his own recent experiences with Gillean to himself. He thought it best to focus his attention on how to help Adara. She'd asked for him. He didn't turn inward for guidance. He wasn't sure he wanted an answer, other than his directive. After all, if a human has the power to summon an angel, it was his duty to remain. She asked not out of malicious reasons, but out of love. He was walking a fine line. He grappled with the decision to tell her what Gillean meant to him, because it was she who had beckoned him and asked that he stay.

He would not reveal anything about Ciar unless directly asked. Adara deserved the truth, but she needed to come to her own conclusions, without any influence from him as to what path she would walk.

The real conversation between the two was the silent dialogue which found expression only with their eyes and gestures. Each longed to speak about the layer beneath the surface of their words, the place where the truth resonated like the final chord of a song. But the phantom of Gillean kept them both circumspect.

The interior of the Faraday house was like a grand church. The air smelled of sandalwood and fresh flowers. Sully paused as Adara led him down a corridor.

"What is it?" she whispered.

"Listen." He cocked his head to the domed ceiling above, painted a summer sky blue.

"What?" Adara followed his glance.

"The breath of sleeping children." His eyes returned to her face.

"And what does that sound like?" She concentrated on the easy hush of the house.

"It sounds like…like peace, serenity. It's the certain knowledge that joy does exist, and they are its purest form." He closed his eyes and breathed deeply. "Do ya know the word 'inspire' literally means 'to take in,' like a breath?"

"I'd forgotten how much they do inspire me," she replied wistfully. "Gillean and I have much to make up for."

"You gave them life. Let them bring some back to you."

"But what happened to the life Gillean and I built for them?" She stared at him with eyes the color of December. "You must know what his intentions are. I don't want to know for myself, but please, Sully, for them." She gestured to the bedrooms above. "I need to know for my children. Where is Gillean? What is he going to do now?"

Reality tugged hard at Sully. Gillean's words echoed in his head. *Your silver wings are tied to my steel guitar strings. You are obliged to follow my wishes.* Gillean had no idea the depth of truth in his statement, or the irony. In trying so hard to cover up his duplicity by acting the bully, Gillean unknowingly had made one of the most honest statements he would ever utter.

He and Sully were bound to one another. Sully had made a vow never to abandon him. After witnessing Gillean's erratic behavior over the past several months, right down to the last few days, Sully was developing a plausible theory as to what was going on.

The task was clear enough. He must find out if his hunch was correct. If so, there would be an epic battle—meaning he and Gillean would need to trust and rely on one another as never before. Since Gillean was close to loathing Sully at the moment, the future did not look promising.

"Come with me." Sully lightly pulled Adara into the nearest room.

"Aren't you going to turn on the lights?" she asked in a muted voice, as Sully led her to a couch. She took a seat on the edge.

"It's best I don't." He kneeled on the floor in front of her. "As long as *you* can see me, anyone else can, too. I need to ask something of you."

"Alright."

"Remember the day ya danced for me?"

"Yes, I do."

"Concentrate on how ya felt when you were dancing and hold it in your heart. I can't say anything more right now. Will ya do this much, not for me, but for yourself?"

"You can tell me more about what is going on, but you're afraid to." She leaned closer to his face. "Don't misjudge me. I don't need to be protected. I can handle the fact that Gillean loves another woman. I just ask that you be decent enough to tell me."

"Sweet Adara, that is between yerself and Gillean."

"I see." She leaned back as if the weight of his words was too much to bear.

"You believe in the Divine forces of this world, don't ya?" Sully posed.

"Yes…"

"Then ya must believe there are dark forces at work as well. And they exist only to tempt and torture those who are most vulnerable."

"What are you getting at?" she asked, her voice a tired whisper.

Sensing her fatigue, he spoke softly. "I'm sayin' it's late. You lay down now and get some rest."

He took off her shoes and gathered a quilt around her.

She didn't resist.

"Listen to me. This is important," he pleaded.

She quietly waited.

"Please don't forget you are a dancer, *please*."

"I'm…I'm just so tired."

He had to respect her own desires, would abide by her wishes and censure what was in his heart if he must. He drew in a long breath before asking the difficult question: "Do ya want to be with Gillean? Do you love him?"

"I loved a fantasy. How can one have a life with a fantasy?"

"Take this time to decide what ya want for yourself."

She fought against the heavy hand of sleep. "You're leaving, aren't you?"

"I need to be sure of something. But, I'll be back." Sully shut his eyes, willing the wisdom to keep himself from becoming too entangled in these human lives. "I promise."

"I believe you, Sully."

Chapter Eight

Bonds

Gillean reclined in the private aircraft that cut through the darkening Irish sky. His destination was a small, infrequently used landing strip in Prague. He was risking everything for this inscrutable woman.

Gazing out over the wide expanse of green, he noted the puffs of white sheep grazing peacefully in the fields. Their coats, streaked with red or blue, meant that someone took care to keep them safe, making sure they would not fall victim to a hungry predator.

As the plane took Gillean further from all that was familiar, his thoughts were not of Sully, Adara, or Ciar, but of his birthplace and his childhood in Brazil. The bittersweet combination of loneliness and freedom filled his heart, just as it had filled the heart of the nine-year-old boy running under a throbbing, hot sun, the soft, gritty sands of the streets beneath his bare feet.

He traveled back to a warm day with a balmy breeze following him like a devoted friend down the narrow paths. A man whose age was difficult to ascertain with his sinuous, black hair and mocha-colored skin sat on a crumbling cement wall, his agile fingers picking sultry music from a much-exercised guitar. It shone dazzlingly as rays of light bounced off its wooden belly, casting a spell on the untamed Gillean, luring him closer.

Tourists sat outside local cafes sipping strong, fragrant coffee. They smiled at Gillean, looking every bit the local scamp with his golden-brown skin and light cotton pants which hung loosely from his small frame. He ran with his shirt unbuttoned and the sleeves rolled up. His uncombed hair needed a good washing.

"Little Gilberto!" the guitarist called to him, without losing tempo.

Gillean rushed over to the musician, easily fitting himself in the space between the man's arm and his guitar.

"Sing for them, Gilberto. Go on, like I teach you." The man laughingly nudged the young boy.

Gillean jumped from the wall facing the few seated nearby. "A note, sir, give me my note!"

The man nodded and played a C chord, strumming with great fervor until the boy was ready to begin the song.

It didn't take Gillean long to find the key, or his voice. With a knowing smile he began to sing in Portuguese, his body swaying to the rhythmic guitar. His eyes met the gaze of each and every person who stopped to listen. By mid-song, a small crowd had gathered. By the time he had finished with a dramatic bow, offering his acknowledgement of their praise, they were clapping and enthusiastically requesting another tune.

But his joy was short-lived. Cutting through the small gathering, his father was unexpectedly at his side, grabbing at his bare arm.

"*Gillean!*"

His father spoke with authority, turning himself and the boy from the hushed assemblage. The carefree guitarist ceased playing.

Gillean's face flushed red at his father's disregard for his son's obvious talent.

"Da..." He struggled against his father's firm grip.

"Gillean, you were instructed to collect your brother an hour ago to help me at the dig."

His father was not a violent man, or one to raise his voice, but he demanded unquestioning obedience from his children.

The tourists, who only moments ago had showered Gillean with approval and appreciation, began to disperse. They returned to their coffee and conversations, clearly uncomfortable at witnessing a private matter between father and son.

"No, no, is my fault, *senhor*." The tall, slender Brazilian approached the two. "I ask Gilberto to stay. Please, do not blame the boy. My fault, okay?"

He extended an apologetic hand to Gillean's da, and Milo Faraday accepted it.

"Right then, I appreciate your attention to my son, but he has his duties, you understand, and entertaining others isn't one of them."

"Yes, *senhor*. I make sure he remember."

The well-meaning guitarist mussed Gillean's hair with his hand. "You mind your *pai*, Gilberto."

Gillean would have gladly traded his well-respected and educated father for the passionate, street musician, if given the chance.

"See you soon, Ernani!" Gillean called out. "Save my place!"

The man had taken up his guitar and was moving on.

"Your *place* is with me and your family," his father reproached. "You must learn that family and respectability always come first. That is the true measure of a man. No matter what is in your heart."

Gillean jerked away. "*Voce nao me compreende, Pai!*"

"I've asked you to speak English to me, *Gillean.*"

The rebellious Gillean translated the statement only in his mind. *You don't know me, or my heart!* To further anger his father would only bring unwanted repercussions.

"I forget where I am sometimes, *Father,*" he said. His expression was both innocent and shrewd.

"I shall have to remind you. Starting tomorrow, you will be working with me on the dig for the next week."

Not caring about consequences, Gillean shouted after the man who had started the walk back to their home.

"Why don't you hear *me?* Why don't you know *me?*"

Gillean turned his head from the window of the plane, and away from the hurtful memory. He wondered how he could muster the nerve to stand in front of strangers, night after night, baring his soul to them through his music, but had never found the courage to ask his father the one simple question that besieged him day after day: "Do you love me, Da?"

Chapter Nine

Payment

"**W**ild horses could not have kept me from you tonight." Gillean kissed her face and neck while she unbuttoned his shirt, running her sharp, painted fingernails the length of his chest, sending shivers down his spine.

"I was afraid you might have changed your mind about me," she cooed.

He brushed her hair with his hands. "Forget what I said earlier. I don't doubt you, Ciar. I need you, *so much.*"

He unlaced the front of her dressing gown, kissing her wantonly. She was in the process of breathlessly undoing his belt when the golden guitar vase crashed to the floor, sending water and shards of gilded glass to the carpet. Gillean jumped back, releasing Ciar from their half-dressed embrace.

The CD player filled the room with music by an artist of legendary status. Gillean had idolized the American singer-songwriter, like most teenage boys of his generation. Oddly, the voice was familiar enough to his, but not the words.

I know you can feel me, I've long since realized. You know I can read you, cause you've seen me in your eyes.

"What the hell?" Gillean spun around the room.

"You didn't come alone, did you?" Ciar yelled at him over the music.

"*What?* Of course I'm alone! Who did you think I brought with me, George Michael?"

He fumbled with the player but had no success in shutting it off.

Who is this mystery that stands before me? A beggar, a fool, a fantasy? You hide in the darkness afraid of the light, but you are not free until you make it right.

The song continued its musical accusations. Ciar pounced on the

CD player, sending it smashing like the vase to the floor. Gillean didn't have time to react as she furiously crossed the room and took him into her arms, squeezing him with the inescapable grip of a python.

His eyes widened as her hold tightened.

"You brought the angel, *didn't you?*" she spat.

"Ciar...please, let go..." He feebly struggled against her. "I... can't..."

"You brought Sully here to trap me."

The pain in his chest was excruciating. His knees buckled. His voice was little more than a gravelly whisper. "No... Look... He's not—"

She relinquished her death grip only slightly, sufficient enough to enable the interrogation to continue. "You fool! Who do you think tipped that vase and set off the music? Who else would be so determined to put a stop to us being together? I tried to warn you about Sully, but you wouldn't listen." She pulled him to her again. Each time he tried to inhale, the crushing sensation came.

"No..." he begged. "Please, stop."

"*Shut up!*" she screamed.

A third voice cut through the air. "Leave go, Ciar! Now!" Sully materialized as the uninvited guest.

She glared at him. "You can't ask me to stop what you have begun, Sully."

Sully strode heatedly forward, clearly intent on protecting Gillean. "I didn't begin this; you did when ya caught him in your black net of lies."

"Caught him?" she chortled. "He begged me to take him in. And now he will beg me for his life."

The pressure in Gillean's chest was too much. He felt as if his ribs were about to push through his skin. He prayed for unconsciousness so the pain would cease. His strength waning, he angled his head, "Sully, please..."

Gillean was sure he was hallucinating when Sully took hold of Ciar. She was like an open flame. As Sully gripped her arms to pry Gillean free, the pungent smell of scorched skin stung Gillean's eyes. Sully's hands were burning! He refused to let go.

"That will do no good," she said coldly. "My power comes from Gillean, from the choices he made to hurt those he has loved in his lifetime—most of all himself."

The words came to Gillean through a haze of agony. He couldn't sort out what was happening to him. One minute he was about to make love to this woman, and the next she was slowly torturing him. How could he not have known of her potent combination of cruelty and strength? Why had he not heeded Sully's numerous warnings? And what was it she'd said about it being his own fault by his misdeeds?

Their voices traveled down a long tunnel, far away from where his mind was receding. The pain was abating at last. He was no longer in the room with them, but traveling a cool, shadowy passageway. Voices echoed off the opaque walls, voices from his past.

Was that his grandfather he heard? *Come now, Gillean, I'll teach you how to fly that kite properly.*

The lads at boarding school taunting him, *Look at the poor, little mutt. Not enough pounds to buy a pedigree, eh?*

The screams of unknown fans wanting his autograph; Adara vowing to love him as her lawfully wedded husband, the cry of his only daughter taking her first breath of life, and the seductive voice of Ciar promising pure pleasure.

Finally, Sully's profound question the night he gazed devotedly into Gillean's eyes. *"Do ya see it?"*

"This is not how it ends." Sully forced the words out, his hands still on Ciar, but no sooner had he spoken than Gillean slid to the floor with a deadening thud.

Sully dropped down beside Gillean, placing the back of his blistered hand over the man's heart. There was barely a rhythm.

He addressed Ciar, keeping his eyes on the musician's ashen face. "Not even you can take a life without losing your own, Ciar."

She stood above him gloating. "You don't think so, little boy?"

"I am certain of it." He took his swelling hand from Gillean and rose to face her.

She rested on the bed, uncharacteristically covering up with a robe. "Alright, I won't play ring-around-the-laurels with you. I have the advantage now, as he made the choice to abandon everything for me tonight. But it gets even better, you see," she sneered.

Ignoring the swelling skin of his severely wounded hands, Sully defiantly sat down next to her. He'd already seen the worst. He was resolved to do what he must in order to bring Gillean back. Sully surmised this was what Ciar had depended upon.

He wasted no time. "Let's have it, then."

"It's not so complicated really," she replied amiably, swinging her legs over his. "Poor, desperate Adara tried to tell you what she had done for Gillean but couldn't bring herself to. Perhaps she was worried that she would disappoint you. She quite fancies you, Sully."

"So you're just gonna spin more lies?" he snapped.

"I'm not blind to the truth as others may be. You were the one who left Gillean. You were the one who forced him into my bed. You're lucky I even want to help you now."

"Considering ya ran me over, you'll forgive me if I don't take your offer of help to be genuine."

"Yes, that's right, because *you* interjected yourself into my business and his life. *You* took my letter, remember? I was simply the means of your punishment. But maybe if you would have waited around for Gillean…"

Sully was growing more nervous the longer Gillean spent unconscious. "What is it yer after?" he demanded.

"What is rightfully mine, of course."

"As if ya had a *rightful* claim to anything."

"But I do, free and clear. What Adara neglected to tell you, or her *dutiful* husband, was that she made a deal with me. She came to me of her own accord."

"Adara wouldn't ask *you* for spare change."

"You don't know the lengths a woman in love will go to. But as I said, if you play your cards right tonight, you might find out first hand."

She stretched out her legs and threw her arms around his shoulders. "A long time ago, Adara came to me. I was a successful and influential French businesswoman."

Sully's face contorted in disgust.

"Once Mrs. Faraday got wind of what I could do for her," Ciar continued, "or rather for her new husband, she asked for my assistance in getting Gillean's musical career started."

"That's utter—"

"Naturally, she wanted this kept between her and me—didn't want to hurt dear Gilly's pride, you understand." She placed a hand to her cheek, appearing deep in thought. "As I recall, her exact words were: 'You and Gillean were once lovers. If you help him, and he wants to be with you, I won't stand in your way. I want what he wants, his success. He's worked so hard for it.'" She sniggered, her black eyes dancing with mirth. "Can you believe Adara actually granted me the use of her husband's body? Where's the fun in that, I ask you?"

Sully fixed her with a stony stare as she happily continued.

"I didn't take her up on the offer at the time—to have Gillean, I mean. But I did manage to whisper into a few of the right ears, and secure his first recording contract; signed, sealed, and delivered. He never knew who was behind it." She tossed her blonde head towards

Gillean's prostrate body. "Fulsome little man always believed it was his talent that opened the door."

"It *was* his talent!" Sully retorted over the relentless torture of his burned hands. "Nice little fairy tale. I don't believe you."

"That's entirely up to you. Didn't you just claim that I don't have the power to take a life? You're correct, I don't. Not unless someone offers it up." She pointed to Gillean. "Well, look at him. There is your proof. His wife offered him to me, you rejected him, and he willingly gave himself to me, and now I wish to keep him."

She took a weighted breath before disclosing her leverage. "It doesn't matter to me if I get him in this life or the next." She eyed Sully with curiosity. "You really don't know how strong the connection is between the two of you. Obliviously you are unaware as to what your leaving did to him." Ciar stroked his leg, her hand coming to rest on his inner thigh. "Poor Sully. You don't understand humans at all. They lack courage. They will do anything to fill the great void and evade suffering. I am infinitely stronger because they are miserably weak." She gave his leg a stiff squeeze. "And little twits like you get squished underneath my fingers. Look at where your dedication to selflessness has gotten you. Gillean chose me over his wife *and* you."

He shook her off, rising from the bed, careful to keep his hands and face from her. "Right, since I'm obviously of no use to you, or Gillean, I'll be on my way then."

"Give my condolences to Adara."

"How's that?"

"Once you take your leave, there will be no second chances for your soulmate. He's dying, and he won't be making any encore appearances."

Soulmate. The word filled Sully's heart with longing, a yearning he was certain no angel should harbor. He had to keep his wits about him. He could show no signs of weakness for Gillean's sake.

"You won't let him die," he said coolly. "What purpose would that serve?"

She stepped over Gillean, the lace of her robe brushing against his colorless face. "I dare say. I'm actually proud of you, little boy! Yes, why should you be the one to pay for Adara and Gillean's stupidity? Save yourself. Good on you!"

Sully willed his voice from quavering. "And ya mean to do what with Gillean?"

"His body may be mortal, but let's not forget, not so his soul. Didn't they teach you in *angel school* that if a human surrenders his soul, there is no going back?"

"Gillean did not willingly hand his soul over to the likes of you."

She forced him to face her with a victorious glare. "I beg to differ. Gillean sealed the deal himself." She circled him like a druid's fire. "More to the point, he disowned you, his soulmate, so he could have the freedom to be with me. It's not my fault he was dimwitted enough to choose a demon to give himself to. I should think the question you ought to be asking is, *why*?"

His eyes didn't leave her impertinent face. "Because you're an expert at distorting the truth."

"Ah, you regard the truth so much, here's a whole heaping of it for you to choke on, ignorant angel!" She all but spat at him, "You took Gillean to the precipice, and then asked him to jump, but you weren't there to catch him. You can't deny *that* is the *truth* of the matter."

She was correct; this loathsome, perfidious being had ensnared Gillean in a net not entirely of her making. Gillean had provided her with the rope. Sully tried to save Gillean from a love he did not understand, and grant him time, but instead he walked directly into Ciar's trap.

Sully glanced once more at Gillean—still as a stone, a tormented expression frozen on his face. Sully knew all about the shadowlands the musician now walked. He knew the place where the muddy earth sucks the feet like quicksand, every step closer to nothingness. Where the stagnant air is weighted with the stench of decay and the infinite sky is devoid of all color or light. The only sound is from the inner voice, screaming for help.

Silver wings and steel guitar strings, Sully considered. *Sod Gillean for being so obstinate!* Sully turned his back on the man he was entrusted to guide and assist. Gillean had insisted on isolation so that he could be with Ciar. What action *could* Sully take now? Gillean had already made his decision. He no longer trusted Sully.

What of Adara and the fragility of her current situation? She had carried the awesome weight of her secret for many years. She wanted to be free from it. Sully could feel that as acutely as the burns on his hands and his love for Gillean. He had his answer.

"I suppose ya have an offer to put forth." He dreaded her response.

She sat down on the bed once again, speaking in the brusque tone of a businesswoman. "You will have to remain human once and for all. You will have no powers, no connection to anything other than your fellow human beings."

"Why this?" he asked.

"Because Gillean has wished that you could know what it is like to be a real man. He believes that if you experienced a life closer to his own, you would have better understood him, and judged him less harshly."

Sully looked at her askance. "And why would ya care about what Gillean wants?"

"I do have my limits. As I said, I derive my power from the souls I encounter. My granting his desire is what keeps him tied to me."

"So, if I become human, you still have yer bond with Gillean. Where's the payoff?"

"I may exchange one life for another. You relinquishing your angel status will restore Gillean's mortal life. That's the deal. You want to haggle with me?"

Sully dipped a toe in the water of her patience. "And what kind of life will he have saddled with you?"

She grinned generously. "Firstly, he will have no memory of what has taken place here tonight. He will wake in my bed and will only remember what happened up to the point he came through my door, nothing else. The troubles he has with his wife will still be present. He may not, however, receive any intervention from you."

She paused, presumably to give him time to digest what she had said thus far. Ciar fed off his pain. She continued her exposition. "He will have no memory of you whatsoever. And you must never communicate with him."

The clock struck quarter to midnight, its toll like an omen.

"And one more thing," she added lightly. "My women's intuition tells me that Adara will be coming for you soon enough."

"Because you will have manipulated her."

"No, not me, dear child, but you. You turned her head. Best be mindful in how you...how shall I say, *handle* her."

"Leave Adara out of this!"

"That pathetic creature will come to you of her own volition, I'm sure."

"And I'm sure I don't trust you as far as I could throw ya!"

Trying to maintain composure was growing more difficult. He feared he would soon lose consciousness from the peeling flesh on his hands.

"Listen to me, you piece of wasted energy. You think you can read people's hearts so well? You think you understand the people you care about and can protect them? Your faith in those humans and your nonexistent capabilities will bring you all down."

The room was beginning to spin.

"Spare me the histrionics, Ciar. What do I need to do to keep Adara safe?"

"'Tis not the time for you to know yet!" she crowed. "But when that time does arrive, your decision will make all the difference. It could mean her life too."

"Am I asking too much for a little more clarity?" He propped himself against the wall for support. "You are asking for my existence here."

She followed, shoving her body against his. "I will make things crystal for you, lover. But since I do so treasure our rendezvous, I'll come to you later to clue you in. This is your test, Sully. We'll see if you can actually live up to the moral imperatives you so readily espouse."

He squirmed. "Ya expect me to agree to a deal when I know half the cost?"

"Need I remind you of your penchant for disobedience? This way I'll have assurance that you will keep your distance from Gillean. Agree, or you can forget about him taking another breath."

He was going to play the hand he was dealt, but not before slipping a little something from up his sleeve. "I'll agree." This time he didn't look away from her contemptuous eyes. "Provided that *if* Gillean should want to leave you, ya must promise you won't stand in his way." His face mirrored composure and purpose "Your *contract* with him and Adara will be null and void."

She glowered at him. "You have the gall to place such a condition on me when I am being so generous as to give you this chance?"

Sully moved to the other side of the room, away from where Gillean lay. "Why so incensed? I mean, unless there is the possibility that Gillean would decide to leave ya."

"As if you have any ability to play me, miserable boy."

"I suppose we're done here."

Ciar's lips twitched slightly. "You can have your special consideration. He'll never leave me. And you cannot make contact with him. You should also bear in mind that, being human, you will die at some point. And because you will have, for all intent and purpose, made a deal with the dark side, you will have to answer for that when you do expire."

He eyed her with wariness. "How do I know I can trust ya to keep your end of the bargain?"

"I am bound by the same powers you are."

"Clearly you and I don't work for the same side."

"No, but we are obligated by some basic laws. If either of us were to break the promise, we would be subject to punishment from our higher powers. Which means you cannot, under any circumstance, reveal to Gillean who you are, or were."

"And if he seeks me out?"

"He won't remember you, but if your paths should cross, you are obligated by the truth of your vow."

"I am already bound to the truth!"

She purred in his ear. "You don't know how far you have to fall, my sweet. You will be impelled only to your vow to me. As a human, you can do whatever, and whoever, you want. It won't much matter, considering where you will end up when you die."

"What if he should remember me?"

"He won't. Now make up your mind. I'm not waiting around here much longer." She paid no heed to the unconscious Gillean as she made her demand.

Sully cast his eyes on Gillean's prone body. He was sure. This was not how it was supposed to end for him, even if Gillean had come to Ciar willingly. He must furnish Gillean this one last chance.

"Alright." he confirmed. "Ya have a deal."

Ciar squealed with delight. "Very good! And since you are being the martyr, I'll allow you to keep your memories and experiences with him and his family. But, as I said, Gillean will have none of you."

"That's big of ya, I'm sure."

"And you can keep those burns as a reminder of your contemptible humanity. You won't be playing your fiddle anytime soon." She puckered her lips like a spoiled child. "And you and Gillean will have nothing to create together."

"Get on with it! Bring him back!"

She pointed to where Gillean lay. "That's something you have to do, your life in exchange for his. Put your hands over his heart."

Sully did so, resting his ruined hands against Gillean's chest. He silently willed the man to open his eyes.

After a few seconds that seemed more like hours, Gillean began to moan and stir. His eyes fluttered open, then shut as he struggled to awaken.

"That's it, Sully, say your goodbyes."

Her voice was fading, as was everything else in the room. He leaned into Gillean's ear, as if following her directive to bid farewell to his charge. Ciar unwittingly provided the key. He used the last of his powers to whisper words that only Gillean would understand. Sully prayed Gillean would remember.

His world went dark. He woke shivering in the middle of a field at sunrise, unable to move his useless, charred hands. A not so welcoming farmer was standing above poking a shovel at him.

"Blasted no good tinker! Catch up wit da rest o' yer caravan and get off me land!"

Back in the world Sully had just left; Gillean awakened feeling exhausted and sore. The exploratory hands of his lover did much to sooth his mind and body.

"Good morning, sweetheart." She kissed his warm cheek.

But something else cradled him, something close to a memory but without recognizable form. Words? What were they—Irish? They eluded the focus of his mind, hiding just beyond his consciousness. But he could hear their cadence, like a song. Was it a song?

"Why do I feel so…strange?" He touched her face.

"Does this make you feel better?" Ciar pulled him to her.

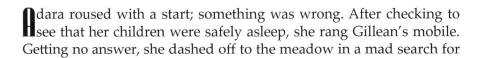

Adara roused with a start; something was wrong. After checking to see that her children were safely asleep, she rang Gillean's mobile. Getting no answer, she dashed off to the meadow in a mad search for an angel.

Chapter Ten

Wicklow, Ireland

Paths

Charlie the Archangel lumbered up the steep hill. The stocky man, tall and built like a bull with black Wellington boots, trampled the early spring flowers with the power of a road roller. Being somewhat preoccupied, he failed to notice the lovely bloom of clovers, daffodils and harebells standing out in splendor against the fresh green of the meadow. Pale blue eyes, the color of his well-worn overalls, rested beneath full, white brows. He set his sights on the dirt road ahead.

The morning sun, aligning perfectly with the horizon, shone directly on his weathered, but clean-shaven face. He lifted a callused hand to block out the blinding light. The lost one he was searching for must be near. Charlie's instructions provided scant additional information. He'd been informed that he must locate a former angel and take him in. This lost one had ventured into unexplored territory as far as angels were concerned.

The robust, heavenly being with a shock of white hair stood six feet five inches tall; he cringed as he recalled the story of the treacherous route the renegade angel had embarked upon by making a pact with another man's demon.

Charlie had been an angel for over a hundred years. He lived among humans, working alongside them, and appearing as any other mortal, assisted them within the well-established parameters he was given. There had been some challenging assignments to be sure, and yet, he had not once felt the temptation to step so far into a human's life as to be forced to exchange his own existence. The very idea made him quiver.

This staid quality made him the perfect candidate to handle such an intricate job. Charlie did not question orders, never bucked against the tide. He was nothing if not faithful and reliable. He was certainly curious, and a bit nervous about meeting such a gutsy and cavalier angel. What would such a being be made of?

Stumbling over a soft, unmoving object huddled in the dewy grass, Charlie swung round to see what his foot had touched upon, expecting it to be a chunk of loose peat. To his horror, Charlie was standing over a person.

The stranger's clothes were covered in dirt. Greasy, dark hair fell across the profile of a face, making it difficult to judge his age. But what struck Charlie most was the vulnerable nature of the individual. It appeared he had been set upon by thieves and left for dead. He assumed the man must have been beaten into a state of unconsciousness.

Bending his huge frame with some difficulty, Charlie knelt and placed a hand on the victim's shoulder. He did not stir. Applying slightly more pressure, Charlie shook the lad, who shivered uncontrollably. He moaned and writhed in the grass.

Turning on his back and in a defensive gesture, the young man placed scorched hands bubbling with blisters over his bruised face.

Charlie gasped. "Bless us, son! What happened to ya?"

The man mumbled incoherently and rolled over, trembling and keeping his back to Charlie.

"Ya need help, lad. Where are ya from? Can ya tell me yer name?"

Charlie wasn't sure if the wounded man was conscious enough to understand him. He repeated his last question in Irish. "Please, what's your name?"

The reply came from chattering teeth. "S…S…Sully. L…l…eave me…"

Charlie placed a hand over his gaping mouth. *Sweet goddess Brigid,* he thought. *So this is the lost one. The Powers help us both.*

———————————◆———————————

"**H**e'll be lucky if he makes it through the night. 'Twould be no use for hospital."

The words settled over Sully like an obscure fog. He was unaware that Charlie had carried him a full two miles, back to a modest cottage, and summoned the local doctor to attend to his grave state of health. The physician followed his pronouncement with a somber shake of his head.

Fever raged throughout Sully's body due to the severe infection brought on by the burns. He spent the next four days shivering and sweating, tossing in and out of a restless, disturbed sleep. Charlie stayed by his side, administering medication and intercession.

During this time, Sully experienced the most vivid dreams. The two participants consisted of himself and Gillean, the latest being the two in a curragh. Choppy waters roiled with viscous, hot liquid. The two men did their best to navigate the unsteady vessel, not knowing in which direction they were headed. The sky above was an illegible map of smoky darkness.

Sully shouted to Gillean that he needed to apply more muscle, warning that it would take their combined efforts to free the boat from the muddy waters. But Gillean simply folded his arms across his chest, looking spent and beaten. He sat humming a melancholy melody, all but forgetting Sully was there.

Sully did his best to steer, but the wooden oars imbedded themselves into his hands. The pain was awful, yet he could not release his grip. He feared that if he did, they both would be lost to the ravenous waters.

They traveled into rougher seas, the little craft threatening to capsize, but Gillean remained unresponsive. A dense mist impeded Sully's view. His hands began to smolder. He cried out in horror.

"Let go, Sully." Gillean's melody took on words. "Let me go." He sang as if rendering a lullaby.

"*Gillean!*" Sully called out.

Waking from his frantic dream, Sully thrust his hands into the air, his bleary eyes bringing into focus two white clumps in front of his face. He tried to speak, but his tongue was trapped inside his mouth. His cracked lips parted, allowing only a guttural sound.

One large hand belonging to a towering, older man tilted Sully's damp head towards a tin cup.

"Take a sip of this now, lad."

With no choice but to drink, Sully opened his mouth, feeling the cool, fresh water trickle down his parched throat and chin.

"That's got it." The man let Sully's head rest once again on the pillow.

Wondering if he had the ability to speak, and if he were still dreaming, Sully attempted to form a word. Looking at his bandaged hands gave him the impetus to release the question: "What...ha... happened to me hands?"

His host dragged what looked like a carpenter's bench across the room, sat on the edge, and peered into Sully's face.

"Ya burned them pretty badly, son. Doctor said he never seen anythin' like it. Yer lucky to have any skin left on 'em at all."

Fresh pricks of pain stirred beneath the bandages at the man's words. His companion leaned over the bed. "Can ya tell me what happened to ya?"

"I..."

The entire incident with himself, Gillean and Ciar played itself out in a matter of seconds in his mind. It was too fantastic to believe. Although his recall rang true, there was an undercurrent of doubt. His eyes teared as he tried to stay focused on the anonymous man. How did he fit into the mix?

"Ah! Don't bother yerself with it now, man," the sizeable elder interjected into Sully's thoughts. "Ya have come through the worst of it. That's what matters. There will be time to talk later. For now ya should rest." He began to rise from the bench.

Sully, too weak and disoriented, merely stared at him with pensive green eyes.

"Do ya want me to notify anyone of yer whereabouts?" the man asked.

"I don't think so."

"Surely there is family to be missin' ya."

Sully closed his eyes. "No," he said above a whisper, "no one."

Charlie scratched at his silver hair. "You were callin' out for Gillean in yer sleep. I imagine she is someone who would want to know where ya are."

If he had enough spirit, Sully would have laughed at Charlie's assumption. Gillean's face was all Sully could see. "It must have been a dream. I don't know anyone by that name." He kept his eyes shut tight.

"I can't imagine ya know much of anythin' right now," Charlie offered with understanding. "Get some rest, and it will become clearer to ya." He pushed the bench back against the wall. "By the way, me name's Charlie. Looks like you'll be stayin' here for the time bein'. I could use the company and the help."

"Help?"

"Sure." Charlie's smile was as expansive as his chest. "While yer on the mend, I'll be puttin' ya to work. Not right away of course. Good, honest labor does wonders to get a man back on his toes. You'll see."

Sully was shattered. He couldn't imagine taking a step out of bed, let alone performing any kind of task.

"I'll be back shortly to fix ya some tea and toast. I just need to tell the doctor yer awake and alive. He thought ya wouldn't last a night, but I knew better. I told em ya must be a fighter!" Charlie's tone was light, but his face somber. "Ya must be quite the fighter indeed, Sully."

Chapter Eleven

Stranded

The following few weeks passed slowly. The heavy hours dragged Sully along like an unwilling passenger.

Time was something he had in spades—too much for reflection. Seated in a beautifully crafted rocking chair, Sully surveyed his cramped surroundings. Charlie was in the habit of leaving after their morning tea, explaining that he traveled into town to take work orders from those who needed furniture restored, houses or barns painted, or the odd repair job undertaken.

Charlie was the local handyman, getting his work where and when he could. This would account for the sparse cottage the older man called home. The impressive number of tools scattered about—hammers left on the kitchen table, rusty handsaws set on benches, coffee cans resting on windowsills filled to overflowing with assorted, variously-sized nails—were in direct contrast to the Faraday mansion. No freshly cut flowers scented the stale air. Sully rested in one of two modest rooms on the first floor, a far cry from the numerous, professionally decorated rooms of Gillean and Adara Faraday. No pictures of beaming children or relatives of any kind adorned the aged walls that were in serious need of stripping and new paint. The floor above served as Charlie's workshop. Sully had no desire to explore what he imagined to be a dusty, tool-strewn loft.

It was obvious that Charlie felt it more important to see after others than to serve his own needs. Sully was uneasy about the fact a man of such humble means would be saddled with the burden of a failed angel, although Sully had no reason to believe that Charlie knew the truth.

The minutes of each day could be counted like the beats of an ailing heart, deliberate and determined—pulsing, tormented memories, lucid and petrifying, inside Sully's head. He'd fallen woefully short of all his lofty goals. Yes, he offered himself for Gillean, but it was purely a calculated risk in an elaborate, spiritual game of chess.

Ciar, despicable as she may be, could correctly read Gillean, whose life had become like a foreign language to Sully. The musician and the music that had once spoken so clearly to Sully's soul had devolved into a jumble of odd and disconcerting notes. Sully's offering had, no doubt, been made in vain, like so many superstitious sacrifices.

The Celts were a people long believing in spirits that inhabited all things: the ancient trees, the ever-present wind, and the delicate blades of grass. But even these munificent agents of good had abandoned Sully, he supposed for the disgraceful display of verve in thinking he could take on the likes of Ciar, and the awesome potency compressed into the desire of one unfulfilled man.

He stared at his fastidiously dressed hands. The unrelenting pain was most peculiar. He wanted to refuse the little blue tablets Charlie foisted upon him every few hours. The pain should be part of his punishment. Hadn't Ciar told him it was to be a constant reminder of his humanity? He felt every ruined nerve ending, locating each by the steady pulsing of their fire.

The door opened, blowing in a sudden spring rain and a sodden Charlie. Wellies and mac were off in a hurry, tossed into a pile near the hearth by which Sully waited.

"Agh! Sure I hate it when the sky hurls down a shower on a man without warnin'!" He shook his body like a sheep dog.

Sully smiled knowingly. "The universe has its way of stayin' one step ahead of us."

Charlie placed a soggy paper sack on the kitchen table, giving Sully the once over. "I'd say ya are a notable opponent to the powers of the universe, young man!"

"I hardly think so."

Charlie primed the small indoor pump and readied Sully's medication. He then stacked the hearth generously with dry wood and started up a warming fire. Rubbing his arthritic hands briskly, he addressed his despondent guest in the rocker. "Now don't start talkin' like a man's who's been beat. That for sure isn't yerself!"

"I can barely use me hands to hold a teacup!" Sully objected. "I won't be boxing anytime soon."

"Yeah, well, open up there champ!" Charlie commanded, as he held the tiny pill and cup in front of Sully's mouth.

"I don't—"

No sooner had Sully parted his lips to speak than Charlie delivered the pill and water in one fell swoop.

Sully gulped helplessly. "Ah! God! Ya should have been an Army commander," he choked out.

The stout man laughed, turning back to the groceries he'd brought from town. "We each have our missions in this life, don't we?" Charlie put to him.

Sully didn't wish to continue the conversation, or his thoughts that perpetually drifted back to Gillean and Adara.

His host approached him in stockinged feet, kneeling in front of the chair and taking hold of the sides. "I asked after ya in town. Seems no one will lay claim to ya. Yer clan must be in another county, is it?"

"Another world is closer to the truth."

"I know all about that feelin', son. Why do ya think I live here in this shanty of a home by meself?"

It was true enough that Sully felt like an alien, and yet the man kneeling in front of him gave the impression that he did understand.

"You have no family either?" Sully inquired in a hushed tone. "None to share a roof with?"

Charlie stood with a grunt. "What is family, but those we hold dear in our hearts? In this way, I have many relations." His eyes rested on Sully's face. "And I know of at least one person ya hold in yer heart."

Sully did not respond. He could not speak his name—to do so would give his muddled feelings order. He preferred the chaos. It felt safer.

Charlie planted himself directly above the chair. "Why don't ya tell me who Gillean is so I can find her for ya? I know she wasn't just some feverish dream, lad. And I'll bet an entire cow that Gillean desperately wants to know where ya are."

"I'd like to lie down now, please."

"Ya don't mean her to suffer with worry do ya?" Charlie prodded.

"Now look, ya forced that blasted pill on me, and I'd thank ya kindly if I can get the sleep that it's bringin'," Sully retorted.

Charlie nodded, helping Sully to his feet and lending support as he shuffled unsteadily back into bed. "Yeah, okay, yer right, son. Sleep on it some more."

As was his custom, a small tri-colored terrier, (*Potcheen*, he was called by Charlie) jumped from the floor, alighting at the foot of Sully's small bed.

Charlie, pleased that the dog had adopted Sully, chuckled, "There's company for ya!"

"He's too pure for this world." Sully muttered.

"Sweet dreams. That's how the spirits visit us. Maybe they will help to loosen yer tongue and yer heart."

Chapter Twelve

Shadows and Light

"**A**nd so I think this would be the best way to handle the situation for the time being." Gillean concluded his well-rehearsed speech. He went over it dozens of times, alone, pacing an empty room. He practiced it more than any song he'd ever performed.

He cautiously explained to Adara about Ciar, hesitantly laying out the words, like setting a landmine between himself and his wife. He admitted he didn't know what the future held. For now he would get a flat of his own in Dublin, remaining in Ireland for the sake of their children until he was able to clear his head. This was the time of year when he did not tour. Gillean typically remained sequestered in order to develop new musical material when the air turned cooler, and people prepared for autumn and the coming winter celebrations.

"You mean this would be best for your career," Adara objected. "You don't give a damn about what this is doing to your children. You want to avoid being splashed all over the tabloids, and the like; your gilded reputation would be flushed down the loo. I suppose you wouldn't seem half as attractive to your lover then."

Gillean should have known that Adara would be able to read him so well. He was like one of her dog-eared paperback books that rested on the nightstand by their bed. Ciar had implored him to divorce his wife as soon as possible. Then she and Gillean could go anywhere they wished.

"The world will be ours for the taking," Ciar whispered to him in bed one gray morning. "You will shine even brighter than before. I will be your muse, and you will write the most visionary music of your life."

He hadn't written a single piece of new material in weeks. When he sat with his guitar or at the piano, he heard nothing. The music that filled his head ever since he was a child had fallen silent. His fingers scuffled over the strings as if they weren't part of his body. He hopelessly groped for some point of contact with the gift he had taken for granted. It seemed that whoever had bequeathed it to him had decided it was time to renege. Perhaps he had upset the spirits at the *Teach na Spioradi*, and this was his sentence. He wasn't proud of what he was doing to his wife and family, but he could see no other way. He was not a genuine partner to Adara, and he feared for how that would reflect on him as a father.

"And so you have chosen to run away," Adara was saying.

He left his thoughts to retaliate. "Given what I have said, would you prefer me to stay here with you?"

"Do whatever you want, Gillean. You always have. Be sure to remember you do have four children who would like to see their da from time to time."

She was already in the doorway, her back to him.

For one brief moment he saw her as she was at seventeen, full of vim and intrigue. She had walked away from him then, dismissing him as a rover and a player. He had wanted to run after her, prove that she misjudged him. But he kept moving, relentlessly searching for an unspecified ideal. Unlike his father Milo, Gillean embarked on an emotional expedition. When the urging of family and friends for him to settle down and "do the right thing" became too much, he asked Adara to marry him and forgo the trip to America and her dancing.

The resentment rose up inside him. After all, if he had to give up his search; she should have to make some sacrifice as well. He wasn't searching for the perfect woman. Adara was more than he deserved. Gillean didn't register the fact until this very moment; he hadn't a clue what he'd been looking for. Still, he would not accept the blame for what was happening to them now. Sometimes things simply fall apart and can't be mended. It happened to the best of people, even to some of their dearest friends.

But something nagged at him, told him this wasn't the full truth. There was no music to drown out the uncomfortable thoughts, so Gillean simply went about packing up more of his things, then kissed each of his sleeping children.

Adara entered the garage as her husband was opening the trunk of his SUV. He turned in her direction as she came through the door. His face offered a glimmer of hope. Maybe she wanted to leave things on a peaceful note after all. But seeing the look of resolve on her strained face, and the purpose in her step, he realized she was not going to offer an olive branch.

"Adara, are you alright?" The words sounded utterly useless.

"Why should you suddenly care about my wellbeing?" she snapped.

The concern vanished from his face as he disabled the car alarm. The two quick beeps bounced off the concrete walls. He opened the door. "Haven't we said all there is to say?"

She rushed at him, grabbing at his arms and preventing him from getting into the vehicle. "Where is Sully?"

Unsettled by her forcefulness, he regarded her with eyes that registered no knowledge of the name. "Who?"

She pressed herself against him, as if the slight weight of her body could pry the information from him. "You know *exactly* who I mean! Now you get this, *husband*." Her eyes mirrored gray shards of ice. "You have lied to me, cheated on me, disregarded every promise you made to me and this family."

He flinched at the biting veracity in her words.

"Don't you lie to me now when an innocent's life may be in danger." She swallowed hard. "And someone I happen to care about."

His lips formed a straight line of silent anger until he was able to speak. "You have the audacity to ask me about your lover?" he shouted at her. "How dare you?"

"You have grown accustomed to, and expert at, I might add, hiding the truth when it suits you." She was unmoving in his face. "I call your bluff. You know exactly who I'm talking about. I can't believe you have become so cold as to not care about the life of another. You know full well Sully is not my lover, but he is your good mate. How can you not care what has become of him? I know you've seen him, he told me as much."

He massaged his stinging eyes. He didn't want to fight with her. He simply wanted to take his leave with the shred of dignity he possessed. "You may not believe a word I say. And I am truly sorry that things are in such a muddled state. I did not set out for any of this to happen. But as to this Sully person, you have to believe me when I say I have no idea who you're talking about. I simply don't."

She backed away from him. "You're a liar. You've shown how far you will go to maintain your double life. You would bring down every innocent person around you for a young bit of skirt." She went towards the door. "Go back to your mistress. You can both have a good laugh at my expense. But you tell her something for me, will you?"

Underneath his leather jacket his heart pounded in anticipation of her words.

"You tell her she is welcome to you and your life of deceit. I'll find Sully on my own. The Lord help you both if something has happened to him." She exited the garage, not giving him another word or glance.

Gillean gripped his keys and climbed into the front seat. His mind was on autopilot. Adara had come to care so much for another man as to threaten her own husband with such contempt. His mind searched through names, faces and memories.

Sully? No, he simply had nothing to go with the name. Yet Adara had said this man had been a good friend. How was that possible? What was she trying to do to him? If this was some sort of game she had set about in order to throw him off balance, she'd succeeded with flying colors.

"I won't let you do this to me." He wiped at the tears in his eyes. "I'm not a complete monster."

He pushed a button opening the door to the garage and shifted into drive. As he stepped on the accelerator his mind caught something— something too sheer and fragile to be certain it was a memory. It was like a mother standing on a back porch, calling to her child to come in from play. So familiar was the sound, and yet, like the evening breeze, the words which floated through his mind dissipated into the night.

He wanted so much to latch on to the sound. Maybe then he would know what Adara was talking about. But he could hear nothing more than a faraway cry down a blind tunnel. He pulled the car onto the street, watching his house fade into the blackness of his even darker heart.

Chapter Thirteen

Ghosts

Maggie, Joseph's wife and Adara's sister-in-law, took a sip of her coffee, washing down the sorrowful tale Adara had just spun.

"But I still don't understand why you have to leave the children. Your stellar husband doing his predictable disappearing act; those darlin's need you."

"I know it's a lot to ask of you and Jos to stay here, but I'd prefer not to upset the children's routine as much as possible. I especially do not wish to involve Ena. You know how she can be. I'm sure Gillean hasn't said anything to her about his *situation*." Adara absentmindedly pulled at some stray threads on the tablecloth. "And if it's too much for you—"

"Gillean is a gobshite!" Maggie placed her mug on the table. "Don't you worry about the children. Joseph and I are more than pleased to stay with them. I won't even nag ya about that pack of mangy dogs!"

Adara chuckled, "*Four* dogs."

"Take care of what you need to. But I don't understand why you're leaving." The raven-haired woman leaned in, speaking in a conspiratorial tone. "Does it have to do with this Sully bloke Gillean grilled Joseph about?"

"You mean to say Gillean actually asked Joseph about Sully?"

Maggie grinned in her knowing way. "Whatever age your husband may be, and despite all the fun he pokes at his older brother, Joseph has always been, and will always be the first one Gillean runs to when he's made a right bags of it."

"I suppose Gillean informed Joseph about his lover?" Adara didn't mean the question to be as derisive as it sounded.

Maggie's eyes softened. "I'm sorry, luv. This must be absolutely dreadful for you. I could throttle that little eejit Gillean Faraday!"

"Mags, did Gillean ask Joseph about Sully?" Adara pressed.

"Da's seen Sully too?" The staggering question came from Arlen who emerged in the doorway, drumsticks in hand, his fathers' smile stretching across his full lips.

"Arlen!" Adara swiveled in her seat to address her eldest son. "Have you been eavesdropping on a private conversation?"

"*Private?* The boy strode over to the refrigerator. "Yer in the kitchen for Pete's sake." Before his mother could correct him, he added, "I was coming in to get a fizzy drink, and I heard ya mention Sully." Without prompting, he continued. "I thought I was the only one who could see him. He was brilliant. I miss him."

Adara measured the importance of what her son may have heard to her need for information. Arlen remained in good spirits, casually opening the icebox to evaluate the contents. She kept her voice bright.

"What do you know of Sully?"

The boy's brown eyes drifted towards the ceiling. "Well, he's a spirit or an angel"—his mother's attention was suddenly engaged— "or some such thing, right? Jeez, Mam! You ought to know! Remember Da carrying on about the ghosts at *Teach na Spioradi?* He made them into bedtime stories for us."

Maggie lifted her head, sitting bolt upright in her chair like an angry swan. "You actually claim to our faces that you saw an angel in this house? That's bang out of order *Argyle!*"

"Mam—"

Adara waved off Maggie. "Is that where you saw Sully, at the castle?"

"Sometimes." The boy grabbed an orange pop and closed the refrigerator. "He's here too. At least he was. I haven't seen him in a bit." He turned back to his mother and aunt, with drink in hand. "I was wonderin' if he took up a new family to look after."

"Arlen Faraday, stop yarning such ridiculous stories!" Maggie snapped. "Can't ya see your mam is upset? You should be in bed!"

"*What?* What did I say?"

"Hold on a moment." Adara motioned for Arlen to come to her. "You haven't upset me. I want to ask you more about Sully."

"Yeah, okay." Arlen approached his mother, but not without turning to stick out his tongue at his Aunt Maggie.

"How…" Adara paused to collect the swell of emotions. "When did you first see him?"

Arlen joined the two women at the table. "Oh, a while ago, maybe a few months." He flipped the cap off the soft drink. "It gave him a right shock that I could see him too."

Adara struggled to comprehend but gave her son an affirming nod.

"One day I felt this kind of…I don't know how to describe it really." Arlen's brows furrowed just as his father's would when considering something significant.

"Presence?" Adara offered.

"Yeah, right, exactly!" The sunny expression returned. "I felt this presence in the upstairs hallway, and I called out. I was joshin' when I shouted, 'make thyself known!' Ya know, like Da does when he's acting gee-eyed." Arlen nudged his mother with an elbow. "Then this man appeared out of nowhere. I can't explain it other than one moment I *felt* him, and the next moment I *saw* him. Does that make any sense?"

"Perfect sense." Adara gestured for him to continue.

"So, he, this man, ya see…" The boy paused, apparently to make sure Adara was truly following. "He almost jumped over the landing. He was like you are now, Mam, he couldn't believe I'd called to him."

"And what did he say to you?"

"He said something like, being an 'innocent'? Let me think now, was that the word he used?" The lad took a pull from the bottle. "Yes!" Arlen continued. "He said being an innocent, it made sense that I would know he was there, because children have the eyes to see things most adults can't. I thought he was talking daft, so I asked his name. Oh, and I told him since I'm fifteen I'm not a kid like Antonia and Atty." He was referring to his six-year-old twin siblings.

Adara could not help but laugh. Of course, if Sully were some otherworldly being, Arlen would be the one to sense it. He was the most trusting of her four. He still possessed the curious wonderment of childhood. The boy didn't have a dishonest or mean bone in his body.

"Think carefully." Adara tried to impart the serious nature of the discussion without alarming her son. "Did he tell you anything more, like why he would have to leave?"

He sat quietly, mulling over his mother's question. "No, he just told me he was here to help. I asked him how he meant to do that, and he said he was thinking on it. That's why he needed to hang around—to figure it out. He made me promise not to tell anyone I could see him, otherwise he wouldn't be able to help."

"And did you promise?"

"Sure, I liked him. He said he'd be looking after us." Arlen studied the scone he'd grabbed from the plate in the center of the table. "Sometimes we'd take walks together, and talk. He'd ask me about school and stuff, how was I gettin' on. We'd play a little football."

Arlen took a generous bite. "He had a wicked shot on him, too!" Arlen chewed and spoke, "Are ya going to collect him, Mam? And Da, where is he?"

Adara stroked her son's chestnut hair, wishing their lives were not in such shambles.

"Yes, I'm setting off to find out what happened to Sully."

"Do ya suppose it was my fault that Sully had to go?" He asked with a look of apprehension. "I swear, I didn't tell anyone about him. Well, not until tonight."

"No, sweetheart. You aren't the reason he had to go."

"What about Da? Why did he leave without a word?"

"Your father and I need to spend some time apart right now." She looked to Maggie, helpless to further explain why she was separating from Gillean.

"Come on, my fuzzy argyle jumper." Maggie rode to her sister-in-law's rescue, playfully jabbing at her nephew. "You'll be stuck here with me and Uncle Jos for a short time. Swear to your Mam you will mind me, so she won't worry."

Arlen's face clouded. "You and Da will be apart? For how long?" He looked from his aunt to his mother. "I'll mind Auntie Mag Pie, if ya swear you and Da will come back."

"Of course, you will see your father and me soon." Adara squeezed her son's hand. "We both love you very much."

"That's what Sully said."

"What?"

"He said no matter how batty Da may seem I should remember that adults can be a little batty sometimes, but Da and you would never stop loving me."

Adara pulled him to her, thinking of how Sully had saved her son's life with his own, and yet Arlen had not reclaimed the same memories she had. Perhaps Sully had spared him those horrible recollections.

She felt the hot prick of indignation. Once again she had to take on the role of both parents because of Gillean's dalliances. He left her to deal with the fallout of his leaving, offering the same, weak excuse that he would speak with his children, "when the time was right." She was more than angry; she was simply finished with his selfishness and their life of lies.

Adara could see the disappointment etched in her son's once-bright face. Just as she had seen it so many years ago in her husband's whenever his father, Milo, was mentioned.

"You'll call us though, like Da does?" Arlen, a proud teenager, refused to cry, no matter how frightening the prospect was of his parents separating.

"Only if you'll be a gentleman and escort your Aunt Mags to her car. She and Uncle Jos will be back tomorrow afternoon." She kissed both his cheeks and lightly nudged him towards his waiting aunt.

Arlen latched on to his aunt's arm ready to walk her out.

"Good night, Dara. See ya tomorrow, dear." Maggie blew a kiss. "I pray you find what you're searching for."

Once in the hallway, Arlen called back to his mother: "Oh! And when ya see Sully, tell him I said hello. But don't tell him I broke my promise!"

<hr />

Gillean tried in vain to get comfortable in the economy class accommodations of Air Lingus. He was lucky to get a seat so close to departure time. After hours of driving aimlessly around the rain-slick streets of Dublin, a city he often roamed to take in its artistic pulse, he unexpectedly found himself in the car park of the airport.

Throughout his drive he had wrestled with his conscience about meeting Ciar. He must be firm with her about living on his own for the time being. He dreaded what was sure to be a heated argument on the topic.

Ciar was the embodiment of a fiery disposition. At first, he had found the experience invigorating. Making love with her, simply being in her presence, was intoxicating, a hit of premium Ecstasy.

The downside was when anger or discord charged her passion. The unpredictable, intense emotion that inspired her to create such spectacular art stemmed from the same manic fervor that colored everything she did. She was a force unto herself. The slightest pangs of doubt stirred within him. Gillean wasn't sure he had the reserves for such a demanding woman.

Adara and her ever-present support had been at his back for most of his life. But try as they might, the couple had failed to create a solid place for one another to flourish. Their lives were planted into rocky ground. Each stone marked the resting place of a dead dream.

Gillean forced himself as low as possible in the back-breaking seat in an attempt to avoid curious glances from the few passengers still awake and suspecting a celebrity in their midst, but no one paid him any mind. The flight attendants were at the rear of the plane quietly chatting whilst they prepared the next series of refreshments.

It used to be when he boarded a commercial plane, every pretty young thing on the flight would be at his side, giggling and pleading for an autograph and anything else he'd like to share with them. And he had shared plenty in his day. Adara's accusations echoed in his ears like a priest's admonishments in a confessional.

Bless me father, for I have sinned.

A voice crackled over the speaker system, intruding upon his uneasy meditation of things to come. "Please excuse the interruption, ladies and gentlemen; this is yer captain, Timothy Sullivan here. Just wanted to give ya an updated weather report for our final destination..."

Sullivan? Sullivan. The name resounded like a bell. *Sully.* Adara had been fixated on this person. He didn't know anyone by that name. Did he?

One of the attendants came to him as he squirmed in his seat. "Is everythin' okay, sir?" She brushed his arm with her hand.

"*What?*" Gillean's excited exclamation caused the heads of some of his nearest neighbors to turn in his direction.

"Do you need anythin', sir? Ya seem uncomfortable."

"I think I'd like a Jameson, if you please."

"Of course, I'd be happy to get that for ya."

"Ah, wait!" he called after her.

"Yes, sir?"

"Your Captain Sullivan... Is he... Does he live in Dublin?"

She looked confused for a moment and then nodded, the smile returning to her red lips. "Oh yes, ya don't have to worry. Captain Sullivan has been flying planes for almost forty years now."

"Forty years? How old is he?" Gillean was wishing for the Jameson so much that his hands were beginning to shake.

"I don't think anyone has ever asked such a question! But for sure the Captain wouldn't mind me tellin' ya. He's sixty, and won't admit to bein' a day over."

Gillean sat back in his seat, mildly relieved. It was unlikely a sixty-year-old pilot was the object of Adara's fancy. He was quite certain he had never been friendly with, much less good mates with one. Was someone seeking him out? If so he was being chased by someone he could neither see, hear, nor possess any recollection of. Yet this Sully person was there, invading Gillean's attentions.

At any rate, the moments were sure to be anything but meditative when he arrived at Ciar's.

"Would you please bring me another?" Gillean asked, after swiftly knocking back the stewardess' first offering.

"Yes, sir." She rolled her eyes as she walked back to the mini bar. "Poor sod is losing his mind," she commented to her co-workers.

Chapter Fourteen

The Song of Silence

Weeks passed. with Charlie and Sully falling into a routine of sorts. Charlie would leave to gather and deliver his work orders in the morning, while Sully took to looking over Charlie's woeful book-keeping.

Sully happened upon a way to help Charlie one morning when glancing at the almost illegible financial ledger. Sully hadn't regained the full use of his hands. He now wore a pair of smooth black gloves to hide the scars intersecting in chaotic, angry lines across sections of ruined skin. Sitting down to look over the figures, Sully discovered his facility with numbers. He could easily compute sums and differences without the use of pen and paper. Both men were amazed with what Sully accomplished that first morning.

Graduating to the ability of holding a pencil, Sully painstakingly reworked all of Charlie's accounts. Sully was happy for the opportunity to be useful and was a bit proud of his acumen in saving Charlie quite a tidy sum; his new friend was so impressed that he directed the saved amount to be put aside for Sully's future. Sully did not have the heart or energy to imagine any other life other than the one he currently occupied. Charlie was a kind and humorous host, and Potcheen loved Sully unconditionally.

But during the late afternoons and evenings, Sully was at his most vulnerable. Charlie suggested numerous times a walk through the abundant woods surrounding the property. Sully demonstrated an inexplicable fear of leaving. He would get as far as the doorstep where the little dog would be waiting, but upon reaching this point he would tremble and retreat to bed.

He enjoyed reading, and Charlie accommodated this passion by bringing him an array of books from the modest library in town.

Sometimes in the evenings, when he wasn't inclined to sleep, Sully would sit in the rocker by the fire and regale Charlie with tales from Thomas Moore, G.B. Shaw and Oscar Wilde. Sully possessed the magic of bringing a story to life with the animated cadence of his voice. With his eyes closed, Charlie could easily picture in full vividness the events Sully recounted.

Charlie did not press for the story of why he'd found Sully lying unconscious and near death in that field. In fact, Charlie remained in the dark about the cause of the terrible burns, and the identity of the human for whom Sully relinquished his powers. Charlie didn't even know how the exchange had come about.

For the first time in over a hundred years, the veteran angel questioned his superiors out of frustration and apprehension for the despondent lad. Charlie was told to be patient and allow events to unfold in due time. Charlie was learning a universal truth: that every being is limited in what he can and cannot do for another, and that each is entirely responsible for the choices he makes, both good and bad. Charlie begrudgingly trusted in his orders.

One morning while out on his usual work run, Charlie chanced upon, or rather was given, a huge piece of the puzzle that was Sully. And like most well-intentioned beings, Charlie did not bother to question the source of the information. He was immediately willing to believe that he was finally on the right track. Charlie had no idea of the speed or strength of the train he was jumping aboard.

A placid looking woman, tall and appealing in a curious way, sat in front of a weathered kiosk taking part in the weekly outdoor market. She was modestly dressed in a denim skirt resting just above her bare feet, and a frayed, long-sleeved blouse. Clutching a black shawl around her boney shoulders, she called out in a hopeful voice to those who might buy her used goods.

Sorry for her situation, Charlie decided at the very least to strike up a friendly conversation with the young woman.

"Business good for ya today, lass?"

She smiled at him. He noted the darkness of her eyes, more animal than human. If it weren't for her innocent demeanor, the shade and frigid expression of her eyes would have set his teeth on edge.

"Could be better to be sure," she answered.

Charlie placed his toolbox on the ground and moved in closer to get a look at her wares. Various trinkets, rings and other costume jewelry were displayed on a satin cloth.

"Perhaps I may have somethin' ya might be interested in?" She touched Charlie's arm in an intimate gesture.

The energy surrounding this woman unsettled Charlie. He chided himself for being too judgmental. She was sweet enough. He supposed he was sensing the difficult life this traveler was forced to live. He resigned himself to help her with a small purchase. That would take care of the queer feeling in the pit of his stomach.

"Well now, I do have a friend stayin' on who is laid up. Maybe ya have somethin' to help him pass the time and cheer him?"

"Oh, I bet I do." She squeezed his arm. "What sort of things does he like?"

"Can't say I'm too familiar with his interests, but he's young, like you. And he likes to read."

"Oh, my," She cast her eyes downward. "I'm sorry. I don't have any books at the moment." She looked truly dismayed. "But wait!" She brightened again. "Ya say yer friend is laid up is it now?"

"Yes, he was injured pretty badly."

"That is a pity."

Was she attempting to conceal a grin?

"I think I have the perfect thing for him." She bent down and ran her fingers through a crate once used to hold fruit. It was now filled with old record albums. "Yes, here it is." She pulled one from the collection and handed it to Charlie. "Many thoughtful, young men are drawn to this particular artist's music. It's most imaginative. So if yer friend likes to read, I promise ya, he will love the story songs on this record. The singer is Irish as well."

Charlie turned the record over in his hands, amazed that it was in mint condition.

"Looks like it's never been out of the jacket," he observed.

"Indeed, I got it from someone who knows the musician quite well. I've been saving it for just the right customer." Her peculiar eyes held his. "Now I know that has to be you."

Charlie tried to quell the persistent warning inside his head. He read the title out loud, not recognizing the name. "Messages from Orion…"

There was no other writing on the outer jacket. Judging from the intriguing artwork on the front of the album—a tiny musical score resting underneath a starry sky—Charlie thought maybe this would trigger Sully's interest. It held the potential to spark his curiosity.

"Alright! Yer a good businesswoman to be sure. Ya sold me." He reached into his pocket. "How much for the record?"

"Oh, just enough to buy me a cuppa and a sandwich if ya please." The look of innocence returned to her face. "I won't be stayin' round here, but I would like to get a bite before I go."

"Ah now, what kind of a deal is that?" Charlie protested. "Here, ya take this and make sure ya have a hearty meal and somethin' to spare." He handed her twenty euros.

She blushed. "That's terribly kind of ya, sir. Thank you. I hope yer friend recovers. Sure he has a lot waitin' for him once he's up and about."

"Hmm?" Charlie continued to look over the record, trying to convince himself it would lift Sully's spirits.

"I said I'm sure yer friend has a lot to look forward to once he is well." She pocketed the money and pushed the crate with the other albums back under the cart.

"Well, how does the saying go? One day at a time?" Charlie began to back away from the woman and her shadowy stare. "I think that is the best medicine for him right now, one day at a time."

"Yes of course," she deferred. "He surely has the time. See to it he gives a listen to the music. I'm certain it will do him a world of good."

Walking home, Charlie studied the record intently, his thoughts on Sully and how he could get him to finally open up.

"Perhaps a note from Orion will be just the thing to help ya, Sully."

He placed the album underneath one arm and hastened his pace.

Chapter Fifteen

Orion

Charlie entered the cottage quietly with his gift, wanting to take Sully by surprise Instead, Charlie was the one taken aback when he found Sully's head resting on the ledgers. He was sitting at the table, shoulders hunched and sleeping as peacefully as the little dog at his feet. Only his damaged hands gave the impression that he was anything but tranquil. Seeing Sully asleep in such an awkward position, Charlie's heart felt something he could only imagine was close to paternal for the young man.

Sully was a being easily read. His moods were conveyed by his eyes—smooth and clear as a pond at dusk, with the waning sun casting shade upon complicated shade of green onto the water. Sully might claim he didn't wish to discuss the awful thing that had happened to him, or the woman he was so obviously missing, but his eyes said something else entirely. They entreated Charlie to come closer and look deep into their cloudless center.

Charlie hugged the record close, requesting a blessing, then went about making some tea. Sully opened his eyes at the sound of running water and the clanging of cups. His sleepy eyes questioned Charlie.

"'Tis only yer mate muckin' about like an elephant on ice skates!" He placed the kettle on the hob. "I didn't mean to frighten ya, I'm sorry."

"No need for apology." Sully rubbed at his eyes. "When I was last conscious, this was your home, and I your grateful guest."

Like a child unable to contain himself on Christmas morning, Charlie wanted to share his present with Sully immediately. "I brought ya back somethin' from town!" He went searching about for his old turntable.

"Ya didn't have to do that, Charlie."

Sully watched as the excited man shoved tables and benches aside.

Potcheen barked and skittered on the floorboards, a bit put out at the disturbance.

"Now where in the hell…" Charlie continued to root around helter-skelter, almost knocking a standing lamp to the floor.

"Would ya like some assistance?" Sully offered, amused by the man's enthusiasm.

"No! Blast! Ah! Hold on! Here's the old bugger!" Charlie dragged out a dusty record player which looked to be forty years old if a day.

"What would ya be needing that sorry-looking antique for? Don't tell me you're gonna try and sell it! As your financial advisor, I advise ya would be run out of town on a rail for such—"

"Pipe down now, lad!" Charlie's nerves were on edge. He greatly wanted to cheer Sully and establish a connection with him. "Just have a listen to this. The lovely lass who sold it to me said ya were sure to appreciate the vision in the music."

He slid the record from its jacket, brushing his flannel shirtsleeve over the turntable causing a substantial dust cloud. He placed the record down while flicking a switch.

"Music?" Sully stifled a cough.

Charlie's calloused hand rested the needle on the shiny vinyl disc. "Yes, music. Which means ya shut up and listen, okay?"

The room was as quiet as a schoolhouse on Sunday morning until the soft sounds of a distant guitar filled the cottage. Sully's limbs twitched. He shifted in his chair, ready to bolt like a frightened animal.

The singer entered the room with his words. *"There's something out there in the night sky, ageless and endless like the passage of time…"*

Sully began to shake, holding his hands to his chest. "Where did ya get this?" he demanded.

Charlie stood next to the player, not sure what to make of the reaction. "I bought it in town today. I just thought ya might like—"

Sully was on his feet yelling. *"Who gave it to you?"*

Charlie thought back to the unreadable woman at the open market. "What does it matter where I got it? Why won't ya at least give the music a chance?"

"Shut if off!"

"Why?"

Sully crossed the room, teetering a bit but making it to the record player in seconds. *"Shut this rubbish off!"* He raised his left leg and kicked hard at the turntable. Charlie shuddered at the display of raw, human emotion as Sully kicked again. The needle continued to drag across the recording, making a morose scratching sound.

"Black heart!" Sully shouted.

Potcheen whimpered, hiding under the table.

"What's the matter, Sully?" Charlie tried to restrain his overexcited charge, mindful that undue force might hurt him further.

With one final blow to the player, Sully flung himself towards the door as if he were a cadged bird. He grabbed for the knob. He meant to leave what was once his sanctuary. The voice on the record drove him onward, past the threshold and further out into the woods. He said nothing as he made his way, weaving unsteadily like a drunkard.

Charlie was too shaken to protest Sully's exit. He grabbed for the album cover, wildly searching every square inch of it, hoping to find something that would explain Sully's desperate actions.

"Oh Sweet Jaysus, no," he gasped, as his glance fell across words he could hardly make out, they were so small. In the liner notes was the dedication from the artist: *To my wife, Adara Faraday, with gratitude, Gillean.*

"It was him ya gave yer wings for—Gillean Faraday."

Charlie watched sadly as Sully's figure grew smaller in the distance. He seemed determined to walk to the other side of the earth.

"And 'tis him who ya love. Oh, Sully lad, why didn't ya tell me?"

It was going on twelve hours since Charlie's disastrous attempt to cheer Sully with the music of Gillean Faraday. Sully continued to wander the perimeter of Charlie's home long after the wan orange sun had dipped below the horizon and the cool wind of evening once again stirred disembodied flower petals. The night birds, wheeling low around Sully's head, kindly persuaded him with their delicate flight that it was time to go back and face the real music of his new friend's concern

But once inside the cottage and bombarded with Charlie's cautious questions, Sully found himself mute. When he tried to speak, his mouth opened but no words would come. Half-formed sentences, images and feelings swirled inside his head like the cloudy river of his perpetual nightmare, leaving a brackish taste between his teeth. He could only look down at his bare hands where unhealed wounds were torn open, leaving fragile layers of exposed skin. They served as explanation offered. As always, his eyes, at least, were able to telegraph his suffering. Charlie ceased his inquiries and got to work re-dressing Sully's hands. Sully was given a tablet for the pain, then sent off to bed. Potcheen required no explanations, gratefully settling under the covers with Sully for a good night's rest.

Sully reached for a towel to wipe his mouth after rinsing out the minty toothpaste. His existence was a series of battles beginning when he woke in the morning and continued unabated until he fell into a drug-induced sleep at night. Even the most minimal of tasks, such as brushing his teeth, was a complex set of newly learned behaviors. Having been previously human for only seven years, he had been afforded insufficient time to know what this unfamiliar state consisted of. And if Gillean was any indication of the evolution of man, Sully deduced that one could walk this planet for over forty years and still be clueless as to how to live a fulfilling life.

If anything, Gillean showed Sully that the older a person gets, the more he loses the sense of his own heart. As a child, Sully knew differently. Despite his father's abuse, Sully still dared to dream of another kind of love. He was forced to grow up quickly in his seven years and learn how to protect himself. Now that he was a man, once again he was denied the benefit of growing naturally into his human years. He welcomed the smarting from his burned hands. It was oddly comforting. The visceral memories of pain were familiar enough to him. It was the emotional ordeal of being a lost and lonely man with an untried moral compass that Sully felt he could not undertake.

Staring at his unshaven face in the mirror, he was stunned by the image in the misted glass. At first glance, Sully thought the marked disparity between what he'd imagined and what he saw was due to the scruffy dark beard he'd allowed to grow. He did not trust his worthless hands to hold a razor. This was the one thing he refused to let Charlie do for him. But his shock was due to something more than just facial hair. He rubbed his sleeve over the misted medicine cupboard, leaning in to get a closer look. The man gazing back was like a familiar stranger, someone met in passing, causing one to think, *I know him!*

Harrowed green eyes which threatened to spill over at any moment with tears and awful secrets dared him with their naked veracity to look deeper. Even the pale, sunken cheeks hidden underneath black hair could not disguise the character of his face. It was the same one he remembered as a child. Gone were the similarities to Gillean that had existed when Sully was a re-encounter. He was now indeed his own man with a distinct past, however tangled and unusual. It showed in the appearance of the distressed, broken little boy who had defied the natural laws, and grown into an adult.

In spite of everything—the pain, the fear and the enervating incomprehension—he laughed. He was riveted by the grin reflecting back at him. He could recall the few times in his brief life when he had laughed. He assumed this was what he must have looked like. He gingerly stroked the mirror with his hands, as if touching his reflection would make it seem more real to him. Stepping back, still watching his movement in the glass, he touched his face in awe. Words that still could not cross over into the spoken form begged the question from the safe harbor of his mind.

Who will save ya, now Sully?

Chapter Sixteen

Lovers Cross

"This is not about yer husband, is it?" The woman eyed Adara's tiny gold ring. "Ya want to know about the spirit; the one ya asked to summon?"

"Yes, please. I did make contact with him. Even my son was able to communicate with him." Adara nervously folded and unfolded her hands in her lap. "But he—Sully he is called…"—a flash of a smile turned her lips upwards—"He has left us, and I fear something bad may have happened to him." Her eyes clouded.

The traveler listened silently as Adara thoughtfully laid out her story like Tarot cards. The woman's hands, wrinkled and dotted with age spots, held on to Adara's. "I need ya to think of him. Think only of him," she directed.

"Alright."

Adara closed her eyes. Her mind led her to the image of the last time she saw Sully. The picture was so clear, not like the foggy visions of months gone by. She could see the way his eyes entreated her for a promise, hear the hushed, reverent tone in which he spoke about her children and his promise to return.

After a brief silence, the old woman jerked her hands away. She stared intensely into Adara's face. "How can this be?" she uttered.

Adara opened her eyes in panic.

"What? Tell me!"

"No, I don't believe it can be so."

"Where is he?" Adara demanded

"*What* is he?" The gypsy half whispered with apprehension.

She hurriedly got up from the table and exited the camper without another word. Adara grabbed for her purse and followed.

The woman focused on the gathering of trees that acted as a home, albeit a rugged one, for the travelers. The lush forest was ever-willing to provide shelter, unlike the judgmental people in town.

"I don't know how, and I don't know why, but he has crossed a bridge into a world he should never have come to." The traveler spoke as if seeing the mythical and precarious destination.

"What do you mean 'crossed a bridge?' He's not dead. I won't believe it if you say so."

"That's just it, missus. He's *not* dead, but *alive.*" Her trembling evidenced her fear. "He's a livin', breathin', human bein' like you and me!"

Adara could hardly contain her joy and relief. "You act as if this is a bad thing! I was so worried."

"Ya don't understand. 'Tis not what is supposed to be. This once spirit of light is now confined to earth by the most terrible of forces." Her voice crackled. "He's changed, missus. Oh, he's changed. I'm afraid he can never go back now."

Trying not to let the woman's fear infect her optimism, Adara pressed, "I've got to find him. Don't you see? Can you please help me?"

"I advise ya not to." She took Adara's hand, stroking the modest ring Gillean had given her on their wedding day. "Go back home. Speak with yer husband. Ya can't save the one ya seek. He's made a choice. No one can help now. Leave him be, missus. 'Tis not your fight."

"My husband? What has he to do with any of this?" She pulled at the ring, releasing it from her finger, and placed it into the woman's hand. "I don't need this now, and it doesn't matter if you tell me where Sully is. You told me the most important thing—that he is alive."

She reached into her purse and extended a hundred Euros to the anxious tinker.

"I hope this will be acceptable compensation for your help. Do take care. I'll find him myself." She made ready to leave.

"Wait."

Adara turned around impatiently.

"I don't feel right taking yer money, or your precious ring. Please..."—she held out her hand to Adara—"take this back."

"That won't be necessary."

"Ya mean to find the lost one, and if there's nothin' I can do to stop ya, the least I can do is tell ya what I know."

"I'd be grateful."

"Look for him in the place ya would least expect his other to be."

"His other?"

"Excuse me. I meant *the* other, yer husband. You will find what ya search for in a place yer husband would never go—an intersection."

"Intersection?"

"The rest is up to you. I can't say any more. Good luck to you all."

The woman quickly stepped back into the camper, and for the first time in her life, she locked the door.

---

*T*he Meeting of the Waters!

After sitting in a café for hours staring into the busy street, her tea and biscuits hardly touched, the words came to Adara. They described the only place matching the tinker's description. It had to be where she would find Sully. Adara remembered the name as the title to an old Irish air.

The Meeting of the Waters was where the Avonmore and Avonbeg rivers came together to form the river Avoca, the dark, wooded river valley of the Vale of Avoca. This secretive place was in County Wicklow. Gillean once said he would never step foot there. When they were first dating he thought it clever to visit the many locations in Ireland that had inspired the great writers and poets. He claimed that perhaps there was something to what his father had always been on about—the significance of places in people's lives. She remembered a conversation from years past. Although it seemed like a lifetime ago, Gillean's words were as retrievable as if he had spoken them only yesterday.

"We're not going to the Meeting of the Waters," the twenty-year-old had declared. His fiery eyes punctuated his feelings. "The very idea gives me the willies."

"I'd have thought you would want to experience something that inspired Thomas Moore," Adara offered, amused at how panicked her lover had become. Gillean was not one to share his weakness, unless he thought it would serve him. "You know Moore is considered the national bard of Ireland. Something you aspire to."

"Good Lord, I do not," Gillean had protested. "I don't want to perform in these provincial venues anymore. Bard of Ireland, *please*! As if that was something to aspire to. I'd have thought you would know me by now. And I'm *not* going to the Vale of Avoca."

There must have been something deeper to Gillean's resistance. Moore was reputed to spend hours at the Vale composing his poems and music. Perhaps this threatened Gillean's sense of confidence. But at the time she didn't wish to recklessly dive into the nebulous undercurrent coursing through Gillean Faraday.

"It sounds romantic to me." Adara tried one last time to convince him with her light kisses.

"Yeah, well, perhaps true love can be found there, but I'm not going." He was adamant, even pushing her away.

Shortly after that heated discussion, she and Gillean broke off their romance for a time. He went on the road as an opening act for a major British band, refusing to be weighed down by a commitment to any one person. She had decided the unpredictable musician was not worth the drama.

She remembered how shattered Ena, Mags and Jos had been when they received the news. Adara was greatly saddened to leave her job at the *Teach na Spioradi*. Gillean's family had become like her own. But she hadn't wanted to cause trouble for Gillean. His family branded him the black sheep. And with the breakup, Ena would be hot on his tail, complete with a solemn lecture on the imperative of embracing adulthood and abandoning his childish notion of being a singer-songwriter.

Gillean pressed on. Even when they were apart, Adara couldn't help but admire his persistence in the face of impossible odds. He wrote her the sweetest, most comical letters during his time on the road. She saved them all, entirely certain that he would one day be a revered entertainer. During one phone call, Adara said how wonderful it would be when she could tell the BBC that she'd known Gillean Faraday when he was just a man with a guitar singing in a castle. So it would seem the same doggedness she once loved and admired in her husband was what kept him determined to have his own way with a new life now.

Chapter Seventeen

Open the Door

"**M**iss? Will there be anythin' else?" The waitress was at Adara's side calling her back to reality with her question.

"Oh! Sorry, no, nothing," Adara reached for her wallet, "unless you can tell me how to get to the Vale of Avoca."

"Sure I can. 'Tis such a lovely place. Are ya a poet?"

"More of an admirer."

Adara took out a pen, handing the girl a napkin and asking for directions as she placed a generous gratuity on the table.

An hour later, Adara's Volkswagen was navigating the dirt roads that would deliver her to her destination. Taking in the loveliness of the vast awning of trees and flowers growing any place they desired, she glanced down at the makeshift map the waitress had drawn for her. So far the young lady had been spot-on with her directions, assuring Adara she should make it to the Vale by early evening.

The sun had nearly set, and its warmth was still locked inside the fortress of the forest. She was about to switch on the overhead light to get a better look at her environs when she spotted a rugged man trudging along the side of the road, a wooden toolbox in one hand and a thermos in the other.

Adara pushed the automatic window release and drove slowly alongside, calling out in a muted voice so as not to startle him. "Pardon me please, sir?"

The man stopped as she put her foot on the brake.

"I'm sorry to trouble you, but I was hoping you could tell me if I am close to the Vale of Avoca?"

The man, who appeared to be twice the size of her husband, leaned in the car window. His eyes rested on Adara's face, as if trying to place a person he'd found in an old photograph.

"I'm looking for a friend of mine. I believe he may be there."

The man nodded. "'Tis not too far. If ya don't mind givin' me a lift, me cottage is just outside the Vale."

Not sensing any danger from the gentle giant, Adara released the lock. "Not a problem. Thank you for your help."

"Aaah!" Adara's appreciative passenger let out a tired groan as he slid into the plush seat. "Forgive me, I don't get much occasion to ride in a motor car, let alone one of such style!"

"I can see you must work hard." Adara took her foot from the brake and coasted down the path. "But I wager you value the beauty here in a way most people of *style* couldn't comprehend."

"I try to see both the beauty and the ugliness of life. After all, without one how could we recognize the other?"

"That's true indeed. You are a philosopher as well as a craftsman, I see". Adara turned her eyes back to the road, not wanting to seem rude by observing her passenger too critically.

He laughed at her compliment. "I don't know about that now. I live a simple life. And most people just regard me as Charlie."

"Nice to meet you, Charlie, I'm Adara."

Charlie showed no perceptible reaction. But his voice carried a note of something suddenly realized as he mused, "This friend yer lookin' for, his name would be Sully, I believe."

Adara's heart pulsed, unable to contain the rush of excitement, hope, trepidation. She stopped the car in the middle of the road. "I hope we're referring to the same…*man*: dark hair, green eyes."

"That would be me house guest to be sure." Charlie waved his hand as if to signal no further confirmation was needed.

"But, how did he come to be here?" Adara had forgotten her wish to be polite. She regarded Charlie closely, taking in every aspect of the older man's ruddy face, looking for reassurance that Sully was truly a short car ride away.

The man's expression was honest, lighting his azure eyes. "I think it best if himself explained it to ya."

Adara shifted the car into drive once again. Coalescence. As if some munificent, universal force was pulling on the sublime strings that connected Sully to her, drawing them ever closer.

"You must be much more than a craftsman, Charlie. You're an angel!"

"Let's hope Sully will think so." He said the words under his breath, indicating for her to bear left.

Charlie didn't say much as he opened the door of his cabin. He switched on a table lamp. Adara immediately swept the room with her eyes, seeking any signs of Sully. A pile of books lay on a small bed by a wood stove. One large hardback was open with its pages facing down on the blankets.

Adara gasped when she saw the author—Thomas Moore! A half-empty cup of tea rested in a mismatched saucer on the floor.

"You can try down by the water." Charlie held the door for her and pointed towards the woods.

"Sorry?"

He rested a hand on her shoulder. "I'm sure ya don't want to stay here and have tea with me right now; ya want to see Sully. You should find him down by the water, just past that patch of Ash trees yonder."

"Thank you, Charlie."

"I want to prepare you," Charlie cautioned. "He's gone through some tough times. He may not be the same as you remember. I don't want ya to be disappointed."

"Sully has given me a few things, but not ever disappointment." She moved away from the bewildered Charlie and on toward the forest.

She practically ran through the maze of trees, the noises of night traveling with her as she all but danced over the sweet-smelling grass. Nightingales began to sing their songs of praise to the silver orb, crickets chirped happily among the aromatic pines, and the heady aroma of dampness pervaded the air. She was nearing the lakes, the place Gillean said he would not ever go. Countless years before, he had blithely predicted true love may be found here.

Nearing the spot where the two lakes united, the trees thinned out, forming a clear path to the water.

She failed to see Sully, who was standing only a few feet away. His body was flush against a wild cherry tree. Just before the sound of his voice joined the chorus of night, she saw a flash of white cutting through the air like tiny moths.

"Checkin' up on me again are ya, Charlie?"

Adara stepped closer. Time kept a different, slower pace here. Sounds and sights were magnified and intensified. She heard her own voice but it seemed dreamlike. "There is not in the wide world a valley so sweet, as that vale in whose bosom the bright waters meet." She greeted him with a quote from Moore.

He didn't move from his place by the tree. "Adara?"

Locating him by his voice, she approached. "Oh! The last rays of feeling and life must depart, 'ere the bloom of that valley shall fade from my heart." She came out of the shadows to stand directly in front of him. Even in the growing darkness by the pale light of the moon, she saw what Charlie had meant. Sully had changed.

His face did not so much remind her of Gillean now. The youthful expression was haunted and pained, his hair long enough to be swept back behind his ears, with some stray curls hanging over gaunt cheeks. His eyes revealed a new sadness.

"Adara, *please*, you can't be here. Go back to your family, where ya belong."

"Don't tell me where I belong, Sully. For too many years I have allowed other people decide that for me. I need to find my place for myself. And you…" Mustering her strength against his cynicism, she continued holding him with her glance. "You asked me to trust you. I did. Then you simply vanished. I want to know why."

"If only ya would have trusted me."

"I have never doubted you, *never*."

He crossed his hands in front of his chest, keeping his eyes level with hers. Cherry blossoms impelled by the breeze swirled about his body like angel's breath. "You didn't feel ya trusted me enough to tell me about—"

"Tell you about *what*?" Her shock was tempered by the image of soft petals at his feet, and noticing the bandages that wrapped his hands, she asked, "What happened to you? Are you alright?"

He was oblivious to his surroundings, focusing his attention squarely on her. "I'm wondering, why did ya so easily forget that you're a dancer? And why do ya still refuse to look into your heart?"

"How dare you!".

Sully stepped away from the tree, until the space between them was no more than a hair's breath. "No, how dare *you!* Those wondrous pictures in your mind… You said ya would bring them to life. You are a beautiful, intelligent, brilliant woman. Why are ya here?"

"Don't presume to know what is in my heart. Go ahead and be harsh if that is how you feel towards me. I would have moved heaven and earth to find you, to be sure that you were safe. Why are you so ready to dismiss me now?"

"The world is harsh, the truth even more so. There is no reason for you to be here. Your concern for me is kind but misplaced. You need only to decide what *your* life is to be about." His voice sounded metallic, like the copper and lead lacing the air, originating from pagan mines centuries before. "You're lucky ya have that chance. Don't waste precious time with me."

He started to walk away from her without even so much as a goodbye.

"Sully, Sully! *Wait!*" She ran after him. "I did examine the photos of my memories. Too many are of Gillean. Wants and needs can so readily be mistaken for love. I disappeared inside of Gillean, and he hides within his songs." Her voice softened. "And with other women," she added regretfully. "But you're not such a man."

He kept moving, his back to her.

But she would not be slighted.

"I can read your feelings. Shall I tell you how? *Shall I?*" she shouted, meaning to stop him with the sheer strength of her words. "I am willing to risk any ounce of dignity I may still possess to say what I hold in my heart is you."

He stopped dead in his tracks, her daring proclamation bouncing off the water and holding him fast with its firmness. His shoulders rose slowly upward, then down. He bent over, looking as if he were about to be sick, but instead he turned to her, his eyes glassy.

"Don't sacrifice your dignity for me. You are far too dear." His voice was absent of joy. "I'm not who ya believe me to be."

"Who broke your glorious spirit? Who hurt you?" She motioned to his hands. "Was it Gillean?"

"I made a choice. It's no more than that. Gillean has no idea where I am. That is how I want it. He did nothing of his own volition to hurt me. Sometimes people can hurt others by their inaction, and by hiding from the truth." He placed his hands behind his back.

"*Meaning?*" She couldn't imagine what he was hinting at.

"I don't wish to talk about it. I've made my decision. I have my path to travel. That is the way of it."

"What if your path, your way, is meant to merge with another, just like this Vale?" She moved towards him again.

He bowed his head as if addressing a queen. "Beautiful Adara, my life is how it is supposed to be, solitary. Neither you nor I can change this. Go home and think about what ya truly want. I suspect 'tis not what you believe it to be at this moment." He took up his walk back to the cabin.

"What I want is to help you"—she followed after him—"because you helped me, and my son. Did you forget about Arlen? Should I go home and tell him you no longer care what happens to him?"

He picked up his pace, not speaking.

By the time they reached Charlie's cottage, her breathing had increased from the brisk walk. Sully backed up against the cottage door as if the panels of wood could enfold him.

"Tell Arlen that I will always care about him. Please do that for me."

"Open the door." She came nearer, leaving only inches between their faces. "I'm not leaving here until we talk."

"Why won't ya do as I ask, and go?" he asked her weakly. "'Tis what is right."

"Ah." She touched his cheek. "Remember, I once told you, what's right isn't always what is."

He placed his hand over hers, closing his eyes as if making a wish.

"You're right." She whispered. "Now it's my time to choose."

His eyes were on her. "Choose what?"

"It's more like, choose *whom*." She softly rested her lips on his.

He pulled away. "Are ya sayin' ya want to be with me?"

She lifted her flushed face to his. "Yes, I do."

The light faded from his eyes. "Then you should come inside."

The door to the cabin opened from behind. Charlie met Sully with the look of a worried father. "I thought because of the late hour, Adara can have my bed. I'll bunk in with you, Sully."

Sully swept pieces of falling hair out of his eyes. "The two of us in that wee thing?" He pointed to his not-so-luxurious bed by the hearth while Adara tried to stifle a laugh.

"It's just for one night, lad." Charlie unloaded the books from the bunk. "I think ya both need some rest, wouldn't ya say?"

Adara noted the solemn glance which passed between the two men. "I'm sorry. I don't want to put anyone out."

"Yer welcome here," Charlie assured. "Yer tote is in the other room, and I've already put out the fresh linen for ya as well." He stood and ushered Adara from the room. "I'll show ya where to wash up."

"Thank you." She glanced back at Sully, who gave her a polite nod which did little to assuage her discomfort.

When she turned the corner into Charlie's room, Sully called out. "Adara! Not to worry. We'll talk in the morning. Sleep well."

"And I prefer the right!" Charlie called back.

"Come again?"

"I sleep on the right side of the bed!"

"Of course ya do," Sully exhaled in exasperation.

Chapter Eighteen

Strange Land

"**Y**ou could let me have a bit more of the covers." Sully turned on his side, yanking at a small section of sheet. "If that's not putting ya out too much."

Potcheen wedged himself into the crack between the men.

"Ah! The problem is ya've no fat on ya!" Charlie relinquished some quilt. "You should eat more, lad, then ya'd be plenty warm."

Sully's voice dropped to just above a whisper. He gathered the little dog against his chest. "Ya suppose Adara is alright? I hope she's not frightened, being in a strange place."

"And 'tis none stranger place than the Meeting of the Waters, eh?" Charlie leaned into his bunkmate's face, a bit too close for Sully's comfort. "I can't say I understand what is happening between the two of you, but I'm worried about ya, Sully, about your heart and soul."

"Would ya mind turning over? Sully moved to the very edge of his side, doing his best not to displace his furry companion. "A man is not permitted to contemplate issues of morality from his bed."

"*What?* Who says this?" Charlie's blue eyes danced.

"It's an ancient Irish law."

"I've never heard of such a law."

"Well maybe ya ought to spend more of your time in research, and less worrying about my soul." Sully gave another tug and captured a quarter more quilt for himself.

Charlie grunted and turned over. The two were quiet. Ciar's "gift" of allowing Sully to keep his memories of Gillean was meant to make him suffer, of that he had no doubt. But it was an affliction he welcomed. He was thinking of Gillean and their ardent kiss. In that moment he was a stranger to himself. He wasn't a child, an angel, or a friend. He was a man experiencing the grandeur of emotions he'd only heard about in songs and read about in poems. All the words and music coalesced into an indescribable yearning which transcended everything else.

How had Adara accomplished the impossible in finding him? Sully's head ached. So much emotion had been spent this night.

The heat of his anger dispelled the chill air. Why was he forced to make the insufferable deal with Ciar? How could he possibly protect Adara and Gillean when it was he who had given himself to an agent of malevolence? Would she try to turn Gillean from his children as well?

Sully had not forgotten Arlen—far from it. He had taken to the lad the first time he saw him. The boy was lonely, wanting of a man to spend time with him, and not just any man, but his absent father. Sully had not intended to reveal himself to Arlen. But, to his astonishment, the young Faraday could not only perceive Sully's presence, but often sought his company.

Once they had connected, Sully greatly enjoyed the time he and the boy spent walking and talking. Arlen was the perfect combination of Adara's loving spirit and Gillean's inquisitive, uninhibited nature. The boy wanted someone to share his secrets with. It honored Sully that Arlen had chosen him.

"Sometimes I don't think Da even hears me when I talk to him," the teen confided, while he and Sully kicked around the pitch one afternoon.

"I'm sure he does, Arlen. Why would ya think otherwise?"

"Because he has so many other things competing inside his head: he hears music, and memories of concerts, reviews, his *precious* fans, and without fail, his next project. I used to think it was cool when he would ask me what I thought of a song he was working on, but it got so I wanted to scream, 'Hey Da, what about what I'm thinkin'? What about what I'm doin'?'"

The boy punted the ball, sending it high into the air, powered by adolescent angst.

Sully tried to ease the boy's mind. "It's not that he doesn't care; your da truly loves you. Sometimes adults feel a little—" He paused to think of the right words a lad of Arlen's age could understand without compromising the truth or Gillean' integrity. It was a difficult balance. "Well, adults can sometimes feel a wee frightened that the people they love most might stop lovin' them. And so they do things to assure themselves that the love will be there without fail. Like how your da shares his song ideas with you. Those are very special to him. He must love and respect ya an awful lot to do that. I'm sure if ya talked with him about it he would understand."

Arlen dribbled the ball further while they talked. "But yer not like most adults. I don't have to ask ya to listen to me, you just do. And ya don't talk *at* me, but *with* me. Now that I have you, I don't need to bother Da. He would say he was sorry, and that he would try to do better, but he'd go back to the same ways. I tell him that I love him— why wouldn't he believe me?" The boy was truly baffled.

"But I'm not your father, Arlen. It's important ya keep the lines of communication open with him. He does know you love him."

"So why is he scared that I don't?"

Sully made a dash to take over possession of the ball. "Did ya ever get a present for Christmas, one you'd waited and wished for the entire year?"

"Sure! The Christmas when I was eleven, I wanted a drum kit somethin' desperate. I would leave Mam and Da little notes throughout the year. I even made a drum set out of cardboard and twigs and set it on their bed."

"And once ya got the kit, weren't ya a wee bit afraid that someone might take it away from ya, or that ya might somehow lose this wonderful thing ya wanted so much?"

"Christmas night, I was so in shock, I slept on the floor next to it, and Da had to carry me to bed!" Arlen's eyes were alight with the memory.

"There's your answer."

"What d'ya mean?"

"You are much more cherished by your da than any gift he could imagine. I'll wager that many times he has wished he was home, so he could check on ya while you were sleeping, or doing homework, to assure himself ya weren't going anywhere."

"You believe Da thinks that much of me?" The boy's voice spoke doubt, but his eyes reflected hope.

"That I do. You'll understand him much better when ya have a child of yer own." Sully mussed the boy's hair. "I promise."

"Do you? Understand yer da, I mean."

Sully looked down at the ball underneath his foot. The more time he spent on earth, the more he learned the one thing he valued most, the truth, was not easy to give to others. It was like a strong, unadulterated shot of alcohol. Few could take the purity without some dilution.

"Me da was a different sort of man altogether. You're fortunate to have the one ya do."

"But you came through okay. I think ya'd make a brilliant da, Sully."

The boy hugged him tight.

"*Sully?* Did ya hear what I said? Ya can't be asleep already," Charlie quipped in the darkness.

Shaken from his memories, Sully answered with some irritation, "Is there a reason ya have for me not getting any rest tonight?"

"It's not me who's keeping ya awake. That's a flimsy excuse."

"What is it then?"

"Look, lad, I'm not takin' the stick to ya. Lord knows I worry o'er ya every day."

Sully turned his head towards his companion. "I'm sorry, I didn't mean —"

"Think about what yer doin'. Think long and hard about who ya are, and what ya want."

"And you think I want another man's wife?"

"She is that. And she has taken a fancy to you. I didn't see a ring on her finger."

"Ring?" Sully recalled Adara's gold band. Earlier when she'd brushed his cheek the ring was absent. "But, Gillean, I wonder if he —"

"I'll be leavin' here a little before sunrise. I'll be gone till the day after tomorrow," Charlie cut in.

"Why? Where are ya goin'? You can't leave Adara and me here alone."

"I have some work to do outside the village." Charlie put his hand on Sully's shoulder. "I can't protect ya from yerself, but you are a strong and good man. I trust you will do what is best."

"What if what's best is a lie?"

"Then I expect you'll find yer way to the truth."

"There are no rules, no laws for my situation. The universe has no plan for me, unless I was meant to continuously do the wrong thing." Sully turned away in shame.

"No, lad, she wouldn't have come lookin' for you if ya weren't someone special. In order to gain the love and trust of another, ya have to earn it. I can see in her eyes that you have proved yerself to her."

"She doesn't know me." Sully finally gave voice to the torment that circled him night and day. "She wouldn't trust me if she knew the genuine article, and what is in my heart."

"Why don't ya tell her? She seems like a wise soul."

"It's wrong. Her husband, Gillean, he was me friend, he is me…"

"What? Do ya want to talk about what happened between the pair of you?"

"I cared about him is the sum of it. I suppose I'm not so much peeved with him, but myself. I failed him. I wasn't able to help him in the way I should have."

"Don't blame yerself. Each man is responsible for his own choices. Whatever Gillean did or did not do is not *yer* responsibility, but his."

"No matter what he may have done, it for sure isn't right—Adara's intention to be with me. 'Tis not right for her most of all."

"Then ya have a challenge to face."

"Charlie?"

"Try and get some sleep. You'll have some time with her to figure it out."

"No words of advice?"

"Yer a much braver man than I. There is nothing I could tell ya, Sully. 'Tis I who have learned from you."

———◆———

Considering the enormity of his task, Charlie cursed his Elders. Why would they have entrusted a young, wild and loving creature to an old, jaded spirit such as himself? There was a time when Charlie believed that having the ability to remain detached from his charges was his greatest strength—what made him a superior angel. Sully, with his passion and intricacies, made Charlie painfully aware he'd merely been playing it safe.

Yes, Charlie had done what was required of him and helped others, but Sully, in challenging the Powers that be, had touched lives in a way the practiced angel could merely marvel at. Charlie wanted to tell Sully his rebellion was what made him special, the most genuine kind of spirit. But Charlie was afraid. He feared Sully might have gone too far in trying to save Gillean, so far as to lose himself in the process. Or maybe, Charlie prayed, Sully would at long last find himself.

Chapter Nineteen

Letting Go

"**Y**ou can't be serious." She stared at him over her coffee cup, amused by his out-of- character pronouncement, and slightly annoyed that he had disrupted their leisurely breakfast.

Gillean carried his mug and plate containing a barely touched meal to the dishwasher. He didn't wish for a prolonged discussion about his decision. He had laid awake most of the night gazing into Ciar's sleeping face. He hoped he would be able to read her expression to guide his direction. She grew more beautiful every day, and also more demanding. Watching her lost to the world of dreams, Gillean realized how immature she was. She possessed the same self-centered drive he'd had in his youth. She had no concerns other than her art, and to have him all to herself. He'd left his wife, a decision that incessantly prodded him with the sharp point of self-reproach. It wasn't that he had left Adara, but how. Ciar's relentless request that he spend less time with his children forced Gillean to take a sobering look at where his life was headed if he stayed with her. He didn't like the ominous shadows.

Wiping his hands on a dishtowel, he was overcome with the sensation that he was an incredibly long way from where he was supposed to be. He did his best to keep a patient tone, knowing full well he'd chosen to come to her.

"I'm quite serious. I need some time on my own. Things have happened too fast for me to process."

"What *things*? Isn't this, aren't *I*, what you wanted?" She slammed her cup against the saucer, splashing coffee onto the lace tablecloth.

He paused, leaning both hands on the marble countertop, grasping for the right words to avoid her wrath. But whatever he said, she was going to give him one hell of a fight. "I want to be sure of these life-altering decisions I'm making. I've already caused enough hurt to those who didn't deserve it."

"You mean *your wife*." She sat back, allowing the front of her dressing gown to open. He paid no heed to the promise of her body.

"For starters, yes. My wife did nothing to merit my deserting her in such an abrupt way."

"I suppose she's as pure as the driven snow."

"Please, let's keep this between you and me. You don't know her. There is nothing to gain by throwing mud at her."

"Alright, Gilly, just between you and me." She got up from the table and stood on the other side of the counter, facing him head on. "What have *I* done that you should decide I am no longer what you want? You use me for your pleasure. You care nothing for me and my feelings?"

"Ciar, no." He massaged her shoulders. "But you refuse to be practical about my responsibilities. I will not desert my children. And yet you seem determined that I should see less and less of them." He stroked her hair. "Maybe time apart will help us both to see things in a different light."

She wrenched away from him angrily.

"I'm sick to death of being used and discarded by men who remember their *responsibilities*. I made it clear what I expected should you choose to be with me, and you didn't seem to mind when you were in my bed. Now I see you for what you really are."

She strutted back, lacing her fingers through his belt loops. "I see exactly the kind of man you are, *and* your priorities." She tugged on his trousers, forcing him forward, and then pushed him away as he attempted to regain his balance.

"You can add me to the list of those you have exploited. I hope you'll remember that when you are in the company of your children. What a fine example to your sons you will be. Maybe I will find someone who truly means it when he says he loves me. Thanks for all your lies. They will make for good company at night, I'm sure." She walked away from him. "Please leave your key when you go."

His heart sank. The little amount of food he had eaten tossed about in his stomach. He had anticipated a fight, a tantrum of epic proportions from his lover, a sure and explicit show of outrage. He was not prepared for her hurt and distress. There was truth in what she said. He had told her he loved her, expressed it freely at the time, wanting the words to bring them closer and save him from the abyss he was falling into. But his proclamation had only made the descent that much deeper.

After gathering the few effects he had accumulated in her flat, he found her tucked in bed clasping a pillow to her chest.

He lowered his tired body next to her.

"Do you mean to go?" she asked in a hushed tone.

"I'm sorry to disappoint you." He was taken aback by the deepness of her eyes. Their color shifted from light to dark. He believed he could perceive the soul of more than one woman veiled in the multihued lenses. "Can't you understand?" He broke his earlier resolution to take his leave with as little drama as possible. But the pointed briar lodged in his heart would not let him walk away—at least not without trying to get through to her and relieve himself of the sting. "Most women would think it an admirable quality for a man to want to be a good father to his children."

"I'm not most women."

"And if it were your child that I was a father to?"

"Are you making me an offer?" she leered.

He sighed, wholly defeated by her evasive attitude. "I'm simply saying if you and I had a child, wouldn't you want me to do right by him or her?"

She sat up and leaned against the silk-covered pillows, her knotty hair falling about her shoulders. "You can't even do right by me. And you expect me to admire your commitment to a non-existent child?"

"I'm trying to do right by everyone I care for." He placed his hand under her chin, lifting her face to his. "I didn't say this is goodbye."

"You've wasted enough of my time. Don't play me for one of your fanatical little groupies." She pushed the covers away to reveal her naked body. "This is who I am." She pressed his hand to her thigh. "I am an artist. I live by my passions. Take me as such, and we will live out our greatest desires together." She leaned in to tease his lips with her kiss.

Gillean's resolve began to waver as she glided his hand over her body.

Her lips were pressed against his ear. "Do you want to walk away from the superb life we can have?"

Words tripped over each other, whispers coming from within. It was not his voice but another, speaking in the ancient Celtic tongue and floating above her beguiling promise. The sounds were both words and notes. It was impossible to separate the music from the language. His mind and body were in unison, responding not to her, but to the resplendent ensemble playing inside.

A black thorn has pierced your heart, but I am the mate of your soul. Look for my eyes, and become whole.

Gillean quickly disengaged from her, rising from the bed as if coming out of a trance. He was amazed to find that her inveigling body was merely a beauteous disguise. There was nothing inside of the gorgeous shell reflecting anything close to compassion or caring. Hers was a dead soul housed within a live being.

"I have to walk away from you, Ciar. You and I are not kindred spirits. We don't strive to create the same art."

She knelt on the bed as if she was a goddess in his eyes. "You don't know what you have to lose if you leave me."

"Maybe not." He backed away from her, blind to her physical attraction. "But maybe my leaving has more to do with something I need to find."

Chapter Twenty

Chaos

Sully woke in a cold sweat, his body convulsed with involuntary shivers. Hauling himself up against the wall, he drew the covers to his damp cheeks and assessed the surroundings through blurred vision. A sliver of dying moonlight across a plank in the floor gave him the indication of where he was. Turning his throbbing head, he noted that Charlie was already gone. Sully's spirit sank. He was too weak to move, and frightened for Adara. She couldn't see him like this. He had no idea what was wrong with him.

"Oh Lord, please," he groaned.

His hands began to itch and burn. He fought to free them from the bandages. Pungent nausea mixed with the sting of open wounds. His mind searched for a reason hands should be in such a serious state, when they had seemed well on their way to healing.

"I told you those burns would be reminders of your humanity and the deal we made." She sat on the one, lighted spot in the room, causing the darkness to envelope her. Or was it she who doused the light? Sully couldn't be sure whether she was real and he truly awake, or whether she was merely a visitor from one of his frequent night terrors.

He spoke over the swelling in his throat. "Why are ya here? You concluded your business with me, Ciar."

She turned her predatory eyes to him. "Did I?" She was a marauder lying in wait for her victim. If this was a dream, there was a fine line dividing it and reality. Sully shivered anew.

"Stupid boy! Beg your pardon, you're a man now! A *stupid, human* man! And you are fair game."

"I'm not playing any more games with you." He lay down, trying to breathe past the scorching of his hands.

She clucked at him, "But our games bring me such pleasure. Having a man's complete adoration, especially a man who is used to being the one adored, is a heady trip." She waited for a response. Receiving none, she continued. "I know Gillean's wife is here. Score one for me. And I didn't have to lift a finger. I can't wait to tell Gilly the identity of Adara's new lover—should put his guilty conscious to rest. Poor bugger was worried about the grief he'd caused her. He'll be relieved to know Adara is doing quite well for herself."

Sully lay perfectly still, believing if he did not give her any provocation she would leave, or he would wake from his troubled sleep and the misery would subside. He summoned all his reserves to wait her out.

Ciar crossed her legs underneath her, sitting like a devotee of a dark and dangerous power. "Adara is a fierce one herself. Found you like a needle in a haystack. Bet she makes good use of that energy in bed, eh, Sully? Where is she now? Indisposed?"

The instinct to pull the covers over his head and wait vanished. She had overstepped the bounds by disrespecting Adara. He swiftly got out of bed and moved towards the blackness. He didn't care about the burst of pain when his hands made contact with Ciar's body, taking her in a mighty grip.

"Let me make something *very* clear." His breath lifted her hair. "If you renege on your deal with me, or if you initiate any contact with Adara or her children, I will destroy you."

Her laugh exposed needle-sharp teeth. "Right—you, a powerless little man, destroy me. Just remember, I've got something you want. Something I know you will be more than willing to bargain for. That is, if you truly love Gillean."

He stared into her eyes as if he were standing on the precipice of nonexistence. He didn't flinch. "You've got nothing on me but a promise. And if you should make the fatal error of breaking it— meaning Gillean is no longer free to leave you any damn time he wants—I swear you *will be* held accountable."

His grasp on the indefinable woman weakened as her body dispersed into the shadows of the pre-dawn. He stood alone in the room, his feet on the portion of weak light upon which Ciar had sat.

Her voice ruined the sound of bird song and tainted the breeze. "I can change anything I want, at any time, *little boy*."

"*I won't let you! I won't!*" he cried out.

He was curled up in a ball in the middle of the room mumbling when Adara found him. She knelt down and wiped his fevered face with her hands.

"Sully, what is it? What's happened?"

He attempted to stagger to his feet, but his legs would not obey.

"Are you hurt?" She folded her arms around him.

His exposed hands had returned to their semi-healed state. But reality swept over his senses with a wide, broad stroke of emotion. "I made a mistake," he answered.

"Don't talk nonsense. You have nothing to regret," she said reassuringly. "Is Charlie not here?" she asked.

"Charlie…had to…leave." He forced out the words with staggered breath. "He trusts me, and I…I am such a selfish man." He was intensely conscious of Gillean's absence, seeing him in the bits of violet in her eyes. "You're Gillean's wife."

He tried to move away from her, but she held him back. "No." Her hair fell against his cheek. "I'm not *Gillean's wife*. I am a person in my own right."

"I didn't mean to imply—"

"I know you didn't, but it's important for me to say it after years of silence. You are the reason I found my voice, why I truly know who I am. You once asked me what I dreamed of—what I wanted. Don't you know that you have already given it to me? I love you, Sully. *I love you!*" She rocked him in her arms, kissing his dark hair.

Behind closed eyes he could see Gillean reaching out one last time for help as Ciar tried to take his life. Sully had never felt so helpless. Ciar's vile words played over Adara's admission of love. Ciar had told him of Gillean's wish that Sully should know what it was like to be human—a man—so that he could truly know what his soulmate grappled with every day of his life. Sully recognized in Adara's affectionate face the fulfillment of Gillean's wish. He knew with every fiber of his being what it meant to be a man in love with another, forced to lie to protect his secret and those he cared for. This wisdom was more unbearable than any wound Ciar could inflict. Sully's heart was opened, frantically wanting to take Gillean inside. But now Gillean's innocent wife was offering herself. Ciar predicted as much. It was up to him to make the right decision. If he only had himself to consider, but his decision was designed to affect those he loved in a way which was not known to him.

"Adara, you have your freedom. Don't make the wrong choice. Don't be like Gillean and me."

"You're nothing like Gillean." She touched a finger to his lips. "No more talk about him now. Can't we just hold one other for a little while?"

He was worn out, feeling as if he had trudged through a blizzard. What was one more decision made while snow blind? Maybe he could allow Adara a few moments of peace before the storm hit full force. "Alright, yes, let's hold each other for a little while."

She tenderly pulled him up from the floor and helped him back to his bed.

Chapter Twenty-One

You Could Break Me

Sully's arms encircled Adara as they lay in his small bed. She had been aimlessly wandering through her life, dedicated to the duties of a wife and mother. But a significant piece of her had been lost. She carried the damage with her—through the lean years, the rise of Gillean's career, the birth of their children, and the charmed life filled with amenities. Though her children brought her happiness, she secretly mourned for the missing part of herself, a part that was not connected to Gillean or family life.

Sully had bravely reached into her heart and leveled the cracks like a patient craftsman restores a forgotten creation. The feelings he evoked were different than anything she had known before. Not since she was a young girl had she identified with what it meant to be free to envision a life for herself, based on the principles and ideals that mattered to her.

At seventeen, Adara was making the difficult transition from the labyrinth of adolescence into the realm of attainable, mature dreams— mainly her dancing. The wayward Gillean had stymied her growth with his incessant need to be at the front and center of her universe. His presence had permeated her life. The stage simply hadn't been large enough to accommodate both the dancer and the singer. Like all Irish girls of her generation, she had been taught that to be needed by a man and to afford unquestioning support in return was the ultimate achievement.

Even though a sexual revolution had been spreading in restive waves across the Atlantic at the time, her inexperience and cultural background were stronger forces than any cry for emancipation.

Adara recognized that to Sully she mattered as a person, not just as a woman. She meant more to him than the fleeting gratification her body could offer, or merely a dependable support system should he falter on his own road.

Sully's light humming soothed her. The rise and fall of his chest assured her of his presence. He, unlike Gillean, wasn't going anywhere. Sully had no place to rush off to, nobody else to please. He was there for her, and wanted to be.

"What a lovely melody. Does it have words?" she asked.

"Take your leave of me, carefully. Remember my heart is on your sleeve. Take your leave of me, carefully, remember you could break me," he sang softly.

His voice was unlike Gillean's, but it could carry an Irish air with all its lilts and complexity. She was touched by the innocence she heard, not only in the words but in his expression. The time she spent with Sully gave her the strangest sense of being with a man who had never fully relinquished his childhood. He was not childish, more that he still possessed a childlike wonder of the world.

Gillean had once sung about the sea and the sky—as a poet sharing his dreams and vision. Reaping the earthly delights that had come with commercial success, his talents had sent him crashing back to earth—as a man, older and jaded.

But the stars fastened themselves to Sully as if he were the velvet sky. He was oblivious to his own nature. Adara knew this was the very thing Arlen must have been drawn to. Her son still carried the secrets of childhood. He and Sully spoke the same, mysterious language, one she wanted to learn.

"Are those your words, Sully?"

"No. I'm not sure where I heard the song, but it has stayed with me, like a prayer really."

"Is that how you feel? Like people...like *someone* could break you?"

"When a person cares deeply for another, that is the unavoidable risk."

"I used to feel that way about Gillean. I was afraid he would take his love from me and I would simply die."

"You were young."

"That I was, and there is no easy way to rid oneself of such a powerful tie. I was so enmeshed in his life that I needed to believe the best about him—that he meant it when he said he was sorry." She lay against his chest once more. "Facing the truth of the matter—that the man I loved, my husband—could hurt me so horribly, so publicly, it was easier to believe in his redemption rather than face the humiliation."

"I believe that love and redemption can only come when the truth is embraced by the heart. Most people prefer to walk through fire than take on such a challenge," Sully observed.

"And I am guilty as charged," she lamented.

"As am I."

"I need to tell you something." She fixed her eyes, gray like the stony admission she was about to reveal, on his. "It's not pretty like your song."

He didn't look away, but placed his hands on her head, like a blessing. "Ya don't have to tell me anything. I'm nobody's judge."

"But, I need to. This is my only remaining tie to Gillean, and I must be free from it." Her cheeks blushed with the rush of how good it felt to finally detach from the burdensome anchor, and a bit fearful of what Sully would think of her youthful misjudgment. "I don't want to keep any more secrets. Please, let me share it with you."

"Of course."

She set her chin over her folded arms, keeping her eyes on him. "There was a woman, a former lover of Gillean's, who was quite important in the business world."

Sully's eyes shifted like a flame flashing from low to high.

"Shortly after our first wedding anniversary, Gillean's mother, Ena, was relentless in her badgering. She kept at Gillean to give up his music, insisting how ashamed he would feel if he could not support his wife and the children that would surely come. I didn't expect him to support me. As far as I was concerned we would support one another. But I knew his mother's words whittled away at his conscience. His father was such a well-respected man in his field, and Gillean's brother was a successful professor. These things must have taken a toll on Gillean's confidence."

She paused to sweep the hair falling over her eyes and took up her confession. "And so I decided I would help him. I would find a way to assure his family that we would never want for anything, and my husband would at last be able to share his music with the world."

"Because you loved him," Sully said, without anger or difficulty, only compassion.

"Because I thought that love meant letting go of who I was, what I wanted for myself, and placing Gillean above all else; that was the true nature of our relationship." She exhaled, releasing the shame of her arrested development at her own hands. "He put to me once during that first year together, if I wanted to leave him, he would let me go. He said he was devoted to his music. He was ready to suffer for it but didn't expect me to. That was a lie."

This time there was an edge to Sully's voice. "But it was too little too late."

She looked away.

"I'm sorry. I shouldn't have said that. It's not me place. Please, carry on."

The certainty she had denied for the last twenty-some years was almost too much to bear. "He had every reason to believe I'd remain with him. I didn't think either one of us could make our way in the world without the other. He needed my faith in him, and I needed a purpose. I made the choice to give up my dancing for him. And *I* made the choice to seek out his former lover and ask for her assistance. I went so far as to tell her that if she wanted to—" Embarrassment prevented her from continuing. She looked to Sully's face. There was no appearance of judgment, only empathy for her. "I told her if she wanted Gillean once again as her lover in exchange for helping him, I would not object—as long as she made things happen for his career. It was one of the most difficult and humiliating things I have ever done, offering the man I loved to another. And do you know what?" She laughed at the ugliness of the memory. "This gorgeous, worldly woman looked at me for the inane child I was, and told me she wasn't interested in used goods. But she liked Gillean's music enough. More to the point, she could get a tidy cut of the profits, so she did make things happen. A few weeks later he received a call from a major record label. They wanted to produce his first album. And the rest, as they say, is history. I suspect the woman took her cut in secret because Gillean never knew about her involvement. I certainly kept that hidden from him."

She gently touched her fingers to Sully's face. "I wanted you to know this because, since I have met you, I understand what love truly is. It's not about giving up who you are and allowing another to overshadow your light. Love is light. Please say you understand what I did for Gillean, even though it was because of my own weakness. I honestly thought it was love back then. But now I acknowledge the inherent dependency of our union. I treasure the children he and I created. At long last I can show them what it means to be an individual. They will be strong because of what I've had to learn. And they will be better people than their parents."

Sully's eyes were like the rolling sea before a storm, turbulent and tormented. "Why aren't you wearing your wedding ring?" His tone carried a note of disappointment, dejection even, as though he regretted the fact.

Adara's spirits sank. Her reply echoed with a hollow disappointment of her own. "You still believe I belong with Gillean. After what I've shared, you think I should stay with him. Is it because you believe I deserve to be punished for what I did?" She didn't wait for his answer. "No matter what you believe, no matter how much you feel you owe Gillean your allegiance, I don't. And I'm not ashamed. I want to walk the road with you, because you will allow me to be who I am." She sat up, her nightshirt slipping to expose a freckled shoulder as she turned her back to him.

"Regardless of your answer, I will not return to Gillean. I hold no animosity for him now. I care deeply about him, but, I am not, nor will I ever be again, Mrs. Faraday."

The words came from Sully just as the candle by the bed burnt out, releasing a high wisp of smoke into the air like a dying breath. "You're truly a beautiful soul, Adara. If you mean to take your leave of Gillean, be careful. Don't be so quick to take up the path of another, flawed being. I only ask that ya take some time to be sure of your choice."

She glanced over her shoulder, an uncertain smile budding across her face. "And if I said I wanted to be with you, would you have me?"

"Let's sleep now." He settled her down against the pillows and lay beside her. "We'll share the dreamers' sky for the time bein'. Everything else can wait for the sun."

She nestled her body against his. "I'd be happy to meet the sun with you."

Chapter Twenty-Two

Rain and Blood

Sully jolted awake. His earlier encounter with Ciar had evaporated into a vague, disturbing impression of a hellish dream. No details were provided by memory, only the overwhelming sense of sinister threat. Trembling with residual emotion, he turned to check on Adara. She was sleeping peacefully. Keeping watch on her, he carefully moved up from the bed. Putting on his boots with some difficulty, his hands stiff and sore, he reached for an old jumper of Charlie's.

Sully needed to think. He ached for Adara, because she believed herself to finally be free, but she was walking into yet another life of lies. His love for Gillean would only continue to grow with the passage of time. He needed to be tranquil within himself. He had to find a way to push his great love aside so that both Gillean and Adara would be safe. He had to make a commitment blindfolded and with his hands tied behind his back because of Ciar's "test". He knew too well what failing one of her trials would mean.

His hand on the door, he watched Adara sleeping. He went to her and stroked the fine hair fanning out over her pillow.

The words came soft as a wish. "Please make the right choice for yourself."

Still caught between the world of sleep and wakefulness, her eyes were closed. "Sully…" she breathed.

He passed his hand over her face, like casting a spell. "Sleep now. I'll be back shortly."

She offered a drowsy smile and let him go with the confirmation of her trust.

He made his way to the Vale, the sacred place of poetry and lovers. Taking deep breaths of air scented with pine, lavender, and the potent remembrance of his soulmate, he captured the dawning sky with his accusing glance. Without being aware of the process unfolding, this once damaged child—the flawed, repentant spirit, now wounded man—found himself submerged deep within the inviting, exhilarating ocean of love. It was inconceivable that what he and Gillean shared could be wrong. It was a most adult realization lying next to Adara. Her warmth against him, her delicacy and affection were keenly felt. She was a fellow lost soul, a starling searching for safe haven. He cared for her in this way.

But his pathos for Gillean was altogether different. It existed paradoxically both within and outside of the sensual. Their bodies were the vessels of one expression of the many stratums of their unity. The hunger for Gillean's person was the desire to consummate their union on the physical plane where they now existed together at last. The flesh was a means to delve deeper into everything that existed beyond the body.

Sully reckoned most people searched their whole lives hoping for such a connection, but he felt cursed by the Powers to never truly embrace the life he had taken on. Given what Adara shared with him about her own tumultuous past, it seemed she too was cursed. She mistakenly believed she belonged with Sully. He performed a mental sweep, trying to clear away the reservations from his mind. He must surrender himself totally to his deal with Ciar. Life for him began and ended there.

Semi-darkness clung to the land. The moon took its time relinquishing the sky. Sully exhaled white bursts of breath that quickly disappeared into the chilly air, like the hope in his heart. The stillness of the land was punctuated by the absence of the morning birds' calls. They sensed the arrival of rain, which began to fall in generous drops. He stopped walking and pulled Charlie's sweater over his head like a shroud. He listened as the rain pelted leaves, grass and wildflowers, offering its life-giving sustenance. The rain also offered Sully the opportunity to release his tears freely. They were brusquely washed away like the dirt from his boots. But the water left a muddy residue, the emotion that remained after the tears. He knelt down and scooped up a handful of soft earth. One tiny violet sat in his palm. He tossed his offering onto the imaginary grave before him, which contained the life that could have been with Gillean.

He stood and shouted into the wind, "I'll do what ya ask of me! But he will always be my music!" he informed the resolute moon.

As he reached the intersecting lakes, an all-encompassing mist, hot and sticky, wafted up from the waters. The land, water and sky were depleted of their recognizable features, seeming to become odd shapes of abstract art. The mist continued to thicken until visibility was reduced to a mere few inches.

Disoriented, he relied on his feet to navigate the ground. Shaken by the eclipse, he stumbled over a thick root protruding from the forest floor. It was then he saw a figure among the trees. He squinted, trying to identify if what he saw was a person or a phantom.

The form did not move but communicated an overt vibration of destruction.

"Who's there?" he called out, attempting to sound fearless.

It moved forward, the mist obediently falling away to expose the woman.

"Top of the morning, little boy." She stepped over wet leaves with bare feet. "Up and pining before the dawn? You must have had an eventful evening."

His heart sank. She imprisoned all the loveliness of nature by her mere presence. The air carried the stench of decay.

"So you *were* in the cottage earlier!" he demanded. The malignant dream had a face now.

"You can't stop thinking of me, can you?" she teased. Waves of blonde hair clung to her supple body, making her appear like a rejected siren regurgitated by the sea.

He shoved numb hands into his pockets. "I'd say you're the one obsessed with me." "How is that, when you're supposedly so consumed by Gillean? I wouldn't think you'd have the time, or the interest, for a little boy."

"Oh, I'm indeed pleased with my singer, and he with me, but I'm a woman of varied interests, and I have other things to tend to. You see, these other areas may well be of benefit to the whole Faraday clan. That is, if you are still thinking with your conscience these days and not some other part of your anatomy."

"There is nothing about you that interests me. I've made my deal with you, kept up my end of it, and the next time you intrude on my life will be the last."

"HA! HA! Bravo!" She clapped her hands together, the sudden sound frightening off a gathering of grouse. "All that testosterone has made a man out of you." Her tongue leisurely traced the outline of her plump lips before she spoke again. "I've come to discuss how you may assist the family you unendingly profess to love."

"Bugger off, Ciar!" Despite the undoubted power and menace that Ciar exuded, he turned his back on her. "You and I are done."

Before he had moved a single pace, Ciar was standing only inches in front of him, catching him as he lost his balance. "You'd better watch your step. You're coming dangerously close to voiding our deal."

He righted his footing and took a step back. "You're header mad."

"I told you I would be back to reveal the other half. Now is the time."

"I don't intend to make Adara a pawn in your sick game."

"Don't screw with me, Sully. If you refuse to do as I say with regard to Mrs. Faraday, you know what will happen to Mr."

"I'd never screw with *you* darlin'." He spat into the rain. "I meant to keep my word, but your being here shows me that ya just want to jerk me around."

"Centuries upon centuries and you still can't anticipate me. I like that." She smiled. "To the contrary, I came here to deliver the way in which you can be done with this whole business, the final part of our deal. I saved the best for last."

"You're a liar."

"Or, I can continue to hover about your life. The pact didn't preclude me from making contact with you. You can't do a damn thing to stop me, and you know it."

He tried to step away again, forcing her out of his way. She was impervious to his feeble attempt to be rid of her.

"You doubt the rightness of your decision." Her words caught him like a viscid web. "The remnants of that idiotic angel conscience of yours tells you one thing, but your heart is still wondering, still feeling the connection to Gillean. This is your way out, your chance to do the ultimate good for him, Adara, and their children."

With his head raised, he demanded an answer from the ominous sky as much as from her. "*What do ya want from me?*"

"That's quite the Irish temper you have acquired as well." Her black eyes revealed her delight at his outburst. "I should think you would be angrier about what is on the way than anything I would exact from you."

"And what *is* on the way?"

"Here's what's going to happen to Gillean Faraday." She took her hands from behind her back to display a stunning diamond set in gold positioned on her left ring finger. "He will divorce his wife, and his marriage to me—the spectacular, much younger artist—will become fodder for every form of media in the UK for starters. He will be totally dependent upon me for support. You and I both know the git needs someone ever ready to sustain him. Then, I will make absolutely certain that he won't be spending any time with his children." She scraped the ring against Sully's cheek; after a few seconds, a thin, red line appeared along the grazed skin. "You are aware that I despise children. I can convince a man to—"

"Gillean gave ya that ring?" Sully spoke over a rush of bile in his throat. "He said he wants to marry ya?"

"Your confidence that he would leave me is charming. I told you before, he's a done deal."

"What of Adara and the children?"

"They will have so much alone time they may have trouble remembering what the old man looks like." She breathed on the ring and polished it on her skin. "Ah, well, they'll get enough of him in the tabloids for a while anyway."

Sully was horrified. He hadn't fully considered what effect Gillean remaining with Ciar would have on his family. Sully doubted that even Gillean had a clue at this stage.

"It's making sense to you now, isn't it, lad?"

Sully remained steadfast. "You can forget about any further involvement from me. I did what ya asked. Gillean is free to do as he likes. There is no sequel to our deal. You're over the bend if ya think I will continue to be a bargaining chip for you. And I sure as hell won't let you anywhere near Adara and her children."

"We are both of the same mind on this." Her spiteful grin broadened. "As I said, I have other matters to attend to, matters which have nothing to do with Gillean Faraday. Besides, he is beginning to bore me. There's no challenge in blind adoration. This is the last time I will come to you. You can be sure that what I have to offer is a gift for you."

"I don't accept gifts that can't be returned."

He tried to find calm within the rhythm of the rain, but the woods were silent as a tomb.

"Not even the ability to save Gillean's career? Or how about my leaving him, Adara and their children alone for good? Of course it would take some doing—the little musician is mad about me—but I will do my part, if you do yours."

"Which is?"

"Denounce Adara. Send her away. Tell her you do not now, nor will ever, love her. *Break her heart!*" Ciar was gleeful in her request.

Coldness entered his body as the warmth of humanity drained away, leaving only the endless cycle of debt and payment to this wretched being. "You're out of your bloody mind!"

"You still have a lot to learn about good and evil. I thought you would at least have a better understanding of it because of Gillean."

Was there a shade of contrition in her voice when she spoke his name? "What do ya mean about Gillean?"

"Would you say he is good or evil?" she posed.

"He does not play for your team, if that's the question."

"And yet, here you are with his wounded wife, wounded yourself because of him."

"He's not evil, he's just—"

"Embraced the truth—that his life is not how he pictured it to be, and his marriage is a sham. He longs for passion and love. He faced his own truth, and look what it brought him. You see, the truth doesn't always set one free."

"Ah, the fiend-philosopher; what a lovely combination of evil and bullshit."

"I will break Gillean's heart. I'd say it's par for the course that you do the same to his wife. It is our task, each in our own way, to *persuade* them to resolve their issues and move on."

"*Our* task? As if ya gave a tinker's curse about either of them!"

"Good and evil, my friend, two sides of the same coin. Both Gillean and Adara can relate to temptation and honor. They have shown us as much. He wants me, and she wants you."

"He loves me and I love him! It's not the same sordid thing as you have."

"Love?" she nearly gagged on the word. "You can't be so stupid, can you? Do you actually believe that Gillean would have the daring to love *you*?" Ciar eyed the magnificent ring once again. "He is smarting over your rejection. And Adara told you herself that she gave up her bloody life for him, and he turned his back on her for his music."

"Let me see," Sully said, playing with her words for more time. "Gillean is *smarting over me*, even though you swore vehemently that he would have no memory of me. Which is it?"

If he wasn't looking directly at her, Sully would have missed the slight flinch. "I was referring to your deluded concept of the everlasting torch the pair of you idiots carry for one another. Remember, he did ask me to marry him. Even you can recognize the only fire is between him and me."

Sully came at her from a different angle. "You recommend I should crush Adara to help her through your blessed nuptials? Speaking of idiotic ideas…"

"Oh, dear, you mean your good intentions will?" she snorted. "Ignore my offer, and I will always be close at hand. Now what kind of a life would she have? Tormented by someone she cannot see. And what about Gillean, your soulmate? His fall from grace will be witnessed world-wide. And his sweet, innocent children…both parents shattered people."

"STOP IT!"

He lunged at her, halting short of throttling her when his hands squeezed her flesh. She felt like a woman, and he was appalled by his violence towards her.

She rubbed at her arms, acting as if he had caused trauma. "You *can* stop it, Sully. Stop the cycle and have me out of the Faraday's life forever."

Sully wished he held the remedy to rid himself of this monstrous creature. Ciar's suggestion that there would be another part to their contract impelled him to get an unbreakable vow from her in any further negotiations.

"If I agree with your proposition, I want a clear-cut guarantee that you will not so much as breathe within the vicinity of *any* Faraday *ever* again!"

"I'll give you clear-cut proof of my sincerity." She removed something small and sleek from the pocket of her dress. Holding out her thin wrist to him, she waved the object in the air with her other hand. It clicked once to reveal a single, silver blade. She sliced into her skin. Blackish-red fluid poured immediately from the substantial cut. Without hesitation, or giving him any time to react, she reached for his arm and did the same, placing their wrists against one another.

"My blood mixes with yours. It binds me to the promise I will make you. If I break it my essence, my being, will be at your disposal. Do you accept?"

Sully rocked back on his heels flabbergasted by her action. "Swear to me, you will let Gillean go, cease to exist in his life, Adara's and their children's!" Dizzy, he glanced down at the fluid dripping from their enjoined wrists.

"I am as good as gone—so long as you march back to the cottage, rid yourself of Adara, and I will do the same with regard to the Faradays. As far as that family is concerned, we will both be nothing more than residual energy." She derided him. "I told you, human desire will always ruin the best of intentions. I'm right, aren't I?"

Desire. The word pinned his heart like a butterfly under glass. Was this what he was feeling for Gillean? Desire?

"You can be the better man, the stronger man, Sully. Aren't you the least bit curious to see if Gillean can right his relationship with Adara without our interference?"

Sully closed his eyes. He felt the blood, that a moment ago was beating forcefully through his body, drain away. "This is the end of the line for me and you, Ciar." He no longer fought, but pulled her wrist tight against his. "Full stop. I'll say yes to you, and you vanish from my life *forever*. Mind you, I will find you, and make sure ya pay should you make contact with the Faradays!"

"I was the one who suggested this!" She tossed her head back. "I'm putting my existence on the line. I'm not so hard up to risk that for a Faraday or you."

"Then get out. Get the fuck out!" he yelled. His blood fell onto the leaves around their feet.

She backed away slowly, saying nothing, seemingly content to let him have the last word in their protracted war. Sully looked to the fog rising from the water, dispersing into the first, temperate rays of the morning sun. When he looked again to the trees, she was gone.

———————◆———————

Sully sat on the step in front of the cabin door, his head in his hands, hands that bore no evidence of the insufferable burns. All that remained was a pronounced scar across his left wrist: no blood, no pain. Flesh covered the once deep gash, giving the scar an aged look. Another reminder of the deal made with Ciar, their final transaction. The inner stillness he had hoped to elicit during his pre-dawn walk had been snatched away.

His ever-certain feelings for Gillean lingered. It was a reticent recognition of the definition of love that he had gained.

Adara had said love was sacrifice, believing the idea to be only a misconception of youth. Perhaps because he was young and inexperienced, he was required to pay his dues, make his own sacrifices in the name of love. Maybe the fruition of real love came only with time, like the fruits of a dedicated farmer ceaselessly tending his soil through seasons of flood and drought, the waxing and waning of the moon—patience and the knowledge of how to read and respect the natural cycle of things.

Sully wanted the permission to love, the freedom to dismiss the concerns of right and wrong, and the chance of a joyous life. The tears falling onto his hands were those of resolution and begrudging acceptance. He was not meant for any of that. He recognized the one duty he could not dispense with was his obligation to protect Gillean and his family. Adara was free to walk away from her husband. It was right that she should want a life for herself, a life where she was valued for the remarkable person she was. Sully hoped she would make the decision on her own.

This life was his last go around the great wheel, his final chance to live in the light and prove what he stood for as a human being. A short time ago he'd stared into the looking glass wondering who would save him. He'd been gazing at himself all along.

Chapter Twenty-Three

Balancing Ledgers

Adara opened the door and stood above Sully. "I've put some coffee on." Her voice was bright and she gave his shoulder a playful squeeze. "Poor old Charlie, he doesn't even—" Her observations on Charlie's housekeeping were cut short as Sully raised his tear-stained face to her. "Why are you crying?" Her question came with total surprise. "Come now." She took his hand. "Come inside so we can talk."

He followed her into the cottage. The strong smell of coffee punctuated his reality and the thought of the vile task at hand.

"I've thought a great deal about what you told me," he said, as she brought him a steaming mug. "I want you to know that I appreciate and respect your honesty. I in no way judge what ya did as good or bad."

"You appreciate my honesty?" She put her mug on the table. "Would you please tell me what is going on? The last thing I remember, you were going for a walk and promising you would return shortly." She stood near the kitchen window as if bracing herself against his somber mood. "What has gotten into you?" she demanded.

"I've had time to consider what you said regarding your past with Gillean." He sounded disconnected, not only from her but from himself. "Given what you have told me, I don't see a way for us but to part now."

"W…*Why*?" She stammered.

"You admitted you gave up your life, what you wanted for yourself, even offered your husband to another woman."

"I tried to explain to you." She wrung her hands. "I was young and incredibly naive. I truly believed I was helping Gillean. It was wrong. I know, and I…" She choked on the words. "I thought you understood."

He sat at the table next to his ledgers. This was the most complex of problems. How to convince her to go, when what he wanted was to set her mind at ease. Of course he understood, of course he wanted to help her. "I have great empathy for you," he spoke, absently picking up a pencil. "I'm like you were then, young and not of the best judgment."

"What?" She was at the table gripping the edges with both hands.

"You said there would be no more secrets when you told me about what ya did for Gillean. You said that you loved me, but there are still secrets. Love cannot exist within lies, even if they are well intentioned."

"What secrets are you referring to? I've told you all there is to know about my life." She rounded the table to kneel in front of him. "Surely you know you can share anything with me. I don't presume that things will be easy for us, but I'm ready to face whatever comes—together."

Sully remained impassive. The silence between them was almost physical for several minutes, weighted with the agony of despair.

Adara was the first to move. Without raising her head, she laced her fingers through his, sighing she looked up into his eyes. "Sully…" she said with a note of wonder, "what's this? The burns are gone! It's an omen." A faint smile broke on her lips, and her eyes reignited with hope. "You see, you and I are good for one another."

What could he say to her to make her go? He couldn't find the words to utter such a potent command. He had to weave the opaque cloth needed to suffocate the truth. He couldn't tell her of his love for Gillean—that would be a betrayal of the man. He could at least offer a half-truth in which he held some faith.

"You and I together would be wrong."

Her face became a sheet of blank paper, white and creased with lines. It was time to write the ending of their story. He did not wait for her reply, to make the next notation. "You asked me if I still cared about Arlen. I do. I care about your family." He watched her lips tremble. "Your place is with them now."

Her expression darkened like fast-moving clouds masking the moon. Nevertheless, she spoke calmly and with a hint of remorse. "This isn't about my children. They are wise beyond their years. They've had to be. They sense every bit of tension between Gillean and me." She placed her hand beneath his chin, preventing him from looking away. "Is this about your misplaced sense of loyalty to a man who does not deserve it?"

Sully's brow furrowed. She wasn't going to make this easy, and he admired her all the more for her fight. "My task is to stand back and allow Gillean and each one of you to make your own way in this world."

"Did you not hear me before? I have chosen my path. And, as for

Gillean, he does not deserve your respect. He has hurt you deeply. He denies ever laying eyes on you!" She was fighting against her anger, offering it to Sully to unravel like a string of entangled beads. "Why in God's name should he be a factor in this?"

The dam of emotions he was trying frantically to hold back pressed against him like a great cascading wall of water. He sank to the floor and took hold of her. "Don't ya see? We must be careful with those we love, no matter how careless they may be with us. We must be careful how we take our leave of them. Your children could pay a heavy price, and none of us—you, me or Gillean—wants that."

Her voice broke. "Is that what you are trying to do, take your leave of me?"

"Yes." He tried to release his arms from hers.

She raised her lips to his, whispering, "I don't believe you."

"Adara—"

She wrenched away, her eyes teeming with questions. "It's Gillean, isn't it?"

The words pushed against his teeth. He could not allow his lips to release them.

"Gillean is responsible for your wounds, isn't he? He is the reason you ended up here, with Charlie."

Scraping the bottom of what remained of his stockpile of fortitude, he pushed onward, like Sisyphus with his boulder. "Gillean has no idea what happened to me. You mustn't blame him for every misfortune." He inched away from her, his voice low and sharp. The words he was about to offer cut through his lips like broken glass. "You aren't ready for another relationship, Adara. You savor your anger for Gillean, and it's your anger that ties ya to him, even now. You can no longer blame him for your not being a dancer."

What he said may have been enough to impel her heart to let him go. Her offended eyes regarded him with uncertainty. He needed to be sure that she would leave and be safe. "I'm not interested in used goods." He threw the words Ciar had said to her so long ago, meaning to rip apart what was left of her trust in him.

His exacting choice of words electrified the room. She moved as if in shock. Her eyes darted from his face to the window and back again; her lips tightened in concentration. She was trying to quickly connect all the disjointed clues from Sully's incongruous statements.

"YOU'RE LYING!" she shouted, as the tears fell. "I saw you in the woods with her!"

"Oh, God, Adara, no…"

"How can this be?" Her penetrating eyes posed the question more forcefully than her voice. "She is the same woman I sought out years ago. I could never forget her."

Sully was frozen, his mouth gaping, his eyes set in a wild stare. He could do nothing to prevent Adara, who by some stroke of genius or madness seemed to be untangling the threads connecting three individuals with one egregious woman.

"What reason should she be here with you?" she confronted him. "How can you know her too?"

Sully lurched to his feet in a reflex action. He had to take advantage of her doubt. An image of Arlen, the spirited, troubled young man, shone in his mother's eyes. Reflected in the reticent shades of gray and violet were pieces of both Gillean and his son. Sully had come to a crossroads. He wanted to give her total honesty, to present it to her like a knight lays down his sword, but he could not bring himself to risk the lives of Adara, her children and Gillean. Yes, love was sacrifice, and it was at that moment Sully knew the exact cost of loving.

"That is what I have been trying to tell you." He spoke as if she were a child not yet mature enough to comprehend. "I have my own secrets, and they aren't ones I wish to share. Now will ya please return to your family and leave me be."

The last few words tasted like salty, warm blood, as if a potent fist had just struck him in the mouth.

"Is this the real reason you want me gone?" Tears restricted her words. "Because of her?"

"I can assure you that Gillean will be on his way back to you shortly."

"She told you this?" Adara countered.

"That she did." His confirmation was offered without the cushion of kindness or caring. "It's time for you and Gillean to stop running away, and be on about making your lives better. Your children deserve as much."

Adara was shaking. The sun paled in her wretchedness, taking its warmth from the room and casting long shadows. "Don't you tell me what is best for my children! You knew she was Gillean's lover the entire time, didn't you? But how could she—"

Sully stood back, closing his eyes to suppress the veracious nature that was sure to betray him when he looked at her pained face. "You didn't hear what she and I were discussing this morning?"

"No," her brow furrowed. "I mean—I don't remember if I did."

She faltered, appearing to finally stumble over a stone of indecision. He hurriedly took over the conversation, fearful that she might remember his deal with Ciar. "I also told you there are powers greater than you and me. She is a powerful and persuasive woman."

She regarded him like he was the worst kind of criminal. "You've said quite enough. And here I thought I had gained wisdom over the years. No wonder you and Gillean got on so well. You are so much alike."

"Neither you nor Gillean will have to worry about her being a disturbance in your lives any longer. 'Tis me she's been after throughout, and 'tis me she will content herself with."

"No doubt you will be happy together. You can both go to hell, Sully. I hope at least you relish your victory over my heart." She retreated to the back room to gather her things.

When she returned, he was holding the door open for her, his face a mask of coldness. She asked one final question: "Tell me this, since you and Gillean have shared so much. Did you share her as well?"

"Goodbye, Adara." He turned his back and walked away, counting the seconds, holding his breath until he heard her car start up and the tires grind down the dirt path. Kneeling on the floor, he was seized by an ache more terrible than he'd ever experienced in any lifetime. He had won. The Faradays would be free from Ciar forever. But he had lost the one connection that made him feel genuinely alive and human. He lay on the floor and wept, a broken, beaten man.

Chapter Twenty-Four

Ribbons and Diamonds

Adara drove with one hand trembling on the wheel, the other wiping the rush of tears blurring her vision. She steered the car to the side of the road in order to collect herself. She felt she may be sick. Sully's repulsive words churned in the pit of her stomach. He had stolen her last shred of hope and dignity.

With eyes still unfocused, she caught a flash of movement among the trees. Sunlight illuminated the sparse patches of forest floor. It was a maze of light and shade. There, among the play of daylight, she spied the flowing of a white, diaphanous garment—the hem of a small girl's dress. Rubbing her eyes, Adara spotted the edges of a green ribbon waving in the breeze like a tiny sail attached to a head of red hair. She blinked and saw a child running into the woods.

Stepping out of her car, she heard a little girl's laughter and whispers, like that of a group of children passing round a secret, their voices faint and feathery, their suppressed giggles suspended in the morning breeze. With mounting curiosity, Adara followed after the voices, moving deeper into the glen.

Running at a good clip, sweat, not tears, obscured her view. The last bit of white and red wove its way through the green of the trees.

"Wait!" she called out, breathless. "Please, wait!"

The laughter coasted further and further away. Woozy from hunger and emotion, Adara bent over, clutching her knees. Her mind must have been playing tricks on her. It had been one of the worst mornings of her life. Why shouldn't she also be having visions of wood fairies to top things off, she considered, as she took in deep gulps of air. The crisp taste of nature soothed her.

Looking down, her eyes rested on a patch of wet leaves. Their color was striking, the rusty brown dotted with bright red drops; an artist's brush had dripped its crimson contents onto the foliage. Underneath the leaves, something glistened as the sun's rays stretched down from the indigo sky. Picking up a leaf and bringing it to her nose, the musk of wood and peat tickled her senses. But when she touched it, the red clung to her fingers. Blood! Covering her mouth, her stomach threatening to wretch, her eyes fell upon the object concealed by the leaf. Adara could hardly believe that here, in this forgotten place, someone had left behind the most superb diamond ring she had ever seen. She held it up towards the light, its sparkle catching each and every hue of the color spectrum.

"Oh my God!" Adara gasped, as the light momentarily blinded her. She crushed the bloodstained leaf in her hand as the missing early morning hours inundated her consciousness. It was a terrifying dream in which she had secretly followed Sully into the darkness of the wood and witnessed him engaged in a conflict with a powerful, female adversary. Upon waking Adara shuddered at the vague recollection of sliced skin and flowing blood. Only now she realized what she had been privy to was not a dream, but a cogent recollection of a real event.

I'll give you clear-cut proof of my sincerity, the woman was saying to Sully while she savagely cut into his wrist with a blade. *Ciar*, Sully had called the woman. Ciar. Adara remembered him staggering back, his blood dripping onto the leaves.

"Oh, Sully, why?" Adara cried, as the memory unfolded.

Denounce Adara. Send her away. Tell her you do not now, nor will ever, love her, Ciar had demanded of him.

The look of torment on Sully's exhausted face was as obvious as the morning light. Adara wanted to run to him then, but was petrified of the sinister woman.

When Adara opened her eyes the woods were hushed, save for her own voice speaking calmly. "You love Gillean."

The flecks of crushed leaf fell from her hand, blood clinging to her palm. She groped around for the diamond she had dropped in her distress. Locating it by its sheen, she scooped it up and placed it in her pocket. She looked once more to the awning of trees, where she noticed a curl of copper hair trailing in the wind. A little girl whispered the words, *Be a dancer!*

Adara ran to her car. The tires kicked up a massive cloud of dirt as she shifted into reverse and headed back towards Charlie's cottage.

Everything was made known to her now. It was as if someone had handed her a key to a door deep within the tunnels of the *Teach na Spioradi*, a door to a room where all that connected Gillean and Sully was stored. Love had unlocked it. The burdensome contents contained within tumbled forth.

Potcheen drowsed peacefully in Sully's lap. Man and dog slept in the rocker by the stove. Sully woke to the sound of Adara removing her mud-caked shoes by the door. Walking on the tips of her toes, she knelt beside him. He silently regarded her as she reached out and took his left hand into hers. Pushing back the sleeve, she saw tiny droplets of blood had stained the white cuff. His wrist bore a scar about three inches long; the proof of Ciar's demand of a blood promise to secure the safety of the Faraday family.

Her attitude was one of pity. "You wanted to save us."

He believed he was hallucinating. "You came back?"

"Am I so easily rid of?"

"What are ya doin' here?" His voice was raspy with sleep and spent emotion.

"I know what happened between you and Ciar this morning."

Sully sat up. Potcheen resettled himself under the table while Adara waited for Sully's reply.

Sully stared at the woman he'd so cruelly sent away only hours before. "How could you know about her?" he asked.

She traced her finger over his scar. "Would you believe I remembered what I saw and heard earlier with the help of some fey?"

He sighed. "Then you know how I feel about Gillean."

"Yes. I suspect he feels the same for you but is too afraid to admit it."

He wanted to put his scarred hand to her cheek. He wanted some way to show his contrition for having hurt her. "I'm sorry I lied to you. I'm so sorry."

"You had your reasons. It's like you said, there are forces greater than you and I, forces of good and evil."

"Which am I?"

"I don't hate you, if that's what you're asking."

"I wouldn't blame you if ya did." He got to his feet. "I'd like to tell ya the whole truth."

"It doesn't much matter now."

"Adara, *please*."

She rose to face him. "Why?" Her eyes disclosed a strength he had not seen before. "Are you so troubled about Gillean? The sum of your sins is that you are guilty of loving him. What power could punish you for that?"

"My sins are much greater than simply loving someone. Maybe I should be punished. I do know that punishment is administered by Ciar. And she has no love in her. She almost killed Gillean." He intended to give her the full story, hoping his offering would bring her some comfort.

"What do you mean she almost killed Gillean?"

"That is how I burned my hands—trying to save him from her. I made a deal with Ciar then as well. It prevents Gillean from remembering me. He isn't purposefully denying me as you said. He had no control over any of it. She demanded it to be so in order for him to live."

The light of growing comprehension grew in Adara's eyes. "That's why you are no longer a supernatural being, but a human—because you wanted to save Gillean. Is that the bridge you weren't supposed to cross?"

"I wasn't supposed to let any of this happen. Cross a bridge, ya say?" He laughed bitterly. "Well hell, I blasted it to bits."

"Right, and now you're going to tell me that Gillean had no control over being with her in the first place. She held a gun to his head, did she?" Adara repeated the story revealed to her—that of Gillean, Sully's other half. "You care for Gillean. You two are connected in spirit. But I know Gillean Faraday—the man—better than anyone. I'll bet my own soul that he gave himself to Ciar because he is a coward."

He said nothing, remembering the unadulterated anger, not the unconditional love of an angel he had felt upon finding Gillean all too ready to give himself to Ciar.

Adara persisted. "Why are you determined to view the situation in terms of what *you* did wrong, what *you* could have prevented? Don't you get it? She pursued Gillean because she has knowledge of his precise nature, and yours." She touched his chest. "Ciar read me like a book as well."

"You're not to blame for any of this," he asserted.

"Why did you come to my home? Did you simply want to be near Gillean through me?"

"*No!* I thought it was fate. I didn't..." He sat at the table feeling useless and tired. "I was such a fool. When I saw you, I thought I could make a difference." He laughed at his naiveté. "I sure as hell made a significant difference, didn't I?"

"What did you see when you looked at me?"

"I saw the power you possess. Underneath the years of snow and ash, I saw roses. I wanted you to see them too. I care for you, Adara, that won't change, but ya don't know Ciar as I do. I did what I thought was right. I wish to God you could believe that it was not my intention to deceive you for my benefit."

"You did help me. I found something of value underneath the ashes." Her voice held no resentment. "You should go to Gillean and speak with him. Make sure he grasps the consequences of the choices he has made. Maybe now he'll be ready to hear you, as I have."

Sully lowered his head. "I cannot break my word. It would mean chaos for your family. Gillean will have to find his own way. I hope he does so with as much grace as you found yours."

"To hell with grace!" She pulled out the chair next to him and leaned into the table. "Ciar won't be demanding a damn thing of anyone any more. Her power feeds off the vulnerability of others. It's very clear what she is about and how she operates. I have the advantage because of you. She won't have the chance to even breathe the same air as my children." Her stance was that of a lioness protecting her cubs. "We'll manage just fine."

"No, Adara—"

"*We'll manage just fine.*"

"Can you forgive me?"

"I believe you did what you thought was right." Her fingers rested briefly on his wrist. "Give me some time to accept that is what 'tis."

"**W**atch over them, I beg you," he asked of the boundless sky, as Adara drove away.

Surely the mother of such infinite beauty would identify with a woman wanting only to keep her children safe. The silky white clouds were the pillows on which the stars, the children of the heavens, could rest protected from harm. Nature's predictable rhythm gave him some sense of hope. He tried to reconcile the sad corner of his spirit where an image of Gillean kicked about like a restless child.

He headed back into the cabin, wishing for Charlie and his homespun guidance. Adara informed Sully he would be able to catch up with Gillean on the second night of his tour of Cork. Gillean was set to play the next two nights at The Stars and Ploughshares Theatre.

Sully was grateful for her generosity, but he would no longer defy "the Powers that be." He had hurt enough people for a thousand lifetimes.

Chapter Twenty-Five

See Me

No sooner had Gillean stepped from the private plane into the airport catering to Ireland's elite, than his mobile rang. He thought it would be Adara, since he had just left a message on their answering machine saying he would be home within the hour. He'd thought it odd that nobody had picked up at his prodding while he spoke. "Oh well," he'd concluded his message. "Perhaps my family is out having a good time without the old man. I look forward to seeing you, my dears."

He answered the mobile with lifted spirits.

The voice of his irate manager, Noel, shattered Gillean's hopeful mood. "Did you forget about the show you have tonight in Cork?"

Gillean held the phone away from his ear, taking deep breaths before speaking. "Noooo..." he said, drawing out the response. "But I would like to spend some time with my family before the show if that meets with your approval."

"That's a load of tosh!" Noel snapped. "Your family is scattered in the wind. Don't pretend you know what's going on in your home. It's me, Noel. I've known you for fifteen years. And you will get your little musical ass to Cork, even if I have to drag you there myself."

"What do you mean my family is scattered?" Gillean slowed his mad pace and found a quiet corner of the airport to continue the conversation.

"I'm told that your wife has been gone for two days. Mags and Jos have been carting your children round to their activities. You're not needed."

"Where is Adara?" Gillean couldn't decide if it was apprehension or anger he felt.

"Apparently only Arlen knows the answer, and he's not offering up the information. Protecting his mother is of the utmost importance."

"Protecting his mother from whom? *Me*?" Gillean barked. "I wasn't aware my family was at war with one another."

"You aren't aware of much, old boy. But then again, how could you be when you've got your head buried in the jubblies of that artist?"

"Fuck you, Noel!"

"Fine, I'll arrange for that, right after I get you to Cork. I've got a car and driver waiting outside the airport. Don't even think about running. You're Gillean Faraday. You can't disappoint your fans. I'm here to make sure of that. You'll thank me in the morning."

Gillean abruptly hung up, knowing full well there was no escaping Noel. He would have to go to Cork and play—play his music and play the part of the charming, happy-go-lucky Irish bard. The thought made his stomach turn. Adara was gone and his own son was protecting his wife's secret. How had he lost the unity of his family?

Noel's words pricked at him. He hadn't lost it, he had driven away each of them—Adara, Arlen, even his wee ones—by his own selfishness. They were all wiser now, not so willing to believe their da and provider possessed the magic to make the bad things disappear. They had pulled down the curtain, seeing him for who he was—a man with more vices than virtues. But he loved them. Could they see that too? Or did they simply see a lying, desperate stranger, one who had broken faith too many times?

Following his manager's demand, Gillean allowed himself to be driven to Cork, arriving a little over two hours prior to show time. He dismissed the driver, giving him the best gratuity of his life. He did not want to be bound by anyone else waiting on him. He was promptly ushered into the dressing room by the domineering Noel, whose goal it seemed was to push Gillean nearer to a total breakdown.

"Look." Noel put his hands firmly on Gillean's shoulders. "All you have to do is get through tonight, okay? I'll do my best to help you sort out things with your family."

"My family is none of your business, Noel," Gillean retorted, irritably turning away from him.

Gillean and Noel had been through the muck and the glory over the years. Noel was known as "the gardener." He nurtured the potential in burgeoning musicians.

"Remain cool, babe," Gillean's manager reassured him in his glam rock lingo. "You're my glitter man." Noel left Gillean to prepare for his sound check.

Gillean stared into the mirror encircled with white lights. The illuminated bulbs shone on the purple circles under his eyes and his depleted expression, revealing a man who had aged ten years in the span of a few months. He had seen this face before, had come to view himself in the cold, hard light of reality—but when? Where? The distant whistle of a train issued a long, lonely call inside his head. The sound had always brought him comfort. The drawn-out, distinct wail conjured up images of faraway, unexplored places. The echo faded, but the loneliness intensified. He feared the unexplored places of his guarded heart.

Ciar's flawless face came to mind, shielded by the temporary armor of youth; she looked upon him as an artist, able to turn a blind eye to his age, his shortcomings and his marriage. But she demanded so much in return—too much. His wife had loved him in a different way. Her body had gone through hell to bless him four times with children. Gillean hung his head in disgrace, remembering how he had walked out on Adara. He hadn't even bothered to sit and talk with his children to explain why he was vacating their home. He'd loaded it onto Adara's frail shoulders. No doubt she was ready to rid herself of her unreliable, self-centered husband. Was it for this unknown man, Sully?

A knock at the door ended his musings.

"Can't you give me at least five minutes alone, Noel?" Gillean called out.

She let herself in, striding up to him with confidence and kissing him full on the mouth. "Hello, darling, isn't Ireland lovely this time of year?"

He tripped over the carpet to get away from her. "I thought I explained that you and I are finished. You can't be so desperate as to make a fool of yourself over me."

The emptiness of human feeling in her expression turned his blood cold.

"You're the only fool here, little Gilly." She nonchalantly fingered a flower arrangement from an adoring fan. "All those people who come to see you, to hear you. They have no clue as to who you are. They think of you as a prophet."

"Ciar, please…" He raised a protesting hand to cut her off.

She pulled the flower from a red rose, leaving the headless stem in the vase. "He loves you…" She began to tear the petals one by one, dropping them to the floor. "He loves you, not!" She ripped several petals and tossed them in his direction. "Sully…" She came towards him. "…loves…" She pinned him against the wall. "…Adara!"

Gillean's head swam. Despite his current assessment that Ciar was only out for herself and not to be trusted, he didn't disagree with what she asserted about his wife. It was fitting that the universe should confirm his suspicions through the words of such a dark-hearted messenger.

"Senseless little Gilly, you don't even know who the man is—what he meant to you; a younger, virile man who has taken your wife to his bed and won the trust of your precious son."

She pressed her body against his, forcing his back into the unyielding bricks. "You haven't been able to reach her, have you? That's because she is with him, making love to him." Her eyes were empty hollows shining with the pleasure of his misery. I'll bet they are horizontal as we speak." He pushed at her, meaning to assert his full autonomy and evade the darkness she represented. "For the last time, I'll ask you to leave me alone."

She backed away. "Or what?"

"Or I will be forced to do whatever I have to in order to ensure that you will not invade my life ever again."

He was invulnerable to her extraordinary figure wrapped in an elegant, low-cut red dress. His attention was for the mangled flower petals her fingers had so callously crushed: an offering from a well-meaning stranger, destroyed by a heartless woman. He was on the verge of a sea change. The words of the great Bard brought comfort.

Full fathom five thy father lies, of his bones are coral made. Those are pearls that were his eyes. Gillean was approaching a turn of the helm. He could either steer it with great care or take his hands from the wheel and continue towards a breach. *Nothing of him that doth fade, but doth suffer a sea change, into something rich and strange.*

"Please leave." He addressed Ciar. "I was wrong to think I cared for you." He bent down to retrieve the petals as she looked on, open-mouthed. "I was wrong about a lot of things." He stroked the soft edges of the ruined flower. "And if my wife is being loved by another man, I cannot fault her. She deserved better than a husband who demanded she be someone she was not. Perhaps you're right. Perhaps she is happy with him." He closed his hand around the petals. "I hope so."

"Sully is no better a man than you. Worse even, because he knew exactly what he was doing and who he was betraying."

She held him in a long stare. Her eyes had the power to touch him like fingertips to his naked body. "You will remember my words soon enough. You won't feel as generous towards your wife knowing what she has done. As for me, I leave you to your own destruction. There will be plenty of people interested in spending time with me, and the story of my time with you."

She stroked his cheek with false affection. "Think of the fodder I can feed the hungry media about what I know of your wife and her pubescent lover. I will be much more in demand without you."

She was at the door, grinning.

He spoke almost as an afterthought. "I am thankful to you for one thing, Ciar."

"Oh?"

"I've accepted that I have been a selfish, self-serving bastard, most likely from the day I was born."

"Aren't all humans?"

"No, in fact John Locke theorized humans are born tabula rasa. A bla—".

"A blank slate," she finished his thought. "Apparently, you theorize that I'm not very astute."

"I believe you haven't had the same honor as I've had: to be in the company of humans who are born open to every possibility and make the choice to be selfless."

"You mean self-actualized," she sneered, "according to Abraham Maslow."

"You've just proven my point," he said, turning away. "You make me ashamed of myself."

He had given her pause. "This is why you are grateful to me?"

"Partly. Also, I can console myself with the fact that I am desperate to make amends. You have no clue how evil you are, and you don't care much for self-reflection."

"I suppose that makes you the bigger man, as it were."

"Wiser. There's a difference."

"I'll watch your demise from a respectful distance," she predicted, slamming the door as she exited.

His eyes focused on her high-heeled shoes. For one brief moment the sound of the train whistle, combined with a memory, dropped into his mind as softly as a leaf. He was twenty, sitting on his bed at the *Teach na Spioradi*, watching an older, cultured French woman's pink stiletto heels clicking on the floorboards of his room. She was gathering her things in a huff, upset with him because he had declared the end of their affair. He was promised to another woman, Adara. The last thing he recalled was the Parisian's saffron hair as she slammed the door behind her.

A black thorn has pierced your heart, but I am the mate of your soul. Look for my eyes, and become whole. The cryptic words uttered in Irish, the unremitting whistle, and the memory of a sphinxlike woman circled Gillean's cloudy consciousness like a ring of smoke. He shook uncontrollably. He looked around, but there was no alcohol in the room to steady his nerves, only bunches of flowers, boxes of chocolates, and various trinkets of appreciation. Where was the wine, for Christ's sake? Some smitten fan always gifted a bottle of the finest.

Tottering on unsteady legs, Gillean tripped over a guitar standing by the door. He was due for his sound check. Noel would be coming to cart him off shortly. Gillean reached for the instrument, thinking a song might be just what he needed. *Don't forget this.* It was a memory: the whisper of a little girl, but it was not his daughter's voice. *It has always taken you where you need to be.*

The whistle in his head grew louder and more haunting. Bells clanged like a train lumbering into a station. He stumbled back onto a small red couch and examined the mirror closely. His eyes teared; palming one eye, then the other, he gazed back into the glass transforming into a train window. Slowly two faces emerged: a wee girl, her red hair in braids, and a young man with fervid green eyes. The haunting pair observed him from the other side of the window, but their ghostly quality made it seem as if they were on the other side of a nether world. Gillean's heart wrenched, an entity was trying to break free from the layers of lies he had buried over the years. Whoever these two phantoms were, they could see right into his soul.

He gripped onto the guitar's neck like a vice, the steel strings biting into his fingers. When he looked at the window again, it had reverted back to a stage mirror. The faces, noises and memories were gone.

Gillean's life was chaos, the havoc created by his carelessness. He was losing everything and there wasn't a damn thing he could do to stop it. Not even the much- adored Gillean Faraday could salvage the disintegrating composition which took the bulk of his years to create. His father had spent a lifetime sifting through the lives of others with the absolute certainty his work was crucial. Gillean had only ever wanted his father to lavish him with as much attention and devotion as he did those old, dirty bones and artifacts. He spent his entire life hopelessly searching for that acceptance. And now came the truth, piping hot like a cup of black coffee poured down his throat, burning with irony. Arlen wanted the same from his father. But Gillean had been too busy listening to the music in his head to hear his son's plea.

"Damn you!" He raised the guitar over his head and slammed it to the floor. "God damn you!"

He choked out the protest from his ragged throat as he continued to smash the instrument against the walls, sending flowers from their vases scattering into the air, the chunks of glass pulverized by his step. Splinters of wood flew out like embers around him. The room filled with the awful sounds of his banshee wail, the popping of guitar strings and the smashing of wood.

With waning energy, Gillean inspected the remaining piece of ruined guitar in his hand, a severed string lolling from it like a tongue. He threw the last piece of what was once his treasure against the door.

"Here's to you, Gillean Faraday! Bravo!" he cried, falling back against the velvet couch weeping.

"What the...?" Noel rushed in, looking incredulous at the devastation and the crumpled remains of his friend on the couch.

"Get out, Noel." Gillean continued to sob quietly.

"Gillean, talk to me."

"Please, get out." He was utterly defeated.

"Jesus, Gill," Noel mumbled. He hesitantly backed out of the ravaged room. "I'll be with you shortly. I'll need to see about rescheduling the show."

Chapter Twenty-Six

An Angel's Coat

Elsewhere in the grandiose hall, Charlie nervously paced about the lobby. He looked as out of place awaiting the commencement of a Gillean Faraday concert as a fisherman tilling the land. He chuckled, amazed at his own bravado in not only finding where the show would be, but also his resourcefulness in renting a car for transport. Granted, the motor car was an older model from a less-than-reputable dealer, and one that any reasonable person would have haggled over regarding the cost. But Charlie was proud of himself nonetheless.

He'd procured transportation and a ticket for the show at short notice. Decades had passed since he'd left the secure confines of his little village, but it had also been decades since he'd met the likes of Sully. Charlie welcomed the challenge. He'd gone through the necessary motions like many of the humans who were seated in the theatre. To them, this was an opportunity to escape their individual realities within the music. But for Charlie, it was the chance to prove to himself that he possessed the courage to tempt fate in order to save another.

Because his mission was self-imposed, certain facts that the Powers deemed necessary were kept from him. Charlie's success depended upon getting to Gillean unimpeded, and, the Powers willing, deliver Gillean to Sully. This, Charlie believed, was the only hope of helping his charge. Sully was like a mountain, stoic and unmoving in his convictions. Charlie took stock in Francis Bacon's proclamation, deciding to bring Mohammed to the mountain.

Leaving their seats, a group of people trickled out into the lobby, joining Charlie in his anxious waiting. He heard fragments of conversations as several members of the audience paced about the lobby, clearly irritated by the delay. Charlie sweated in his overcoat. He was about to remove the garment when he heard a voice over the loudspeaker. The announcement came first in English, then in Irish.

"Ladies and gentlemen, we regret to inform you that this evening's performance has been cancelled. Mr. Faraday sends his deepest apologies. He is too ill to perform. Please retain your tickets. The concert will be rescheduled as soon as possible. Those who prefer a refund will have the opportunity to do so. Again, Mr. Faraday and his management are extremely sorry for any inconvenience. Please exit the theatre in a timely and orderly fashion. Thank you."

An older woman attired in a sequined evening gown, toting a bottle of champagne in one arm and a large bouquet of roses in the other, turned to her younger companion with a ridiculous fur cape draped around her neck. To Charlie, they looked more like burlesque performers than concertgoers.

"I cannot believe, can you?" the elder quipped in an Italian accent. "I spend much money, follow him my entire holiday, and he do this—cancel a show at the last momento?" She scanned the lobby filled with disappointed guests. "And where is Max for God sake? The man is a useless arm!" She turned back to her fur-clad friend. "I wish to give Mr. Faraday una piece of my mind. Then sarà malato!"

Charlie knew little about Gillean Faraday. So far, he had learned two things: Gillean was the less-than-devoted husband of Adara, and had been responsible for Sully entering into a terrible pact with an instrument of darkness. Such scant evidence cast Gillean in a dubious light. Still, standing among so many demanding and unreasonable 'fans', Charlie pitied Gillean. Charlie had enough sympathy to imagine that year after year, this kind of life became a slog. It would take a toll on any reasonable person.

This was another first for Charlie as he offered his unsolicited advice to the disgruntled woman. "Maybe ya should focus more of yer time on the people who are real to ya, rather than some fantasy of a man who owes ya nothin'."

"Scusa?" she asked indignantly.

"The young folks call it a reality check. Life is more than one singer with a guitar. And I suppose whoever Max is, he would agree, so get to livin' a real life while ya have the chance."

Charlie left the mortified woman to see if he could sneak his way into Gillean's dressing room. He had a hunch the musician would still be in the building, waiting for everyone else to leave.

The confusion and crowding of concertgoers was enough to keep the security workers' attentions diverted. The ease of slipping behind stage was a relief to Charlie. He walked down a dimly lit corridor, feeling sure that Gillean was in one of the rooms, the only quiet space in the venue. Spotting a door with a small gold star, Charlie trusted that providence worked in his favor. He prayed it was a good sign that he was able to locate Gillean without much trouble.

Hearing no sounds from the other side of the door, he knocked softly. There was no response. He pressed his hand a little harder. "Mr. Faraday?" After his third attempt at calling after the singer, Charlie tried the door. As he suspected, it was locked.

"Well, I hope it's not against the rules to use me physical powers."

He shoved his imposing frame against the door. It took little effort to tear it from its hinges. He stumbled into the darkness of the room; a nightlight from the adjoining lavatory cast a meager glow, but enough for Charlie to see a man lift his head wearily from a couch.

"Who the hell are you?" His tone was angry, but his voice weak.

Charlie propped the door back against the frame. "I'm sorry to impose, Mr. Faraday, but I believe I can help ya."

"Help me?" Gillean regarded Charlie but showed no signs of fear. "Would that be by breaking into my private dressing room, or by demolishing the venue's property?"

"Ah, well now…" Charlie timidly walked to the center of the room, his boots tramping across wooden shards…and something else. He wondered if he had done so much damage to the door. When he knelt to examine what was underfoot, he found the remains of a shattered guitar, the strings stripped from the body of the smashed instrument.

"Looks as if ya have done a good job of demolishin' as well. Why did ya do it?"

"Because it was there." Gillean lay back down, placing a wet cloth over his head.

"Like a mountain."

"Precisely."

"You aren't makin' much of an effort to get rid of me." Charlie came closer. Gillean's sadness clung to the very walls of the room.

"Should I?"

"You don't seem to care much about anythin'."

Charlie eyed the surroundings, taking in the shredded bouquets, headless stuffed animals, and crushed boxes of chocolates strewn about.

Gillean lay like an injured man in hospital—a causality of war. Although it was a battle of the musician's declaration, Charlie's heart went out to the man. Gillean appeared broken, like Sully when he'd first arrived. The two men decidedly had much in common. How was it they were enemies? Charlie wondered.

"Take what you want, then please go." Gillean's voice was barely audible.

Charlie said nothing.

"Is it an autograph you're after?" Gillean sat up slightly. "Alright, bring me pen and paper."

"No. I don't want anythin' from ya." Charlie searched for the words to convince the man of his desire to help.

"That's impossible. People always want something from me."

"I know of one man who only wanted to love ya. In fact, he gave up everythin' to do so."

"I see. You're some kind of Jesus freak. Worried I haven't accepted Him as my personal savior? Well, you're a little late. I'd ask you to leave your literature at the door, but seeing as you obliterated it—"

Charlie laughed a big hearty sound that filled the room. "Fair enough! But I wasn't referrin' to Jesus, but to someone a little less divine, someone ya had a friendship with. Someone a lot like yerself, I would say."

"I have no such friends. No one would give up everything for me. If they did, they would end up resenting me for it."

"Friendship and love are two-way streets, I'm afraid." Charlie didn't bother to ask, but sat on a chair next to Gillean. "In fact, so is war. Ya should know that though. I believe ya have sung about all three."

Gillean removed the cloth from his head. "How so?"

"In order for peace to exist, one man has to lay down his arms. It can only work if the other is willin' to do the same. And a person has to be ready to open up his arms for love and friendship to happen. If not, someone gets hurt."

"A wise observation. What did you say your name was?"

"Oh, excuse me ignorance. I'm Charlie, Mr. Faraday." He held out his chafed hand.

"Pleasure, Charlie." Gillean returned the gesture with a weak handshake. "And I'm Gillean. Mr. Faraday, my father, has been dead for years."

"And yet—" Charlie thought better of voicing his thought.

"What?"

"'Tis nothin'." Sitting next to the desolate man, Charlie's sense of purpose grew. He was beginning to understand why the singer had been so important to Sully. "I meant to say that most people wantin' to be famous usually change their names—ya know, try to create an

BLACKTHORNS OF THE FORGOTTEN

image for themselves. But ya kept yer father's name. Must be important to ya, part of who ya are."

Gillean's laugh was one of mockery. "My father knew nothing of little Gilberto, nothing of me."

"And who might little Gilberto be?" Charlie asked with a sympathetic smile.

"Damned if I know. It's all a bloody mystery to me."

Charlie hesitated but decided to take what seemed to be the perfect opportunity to explain his presence. "Just like Sully, eh?"

Gillean sprang up from the couch. "How do you know Sully? Did he send you? Where is he? With my wife...with Adara?"

"Easy now." Charlie reached over to steady the overexcited man. "Ya don't remember him, do ya?"

"How can I remember a man I never met?" Gillean posited. "Is everyone trying to drive me mad?"

"Thisa way, signores! I hear him!"

The two men were startled by the woman's call from the other side of the broken door.

"Now look what you've done," Gillean lowered his voice. "They'll descend like a pack of hungry vultures. Thanks ever so much."

Charlie towered over the irate singer. "The hell they will. Get up!"

"What?"

"I said get up, *Gilberto*."

There was no time to consider the options. Gillean obeyed.

"Now, ya just stay with me and don't say a word. Agreed?" Charlie put his coat around Gillean. The massive garment enveloped the singer, allowing only his feet to protrude from the bottom edge.

"Do I have a choice?" he protested, his voice muffled by the thick material.

"If ya want safely out of here, I'm afraid yer stuck with me, lad. Let's get a move on."

Charlie led Gillean to the door, holding him tight, like a child he didn't want to lose.

Charlie successfully navigated the clutching crowd and whisked the fugitive performer into the back of the rented car. Gillean sat in dazed silence as Charlie worked furiously to master the clutch and gear lever for the open road.

"The devil take this piece of machinery!" Charlie cursed, as the gears ground and his ill-practiced footwork sent the car into a series of quick jerks.

Gillean spoke in monotone. "Where are you taking me?"

233

"Beg yer pardon? Ah blast! I'm sorry, it's been a while since I drove an auto and…" Charlie viewed Gillean through the rear mirror; his mussed hair and pale face gave him the look of someone who'd seen a ghost. "Are ya quite alright now?"

"Where are we going?"

"I'm takin' ya to the Vale, to Sully. Maybe then, Gilberto, you will be able to open up your arms."

Making the drive back to the Vale, Charlie concentrated on both onerous roads before him—the physical one, and the even more difficult path of thoroughly explaining his identity to Gillean. The angel revealed all but one piece of information to the incredulous musician. He shared what he knew about himself, Sully and Ciar. He then made a snap decision as the road rose up to meet him, not peaceably as in the Old Irish blessing, but as a twisting path needing to be routed with the greatest of care. He believed it prudent to allow Sully and Adara the chance to explain to Gillean whatever they had come to decide for themselves.

Charlie was more apprehensive than his mellowed passenger, who accepted the jarring car ride to the one place he had resolved not to step foot. This was the single piece of information Gillean shared during the journey.

Gillean caught Charlie's eyes in the rear-view mirror. "Please explain something to me."

"I will if I can."

"You said this Sully was an angel, like you, but Ciar told me he has been with my wife as a man. Is this true?"

Charlie redirected his eyes to the road.

"Charlie?" Gillean leaned forward tapping the man's shoulder.

Charlie cleared his throat and offered an answer. "'Tis true. Sully was once an angel, but he is now a human—a man like you. How he came about his present state of existence is for himself to explain. But I will tell ya that he is as good a man as you would find in field or city. Considerin' the nature of Ciar, I wouldn't place much stock in what she said."

Gillean stayed over Charlie's shoulder, growing more agitated the further they drove.

The elder angel reached around to pat Gillean's hand. "Rest easy, Gillean. We're almost there. I trust Sully should have the answers to yer questions."

Chapter Twenty-Seven

The Vale

"**D**on't just stand there with yer teeth in yer mouth, lad," Charlie nudged a dumbfounded Sully who had risen nervously from the step upon seeing a strange car pulling up to the cottage and depositing Gillean Faraday.

"I got him here; the rest is up to you." Charlie advised the men. "Take yer time to talk. I imagine ya both have a lot to say to one another."

Sully's apprehensive eyes followed Charlie as he entered the cottage and shut the door without another word. He was taken aback by the sudden impact of the voice he'd grown to simultaneously love and despise.

"Is Adara here?"

"She's gone."

"Gone? As in—"

Sully wanted no more misunderstandings. It was too easy to get lost in what was not said, but assumed. "As in she's home with your children, waiting for you."

Gillean closed the gap between the two. "What was it you said to me?" He shook as if a winter wind cut through to his bones.

"I said Adara is home with—"

"No!" Gillean was on the verge of shouting. "What did you *say* to me?" Sinking to the ground, he reached out to Sully.

Sully intuitively placed his arms around Gillean's shoulders, trying to hold him steady. His trembling hand rested on Sully's scruffy cheek as his eyes probed Sully's.

Gillean's pain was like a thousand lashes of leather against Sully's skin. He understood the question and translated the Gaelic phrase he once hoped would free Gillean's entrapped heart. "I said, a blackthorn has pierced your heart, but I am the mate of your soul. Look for my eyes and become whole."

Gillean rose to his feet. "You are my soulmate, aren't you?"

Sully looked away.

"Is it Adara?" Gillean powered up from the ground. "Are you in love with her?"

"You haven't changed, have you?" Sully didn't have the energy to be angry, although the question from Gillean offended. "After everything, you're…"

"I'm what?" Gillean prodded.

"You're here with me when you should be with Adara—"

"You don't honestly believe that." Gillean dared Sully with his eyes. "Both Adara and I are changed people. You more than anyone should know that."

Sully waved a dismissive hand. "Leave it out."

"I can't." Gillean spoke softly. "I sent you away in anger, but nonetheless you stopped her…" He inhaled, then slowly released his breath. "You stopped Ciar. You saved my life."

"You remember? She swore it wasn't possible!"

"You believed it was." Gillean smiled warmly. "I wasn't certain until Charlie. Yet I felt you with me even if I didn't have a clear memory of you. But, as soon as I saw you walk towards the car…" Gillean placed a hand over his chest. "It confirmed what my heart would never forget, even though my head needs a thorough examination."

"It wasn't your head misleading you, but Ciar."

"I know that now. But I provided her that power because I was weak."

Sully rubbed the scar on his wrist. "Are ya still with her?"

Gillean chortled. "I left her before Charlie arrived and explained her true nature, and about the pair of you."

Sully didn't understand the connection. "The pair of who?"

"You and Charlie are both angels—well, you once were, and he still is."

"Charlie is an angel?" Sully staggered back at this unexpected revelation. *"Son of a bitch!"*

It was in the mixture of mourning and love reflected in Gillean's gentle chuckle that Sully identified the delicate balance of his situation. He loved this man, but he would never again try to influence Gillean's decisions. Sully averted Gillean's stare. "You felt ya had reason enough to send me away."

Gillean's cheeks flushed. "I took the easy way out. It was a coward's choice."

Charlie had taken to setting a tallow candle in the front window of the cottage every night that Sully had been with him; the realization that he and the old man shared something all the more unique that he hadn't seen until tonight imbued the flickering flame with additional significance.

"Gillean, I don't require an explanation from you. If you have truly seen Ciar for who she is, then the whole lot was worth the price."

"But I need..." Gillean corrected himself. "I would be grateful if you would give me time to speak with you."

Sully nodded, even though he was not certain he wanted to hear more. He could retreat into the cottage with Charlie where there was a better chance Sully's world would be put to rights.

"Come." Sully motioned for Gillean to follow. "Let's walk."

Sully led them further into the woods. The reed and sedge warblers brought comfort with their wonted night songs. Gillean followed a slight step behind, saying nothing for several moments. Eventually, he spoke in a quiet voice to which Sully was not accustomed.

"My grandfather said that everything a man needs to know he can find by reading the stars." He motioned with his hand to the sky, as if in greeting to his beloved relative. "I believe that. But Granddad failed to tell me it's just as important to pay attention to the words in a person's eyes. They show what is in the heart."

Sully continued walking.

"Adara's eyes hold a different look than yours," Gillean called out. "I didn't see it before. How could I not have seen what she was trying to tell me?" Gillean slowed under a Yew tree. "I see now she was telling me goodbye."

A strange moon shone a purplish tone on the gray of the Yew leaves, the distinctive color of Adara's eyes. Sully's hands slid into his pockets so that Gillean would not notice their shaking.

Both men proceeded towards the juncture where the two lakes met.

"Funny thing is," Gillean continued in his ruminations, bending down to pick up a fallen tree branch and using it as a walking stick, "I thought I was the one who was leaving her."

Sully stopped. "You did leave her, Gillean."

"Yes, but I thought it was because of Ciar."

Sully fought the urge to turn around.

"I've been avoiding what I saw in your eyes that night in my study. It scared the hell out of me."

Sully wanted the truth—Gillean's truth, as if it was a riverstone he could slip into his pocket, gliding his fingers over its smooth surface whenever he needed. "Why?"

Gillean grinned and settled with a slight groan onto a knotty log nestled in the ground, and pointed to the moon. "Apollo 8. I did some reading on the subject." He traced circular patterns in the dirt with his stick and took up his account. "December 21, 1968, the first time earthlings orbited a celestial body. The dark side of the moon…quite an amazing happening. Did you know that was not the astronauts' intended destination? They made the trip by default. Their original mission was to test a piece of equipment, but it wasn't ready."

"You think this is news to me?"

"Sully," Gillean extended his arm. "Come here to me."

Sully kicked at the dirt. He strategically lowered himself next to Gillean on the log, saying nothing more. It was his cue for Gillean to continue.

"Those men could see the Earth in a way that no one else had. Our planet was a meager blue sphere hung in a sprawling galaxy. But they weren't afraid of what they saw." Gillean kept his eyes fixed on Sully. "They saw more than our limitations. They observed that we are one, complete entity, not simply the many, little spaces we carve out for ourselves and believe to be so bloody important."

Sully pivoted to face Gillean. "What are you telling me?"

Gillean's eyes sparked the same fire as the night Sully and he squared off in the study. His fingers caressed Sully's face with unspoken devotion. "You made me see, Sully. I spent my whole life out there on some misguided quest." He angled his head towards the sky. "It wasn't until I really looked into your eyes that I saw not only my long ago self, but who I could be with you. I found my home."

"But Adara…" Sully's eyes glistened with tears. "You love her."

"I do love her," Gillean confirmed. "But not in the way she deserves." He paused long enough for them to hear the whistle-song of a lone nightingale. "He's a little bird with a loud voice." Gillean remarked. "That was me when I met and married Adara. I had no faith in myself. My father was forever disappointed in me." Gillean flung the tree branch. "He understood books and ancient bones and working for respect. He was ashamed to have a songbird for a son."

Sully brushed away the tears on his cheek, "How terrible for you."

Gillean shook his head. "I made it terrible for Adara. My being twenty-two, I sought adoration and called it love. How could she possibly be expected to…we didn't have a chance to rightly appreciate one another, let alone love properly."

"I believe with time she can forgive you."

"I hope so." Gillean grabbed hold of Sully's hands. "I'm fully aware that in any universe I do not deserve to find the love of my life when I have orchestrated such havoc."

Sully's heart spilled over with love and pain. Being human was like running naked into the rush of the ocean, the ecstasy of the white-blue waves crashing against the mortal body, and the incessant threat of being pulled under by the very thing that brought such rapture.

Examining the unguarded, dark eyes upon him, Sully asked, "You're not afraid—of this place...of me?"

Gillean reached down, pressing their joined hands into the dirt. "Look at this natural beauty." He held a crimson fistful towards Sully. "Incredible red earth, right underneath our feet."

Sully chuckled, "'Tis only the copper."

"And yet, here we are, in this place, at this time in this entire vast universe." Gillean's thumb traced a streak of the soft earth onto Sully's forehead, an anointment of love. He pressed his face to Sully's and whispered, "This site is intended for two entities to intersect and merge into one another."

"Is that what we are, Gillean?" Sully bit his lip against the kiss he eagerly wanted to offer.

Gillean's hands laced through Sully's hair, the damp, red earth blending with black curls. "We are so much more." Gillean's lips tentatively sought Sully's. "We are soulmates."

The words stirred an entirely new feeling deep in Sully's core. A bridge was collapsing inside. He hungrily returned Gillean's kiss. The more intensely they explored, the more Sully wanted to free fall.

"I recognize your heart, Sully," Gillean breathed. "You have mine, always." He confirmed his commitment with kisses as resonate and pure as the water that surrounded them. Kisses tasting of honesty, the pungent earth, stars, and love.

Gillean leaned against the borrowed car which had been entrusted to his care with Charlie's great relief.

"Take all the time ya need with your family," Sully insisted.

"Are you sure you won't come too?" Gillean physically ached at the thought of leaving. The creative dam inside his head had burst. Music and lyrics came rushing forth. They were songs of love, gratitude and passion. "It would be wonderful to have you with me."

Sully shook his head but couldn't conceal a grin. The past three days had passed in a haze of warmth and happiness, as if he and Gillean were wrapped up in a Luna moth's cocoon. They shared impassioned kisses, loving embraces, holding one another as they talked and laughed into the wee hours of the morning. Both men agreed not to give themselves fully until Gillean could speak with Adara. "You have to go this one, but *only* this one, alone."

"I suppose I do," Gillean acquiesced. "You'll be okay here?" His eyes nervously swept the wooded homestead for any sign of a threat.

"Of course, I'll miss ya like hell, but my comfort is that you'll be missing me too." Sully's eyes narrowed. "Am I right?"

"Come here to me," Gillean said threading two fingers between the buttons of Sully's vest, pulling him into languid kiss. "What do you think?"

Sully rested his head on Gillean's shoulder as his hands played through Sully's hair.

"Promise me you'll be safe here."

"Gillean, I've done okay so far, wouldn't ya say?"

Gillean asked the unbearable question: "What about Ciar?"

"Sod her! I've got Charlie!"

"Where do you suppose he was these last few days?" Gillean whispered.

"'Tis not for us to know!" Sully took a step back. "If you should change your mind, if you come to find this is not what ya want, or your family—"

"Are you trying to be rid of me already?"

"I'm just sayin' I'll be here no matter what."

"Good! Because I intend on coming back post haste. Faradays are stubborn like that." Gillean jingled the car keys in his hand.

"That come from your grandfather too?"

"Nope, my father, Milo Faraday was the most stubborn sonofabitch I ever knew."

Sully opened the door, waving Gillean into the front seat. "Be on your way! Take this altogether ridiculous car and get to those wee Faradays. Meself and the old angel will do fine."

Gillean took his seat and started up the gasping engine. "Wait for me." He winked.

Sully shut the car door. I'm standing here, aren't I?"

———⟨✕⟩———

A wistful stillness settled over the Vale, a respect for the holy alliance between two eternal souls. Sacred energy encased within the confines of two mortal men, both desperate to stay connected and walk their path despite earthy limitations. Both looked to the stars, the heaven's eyes, for answers.

Chapter Twenty-Eight

Rest Stop

The highway was empty. Not much traffic moved through the cluster of villages this late in the evening. Gillean considered himself fortunate to find a service station open. He laughed outright exiting the less-than-luxurious rental car to pump petrol. He reflected that Charlie, resourceful though he obviously was, probably didn't know enough to make certain the tank was full when they had absconded from Cork.

"Must be magic that we made it back to the Vale without having to push this old clunker," Gillean spoke to the night as the fuel dispenser registered the gallons in a series of short clicks. He entered the dimly lit convenience store to pay for the petrol and grab a cup of coffee. When he reached the counter, a display of chocolate bars caught his eye. It had been years since he'd actually felt a hankering for chocolate. He'd been gifted gourmet sweets from all around the globe. Gillean had ingested so much of it that he no longer savored the taste. Chocolate had become something else he took for granted.

Examining the small bar made by a local confectioner, Gillean had never craved this simple pleasure more than he did at that moment. He set the coffee and candy on the counter in front of a young man seemingly a few years older than Arlen. The lad's buzz cut, reddish scalp, ripped T-shirt, and various piercings were in complete contrast to the innocence of his freckled face.

Gillean's years of defiance gave him to wonder about the young man's perspective. Gillean had once possessed the desire to be a blank canvas, open to the world throwing its colors onto him — thick, striking and messy. Now he was just a regular bloke, pumping his own petrol, buying a cup of store-brewed coffee and his own chocolate bar. He took out his wallet, grateful at simply being another customer.

"That'll do ya then?" the clerk inquired. The name Eamon was printed on the tag pinned to his smock.

"Ya know, lad, why not give me a pack of smokes too." Gillean indicated the brand he wanted.

"Right ya are."

Eamon began to ring up the purchase but stopped midway.

"Hey, ya can't be... No shite, but, are ya?"

"Sorry?" Gillean attempted to dodge the obvious question.

Eamon pointed as if he had stumbled upon a historical treasure. "Aren't ya Gillean Faraday, the musician?"

Gillean's smile reverted back to the polite grin he wore for the public. "Yes, I am," he half-mumbled, thankful the rest of the shop was empty.

"Bloody hell, yer one of the luckiest blokes alive!"

"How's that?" Gillean hoped the youth would give him a straight answer. He wanted to know how this stranger regarded him.

"What ya takin' about?" Eamon took a step back and gave Gillean the once-over. "Ya've got it made! Yer famous, got a brilliant home tucked away from us working sods. Ya got the full treatment—wife, kids, and gobs of cash. Man," he shook his head with a smile, "don't ya know how many people would kill to have yer life?"

Gillean shoved the cigarettes into his pocket. "Don't be so sure about that, Eamon."

"Go on with ya! At least ya can escape this bloody country any time ya like." The young man lit up a cigarette, then held the pack out to Gillean, who accepted the offering. "Every freggin' tourist who comes through tinks dey're in a freggin' enchanted leprechaun land. Eejits." He exhaled a white ring. "I'll be stuck here with the blasted leprechaun hunters and sheep till I die."

"How old are you?" Gillean took a pull on his cigarette. "If you don't mind my asking."

The young man grinned. "'Course I don't. I'm seventeen. And don't say I have me whole life ahead!"

Gillean raised his hands in the air. "I wouldn't dream of it. But—"

"Ah!" Eamon laughed. "Get away now with yer buts!"

"Think about what you really want, son. I paid too dear a price for what I thought I wanted. Your mates and family, they'll be with you till the day you breathe your last. Trust me, that's not such a terrible fate."

Eamon flicked a bit of ash onto the floor. "Yeah, yer gonna tell me yer not happy bein' who ya are?"

Gillean's expression was genuine, reflecting all he had experienced in the last few months. "I'm finally realizing happiness. Ya see, I only just found out who I truly am."

Eamon's puzzled expression made the moment even sweeter for Gillean.

"I tell ya what: I'll pay a visit next month and let you know how it's going." Gillean crushed out his cigarette in a dirty tea saucer sitting next to the register and dug into his wallet. He nonchalantly placed the contents in front of the boy. "Meantime, you take this and treat your mates to a good time, eh?"

Eamon's eyes widened as he noted there were at least one hundred Euros sitting between them. "Ah, no, now, Mr. Faraday, sir, I wasn't after anythin'."

"We all are, Eamon, just be careful what you wish for."

Gillean left the young man staring in astonishment at the pile of notes and headed for home. He switched on the local music station as he edged closer to his affluent community. The song on the car radio was a traditional piece, sung by a group of native Celtic musicians. Their joy was palpable throughout the performance. The men stomped their feet in time with the fiddle, yelped and called out to one another with the camaraderie of brothers sharing in a long-standing family tradition. It was clear the band played for the sheer joy of the experience. More than likely they would tour no further than the confines of their country. If they were lucky they might make it to America once or twice in their lifetime, as a featured import act for Irish-American patrons still proud of the homeland. But it wouldn't matter to these boys. They'd make do on what they had. And if they had to work extra jobs to support their families, so be it. They were doing what they loved most and were able to be with whom they loved most.

Gillean remembered the fantastic feelings aroused the first time he'd heard musicians such as Bob Dylan, Joni Mitchel and Van Morrison. He venerated them as saints. They came from humble beginnings, endured heartache and uncertainty, but their music resonated with people in a way nothing else could. Back then, it didn't matter to him how many people he reached, or how much he could earn. Gillean was sure that if even one starry-eyed girl, one overworked farmer, or one lonely child, could find release—find some jubilance and meaning in his songs—then he would have success far greater than any riches real or imagined. He would have made a difference, touched another's life.

The sanguine girl had been Adara, and the lonely child, Sully. They had both suffered, both given the best parts of their lives for him, to further his achievement and happiness. He had taken what was offered like so many other gifts, never appreciating the sacrifice and devotion.

245

The universe did have order, Gillean reckoned, as he peered out the windshield hearing his grandfather speaking about the eternal power of the stars. Kindred spirits, keepers of the light, would always find one another.

"**Y**a dirty old bird." Sully sat at the table. Charlie was half-asleep over a cup of tea.

"Come now." Charlie cleared his throat and rubbed his eyes. "What are ya on about?"

Sully rocked back in his chair, casting his gaze on the man as if for the first time. "I'm deeply offended, ya know."

"Hmm?" Charlie yawned.

"Ya spill to Faraday about yerself and not me, after all we've meant to each other?"

Charlie pushed his cup away, stifling another yawn. "And yerself havin' once been where I am, ya ought to have known better than to snooker me. I wonder if angels can retire. You and Faraday are welcome to each other, pair of damn obstinate mules. Ya wore me out."

Sully let his chair rest on the floor and endeavored to help his tired friend from the table. "Come on, Charlie, darlin', your job isn't finished yet. You'll need a good night's sleep and then, it's off to Bray for you in the morning."

"Bray?" Charlie was waking up with a start. "What for?"

"You're going to the Faraday estate, and yer gonna make sure they are safe and sound, angel."

"Hold yer horses!" Charlie stopped Sully as he attempted to whisk him away from the table. "I can't get to Bray. Faraday has the car!"

"Brilliant try." Sully's grin extended to his luminous eyes. "You're a resourceful being. I'm sure you'll find a way." He resumed the procession to Charlie's bed.

"Ya ' tossin' me out of me own house? I've got work orders to see to. I can't take up and leave."

"Right, I'll mind the shop. I may be only human, but I think I can handle things for a while."

"I've got you to look after, lad. I... I'd like to stay here." The caring was obvious enough in his hushed voice. "Ya shouldn't be alone now."

"Aren't you forgetting how pissed ya are at me for giving ya such a run for your money? I'll manage." Sully patted the man's arm. "'Tis the Faradays who need some assistance at the moment; be a caring presence is all I ask of you. Please, will you do this one very important thing for me, Charlie, *please*?"

"Ah!" The large man sat on the edge of his bed grumbling. "Yer like a wee, lost cat with those great, green eyes of yours."

"Good." Sully turned down the lamp by the bed. "It's set. I'll wake ya in the morning. Hell! I'll even cook ya breakfast."

"Sully."

"Yeah?"

"Yer a good man, willful as I've ever laid eyes on, but a fine man indeed."

"I love you too, Charlie."

Chapter Twenty-Nine

Homecoming

It was close to midnight when Gillean crossed the front foyer of his home. He hesitated outside the main double doors considering if he should use the intercom system to ask permission to enter rather than his key. Not wanting to wake his family, he opted to enter unannounced.

The house seemed to him like a public library or museum, rather than a place he'd called home for the past ten years. Boxty, a retired racing dog Arlen had rescued, was the first to greet Gillean. His son's heart was as generous as it was good. Once he became aware of the plight of so many of Ireland's forgotten ones, Arlen made it his personal crusade to educate not only himself, but the members of his family, friends, anyone who would listen. Gillean's eldest even convinced his mother to take on additional dogs, and his father to donate a tidy sum to the animal shelter to furnish a new pet health clinic. The public showered Gillean with praise, leaving Arlen once again to fade into the shadows of his father's fame.

Bending down to give the faithful greyhound a pat, Gillean longed to see his son and apologize for not listening for far too long. He wanted to assure his boy that no matter what changes may come to their family, he would make every effort to be the devoted and attentive father his children deserved. Holding the dog close, Gillean cringed at the possibility Arlen might wish for a different father the same way Gillean had once wished for the Brazilian street musician.

"So the circle comes back to the beginning, doesn't it, Boxty, girl?" Gillean looked into the dog's docile eyes, seeing the simple quality of unconditional love.

"Gillean?" Adara switched on the hallway lamp. "What are you doing here at this hour?"

Hair spilled over her shoulders in russet waves. Standing to greet her, he noted the haunted look that had been hanging about her like a burdensome cross was absent, as was her wedding ring. She was a stranger to him now—a beautiful, distant stranger.

"Am I not welcome?" he asked, awkwardly standing with his jacket still on. He didn't blame her. The last time they were together, he was leaving to be with Ciar. It was like an awful dream, one he was glad to wake from. But the residue of a restless sleep would not wash away so easily.

"Weren't you the one who chose to go?" she confronted him. He saw no trace of malice in her stare.

"I did."

"I got your message." Her voice was laced with tiredness. "You said you would be home days ago before the concert, but Noel rang me. He was worried. He said you couldn't go on, and then you disappeared. He tried to get you on your mobile."

"There was someone I had to see," he said quietly.

She sighed. "I know."

The physical distance between them was minimal. He searched for a connection, a way to bridge the emotional divide.

"But we're both here now," he observed simply.

"Your solicitor dropped by, hoping to discuss this apparently new legal proceeding in Ireland called divorce. She glanced at a stack of scattered mail containing a large envelope sitting on a side table. "Is that why you've come?"

He lifted his bewildered head. "Perfect timing."

"Would you like some tea?" she proposed half-heartedly.

"Tea?" he sputtered, laughing spontaneously.

How utterly outlandish this was, conversing in the hallway with his estranged wife, he now committed to Sully. And she was suggesting a cup of tea.

"What is it you want?" she snapped. "My blessing?"

He could offer no legitimate reason why she shouldn't hate him. Here stood the lovely woman who had grown up right before his eyes, reaching eagerly towards the sky with the brightness of a sunflower. But he hadn't bothered to see her once he had claimed her. Gillean shivered. He hoped for the impossible.

"I've come from Avoca. Imagine, Dara-Day," he shared his surprise. "You were right. The place I most shunned held the answer."

"That being Sully." She cinched the tie of her bathrobe around her waist.

"Why don't I make the tea?" Gillean offered.

She checked the clock on the hall table. Gillean's glance followed hers. It was a little after one in the morning.

"Is Darjeeling still your favorite?" Gillean expectantly waited.

"There may be some biscuits left, unless the twins got to them first." She strode ahead of him towards the kitchen.

Gillean set the silver kettle on the stove. Adara took a seat at the table, watching as he opened cabinet after cabinet.

"Hmm…" Gillean riffled through boxes of cereal, leathery fruit roll ups, and cans of condensed milk. "The tea leaves were—"

Adara rubbed her forehead as if Gillean's fumbling exploration was inducing a headache. "On the counter next to the stove you will find the tea bags, sugar and honey."

"Bags?" Gillean closed the cabinet door. "You use tea bags?"

"You'll have to slum it, dear."

"Right!" Gillean rubbed his hands together and jumbled the neatly stacked boxes of tea. Snatching the Darjeeling, he shut off the kettle as steam blew to the air, accompanied by a high-pitched whistle.

Grateful that he made it to the table without smashing cups and saucers, Adara delivered the cream she easily located in the refrigerator.

They both sat quietly at the table, steeping their tea bags.

"There is so much I want to say to you." Gillean cleared his throat. "But I'm afraid it's already too late."

Adara folded her hands. "Too late for what?"

Gillean removed his jacket, hanging it on the back of the chair, "Would anything I say to you matter at this moment?

"Do you plan on being honest?"

"Yes," he firmly concurred. "It scares the shite out of me, but the truth is all I have."

She raised her eyebrows. "That would be refreshing."

"Do you remember you danced to Bob Dylan when we first met?"

She took up her cup, surprised at the unexpected question.

"I remember how incredible it felt when you danced while I played."

"It was." Her lips blew steam from the cup. "We were young. Everything is exciting then."

He leaned in. "You binned your dancing for me. Oh, Adara, you were a brilliant ballerina. You should have gone to America—traveled the world—but I convinced you it was not meant to be."

She rolled her eyes. "Gillean—"

"No, please, let me go on." He pushed his cup aside. "Maybe it won't be worth a damn to you…" He ignored the tears stinging his eyes. "Please let me say it anyway."

She was admirably tolerant. "Alright Gillean, go on."

"I became your prison. I held you captive with my own self-interest for far too many years. I was blind, or maybe I chose not to see how I conducted myself. I stopped playing for you first and foremost." He bowed his head. "There is nothing I can say or do that could come close to making amends."

"I don't expect that." She met his impassioned gaze. "I am curious: why now? Why are you compelled to express your remorse to me now?"

It was about Sully. Adara was blessed in spades with women's intuition. Did she want to dole out the punishment he deserved?

"I may very well have gone on the rest of my years with my head up my arse. I hope not. But by the grace of powers unknown to me, I was given a guide."

Her back straightened against the chair. "Sully," she responded.

"He saw the entirety of the situation. He saw your light. You must know that he desperately wanted you to reclaim it for yourself."

"And you, what do you desperately want, Gillean?"

"As I said, I can't bring us back through time to return what I selfishly stole from you. But I can be—that is, it would be my honor to provide—unreserved support from here on."

"I walked into your life of my own free will. If you were my prison, I didn't try to escape. I don't know what I feel, *felt* for Sully. What matters is how he helped me. I was prepared to bind myself up with another man and call it freedom, but Sully knew better. I can't be anything but grateful to him, I suppose."

Looking at his wife, Gillean understood that he would come to love her in a far richer, authentic way. He would come to know her as an individual, a friend, if she gave him the chance. "Before I left the Vale, Sully expressed his wish for us both to take whatever time we needed to...repair? Rebuild? I won't presume your wishes as to how to proceed."

She tucked her hair behind her ears as if preparing to undertake a laborious task. "What happened between us wasn't entirely your fault. I started the chain of events years ago. I pushed as hard for your success as you did. I didn't have the wisdom then to see what I was doing." She shut her eyes tightly against memory. "I held such anger towards you. I couldn't tell you what I needed. I didn't know how to, and—"

He didn't hesitate. He went to Adara, pulling her up from the chair, and embraced her with the full force of his love.

"You tried to tell me, but you were screaming into the wind. I was brilliant at running away. Sully was meant to teach me something. He is connected to my soul because he forced me to explore the darkness of my heart. Both of you have given me such a precious gift." He took her hands, standing back to take in her lovely violet eyes. "I want the chance to give back to you, if you'll let me."

"I didn't think I could believe, but I see for myself so clearly. It's there in your entire attitude. I saw the exact same expression days ago. You and Sully are in love."

He chuckled through his tears. "I didn't think I could believe it either."

"Does that scare you?" She sounded more concerned than contrary.

"No." A peaceful expression slowly spread across his face like an arrested sunrise. "It feels like the most right thing in the world. I didn't love unconditionally. I hated myself for that. I'm finding it possible to be proud of who I am, because I can love without restrictions." He squeezed her hands. "But, I'm frightened that I'll lose you. I don't want you to walk out of my life. I want to be a real and present father for our children. I have no expectation for you to accept Sully and me."

She exhaled as if releasing all the turbulent years between them. "We have four magnificent children. They are the legacy our bond created. I would never keep them from you. They will be ecstatic to have you to themselves"

Gillean allowed his heart to hope. "And you and I?"

"I want to be happy, Gillean. You and Sully should not ignore the way you feel for one another. Love will appear like the moon, because it is meant to be, not because a person demands it. But I'm not such a perfect being. I need time."

"You shall have that, and whatever else you need." A smile turned up the corners of his lips. "I'm not running away anymore."

Chapter Thirty

Flying

After looking in on his three sleeping children, Gillean walked through the tranquil halls of his home. He must speak with Arlen, thankfully a night owl like his father.

He paused in the doorway of a posh sitting room. A grand piano dominated the space. This precious instrument had been one of his immediate purchases once he had secured his first recording contract. To play and compose songs on such a fine piece of craftsmanship had always given him a sense of awe. At present, the piano was nothing more than a display for family photos and the souvenirs from his years of travel.

Gillean picked up a framed black-and-white photo, carrying it to the window to study the picture by moonlight. The moment captured on film was as rare as any relic his father could have unearthed. A little boy stood flanked by his father and grandfather. The puckish Gillean was missing a few front teeth, but his smile was all the wider to make up for the loss. His grandfather's eyes charmed the camera with their warmth. Gillean raised the frame closer to his face, retrieving his glasses from his pocket.

When he examined the picture again, he paid particular attention to his father. Milo Faraday was not facing front as his son and father-in-law were, but instead was turned, looking at his boy. The vivacious child had his father's full attention. The man's hand had settled on his son's shoulder. Milo's eyes peered down on the lad with a mixture of pride and sorrow. Gillean's heart swelled. Setting his glasses on the piano, he wondered how many times he may have looked at his own son with the same doting eyes as his mysterious and misunderstood father. Sitting at his piano gazing not at the distant stars but the faces of his family, Gillean understood.

The tears fell easily, anointing the image of the two men he had loved during his life, one without question, and one with a fierceness borne of defiance. His finger traced over the faces of his father and granddad.

"Why didn't I ever see before, Da? Why didn't I know?"

Gillean returned the picture and laid his head on the smooth lacquer surface, doleful sobs shaking his body.

"I loved you, Da. I was forever trying to prove myself worthy of you. Why couldn't we say the words?" He wiped at his eyes, choking back an ironic laugh. "What would you think of Sully? He is the most fearless person in the face of love. I'll hear those cherished words until the day I die. And I won't be afraid to speak them often either."

"Da?" Arlen called out quietly.

Gillean lifted his head as his son approached, taking a seat next to Gillean on the bench. "Da, why are ya cryin'?"

"The question should be why aren't you?"

"Why should I be?"

"Because I have been no use to you as a father." Gillean's tearful eyes searched his son's. "Because I've let too much time go by, so much so that you wonder whether I love you, don't you?"

Arlen shook his head. "No, Da, no."

"Come on now. Tell me the truth, eh?"

Arlen took a moment before speaking. "Alright." He tapped his fingers on the piano. "First, ya see how we're sitting here? This is your domain, your world. Come outside with me. Let me show ya mine."

Gillean happily agreed.

They left the house together, Gillean occasionally stumbling over a toy left behind in the wet grass by one of his other children.

"Atty and Antonia," Arlen chuckled as Gillean negotiated his way through this foreign land of children. "Mam's always after them to bring their stuff inside."

I don't even know how my own children spend their days, he realized while stepping over the tiny bodies of colorfully clad action figures.

The remorse of knowing he had simply provided the means for the activities, but was rarely a participant, stared him down with the intensity of the unusually bright yellow moon. The orb's blue-gray craters could easily be seen with the naked eye.

"Here we are!" Arlen stopped short on the east side of the house where a sleek, blue telescope faced the cosmos. "This is a perfect time. Now if ya look to the west, you can easily see Orion and Gemini. Ya don't need the telescope."

Gillean focused on where his son pointed; indeed he could make out the blazing images of the hunter and the twins.

"But, this is grand." Arlen peered down the lens, making small adjustments. "If ya look right between Gemini and Leo, you can see Cancer." He stepped away from the scope and offered Gillean a view.

Gillean placed his right eye close to the lens.

"Look directly above ya." His son's hands were on his back. "Do ya see the five stars of Cancer?"

Gillean squinted and blinked. Just as he was about to step away and reach for his eye glasses, he saw the connected points of light. They were faint but steady, glowing right where Arlen said.

"I'll be..." he whispered reverently.

"Okay, stay focused." Arlen was behind him, excitedly directing. "Look a wee bit further up. You should see two stars directly next to each other and then two more a bit farther out, heading north."

Gillean squinted but could only see a dark void above the well-known clusters. "Where, son?"

"Right above Cancer, four stars. Ya gotta look beyond that patch of darkness to find them."

"I don't think..." Gillean placed his hand on the instrument. "Oh, wait, here now, yes, two stars." Gradually the void filled with tiny dots of light. "And, yes, the other two above! I would have never..." He breathed in the frosty March air, releasing a puff of white mist. "How did you manage to find that one?"

"Awesome, isn't it?" Arlen beamed. "It's the Lynx, one of the last vestiges of winter, and Arcturus rising in the east is one of the first signs of summer."

The lad's hands extended to the sky as if it were a gigantic chalk board and he, an eager professor, sharing his knowledge with his pupils. "Shakespeare referred to the stars as the night's candles."

"You read Shakespeare?" Gillean could scarcely fathom it. This astute young man was the same little boy who had followed him over every inch of the stage during his sound checks as if his father were the Pied Piper.

"Well, no, not avidly," Arlen laughed. "Sully told me that bit one night."

"Sully did?"

"Uh huh."

"You're good mates, you and he?" Gillean kept his curiosity in check.

"Sure, I mean, he's a real decent bloke. Kinda strange, but in a good way."

"Do you...do you remember what he did for you?" Gillean measured out his words carefully, not wanting to rouse unpleasant memories for his son.

"Ya mean how he saved my life?"

Gillean nodded.

"Yeah, I do. I didn't at first, I mean when I first saw Sully. But, little by little, it came back to me. I asked him about it. I couldn't remember the whole lot, just that it was him who saved me from bein' creamed by a car."

Gillean remained cautious. "What did he tell you?"

"He said to put it out of me head, and I should remember to look both ways before crossing the street. Weird, huh?"

Gillean sent out a silent sentiment of gratitude to his soulmate for not revealing anything about Ciar to Arlen. "Sully is an exceptional individual to be sure," he concurred.

"He cares for you too, Da. I guess I should have listened to him about some other things besides Shakespeare."

"How's that?"

"Sully told me once that maybe you were afraid I didn't love ya."

"He did?"

"Yeah. He explained to me that ya wanted to do right by our family, and I should talk to ya more. I'm sorry I didn't—talk to ya, I mean. I should have. You must get desperate lonely sometimes."

"Arlen, lad, that is on me completely, not you."

"No, Da. I was wrong. After I talked with Sully, I felt better knowin' ya weren't as perfect as everybody else says. But, I still should have come to ya. I hope ya aren't ticked at me."

Gillean put his arm over Arlen's shoulder and led him to a set of swings behind their house. Wasn't it just yesterday when he and Adara had installed the wooden play set on the grounds of their dream home? Arlen had grown past the age of swings and jungle gyms, but his younger brother Abbot, along with and twin sister Antonia, gave their older brother many occasions for excise by demanding to be pushed on the "fly chairs", as they called them. Gillean rarely had the time for family play as his career was beginning to soar.

Gillean and his son sat on the vinyl swings, side by side. It was quiet here, not like the Vale with its many night creatures and their songs of praise for the water.

"You said something profoundly wise tonight, something I will remember always. You said I had to look beyond the patches of darkness to find the light. *You* said that, son. Not Shakespeare, not Sully, but *you*, Arlen Faraday. Thank you for being patient with me, for teaching me."

"Actually, Galileo was the first to observe that." Arlen was looking to the magnificent moon hanging like a plump, golden fruit on the tree of night. "But thanks for hearing me. I miss ya when yer away. I'll try to be more patient."

"You won't have to. This here *perfect* musician is retiring." Gillean propelled his swing forward, offering his son a mischievous smile.

"What? Ya can't be serious?" Arlen's swing remained stationary, the boy's feet planted on the grass as Gillean gained momentum.

"Yer not goin' on the road anymore? Not writing songs or recording? Ya can't quit. It's who ya are."

Gillean swung higher still. The cold air rushing against his body enticed him to let go and take flight. Little by little all the weighted objects of fame that had restrained his movement and hidden the knowledge of himself as merely a person in the world were falling away. He was at once like every other man; and yet, uniquely, he was Gillean Faraday—a new being with a new purpose.

"Who I am," he said between staggered breaths, "is a father who loves his children and won't waste another minute away from their esteemed company."

Arlen's amazed expression propelled Gillean to swing faster and higher.

"My son, the brilliant astronomer!" Gillean announced to the sky. "Look out ye stars, planets, and alien life forms." He shook a chiding finger at the heavens, causing his swing to wobble. "You too, Galileo! Arlen Faraday is on watch!"

"Jaysus, Da, have ya gone round the bend?"

"I'm right where I need to be. And there's going to be some major changes round here. I need to know that you'll be okay with them,"

"Not if it means you giving up yer music." The boy started up his own swing. It took him a few good heaves to reach the heights of his father.

"I'm proud of you and what ya do!" the teen hollered back.

"Really?" Gillean let gravity take its course, offering no more incentive to keep the swing in motion. "You're proud of me?"

"Come on, ya didn't know?" Arlen's deep brown eyes, the very same as his father's, stared back, "You inspire people with what ya do. It wasn't news to me when Sully talked of how ya inspired him."

Father and son were quiet, slowly descending back to the ground. When Gillean spoke, his voice was ragged from shouting and emotion, "That means more coming from you than anybody else on this earth."

Arlen dragged his feet on the grass. "I'm sorry I didn't say it before now."

"Don't be. I'm sorry for so many things, enough for both of us. But there's something else I have to tell you. And, it involves Sully," Gillean put forward warily, "Another change that may be a little tougher to accept. I hope you trust me when I say it is the right choice."

"Da, we already had that talk."

"What talk?"

"Ya know, *that* talk," Arlen jabbed at Gillean. "I think when I was like nine or ten. I remember ya weren't too good at it then, either!"

Gillean tightly grasped the ropes of his swing, taking a quick glance at the sky imbued with the stars his son so admired. "I'm sure I didn't cover this bit with you back then." His face blushed red.

"Go on, spill," Arlen encouraged.

"It...it may take time for you to accept this." Gillean's cold hands brushed over his jeans. "You might not be able to accept the idea of Sully and me—"

"Remember when I became a vegetarian?" Arlen interjected.

"Vegetarian?" Gillean was thrown off by the question. "Uh, yes, I do as a matter of fact. You were all of eight years old."

"Yeah, and you were up in arms, sayin' it was just a phase, I would get sick, people are meant to be carnivores and all that rubbish."

"Well, I—"

"And it's been seven years. I'm taller than most boys in me class. I can outrun most of 'em, too." Arlen scratched his head. "Come to think of it, I don't remember the last time I saw ya have a steak. Used to be yer favorite meal, huh?"

"Your point?" Gillean teasingly swatted at his son's arm.

"People aren't *meant* to be anythin' other than who they are. I'm not the only vegetarian in the world." Arlen spoke with the quality of voice that only teenagers possess, the "why are adults so daft?" tone. "And I would suppose that you and Sully aren't the only two men in the world who care for one another, either."

Gillean inched his swing closer to his son's so that they were face to face. "That doesn't make you uncomfortable?" He feared he was placing too much in Arlen's lap. "It must be a bit wild."

"Well, yeah, it'll be a bit weird to be sure, but I'm not a little kid anymore. You and Mam haven't been happy together for a long time. I don't exactly understand how this happened, or how it will be, but, if you and Sully are together..."

"What, son?"

"I don't want ya to think I'll love ya any less, or that I don't want us to be a family—Mam and the rest, I mean." Arlen's eyes shone with tears. "I know there's a way for us to still be a family, all together, right?"

Gillean smoothed his son's hair, remembering the rare nights he was home in time to send Arlen off to sleep with a song. "Somewhere along the years, you turned from a shy, fair-haired boy into an intelligent, thoughtful young man. One who can teach his old man a thing or two about life. I love you very much, so does your mother, and Sully. I have absolute faith that we'll all manage. Things may be a little difficult to start. I want you to talk to me no matter what, no matter how you feel. Promise me."

Arlen cocked his head to one side with a dubious stare. "Ya promise to listen?"

"*What?*" Gillean craned his neck towards the lad. "Did you say something?"

"Okay, Da. Yer so brilliant." Arlen rolled his eyes, looking like his mother when she was seventeen.

"Right." Gillean brushed away tears and stood. "Why don't you come with me when I collect Sully? I'm sure he could use your friendship and help. You're the best one to help him get acquainted with your brothers and sister."

"Sure," Arlen said, rising to stand beside his father. "We should be more worried about those wee fiends freaking out Sully."

Gillean delighted in the idea of Sully being surrounded by the high-spirited young ones. "From this day forward, we will be fan-flipping-tastic!" He gathered his son in a bear hug.

"Da!" The boy playfully wrestled against his father's grip.

Walking back to the house, Gillean's hopes were not of the fragile, easily dashed sort of his youth. This time, what he aspired to be was not gained by painful sacrifice, but by the simple joy of living.

Chapter Thirty-One

Family Trust

"I'm pleased you want to travel with your father. But, are you sure you want to make this particular trip?" Adara spoke to her son from the driveway while he helped Gillean ready for his drive to Acova. "We both want you to be comfortable, no matter what your choice."

Gillean didn't oppose his wife but allowed the lad the chance to speak for himself.

"Mam," Arlen responded with a rascally smile, "it's okay. I owe Sully. Besides, I happen to like him, too."

The boy kissed his mother's cheek and jumped into the passenger seat of the strange, old car his father had acquired. "Ta for now!" He saluted her from the half-open window.

Gillean tapped Adara on the shoulder as he donned his sunglasses, fishing for car keys in the pocket of his faded blue jeans. "Damn fine lad we have there."

A cloudless sky the color of cornflowers cradled a warming, saffron sun.

"Gillean, I appreciate the way you've been these past few weeks; how you're changing. It's, well—"

"You're terrifically proud of me!" He tossed a duffel bag packed with CDs, as well as snacks for the road, over his shoulder.

"I was worried you might lose that healthy sense of ego," she scoffed.

"Some things never change." He winked.

"You actually want to keep this?" Adara nodded to the car. "You said you were returning it for Charlie."

"I'm attached to it." Gillean lightly tapped the boot. "It delivered me. I'll be sure to pay the dealer on the way."

She appeared to have more on her mind. "We agreed the children and I will remain here for as long as I wish," she began, "but you and

Sully…" She pressed a wrist to her lips. "Where will you go?"

"Sully and I will find a home close by. You call whenever you're ready." He cupped her chin in his hand. "Any time you need."

"Right then," she smiled.

He hesitated, not wanting to make their parting more difficult, but needing to give her a final warning. "Please be careful of Ciar." He lowered his voice. "If she should come here—"

"Not to worry. We have what we need to keep her at bay."

He waited for further explanation.

"We trust one another now. There are no more secrets, no dirty little cracks she can slip into. What you are doing now—going back for Sully—she has to know there is nothing left for her to prey upon."

"The very idea she got a hold on me, and I allowing it… I wish you could believe that empty, selfish man is gone for good and all."

"No more apologies," Adara handed him the diamond ring. "We get to write the rest of the story."

"What's this?" He held the flawless ring. Its beauty blinded him, like Ciar.

"You gave it to her, didn't you?" Adara's eyes drifted from him to the ring as if verifying the connection.

"I certainly did not give her a ring!" Gillean recoiled as if the shiny object possessed a nefarious power. "My God, did she make you think… I didn't ask her to marry me!"

"You swear?"

"On my life."

"She told Sully you had." Adara stepped back, motioning for Gillean to follow so their son would not be privy to the exchange.

"She made him promise, Gillean, she wounded Sully and made him promise to stay away from you and our family."

Nervously twisting a strand of hair around her finger, she revealed what had transpired at Avoca.

"Sully didn't tell me this." Gillean rubbed his sweaty palms against the denim of his jeans. "Why didn't you tell me until now?"

"I thought you knew."

Gillean paced the pavement, hands trembling. "I'm afraid only Sully understands what she really wants. He has put up one hell of a resistance to protect us from that knowledge."

"I'll come with you. We should be together now. Maybe that is how we defeat her."

"Hey! Come on, Da. Step it up will ya!" Arlen gave two quick impatient beeps of the horn, jolting Gillean and Adara out of their shared bond of dread.

Gillean held Adara close. "You must stay here with the children. I came to Sully on my own. I rejected Ciar. I can't predict how she will react." He tried to gather courage as if it were as easy as collecting a bundle of twigs. "You be strong, Dara. You were right: as long as we stay united, we have power." He released her and headed to the car.

It was time for Gillean to repair the damage he had caused. He would run head-on into the storm if necessary.

"Hey pal, sorry, but change of plans." Gillean opened Arlen's door. "You stay here with your mam."

"I don't think so. I remember Ciar too." Arlen belted himself in. "If she is after Sully, then I'm ridin' shotgun."

Gillean looked to Adara, steeling himself against the crushing terror he bore. She reticently waved her approval.

"Alright," He shifted the car into gear. "You're with me."

"Be safe!" Adara called out.

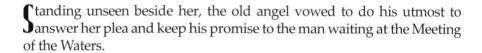

Standing unseen beside her, the old angel vowed to do his utmost to answer her plea and keep his promise to the man waiting at the Meeting of the Waters.

Chapter Thirty-Two

The Memory of Yellow Roses

Gillean laughed easily at Arlen's verbal list of descriptive pet names for his father's new-old car.

"…*Reject Rian*?"

"Reminds me of a failed Irish air carrier."

"Okay. How 'bout…*Great Gobs of Fire*?"

"Too American."

"Right… Wait!" Arlen fidgeted while rapping on the dashboard. I have it! *Space Junk*!"

"Oscar Wilde couldn't have done any better." Gillean quipped.

"Space junk it is!" Arlen popped a crisp into his mouth. "But is this space junk male or female?"

Gillean snatched a crisp from the bag his son held out. "No comment."

The car miraculously plodded its way through yet another significant road trip, seeming to run on the combination of petrol and prayer. It wheezed and chugged along like a terminally ill patient determined to cheat death.

As the vehicle turned off the main road, the sun slipped behind a gathering of bloated clouds. It wasn't long before the first drops of rain hit the windshield, falling like so many tears from the aggrieved universe, only to be swept away by the squawking wipers.

While Gillean heaved the manual window control counterclockwise to keep water from flooding the interior, he commented on the predictability of the Irish weather. Arlen appeared to be mesmerized by something not in Gillean's purview. The remote look in the boy's eyes made it clear he wasn't charmed by the swiftly passing scenery or bothered by the rain alighting upon his clothes.

"Arlen, what is it?"

The slick road and his preoccupied son divided Gillean's attention.

"'Tis right you should do this, Da." Arlen's focus was unshakable as he stared straight into the oncoming rain.

"What do you mean?"

"Help Sully. It was raining the day they laid him to rest. I can see their black umbrellas and smell the roses. They laid yellow roses on his casket." He fixed his disturbing gaze on Gillean but was seeing an altogether different scene. "It was yer music they played. The priest said it was Sully's favorite. Your music was meant to say 'farewell', when in truth it was saying, 'I'm sorry we were too late.'"

Gillean tried to keep the tires from lifting off the road as he veered the car over to the shoulder, shifting into park. He reached across his son to roll up the passenger window before cutting the engine.

"How could you know that? Gillean demanded. "How could you possibly know what happened the day Sully was buried?"

Damp hair covered the boy's eyes as he shook his head, untroubled by Gillean's distress. "I don't know how, but…it's like I was there, like I have a memory."

Gillean shuddered. His son was not one to lie, not even to avoid punishment when he was a child. Arlen was truthful to a fault, sometimes offering his opinion when it was not welcome. It was Arlen who waited up those nights when Gillean entered the then modest Faraday home with the rising sun. It was the sleepy-eyed six-year-old who snuck from the comfort of his warm bed to inquire of his badly behaved father where he had been, and didn't he know that his staying out all night made mam cry. Gillean readily delivered the lies, or "explanations" as he liked to think of them. Although not even old enough to attend primary school, Arlen had a good enough grasp on the ways of his egocentric father, and how he was slowly and methodically breaking his mother's heart.

Dazed, Gillean laid his head against the steering wheel. The patter of rain steadily hitting the car sounded like clatter upon a tin roof.

"Da, are ya upset with me?"

Gillean could scarcely believe the forces that surrounded him, forces of beauty, love and goodness. Forces that were tied to his soul, his bloodline, but he had hidden in the shadows. Sully provided a meaningful explanation on a not-so-long-ago morning splintered with sunlight. They were having coffee. Gillean was laugh-crying at Sully's attempt to skip stones across the lake.

Sully feigned insult at Gillean's complete lack of composure. "You've had more time to practice, ya blightin' bully." He threw a small stone, hitting Gillean's thigh, which made him crumple to the ground in tears.

"Man down!" Gillean shouted. "I need triage."

Sully stepped closer. "Surely you're not hu—"

Gillean seized the moment, tugging on Sully's trousers, upending him. He was quickly taken in by Gillean's eager arms. After more laughing, a fit of coughing and fervent kisses, they lay side by side admiring the sun floating on the water.

"Will you tell me now?"

"Hmm…" Sully savored the feel of Gillean's fingers in his hair. "Tell you what?"

"How do these collectives work? Are there Lords and Ladies of Darkness and Light? Is there one God, or Goddess? Who did you and…" He wasn't sure he could say her name in such a serene moment. "What entity directs Ciar, and did the same one direct you and Charlie?"

Sully's face clouded with worry. "Why are ya askin' me this?"

"You explained it to me once when you told me you were a re-encounter. But it did my head in. My mind is clear now. Can you imagine the situation from my vantage point?"

Sully picked at the grass. "I'm not the one to ask, given me history." He tossed a handful of loose grass at Gillean. "You should speak with Charlie."

"I want to hear it from you." Gillean would not be put off. "We are meant to spend our lives together."

"Does my answer have an impact in that regard?"

"What?" Gillean quickly sat up. "No, of course not, and you know that! Stop trying to buy time and tell me."

Sully sat up slowly, taking a sip of cold coffee. "I can tell you my learned experience."

"Your word is bond to me." Gillean reassured.

"The powers of good and evil are real enough, collectives as ya mentioned. There are numerous collectives. Some members can assume human form, but they are bound by their individual set of tenets, as it were. None can be seen in their purest state."

"Are they like shapeshifters?"

"In a way, Charlie appears to you as he does so he can be seen by you, but, his true form is comprised of light energy, where love, generosity and the Divine are the core. Beings like Charlie—"

"Angels," Gillean interjected.

"Angels are sent to assist human beings."

Gillean gathered up Potcheen, who was busy lapping coffee from his mug. "What about this little beast? Does he have a greater purpose?"

"Without question," Sully grinned.

"Well, you're certain enough about that!" Gillean stroked Potcheen's head. "My son would wholeheartedly agree."

Potcheen returned to sniffing the surroundings while Gillean processed Sully's exposition. "So, if Charlie is an angel, then Ciar must be the other side of the coin. She is the human form of dark energy? But for what purpose?"

Sully rubbed a thumb over the scar on his wrist. "I don't entirely know."

"How could you not?"

Sully darted up from the ground. "Please don't ruin this moment with any more questions."

Gillean took hold of Sully's arm. "Hey, I don't want to ruin anything. I'm simply fitting pieces together." Gillean pleaded, "What is happening here? You are *everything* to me."

Sully closed his eyes. This was the first time he'd conjured the memory of his bleakest hour, but he no longer maintained the terrible, visceral experience of his death at his father's hands. There was nothing to feel. His father was among the dead, taken by time and change.

"You're leaving something out. Please look at me." Gillean gently coaxed, "The reason why you first came to me. You wanted to warn me because you knew what Ciar was capable of."

Sully drew in the surroundings; the trees, flowers, birds, Gillean. It was endless inspiration. "Gillean, you're referring to a history I no longer carry with me; the sorrow, loneliness, the pain…none of it."

Sully's sudden laughter took Gillean off guard. "What the hell is so funny?"

"Everything!" Sully took Gillean's face in his hands. "Everything that has transpired between us; every exchange, every slight, the anger—"

"You mean passion." Gillean grinned.

"That too!" Sully nodded. "It all flies in the face of Ciar's purpose. Did ya not just say we are meant to spend our lives together?"

"Yes." Gillean ardently confirmed.

"Well, then." Sully pulled Gillean into a kiss. "Here we are."

Gillean, left breathless, whispered, "Here we are, meu amor."

"**D**a?" Arlen shook Gillean from his reflections. "I asked if yer upset with me?"

"Upset with you?" Gillean turned to his son, feeling both a master cheat and an ignorant victim. Arlen was bestowed with a special gift, one Gillean could not take credit for. Was it merely an accident of the universe, or what Sully had been trying so desperately to convey — that these men were connected through time, space, heart, and soul?

"The lighted path was directly in front of me my whole life, and yet I chose to drift in the darkness. I believed good and evil were synonymous with some antiquated idea of God and the Devil, and therefore easily dismissed. I didn't search further for answers. I wrote songs."

Arlen listened attentively.

"But each of us has the capability to wield incredible power." Gillean continued. "Good and evil, right and wrong, aren't so neatly identified with two separate beings as God and the Devil, are they?"

Arlen looked as if he were laboring over a complicated equation. "I think I know what ya mean, Da."

"So how do you see it?"

Arlen closed his eyes, apparently sifting through the choice of words to define his thoughts. "It's like we aren't at the mercy of some outside forces, but of ourselves — the powers we choose to tap into. And sometimes we're at the mercy of one another, like Sully was."

"Like Sully is," Gillean corrected.

Gillean could only imagine with compassion and revulsion what the child Sully had endured and how he'd been held hostage by his — Gillean's — mistakes. And yet in a most tangible way, Sully was part of Gillean, like his skin and blood. Sully's tortuous experiences burned in the once unlit corner of Gillean's heart, the space reserved to stow the pain of rejection, failures, and fear. It was in the face of his enlightened son, and the way he extended an open heart to his father — despite all the hurt Gillean had inflicted — he could see his new road. The indestructible nexus to his soulmate wrapped around him, tethering him forever to past lives, the present, and the future he saw in his empathetic son.

"This time I come to Sully an enlightened man." Gillean started up the car, undeterred by the earlier uncertainty of what he may find at the Vale.

"I don't think ya need to rely on any deities tellin' ya what's right, Da. Yer pretty good at figuring things out when ya actually pay attention."

Arlen popped a CD of Gillean's music into the player and settled back in his seat for the rest of the ride.

Chapter Thirty-Three

Dead Things

Sully stared at the plate of toast and cheese in front of him with no appetite. Three months had passed since Gillean had returned to his family.

Time and silence mocked his loneliness, matching him step for step. It was an unseen, unheard presence ever at his heels. He couldn't sleep, eat, or focus. His heart and mind were somewhere else, leaving his body to fend for itself without the spirit necessary to carry on.

He lowered the plate to an obliging Potcheen. Sully wished for news, any word to inform him how to go about living. Gillean loved him, of that Sully was sure. Everything about Gillean affirmed his devotion. The way his scent, like the sand and briny sea, clung to Sully's skin, his munificent eyes taking Sully to a place where he was sheltered and cared for; the taste of Gillean's kisses, like rain on parched lips, granted rebirth in the waters of their shared commitment.

Life was capricious as the wind and rain. Sully understood what his fellow humans, dwelling on this precarious plane of existence, endured in dealing with its vagaries. Love possessed the potential to catapult a person to the heavens or set him falling haplessly from the stars in the wink of an eye. Sully respected his soulmate's vow to be a support for his wife and commitment to being a better father to his children. Gillean was changing and, after all, wasn't that what Sully had been determined to bring about by barging into the musician's life in the first place?

Be careful, Sully admonished himself, depositing a plate licked clean into the sink. *Be careful what ya wish for, lad.*

His words chilled and highlighted the stillness of the cabin that may be his home for many years to come. Growing old with Charlie was a complicated prospect. But it was one Sully felt he must at least consider, given that he'd assented to be supportive of whatever choice

Gillean made. He, Adara, and that remarkable young man, Arlen, were dearer to Sully than anyone else, next to Charlie and Potcheen. Sully knelt down to bestow a kiss on the dog's soft fur. "I wouldn't think of losing you either, sweet boy."

Still, the thought of losing half his heart should Gillean walk away was an even thornier notion, and one he could scarcely bear. Maybe he would take to the road. His broken spirit wouldn't be so noticeable wandering among the countless others. Given time—that wily beast staring him down at every corner—he might be able to master the art of simply living, giving of himself when and where he could.

But Sully didn't feel up to the task of a philanthropist's work at the moment. He was a man entirely who ached for his love. The most he could muster was the intent to help his charitable, but disorganized, host. He would make the trek into the unexplored second level of the cottage to sort through the menagerie of Charlie's things in an effort to get the old codger functioning at full speed. Just last week, the angel had been blustering on about how he could never find the proper tool when he needed it.

"Well, no wonder," Sully had fired back laughingly, "ya keep hammers in the ice box and nails in a biscuit tin. At this rate the house will fall down around us while we starve to death!"

Before setting about his work, Sully remembered to place the tallow candle in the window in appreciation of Charlie's watch over the Faradays. Ascending the stairs creaking in protest, Sully tried to empty his mind of other considerations, save for the task in front of him.

There was much to keep him fully occupied. One glance could scarcely take in the entirety of Charlie's worldly possessions. Dust pervaded the large space filled with rusty tools, peculiar-looking gadgets—some of which Sully could not identify—and newspapers dating back a decade. He was surprised to see a bookshelf which housed several leather-bound first editions by some of the greats: Shaw, Yeats and Wilde. But Charlie, knowing of Sully's passion for reading, had opted to travel to the library each week rather than offer the well-preserved copies in his possession.

Sully reached for one of the smaller volumes. It slipped from his fingers and fell to the floorboards with a resounding thud. His eyes watered from the dust that was kicked up. Sneezing and leaning down to grab the book, he noted an almost illegible scrawl on the front page. It was a dedication.

To my dear friend, Charlie, I cannot write of the people of Eire without your generous spirit rising up in my mind. May it be a great while until you leave this mortal earth. Always, J.J.

Sully blinked several times to clear the dust from his eyes, then turned the book to its front cover. *Dubliners.*

"Well, I'll be..." Sully sputtered. He reverently returned the book to its resting place. "So, ya befriended one of our greatest writers did ya now? And I...I've gone and bungled the life of one of our greatest musicians. No wonder I'm no longer counted among the angels. I should be counted among the dead."

He eyed the priceless work of art one last time before plunging into a pile of dirty, paint-stained rags concealing an aged, gnarled walking stick.

"Who the hell did this belong to, St. Patrick?"

The hours passed swiftly with Sully rooting through the contents of the room, thankful he'd not unearthed the proverbial genie in a bottle. Rubbing his grimy hands over equally filthy trousers, he surveyed the afternoon's progress. He had successfully cleared a small corner, stacking the newspapers neatly in a half-dozen or so separate piles. He didn't want to toss anything until confirming Charlie's approval, but at least the necessary items, such as a well-used sawhorse, levels of assorted size and tape measures were more readily accessible.

The first pangs of hunger nipped at his empty stomach, but physical and emotional exhaustion were uppermost, more prevalent than his constant yearning for Gillean. Moving as if sleepwalking, he closed the windows and practically tripped down the stairs to the main room. Unruly, saturated, black waves of hair obscured his irritated eyes. He maneuvered the kitchen pump with minimal energy, scrubbing over his blackened hands with a bar of peppermint soap.

Before removing his boots, pants, sweat-soaked T-shirt, and mindlessly crashing into the little bed by the wood stove, he had the presence of mind to re-light Charlie's candle. It was his way of keeping the connection, sending out whatever strength the angel might need to keep guard over Sully's loved ones.

"The sleep of the dead," he mumbled.

⋙※⋘

It was the month of June, but there were no fireflies wondrously lighting up the breezy summer evening. The leaves rustled with a swift, uneasy current of cold wind. Limbs broke from the bodies of trees. She carelessly trampled over the splinters in bare feet. The austere night, absent of the moon and his doting court of stars, was the only attire she had need of. The Vale had been spared the earlier gales and rain. The land surrounding her destination was dry as a decayed bone. The fetid air brushed over her unclothed body like the hands of an eager lover.

Nature worked in her favor. This isolated, wooded locale would serve her perfectly, like every man she had enchanted. There was only one man worthy of her attention now, one who would deeply regret having crossed her. She was finished with deals, promises and games. She was at her most potent, but her time was limited. Her waning powers would rise up like the last spray of fireworks, shooting their blinding colors to the sky before descending to earth in burnt-out flickers of dying light.

Behind her she left a trail of dead things. The cottage of the primeval angel lay before her. She grabbed at the silver wind chimes hanging in the doorway. They rang out a final caution as she cast them crashing to the ground.

"Peace to all who enter here," she said, spitting on the chimes and reaching for the doorknob.

Chapter Thirty-Four

Fire and Music

Naturally it wasn't locked. She smirked letting herself in. The occupants trusted they would be protected from any external harm. It was they who offered protection to anyone in need who might come this way.

The first thing her coal-black eyes rested on was the white candle glowing in the window.

"How sweet," she commented. "You think a single light will save you now, Sully?"

Sully's body lay as still as a corpse while she walked about the room, passing her hands over objects. She wanted to take in every detail of these last moments of his life. They would serve as her solace when she was no longer an extraordinary force to contend with, powerless—human, like all the other vile beings she loathed.

Satisfied by the picture of the doomed cottage stored in her mind, she turned her attention elsewhere. Flaxen hair hung about her curvaceous form, swaying with her as she edged closer to his bed. Her lips spontaneously turned upward seeing his discarded clothing on the floor.

"Oh my, little boy," She leaned over, stroking his hair with her pointed fingernails eying his bare chest. "I can make this, your last night on earth, most worthwhile. Standing before you is every man's fantasy of fresh womanhood and yet you sleep, no doubt dreaming of your aging lover."

The candle flickered, casting grotesque shadows on the wall opposite the bed. Ciar's silhouette depicted not the youthful, desirable woman of men's dreams, but a haggard, twisted, demonic nightmare. She slipped under the covers, but he remained motionless, immobilized by the secure net of slumber.

"Sully." His sleek skin was a pleasurable surprise for her roaming fingertips. She whispered in his ear. "I've come to say goodbye."

He turned his body to her, eyes closed. He was slowly making the transition into wakefulness.

"That's it, little boy," she cooed. "Take what you want from me. I won't begrudge you. Since it is because of you and our soured deal that I will soon be human, and you dead, why not partake of one another now? At least you will die knowing what it is to be pleasured by a woman." She held her mouth against his, kissing him with anger and lust.

"Gillean?" he murmured, pulling away and waking from the force of a kiss that was not the tender offering of his soulmate.

"No, not Gillean, it's just you and me."

She leaned forward, resting her chin on his chest.

"Ciar!" His heart pounded in horror as he dove over her, hitting the floor hard in his ungainly landing. He hurriedly located his shirt and yanked his trousers over scraped knees, limping into the center of the room.

She called to him in a sing-song voice from her place in his bed. "You've been expecting me, no? Or would you rather I go straight to the Faradays?" Her smile was one of familiar manipulation as she came up on her knees.

Sully turned his back on her nakedness, thankful for the knowledge that Gillean and his family were safe. "Once again you believe we have unfinished business," he said, maintaining his dignity.

She darted from the bed, knocking over the small table stacked with his nightly reading material, unaffected as several books toppled onto her feet. She simply kicked them across the floor. "Wrong again, our business will be concluded *this* night, in *this* place."

She snatched at him, her fingernails digging into his flesh. "You went back on your word. Imagine that! The man who is supposed to stand for the truth has told one monster of a lie." Her eyes intensified, saturated with a hatred so overt it seemed to splash onto him like a toxin, stinging his skin. "Gillean remembered you and what you two shared. You didn't send him away, but pledged yourself to him. And Adara… You may have managed to be rid of her, but not before having a candid discussion! Yet another lie."

She waved a finger in his face. "Did you forget I'm the *one* person you should *never* lie to?"

"Would ya look at the pot callin' the kettle black!" He pointed a finger at her as if they were two children in a school yard trading insults.

"What?"

"Gillean asked you to marry him, did he? Gave ya a ring that would choke a horse?"

The sight of her exposed body brought nothing but absolute aversion. "He left ya high and dry, paints and all," Sully mocked, positioning himself inches from her face. "Gillean Faraday had zero plans to make you his wife. He saw ya for what ya are—an evil, desperate creature. You made a deal with me under false pretense. I'd say that makes it null and void. You have no one to blame but your pathetic self."

She wrung her hands, shaking with rage. "You promised you would keep clear of him the night I spared his life."

"And so I did."

"Liar!" she shrieked. "He was here, at the Vale, with you!"

"He came of his own volition. I didn't have anything to do with his visit. I didn't seek him out. And he remembered by his own cleverness too, despite your sureness he wouldn't." He walked away, pleased at her surprising lack of restraint. "What's the matter, old girl? Apparently, you aren't the only game in town. Ever think there may be forces out there stronger than yours?"

"You don't mean that absurd, wheezing old angel?"

"I mean goodness, light and love."

"Love." She lowered her voice, sounding more animal than human. "Let me enlighten you about love. Once upon a time, dear Sully, you and I were born worlds apart from one another. We were both granted a soulmate."

Sully looked up, mystified by this latest revelation. "*You*...had... What happened to your soulmate?"

"That's irrelevant," she said, shaking her head and veiling her eyes behind a mass of golden hair. "Even soulmates can betray one another. The bond isn't as unbreakable as you assume it to be. Gillean became a self-seeking, materialistic man of the world and you...well, that's why you two were separated and you were granted special abilities because of your suffering."

"Nothing is irrelevant when it comes to you." Sully picked up a clean shirt of Charlie's from a basket of laundry and handed it to her. "Please, if ya want to be taken seriously, put this on at least."

She silently buttoned up the shirt, which fell to her knees.

Sully's eyes flickered with notions that were lighting like so many sparks inside his head. "Your soulmate betrayed you, hurt you."

"It was the making of me," she hissed. "I would not have traveled the world, inhabited countless pre-eminent individuals..."

"Pre-eminent targets I imagine."

"But the real fun"—she took a seat at the table, pulling her knees to her chest—"was chancing upon beings such as your pitiful, grieving father. A widower saddled with a child he had no clue how to care for. As I said before, I derive my strength from those I grant the privilege of my company. Your father's heartbreak was easy fodder for me to transform."

For the first time he could see her as his equal, stripped not only of her salacious clothing, but of all subterfuge. Pulling up a chair next to her, he boldly pushed the hair from her face, noting traces of misery in her eyes.

"You have wasted your whole existence to avenge the rejection of someone you truly loved."

"You're so sure it wasn't I who caused the break?"

Sully detected a slight waver in her voice. "I wager I am," he said, his own voice softened. "You were granted the same capabilities as I, because of the torment caused by your soulmate. But you allied yerself with destructive forces. Each time you returned, ya made sure to strike first. You thought it was safer, but you've only managed to forfeit any chance to unite with your soulmate." He appealed to her. "Why, Ciar? Why didn't ya learn from your mistakes?"

"Like you did?" she snapped. "Like Gillean did? You're both useless. He'll lose everything with his so-called new insight on life because of his love for you. Is that what you consider compensation for good behavior?"

Despite the heinous past between them, Sully reached out to her in sympathy.

"Don't look at me that way, little boy." She jerked away from her seat, snatching the half-burned candle from the window ledge. "It's too late for you. You won't have the chance of a life with your beloved Gillean. You won't get your just reward." She waved the candle; its flame swayed unsteadily. "I didn't waste my existence. I mastered fire! Your vulnerable flesh can attest to this."

He crossed both arms over his chest, tucking his hands behind his elbows.

Hot wax dripped to the floor, hardening into a white polka dot pattern on the wood. "Thanks to you, I soon will lose my powers. It's been decided that I should receive a significant sentence for misleading you. I will become human with no chance to earn my way back into my collective." She shivered. "No doubt that makes you happy."

"Not for the reason you assume. I hope you will have sense enough to recognize that neither you, nor anyone else for that matter, can subdue the natural world." He followed her from the table. "You merely utilized one of the raw elements to inflict harm. That makes ya its servant. Things can be different; *you* can be different, happy even." He entreated, "Don't be afraid. Let me help you."

For a fleeting instant their eyes exchanged a look of empathy. She seemed to be wrestling with herself. Then the shadow of darkness fell.

"Goodbye, Sully. One last bit of servitude for you to enjoy."

She dropped the candle into the basket of laundry, then tipped the ignited contents onto the floor. At the same instant the needle dropped onto a record playing from Charlie's stereo in the far room. *We run under the stars. But they cannot outshine us.* It was Gillean's album, the same one Ciar had duped Charlie into purchasing. Fire reflected her jubilant expression. *We run naked together, the green earth below us.* Hungry flames chewed at the timber floorboards, traveling up one leg of the kitchen table. *We run with the force of the blue wind behind us.*

"You can't help me, or yourself!" she shouted over the fire and music. "This time you won't be coming back, and you won't ever be reunited with Gillean."

Sully grabbed for the blanket on his bed, trying in vain to smother the growing flames. The fire eagerly sucked at the material, like a lapping tongue drawing marrow from the bone. The dire circumstances hit him like a balled fist as he tried to force open a window. His limited strength could not budge the window in the slightest, and the door hermetically sealed.

Ciar mocked his efforts. "Don't bother. There is only one thing about my future that makes me happy: that you will no longer be a presence to contend with."

He grabbed her from behind and held her against him. "Don't do this. Don't waste the only chance ya have for redemption on me."

"Leave go!" she protested, but did nothing to prevent his restraining grip.

The music played over their words.

We run together; nature's rules cannot separate us.

"Ciar, listen to me! You will be human. You can have an entirely different kind of existence now, one that could surpass your wildest imagination!"

"As if you were interested in my redemption, rather than your own skin!" she snapped.

"Let me help you," he pleaded while the needle, stuck in a grove, playing the last line of the song over and over.

Separate us, separate us, separate us…

"No!" Her elbow jabbed into his stomach. She shoved backward, sending him sprawling to the floor, which was fast becoming engulfed in ravenous, orange flames. He got to his knees, but she passed through the door without another look or word for him. In seconds he was pounding against the wood, hopelessly trapped.

"Ciar!" He called out to her. "It's not too late! Open the door!"

"Stupid Sully," she whispered. "This must be done." She allowed herself a half smile as she listened to his urgent rapping. "But you will be ushered out once again by the music of your beloved."

Ciar ran for the trees straight ahead. She meant to stay and make sure nothing would go wrong. Justice was called for. No matter what he had claimed to believe about her, Sully had to pay for his undeniable sleight. Actions were always louder than words.

As she watched the cabin, lit from within by swiftly moving licks of fire, a car labored up the dirt road gaining speed as it neared the cottage. The headlights illuminated her body against the backdrop of an alder tree. She closed her eyes, summoning the remnants of a dying force for one final lie.

Chapter Thirty-Five

Céide Fields

The devastating sight of the cottage well on its way to an inferno rendered Gillean and Arlen into astonished silence. Gillean's hands trembled as he switched off the engine. He turned to his son, who was already opening the passenger door.

"What's happening, Da?" Arlen asked, his voice quivering.

"Alren, stay here!" Gillean thrust the heavy car door open with such force the recoil nearly smashed his legs. "Call for help!" He took off in a run.

The boy was already out the door, too shaken to check for his mobile phone.

Gillean raced towards a figure standing among the trees outside Charlie's cottage. He took another look at the blaze, then at his son racing towards him.

"Arlen, wait!"

Arlen easily cut the distance between himself and his father. They met up at the tree, greatly relieved to find the person they believed to be Sully disoriented, but otherwise unharmed.

Gillean moved in closer. "Sully, are you alright? Are you injured?"

Sully's hands were hidden inside the pockets of his trousers. He looked at Gillean with an expression devoid of emotion, shaking his head back and forth to indicate he had not been harmed.

The blank look on Sully's face was grossly incongruent with the desperate situation. "This is quite awful, I know." Gillean glanced back to the burning building. "Sweet Jesus! What about Charlie? He's not in there, is he? And the dog?"

Again, only a shake of the head indicating neither Charlie nor Potcheen were in the cottage.

Arlen drew his father's attention momentarily from the bewildered Sully. "Charlie? Who's Charlie?"

"I'll explain to you later."

Gillean grabbed at Sully's arm like a fretful child unable to have his way. "Sully, will you please speak! We've come to take you back to Bray with us. Isn't that welcome news?"

Sully pursed his lips together and looked upwards to the ashen sky.

"What's wrong with you, damn it?" Gillean shook the man. "Say something!"

"Maybe he's too in shock to tell us anything right now." Arlen offered.

Gillean nodded, appreciating his son's observation, smoothed a hand over Sully's torn shirt. "I'm sorry, of course. Why don't you tell us what you can?" he coaxed in a patient tone. "Have you alerted the fire brigade?"

Inside the cottage, Sully tried and failed to extinguish the fire with water from the pump. He frantically attempted to open the window, picking up a chair and heaving it against the glass. But upon impact the chair splintered apart, leaving the window intact. The heat of the fast-moving flames was overwhelming, forcing him to move to the back room. Gillean's record had stopped. The only sound was the licking of flames.

Sinking to his knees, Sully watched in helpless terror as the fire swept through the main room, making its way to him. Disjointed thoughts cut through the haze of flames: he was not getting out, he was going to die here, alone in Charlie's cabin. His fading lucidity grasped on to one thought, one prayer: if he was to die, then Gillean and Adara must look after one another. If they could learn from each other, encourage the positive changes that were taking place in their lives, then at least Sully's time on earth would have meant something.

But the thought of Gillean made him want to fight for his own chance at happiness. Fury blazed within, more stinging than the entrapping flames. He wanted to grow and evolve in the steadfast love they had found. Sully knew with absolute conviction that Gillean intended their union, and he would tell Adara this in a most respectful, caring way. Gillean was the person Sully loved, the being in whose devoted eyes Sully lived. He would fight death itself trying to secure that vision.

He forced the weight of his aching body onto his hands and pushed himself up from the floor. It would be only seconds until the entire room would go up like a tinder box. Something pawed at his leg with human-like cries.

"Potcheen!"

Sully blindly bent down, reaching for the animal. His hands took hold of a tuft of fur. Dizziness and the collecting smoke prevented him from moving once he stood again. The air was tight and burnt, leaving precious little to inhale, but he had to get to the stairs. The hope of prying one of the upstairs windows open and jumping to safety kept him in motion. He remembered the loft door faced the eastern side of the forest. Attempting the intricate dance around the flames leading to the stairs, and the agitated dog threatening to leap from his arms at any moment, Sully crouched lower to the ground, away from the wreaths of rising smoke. He tried to speak words of comfort to the traumatized Potcheen and himself, but even talking required enormous effort.

"No...worries, good boy... You and I will..."

His foot kicked against the bottom stair as tremors of coughing tore through his body. He used his shirttail to cover the yelping animal, then pressed his own face into his shoulder as protection from noxious smoke. The extreme heat was at his back, reminding him of the awaiting fate if he panicked. He mounted the second step, then the third, making his way slowly but determinedly up to the next floor, the place where Charlie's treasures were stored. The fire took on a music all its own. It crackled and popped following him up the stairs. Sully wished for that genie in the bottle. Upstairs the air was even less breathable. The vapors had already found higher ground. The smoke placed its thick fingers around his neck and squeezed.

He didn't think to stay low to the ground once he spied the loft window. He was too focused on getting to it and prying the latch open. He gently placed the dog on the floor.

He touched his hand to the animal's head, "Stay put, wee one," as a fit of coughing overtook him. "I just...have to..."

His shaking hands took hold of the latch, and with one great heave he engaged his entire bodyweight to pull it upwards. The latch gave slightly.

"Yes...please..."

Sweat and smoke stung his eyes. His grip weakened. Impenetrable gases filled his lungs, weighing them down like sacks of water. His hands slipped from the latch, knees buckling under him like a newborn colt.

A hapless boat dashed against the edge of the million-years-old Céide Fields. Sully remembered the place as a boy, how the chunks of moss-covered rock rose up from the water in defiance of the sea. Blue-white waves swirled around the pieces of bog-covered land thousands of acres long. Sully's safe place was in the middle of the fields, where grass, foxgloves, dog-roses and ragged robins welcomed the traveler with their wild beauty. It was this image, the secure harbor of Céide Fields, that Sully's mind delivered him as he dropped unconscious below the partially-opened window.

Adara was waiting for him there. He squinted and covered his eyes as the warm sun shone in all its mid-summer glory. The breeze played through her ginger hair like a fiddler's fingers on the strings. She was calling to him.

"Come Sully! Gillean is waiting for you." Her smile was of unbridled joy. "Come see, I'm a dancer!" Her azure dress snapped like clothes drying on a line. The wind twirled the cotton around her lissome legs as she leaped into the air. Gillean appeared behind her, laughing and waving Sully on.

But Sully was so tired. He waved back, signaling his desire to lie in the tall grass. As he fell peacefully onto the fragrant, wet earth, he could see Gillean coming towards him. Sully closed his eyes, sure in the knowledge that he would soon be with Gillean, his body covering Sully like a velvet blanket.

The lights were hotter than Adara remembered as she pirouetted around the stage, moving in perfect symmetry with the music. She cast her eyes towards the audience but was blinded by the footlights. Gillean was present playing his guitar with the orchestra. There was no mistaking the unique South American spice he sprinkled into the traditional Irish tune she danced to. One by one her fellow dancers exited the stage unexpectedly and she was left to carry on. The music continued unabated. She felt a sense of comfort knowing Gillean was there with her.

But something was horribly out of synch. She was coming to the most important part of the dance, her combination grand allegro. As she began the short run leading into the leap, a single fiddle played horribly out of tune. The bow slid over each string, which protested in an ear-piercing pitch. The sound was so jarring she struggled with her footing. There was no turning back; she had to make the jump. Tremendous fear threatened to immobilize her, but her agile body instinctively took to the air. She landed soft as a snowflake.

Gillean's music echoed off the walls of the theatre. Adara basked in the moment, taking in deep, blissful breaths. She accomplished her goal unassisted, despite her apprehension. She searched the orchestra pit for the rouge fiddle player. Straining against the footlights her blurred vision came into focus, locating him. Sully! He was lying a few feet away from her as if he had fallen from the rafters onto the stage. A crushed fiddle lay by his side.

"Stop!" she protested. The music played on. "Gillean, help!" She coughed out the words like blood. "Help him!"

Adara wrestled her way out of the ghastly dream, her body drenched in sweat and her heart pounding with an unknown dread. The house was quiet. She must have fallen asleep on the couch after putting the little ones to bed. She strained against the stifling anxiety to gather her senses. Gillean's music drifted from somewhere down the hall. It was an old song, one he had written when he was not much older than Arlen. She shook her head, enshrouded with the fog of sleep. Gillean wasn't here. He had gone for Sully. She jumped from the couch and sprinted down the long corridor. Not one of her three children was about, so where was the music coming from?

She covered her mouth in terror as the picture of Sully prostate on the stage flashed through her conscious mind. She dashed towards the phone in the front hallway. Her fingers quickly stabbed at the numbers.

Gillean's mobile was on its last ring before going to voice mail. Seeing it was Adara on the line, he picked up.

"Adara, hallo?" he shouted into the receiver

"Oh thanks be to God!" She practically shouted in a strained and panicked voice. "Where is Sully? Is he alright? Gillean, I know something awful has happened. Please help him!"

The man standing before Gillean showed the first hint of concern upon hearing Adara's voice booming through the phone. He quickly averted his eyes from Gillean's pointed stare.

"It's alright, Dara," Gillean responded in a guarded manner. "Arlen and I are right here with Sully. He's a bit shook up, but he'll be fine once we get him out of here. Are you and the children alright?"

"Yes, we're fine," she quickly confirmed. "I don't care what you say, what you believe about Sully, but something is dreadfully wrong. He's not telling you everything. He's in danger. I know it!"

Gillean faced the roaring fire, turning his back from Sully and his son. His mind swabbed at the doubt bubbling up with Adara's plea. She sounded so certain about Sully being in jeopardy, yet here he was right in front of Gillean seemingly right as rain, even though more subdued than usual.

"No worries. We'll be home in no time. Take care of you and the children."

"Gillean!"

He switched off the phone.

"Da," Arlen was pulling at Gillean's sleeve. "Look!"

When Gillean faced Sully again, terror seized his body.

"This isn't Sully." Arlen's tone was as sure and cold as February.

Gillean probed the man's eyes. They shifted in color, like a prism sending out sparks of vivid hues that grew brighter and sharper by the glow of the fire.

Gillean stepped closer, toe to toe with the man. He'd looked into these eyes before, but the feelings stirred were not the warmth and compassion his soulmate radiated. They held a sinister foreboding.

"I agree." Gillean held the stranger with his scrutinizing gaze. "This isn't Sully."

"You're too late, little Gilly."

As the words were uttered, Sully's likeness fell away like a collapsing house of cards. In a matter of seconds, the image of his beloved was transformed into that of his former lover. In the same instant of recognition, her name about to escape his lips, a sound much like the aftermath of a bomb reverberated through the once peaceful woods. The windows to the cabin exploded from the intense heat. The shattering glass sounded like thousands of bells ringing out a declaration of inevitable destruction. Gillean jerked his head around in time to see the door to the cottage swinging from its hinges.

Chapter Thirty-Six

Valor

The doors and windows which had been impenetrable opened like the gates to paradise. Smoke poured from the building, infecting the once pure sky. The fire extended its orange tentacles to the ceiling of the ground floor.

"He's in there!" Arlen screamed.

Gillean swallowed back the bile rising in his throat as he faced Ciar, the woman he once had claimed to love. He had been simply a means to an end for her, he realized; she'd been determined on one thing only, to get to Sully and destroy him. It was icing on the cake that she might take down Gillean as well.

She lowered her head, half-whispering the words, "He's gone, Gillean. The debt is settled. 'Tis meant to be."

"So you say!" Gillean vibrated with rage. "Well, I'm not finished yet, you evil wench, and neither is Sully!"

Gillean grabbed for Arlen and reached for his mobile as he ran towards the house. He thrust the phone at his son. "Call for help and stay clear of the building!"

Gillean stood a few feet from the front door. It was obvious there was no way in, and if Sully was on the ground floor, there was no chance he could have survived the smoke and flames slashing their way up the stairs to the floor above. The heat was terrifyingly intense.

After shouting at the operator to dispatch help, Arlen ignored his father's second order and jetted off to the side of the building. "Da! There's the way in!" He pointed to a loft window that was swinging open, banging against the stone wall of the cottage.

"I thought I told you—" One look at Arlen's determined expression and Gillean knew it would be a fruitless endeavor to try and keep his son away. Arlen was intent on doing everything he could to save Sully. "I'm coming!" Gillean needed his son's help if there was any chance of doing so.

Gillean fought to maintain his calm. Everything that mattered to him was encapsulated in this moment, trapped in the searing flames. His day of reckoning had arrived. He owed Sully his life. He owed Adara her freedom. He owed his children, especially Arlen, an example of a man of valor. He owed it to himself to reclaim the resilient man he had forgone so many years ago. He hurriedly devised a plan.

"See if you can find a ladder. Charlie must have one stashed outside somewhere."

"Gotcha!" Arlen circled the building; halfway round, he found what he was looking for. A paint-spattered, metal ladder lay against the south side of the cottage.

"Found it!" he cried victoriously. Dragging it over to the east side, Gillean and his son quickly set it vertically against the wall.

Gillean shook a finger of warning to his boy. "You stay put and keep this thing steady for me."

"But, ya might need—"

"I need you to do exactly as I ask. I need you to trust me," Gillean ordered, his foot already on the second rung.

"I do, Da, I trust ya."

Arlen's intense focus was all the encouragement Gillean needed. His son would be there for him, and for Sully. The boy placed his hands on each side of the ladder, pushing his body against the center, and keeping it steady as Gillean ascended. The loft was roughly three meters from the ground.

Gillean's mind raced ahead as he allowed his feet to feel their way up the ladder. He kept his eyes focused on the open window where smoke continued to escape like a mob of angry prisoners. How was he going to locate Sully once he made it into the cottage? He surmised he would only have a few minutes at best before the smoke overcame him.

Midway up the ladder, the mournful crying of a desperate creature carried on the smoke-filled air.

"What is that?" Arlen called up.

"I'm not sure, son. Just keep us steady, okay? I'm almost there."

When Gillean was level with the window the smoke momentarily took his breath and sight. He turned away, shaking and coughing. His eyes watered, blurring his vision. He removed one hand from the ladder and wiped at his sweaty face. Peering into the storage room, he could see nothing but thick, black clusters of clouds and flames edging their way into the room.

"Sully!" Gillean choked out.

The only reply came from the snapping flames.

Gillean stepped gingerly into the room, and the crying started up again, faint but audible. He looked down, just as the wobbling Potcheen gave his last yelp, pitching against Gillean's leg. As he bent down to retrieve the animal he saw the tips of Sully's toes. Squinting, Gillean could make out Sully's entire body as it lay unmoving inches from the window.

"Arlen!" Gillean called out. "Come up here!"

The boy climbed the ladder with haste, meeting Gillean at the window ledge.

"Take this poor creature down with you."

Gillean carefully handed Arlen the semi-conscious dog.

"Did ya find Sully?" Arlen asked, as he gently accepted the animal.

"Yes, and he's got that dog to thank for it, too."

"I'll take him down and be right back with ya." Arlen was midway to the ground before Gillean could protest.

He turned his attention back to Sully, feeling for a pulse. It was barely detectable, but Gillean could count the weak, slow beats that were like music to his fingers, searching for the right chord. By this time Arlen was leaning in the window coughing and trying to direct his father.

"I can help ya get him on his feet."

"No, stay there. I'll need your help to get him down."

Gillean removed his trainers and stood with his feet on top of Sully's. Arms joined, he pulled the unconscious man to a standing position. Sully's body fell against Gillean like a heavy stone. His head lay on Gillean's shoulder.

Gillean whispered the Irish words into the dying man's ear, "*Mo anam cara*. I'm here now. I won't leave you." Gillean's mind ran through the possibilities as to how to get himself and Sully safely down the ladder. Sully was a mere slip of a thing, but due to his age and years of stage work hauling heavy equipment, Gillean's back was hardly ready to take on the weight of any man.

Arlen offered an idea. There wasn't much time; the fire was approaching the center of the room and moving ever closer. "Here, take this." Arlen undid the cloth, tie-dyed belt from his baggy jeans and handed it to his father. "Tie his hands in front of him, and then ya can lift him onto yer back with his arms round yer neck."

Gillean stared blankly at his son.

"Ya know, piggy back him, like ya used to do with me when I was a kid."

Gillean was desperate, and his son seemed to know what he was talking about. Gillean agreed. He began the difficult undertaking, which was complicated by the need to keep Sully's limp body upright. He battled to keep the weight of the near lifeless man centered against his own, while wrapping the belt several times around Sully's wrists, knotting the remainder of the cloth.

"Tell me how this is supposed to go!" Gillean shouted for confirmation.

"His arms bein' immobile, he'll be easier to carry. It works. I saw it in a movie," Arlen called back, offering the innocent reassurance of youth.

"A movie?" Gillean was overcome with a mouthful of smoke. "For the love of Christ!" he wheezed.

"Do ya want me to—?"

"No!" Gillean stifled a cough. "Take a few steps down. You'll be my backup."

Arlen eased himself down a few rungs.

Gillean turned his back to Sully, placing his friend's bound hands loosely around his neck.

"When ya lift him, Da, be sure to keep your arms under his legs; support his knees so he won't choke ya!"

The fire was almost on top of them. As Gillean bent over, his back gave immediate protest at the extra load. Doing as his son instructed, he adjusted Sully's arms, and held his legs firmly. Arlen was right. Sully's arms, secured by the belt, made him less cumbersome to carry.

But no practiced breathing technique could assist him now. Every ounce of air went down his throat like daggers. Keeping his eyes on the fire beating against the ceiling with its relenting flames, Gillean stepped backwards out the window, praying his feet would find their way down.

"Here we go, Sully. You better hang on, luv. I won't forgive you if you leave me this time."

Gillean talked through his terror while Arlen pressed his hands to Sully's back, lending extra support.

"That's it, keep goin'. Don't look down. Steady on," the boy encouraged.

A spasm ripped through Gillean's spine like a stray bullet. He fought to keep his hands around Sully, but could do nothing to stop his own body from its involuntary reaction to the pain.

"Arlen, get off the ladder!"

He forced out the words through clenched teeth, moments before he and Sully tumbled backwards, two shooting stars plunging from the heavens. The earth graciously accepted the fire-driven offering. Ashes to ashes, dust to dust. The blaze had taken the cottage, turning the sky into a decayed cavity, empty of any stars or dreams of men.

Epilogue

Ireland
2001

The train moved at an even clip ambling by fields of wild clover like an elderly gentleman of leisure. But she was anxious; maybe it was the jitters from too much coffee. She ought to have declined the affable server who refilled her cup. Exiting the dining car she took a few wobbly steps into the main corridor. Stopping for a moment, she breathed deeply to gather herself together. She turned her attention to the comforting sound of easy conversations being had all around her. She wondered if they were reading the feature article in today's Irish Times, *Gillean Faraday: Reflections on the Bard of Ireland.*

She had read only the first few lines which stated that after an approximate three-year absence from the music industry, recovering from a near-fatal fire, the singer-songwriter played the occasional, intimate venue within the confines of Ireland. He spent his days with his children and his partner in their unassuming home by the sea.

It was a lovely home, she reflected, more of a cozy beach cottage with soft pastel colors, weathered wood, antique lamps and unadorned windows which allowed the sun and moon to provide brilliant light.

"Pardon me, Madam, but you're in me way."

Adara faced the man whose short-cropped black curls smartly framed his animated face. "My apologies, sir, but I was waiting for you to finish your massive breakfast."

He laughed, "Ah, you forget, we shared that massive meal, and you claimed the entire basket of scones for yerself."

She swatted at him with her newspaper. "That is a bald-face lie."

"I get it. Dancers need to keep up their strength."

She grasped his elbow, pausing to look into the quiet eyes which had been robbed of sight. The critical connections may have been severed, as numerous specialists had attested to—Sully's final sacrifice for Gillean the night of the fire by breaking Gillean's fall—but still an inimitable light shone through the sleeping green lenses.

"Shall we?" Adara offered to escort him from the dining car.

Before he could respond Gillean shouted from the open door of the carriage several feet away. "Sully, come here to me! The view is magnificent!"

"I'm blind, not deaf, Gillean."

"How do you stand him?" Adara teasingly questioned.

"I ply him with scones." Sully winked.

"Would you two stop messin' about," Gillean chided. In a matter of minutes Sully was ushered to his seat, a happy Potcheen scrambled onto his protector's lap.

"Come on, Dara," Gillean eased into the seat next to Sully. "You don't want to miss this either!"

"I can see from here." She settled in across the aisle. Her sons Abbot and Atty, no doubt bored by her absence, were now part of the others crowding around Gillean and Sully. She decided to finish the article while the brood were distracted.

Mr. Faraday is keeping busy supporting a variety of artists to get a fair shake in the business. One of Clondalkin's local boys, Eamon Brennan, formerly a petrol station attendant, now fronts his own band, Pie Monster. *Brennan paid his patron homage for the star's unexpected and generous backing by titling the band's debut CD* Far-Out, Faraday.

The article went on:

The seasoned musician's latest philanthropic endeavor is one shared with his former wife. Their combined funding established a school of dance which works in tandem with children from the Ireland Cares Foster Association. The school is managed by Adara Faraday, who has traveled the globe with her highly successful dance troupe. When interviewed, both Faradays explained their belief in creative activity being fundamental to the healing of scars left by an unfortunate childhood.

Adara closed her eyes, seeing the large, bright, lively rooms of her school. The laughter of children whose lives had been tainted with too much sorrow was priceless; in those moments, when her senses were completely in tune with the pulse of the place, she could swear she saw the sparkle of blue eyes as the tall, white-haired angel moved among the children. Smiling, she took up the article.

Mr. Faraday is now reported to be traveling to Brazil, the place of his birth, for a series of concerts to benefit the artists of his native country. It is difficult to fathom that just a few years prior, news of the beloved singer-songwriter's unraveling life read like a soap opera script. He ended his two-decade marriage to make a home with his partner, a man whom Faraday is fiercely protective of, as well as their shared privacy. As if that wasn't juicy enough, news of an illicit affair during his marriage traveled over every media source like wildfire—the biggest showbiz story of its day.

The alleged "other woman," a little-known painter from Prague, attempted to peddle her story to anyone who would listen. She was later deemed mentally unstable and charged with setting the terrible blaze that almost took the lives of Mr. Faraday, his oldest son, and Faraday's partner. Having been found guilty on all charges and incarcerated, the woman's allegations of sleeping with the entertainer and being responsible for the breakup of his marriage were eventually dismissed as the ramblings of an unsound mind.

Adara paused in her reading once again, noting that no one but she and Gillean knew of the single visitor who faithfully made the trek to the women's penitentiary twice a month. Sully was undaunted in his belief that as Ciar was now human, she had been granted a final chance at redemption. It was this hope and light that Sully continued to bring to her.

He relayed that the woman remained guarded because of her experience with the dark collective. Nevertheless, Sully sensed that something had softened in her. He told Adara and Gillean he was certain that one day Ciar too could step out of the shadows of the past and claim a new existence.

Adara once asked Gillean if it didn't ruffle his feathers a bit that Sully had been doing this. Gillean replied that his soulmate's unwavering faith in the potential of individuals made him love Sully that much more. After all, where would Gillean be had Sully given up on him? "But I won't be extending any invitations to have fucking tea with her in this lifetime!" Gillean was resolute on the matter of Ciar.

Adara resumed the newspaper story where she had left off.

Still, Faraday lost a significant portion of his devoted fan base, most especially because of conservative, religious rhetoric on the "sinfulness" of Faraday's new union and his (and his former wife's) choice to share custody of their children with another man.

But, to his credit, Faraday has risen in popularity with the young adults of Ireland.

"Gillean Faraday is freakin' brilliant!" twenty-year-old Trinity College music student Maeve O'Connor shared. "He's a storyteller of the highest order. He's opened up completely new avenues for me and my music…and not just me, yeah, it's the people of this generation listening to songs from thirty years ago. Freakin' brilliant."

"I feel extremely blessed in my life," Faraday addressed the controversy. "I don't believe in any institution, or any person for that matter, demanding

us to deny our truest selves, and dictate who we can love. I have made serious mistakes and hurt people dear to me, but I was granted another chance to do better—be better—as can we all."

Some fans were disappointed in Faraday's scaled-back recording and touring schedule. According to the reclusive singer, "I record when I believe I have something worthwhile to share with the universe."

The article concluded:

The obscurity that surrounds Gillean Faraday only serves to keep him in the collective consciousness of the mysterious land in which he dwells. Ireland has historically been a haven for those artists who possess that rare blend of talent, humanity and just a hint of the otherworldly. Gillean Faraday has finally earned this writer's, as well as most of his fellow compatriots', respect and admiration. We urge him to play on!

Adara considered the challenge of a crossword puzzle but could hardly concentrate in the midst of such lively conversation from across the aisle.

"I told you this is the perfect way to travel to Brazil," Gillean was commenting to Sully. "A splendid train ride to Paris, and then we fly!"

Gillean insisted on escorting Adara to Paris where she planned to buy fabric in the fashion district for her students. She meant to surprise them. Each child would have the opportunity to make his or her own dance costume.

Her excitement matched Gillean's as he turned to the seat occupied by his three youngest children. "Go on then. Whose turn is it to give Sully a description of the view?"

"ME!" twelve-year-old Abbot leaned in.

The younger Antonia propped her head on the back of Sully's seat. "But I do it best! Tell him, Sully!"

Sully offered the perfect compromise, "Why don't ya take turns? The more eyes the better. And don't leave anythin' out!"

Adara listened as her children tried not to talk over one another in their haste to give Sully a detailed and spirited report of their surroundings. She was a proud mama at the way each child had gladly taken on the task of being Sully's eyes. Considering him their friend had not taken much convincing, either. Much like her children, after spending time in the company of Gillean and Sully, Adara not only warmed to, but whole-heartedly accepted their union.

"How long will it take to get to Brazil, Da?" Antonia asked, echoing Sully's inquiry.

"It's on the other side of the world!" her twin brother Atty teased.

"Da! It isn't!" she protested in disbelief.

"Just pay attention to what's in front of you, Nia, luv." Gillean brushed her cheek. "You don't want to miss any part of the journey."

"Hey, Sully!" Arlen called, as he ran down the aisle holding the hand of a red-headed girl. "This lass says she has somethin' for ya."

"Forgive my intrusion, sir, but, I believe ya left your bag in the dining car." She placed a threadbare satchel into Sully's lap.

His fingers investigated the material to confirm it was indeed his.

She laid a hand on his shoulder. "You shouldn't be without yer fiddle."

Sully took her hand in his. "You're quite right. Thank ya very much, lass." His emerald eyes glowed knowingly in the afternoon sunlight.

"You're welcome. Safe journeys." She took her time walking away, her eyes fixed lovingly on Gillean and Sully.

Adara assumed the girl was one of Gillean's young fans.

"I can't shake the feeling that I've seen that girl somewhere before," Gillean addressed Sully. "It's as though she reminds me of another child I once met, but I can't for the life of me think who. Madness, isn't it?"

"Maybe you have met her," Sully said, removing his fiddle from the bag, "in another time, another place, another train, another life, maybe."

"I'm sure the same is true for all of us," Gillean confirmed.

"Shove over, Sully!" Arlen wedged himself between his two fathers. "Are ya gonna play yer fiddle in Brazil?"

"Well now, I suppose I could take up with a street band." Sully tweaked the strings.

"That reminds me," Gillean added, "we must find a particular busker while we're there."

"Who's that, Da?" Abbot asked.

"'Tis not the time for you to know yet!" Gillean laughed. "Give us a song, Sully!"

"Come on then, get your guitar out, Faraday."

"Ah, a captive audience, my favorite kind." Gillean accepted his guitar from Abbot. He took a quiet moment before counting to three. They began on the same note, their music filling the car with the splendor and grace of fey.

Adara abandoned her crossword, her glasses resting on the bridge of her nose. A freedom so complete resided in her heart, an unbound soul giving and receiving total forgiveness. The dusky sun flowed through the window, tingeing the two men with its purple pallet. The expression of love that passed between Gillean and Sully, and the haunting music they created, was like an electric current surging through each of them. The children's heads rested against one another as they fell captive to the spell of the music. They were united in their strength and diversity, like an aged tree rooted firmly in the earth, its many branches extending in different directions but reaching for the same sky, bound to one center, forever.